THE COIN OF THE REALM

THE COIN
OF THE REALM

ROGER DUBIN

TARSUS
PRESS

This is a work of fiction. All the characters, organizations, and events portrayed in this novel are either products of the author's imagination or are used fictitiously.

TARSUS PRESS
www.TarsusPress.com

ISBN 9780692310663
Library of Congress Control Number 2008906881
Publication date: October 2014
Revised edition: January 2025

for Barbara

PROLOGUE

The Palace of Facets, Moscow—December 23, 1701.

Yaakov Ziskind is ushered into the throne room of
Peter the Great, carrying in both hands a box crafted of
rare green amber. On its lid, the crest of the Romanovs
is rendered in precious gems.

Ziskind, a Polish Jew and master goldsmith, had
wandered Europe for three decades. Betrayed by the self-
anointed messiah Sabbatai Zevi, graced with revelation
and rebirth afterwards, he'd told his tale to anyone who
would listen, leaving behind in the town hall of each
city he visited a miniature masterwork—a medallion of
the Madonna and Child wrought in gold and silver.
Word of his story and artistry had finally reached the
young Tsar, who sent emissaries to escort him to
Moscow. Thus, four years ago, was born a friendship
that mystified Peter's entire court, and led to the Pole's
appointment as Jeweler to the Imperial Crown.

Tonight, at the age of seventy-nine and increasingly
frail, Yaakov Ziskind knows he is about to present his

last and finest work. The slight, stooping figure in austere black shuffles past the phalanx of aristocrats, generals, and dignitaries—his eyes cast down, avoiding the spectacle of their opulence glittering in the light of a thousand candles—and approaches the emperor of all the Russias.

Now Peter rises from his throne, his six feet eight inches drawing every eye aloft. Before his Imperial Jeweler can bow, the emperor, in a singular gesture, descends and greets him warmly. He takes the box, opens the lid, and lifts above his head the extraordinary object inside, proclaiming it the Zevi Coin. The audience applauds and surges forward.

Forgotten in the excitement, Yaakov Ziskind drifts away, his head bowed and lips moving. No one notices when he falls to his knees.

ONE

The Gift

It was a Friday evening in August 1991, and Eli Kagan was working late.

Rick Weisman closed the double doors behind him; the janitor's vacuum in the lobby muffled to a hum. The Chairman and CEO of Kagan Brothers Shipping looked up, waved him in with his pen hand, continued writing. Several filled pages were set to one side.

"Fix yourself a drink, Rick."

"That's all right, Eli. I'll wait."

He settled into one of the armchairs facing the desk, took in the familiar room: the layer-cake view of twilit summer sky, Brooklyn Bridge and East River, wedged between skyscrapers that filled the two walls of windows; the six-foot model of the KBS flagship, *Empire State*; the Mary Cassatt original in the place of honor—a painting at the beach of a mother and child; and, on the credenza, a recent addition—an antique bronze sextant, which partially hid the photo of President Kennedy awarding

Eli the Medal of Freedom.

He finished the last page, stacked it with the others, creased them and stuffed them into an envelope; wrote a single word on the front and stood it up against his desk set. Rick grinned, certain what word his uncle was about to speak.

"There," he said, then began rattling off memos into his Dictaphone.

They hadn't seen each other in seven months, not since Rick had started shipping coastwise out of Galveston. No need to fuss though. They both knew how they felt, just as Rick knew something important was up or Eli wouldn't have telexed him aboard the *Gulf Queen,* asking him to pay off in Tampa. That was no small request; quitting a U.S.-flagged ship likely meant a long wait for another.

"There," Eli said again, replacing the Dictaphone mike in its cradle. "So. How are you, son?"

"A little tired, but—"

"Baloney. You're what—twenty-four, twenty-five? You don't know what tired means. Am I right?"

Rick shrugged; Eli pointed. "I'm right."

He went to his bar and mixed Chivas and soda. Eli rarely drank anything else; friends joked he didn't know there was anything else.

"You still with that beautiful doll," he asked over the clink of ice cubes, "the law student?"

"Renée? No, we broke up."

"Oh, too bad. I liked her."

He brought the glasses, gave Rick one, perched himself on the arm of the chair next to his nephew's.

They touched rims.

"It's rough on a gal, dating a seafarer. How are things at home?"

"Fine. I called Mom and Sid from Florida."

"Rhoda and I had dinner with them last week and Sid seemed, I don't know, kind of down."

"Probably because of Moonraker."

"His boat?" Another pull of scotch.

Rick nodded. "He just sold her. To some architect."

Eli lowered his glass. "You're kidding. You two love that thing."

"Yeah, but she's a pain to keep up, and I can't help him the way I used to, and he's not getting any younger, so..." Rick avoided his gaze. "Well, nothing lasts forever, right?"

He sensed he'd come across as blasé and that his uncle didn't like it.

Eli jostled his glass, gyrating the ice cubes.

"You've been damn lucky to have a stepdad like Sid."

"I know, sir." The nightmare flashed its lurid colors, ghastly roars and heat: still life with blue sky and a streak of red, the antique Stearman biplane falling from it in flames, the sirens of fire truck and ambulance wailing across the runway as the corkscrew of smoke carrying his father drills itself in.

Rick gulped at his scotch.

"He brought you up like you were his own. Better, to tell the truth. I hope you haven't hurt him."

"I don't think so," Rick lied, and it was plain Eli didn't like that either.

"It doesn't have to be this way, son. You could come work for KBS, be close to your family, maybe meet someone and get married. And it would mean the world to me."

"Please, Uncle E."

Rick hated disappointing him, hated the look on Eli's face when he did. Aunt Rhoda couldn't have children and Rick's cousins hadn't shown any inclination to join the firm. Eli and his brothers, Ernie, Alf, and Milton—hard-driving, old-school men, all hearing footsteps, none aging well—couldn't understand why no one in the family wanted to take the wheel of what they'd built from nothing. Rick was Eli's last hope. His best, too, if he were to believe the sales pitch he'd heard time and again, which he didn't for a moment.

His uncle rose and crossed to the Mary Cassatt.

"That's not why you sent for me, is it?"

Eli turned from the painting.

"Of course not. No, the thing is...I'm afraid your uncle has run out of time."

He came back to the desk and half sat on it, one foot on the floor.

Their eyes met.

"I got the word a few weeks ago from that idiot Kaufman, after another of my episodes. He's been on me since forever to kick smoking and drinking, and...now he says the old pump has just about had it. Frankly, I think he's tickled."

He smiled, clearly wanting his nephew to smile too, and Rick made the effort. Eli drained his scotch, took both glasses to the bar, poured more Chivas, brought them back and handed Rick his.

"Yes to all the questions—opinions, options..." He

half sat on the desk again, sipped. "Look, I'm pushing eighty. I've had a heck of a life and I'm going to keep living it as I always have, for however long the good Lord gives me. I've tidied my affairs, resolved the issues here at the company, taken care of everyone and everything. Except you."

"Eli, you don't have to—"

"Stop it. I know you're not interested in money. This isn't about that."

He set down his glass and slipped a cigarette case from his suit jacket; tapped a Chesterfield on it, flicked a lighter. Took a drag then Rick's measure.

"What I'm going to give you is something I've kept secret for sixty-five years. No one knows I have it—not my brothers, not even my wife. To term it priceless would be a gross understatement." Another drag. "So much so that, if you ever try to sell it, you may be putting your life at risk. Yet if you keep it, you may well be risking everything else."

"I don't understand."

Eli started to explain, then stubbed out his smoke. He walked around to the credenza, stooped to the center cabinet, withdrew the lacquer box that held his stash of Chesterfields and positioned it on the desk. Fishing into the cigarettes, three spilled—white exclamations on the green blotter.

"In there?"

"Only since this morning."

He held up a black felt bag, lobbed it across the desk. Rick caught it, opened the corded top and turned it over: the weight of centuries fell into his palm.

It was a thick, burnished gold coin, more than three inches in diameter. On one side were inlaid three rings of diamonds; within the rings, a royal family crest was rendered in intricate white gold, a large star sapphire just below the crown and between the heads of the double-headed eagle. On the reverse side, the rings of jewels were sapphires and within them, also in white gold, was the detailed device of a mounted lancer, a large diamond at the tip of his brandished sword, just above his head. Around the edge of the coin were engraved words in Latin and Cyrillic.

Eli had retrieved his glass and returned to the armchair, watching as his nephew examined the object.

Rick found his voice. "Whose crest is this?"

"The Romanovs."

"And the horseman?"

"That's Ivan the Terrible, the first true Tsar."

Despite everything, Rick couldn't help but be amused as Eli sat back, waxing professorial. His uncle held a doctorate in European History, an abiding passion for the subject, and a not-so-private vanity about both. Which only made Rick love him more, if that was possible.

"Ivan standardized Russian money in the sixteenth century—all the dengi minted during his reign bore that design—but over the next hundred years it was corrupted with counterfeiting. Peter the Great reorganized it, and to commemorate the first stable currency under Ivan and the next under Peter, the Tsar had this coin fashioned in 1701. Peter was so taken with it he had an eyelet attached, and for years wore it on a chain around his neck as a badge of that stability he strove to establish for the Romanov dynasty. At some point—symbolically, it would be said—the eyelet broke. Thereafter the coin resided among the crown treasures, by the Monomakh Cap itself, until 1742, when it vanished. It's been lost to history ever since."

"But how—?"

Eli held up a palm.

"I'm going to tell you all that I know—about the coin, and the man who made it, and how it came to me, and the legend which has followed it throughout the ages: that he who bears the Zevi Coin will be led to whatever his soul is seeking, be it love, gold, glory, or God."

Eli's brows were gathered at the hook nose, hazel eyes aimed and loaded, looking not at him but into him, further than Rick ever had into himself or could or would want to.

"So, what are you seeking, son?"

Rick knew he had no answer, was on the verge of fabricating a fiction when his uncle's expression changed: He didn't expect one, it was just his way of making sure Rick didn't miss the point of the gift.

"Anyway, it's all written down cold inside that envelope. I wanted to set the facts straight in case the scotch makes me forget to tell you something, or in case you forget later, so you can get it right. Because one day you'll have to decide who should have the coin next."

"And how will I do that?"

"Don't worry. It'll be like it was when I realized you were the one, like it was for my boyhood friend Michael when he gave it to me. Somehow, you'll know, and that will be enough."

Eli sighed, drank again, and crossed his legs.

"And now, get ready to hear one whale of a story."

TWO

Here Be Dragons

Through the rain and dark, the corroding hulk that was *Caroline Coast* loomed in the windshield. The taxi pulled up to the gangway; Rick paid the driver. Swish-thunk of wipers, the glow from the dash, Willie Nelson on the radio—

"Hey Mack. You awake back there?"

"Huh? No—no receipt, thanks."

He lugged out his duffel and suitcase, slammed the door. The yellow Checker crunched past the wharf's silos and cranes, cement towers on a cement sky. Up the gangway. Garbage water choked with grain sloshed below the slats; the aluminum stairs creaked. A foghorn.

"Well, look what the cat drug in," said someone from above; then, as Rick reached the deck, "You were scheduled to be here by noon."

"I had to see a man about a horse."

"Oh, smart aleck, huh? Gimme your papers."

They stepped out of the rain, under the overhang of

the boat deck. He shined a flashlight on the Merchant Marine card, grunted "Figures" when he saw Rick's last name. Rick looked him over: greased hair, tight black jeans, a heartland punk in his forties. He handed back the card and orders, led Rick into the main house, made a quick right turn to the mess.

"Stay here."

Rick put down his luggage, slapped water off his hat, glanced around: green chipped paint, worn red Formica, bare light bulbs. She was a C-class freighter, one of the last of her vintage still in commission. Like most of the allied merchant ships built during World War II, she'd been designed to pay for herself with just a couple of convoys; yet here she was, a half-century later, still waiting for a German torpedo. Begging for one, really. She was rusting to pieces, cracking from the pressure of every last drop of profit being wrung out of her. *Caroline Coast* was the type of ship you had to stomach to land your first job in the Merchant Marine, or when you couldn't take the land another minute. Nothing else had been posted on the board when he'd arrived at the union hall after three days at home, but even though jobs were scarce and getting scarcer, no one had wanted anything to do with *Caroline Coast*. No one except Rick. She was bound far away, across the Atlantic and Mediterranean to North Africa, and that's all he needed to know.

"Aye, here's our belated lad."

He turned at the Irish brogue; the owner of it looked wiry tough and sharp at the point, gray eyes matching wavy gray hair. The man from the gangway was slouching at the door.

"I'm Willis Fine."

Rick took the offered hand, got his mashed as he introduced himself.

"Happy to meet you. We'll be watchmates on the eight-to-twelve. I understand you have your 'B' card."

"That's right."

"Good, then you know what's what. I'm union rep here. Any trouble, you talk to me."

The other man snorted. "Don't fret—kid's got a mouth on him."

"Lucky thing too, Jacky, with the likes of you about," Willis shot back.

Jacky flipped him a middle finger and left.

"We get all kinds on this ship, son. Disregard 'em if you can, don't sweat it if you can't."

He had to be in his late sixties, yet the way he snatched Rick's duffel it might have been stuffed with feathers. They hustled from the mess and down the passageway to the 8-12 cabin.

"Quiet now. JJ's sleeping," Willis whispered.

The door griped as it opened. He set down the duffel, indicated the upper bunk above the snoring heap. Rick parked his suitcase, hung his cap and leather jacket on a hook.

Outside again, Willis raised an eyebrow. "You don't know me from Adam, lad, but you'd best take my advice and give our watch mate there a wide, wide berth." He took Rick to the inside companionways and up to the bridge deck. Brass placards on slatted wood doors identified the radio hut, saloon, first mate's quarters, chief engineer's. Willis knocked on the one that read captain.

"Come," was the reply.

Regardless of the name on the door, the office half of the suite, at least, was occupied by the first mate. A marine chronometer on the desk clicked the seconds, light from the single brass lamp hazed onto a gun-metal Moser safe, worn-shiny brown leather couch and chair, framed certificates and photos, shelves with bands of wood securing the books. Save for official-looking papers under weights across the desk, riffling in the breeze of a fan, everything was neat and workmanlike.

As was the first mate himself. He had a pipe stuck between chapped lips, bags of worry under the sort of eyes that seemed always searching for a landfall. And even at midnight, at his desk in quarters where he was unmistakably the master, in spirit if not name, he wore ironed khakis and mirror-shine shoes. Not at all the stripe of officer you'd expect on a scow like *Caroline Coast*.

"The new ordinary's here, sir."

He closed the binder he was reading—a logo with the name Maxton Importers was stamped on its cover— set down his pipe, rose, and came over.

"Jefferson Saint Eves," he said, extending his hand. "Welcome aboard."

There was an air about him older men have sometimes, an understanding of how much they can endure, and that no one else can imagine how much that is.

"You've been at sea—how long?"

"About three years, sir."

"Hm." His forehead crinkled. "Why'd you choose

this line of work?"

"Usual reasons."

He didn't care for the answer. "And just what—?" Now his gaze shifted. "Yes, Mister Abdessalam?"

"Excusez-moi. I did not realize that you were engaged."

Notwithstanding the French, he appeared to be an Arab: bald, in his fifties, with a chestnut face and a rotund shape sleeked by a wine-red silk robe over matching silk pajamas. He wore his simper with a studied flair, the mousse on his thin mustache catching the light.

"Can I help you?" Saint Eves said, too politely.

The hint of a bow in Rick's direction.

"Pardon, m'sieur." Then, to Saint Eves, "Might I ask when we will sail?"

"Before dawn."

"Ah. Merci." He backed out, leaving a fragrance of sandalwood, and delivered his salutation from the doorway. "A most pleasant evening to you all."

Saint Eves flicked his eyes at Willis then returned them to Rick. "Our passenger," he explained, with a tone that meant it was all the explanation Rick needed or should want.

He went to the safe, produced a ledger and the shipping articles. As Rick wrote his information in the book and signed it, and the formalities were executed, he recognized the strains of "Musetta's Song" from *La Boheme* beginning to play from beyond, and presumed it was coming from Abdessalam's stateroom.

Saint Eves returned to his chair, reclined it on its

hind legs, looked him over. Willis left with an aside in his ear, "There's fresh coffee in the mess; see you there." He didn't close the door. Saint Eves' chair plopped forward; he took up his pipe, lit it with a gold Zippo.

"Any questions? About anything?"

"No, sir."

The pipe attended to, he gestured with it. "Good. Minding your own business goes a long way on this ship. Combine that with an honest approach to your duties and you'll do fine. Very well, that's all." Rick had the door half shut when Saint Eves added, "We'll finish our conversation some other time."

Rick peeked back in. "What conversation, sir?"

But he was already immersed in his papers.

—⁓—

Willis was dunking a doughnut and reading the *Duluth News Tribune*; he laid it on the table as Rick entered the mess.

"That was quick. You're lucky."

"How's the coffee in this town?"

"Coffee's fine, it's the water that's lousy."

Rick went to the urn, chose a mug and filled it three-quarters, added cream and sugar. Exhaustion is a way of life in the Merchant Marine, so just about every seaman is addicted to black caffeine and used to the mania's fetishes—like drinking it right before turning in. Rick sat across from Willis, blew into the steam and let his watch mate size him up.

"So you're from New York, eh?" Willis chomped

his doughnut, spoke as he chewed. "I like Broadway, the musicals. My people hail from Dublin."

"Tell me about JJ," Rick said.

Willis eyed him with some appreciation.

"Okay, since you be smart enough to listen. More than I can say for the sap who had your bunk last." He slurped at his mug. "He's been with this ship, oh, maybe eighteen months. Couldn't get no other, I warrant, though he's a twelve-year able-bodied seaman and AB's usually have their pick. Some things people don't forget, you know? But we can't be too choosy here on Caroline, not with this ship's ill fame, not even with the likes of the Butcher of Baton Rouge. Aye, that's what they call him. He's landed more than one man in a white bed and worse. A spiteful, nefarious cur and that's a fact."

Rick absorbed this, drinking coffee.

"With a rep like that, I'm surprised the ship attracts passengers."

"Huh? Oh, the Egyptian." His features shrouded. "He's no passenger, not really. He's what I'd call...a businessman. And I'd sooner you cursed our watch mate to his face than stick your nose in that gent's affairs."

Eli was Rick's model for the breed, so the title of businessman had class in his book. But that wasn't the way Willis had said it.

"So what's his problem?"

"JJ? Can't rightly tell. He likes to brag that he knifed his own dad, which should give you an idea, but I wager he's been simmering so long in his own stew he don't know himself whether it's true, or what's really there 'neath the thin of his skin. It's like those charts the pilots made before the age of discovery. At the frontiers of the ocean, where no one dared explore, they would write, 'Here be dragons.' That's JJ Whitehead, lad."

It was past one-thirty when they tramped down the passageway to 8-12. Whitehead was still snoring. Willis brushed his teeth; Rick stripped to his underwear, hung his clothes over his jacket and hat; when Willis was finished, he used the sink, stuffed his wallet into his pillowcase and climbed up.

The usual, he'd said to Saint Eves. Some joke, he thought now, staring through the porthole, images forming from the harbor lights like clouds of breath on a frost morning...

Black cars and white stones and one small hand in Uncle Eli's; his mother walked beside him, worried because he hadn't cried, not a tear, not once since he'd seen his father crash the red Stearman Rick had flown in so many times. Now under a lowering sky someone began saying words he didn't want to hear so he closed his eyes and swam into the dark. But the dark was not dark. There was a light, or a flame, white with tongues of blue, drawing him in. He opened his eyes and people were laying flowers, yet the flame lingered there, hovering at the rim of his vision. He would see it once more, years later when he nearly died by his own hand, but not again since...

The rain eased. A breeze through the porthole. He bunched his pillow as the wake of a tugboat rocked *Caroline*—like a train switching tracks, like the Long Island Railroad when it breaks out from Penn Station tunnel...

Glen Cove station. Sid waved from the beat-up Ford they'd always used for carrying junk to the boat, or their rifles and gear when they went hunting, or the pistol case when they went to the police range. Today the truck was cleaned out and empty. They drove down the slope of town to the marina.

"That sweet gal Renée called this morning. Your mom really cares about her, you know. The three of us had a heart-to-heart and she told me to tell you—"

Rick's look stopped him. "It's over, Sid."

His stepfather frowned. "So you were, what? Just making sure?"

"Something like that."

They left the truck at the nautical supply store, walked past the rows of yachts to the "ways" where *Moonraker* had sat since she'd been hauled out of the water for the buyer's inspection. The fog was in, thick with seaweed and diesel fuel, turpentine and creosote. *Moonraker* brooded above, her topmast veiled in mist.

"We had great times," Sid said after a while.

Two workmen were prying her propeller from its shaft; Sid's yacht broker and the new owner stood near and watched.

"Greatest ever," Rick mumbled.

Sid had hoped he wouldn't let him sell, that he'd say no, let's keep her, she means too much to both of us. But Rick hadn't known how to do that, how to help him with the boat unless he quit the sea and lived in New York again, which he didn't want to do. So on the day he'd phoned home from the Gulf and Sid had laid out the facts like the gold-shield detective he was, Rick wouldn't let himself hear his stepfather's misery, or remember that embedded in the timbers of that cutter were the best days of his life. Yet he hadn't expected to be home for this last farewell, and now he despised himself for what they'd lost.

They stood in the fog, their guts in pieces.

"God, I feel low, Sid."

His arm on Rick's shoulders. "The hell with it, son. We've loved her a long time; maybe it's best someone else love her now."

He brought Rick over and introduced him to the buyer, one Benjamin Hawken. They chatted just long enough to be civil then drove to Amityville, drank whiskey and shot pool, tried to console each other about the boat and about Eli. That part was okay; Rick and his stepfather were always okay. Sid had taught him everything about sailing and the sea, never lectured him about the three strikes in three colleges, and though he'd tried his best to interest Rick in police work, he'd given his blessing when his stepson decided to ship out. Not Rick's mother, though—she couldn't or wouldn't understand it, couldn't or wouldn't let go of it. Now, because of her brother Eli's condition, it tore at her even more. At first that part was all right too. She loved him, that much Rick knew, and she was trying her best, but after a day or so she couldn't help herself and they went over it all again as they had a dozen times in the past. This time, though, she said something she'd never said before, that she prayed he wasn't turning out like his father.

And then she told him—the truth about Julian Paul Weisman's death. When Rick called home from Newark, waiting for his flight to Duluth and *Caroline*

Coast, she broke down and said she wished she hadn't.

The foghorn; a buoy bell. He closed his eyes and went back to the night after his talk with Eli...

He'd checked into a suite at The Plaza. Wages are good in the Merchant Marine, room and board are free, and seafarers can't spend much until they pay off their ship. Married men go home but, with wallets bulging, each single man has his kinks, his tastes, and most are bent on slaking them in port before the sea calls them back. Rick always stayed in the best hotel, flew first class, dined like a prince, making sure he was bust or close to it by the time he shipped out again.

He ordered room service then phoned her.

"Hello." She sounded tired.

"It's me, Renée."

Slow exhale.

"Are you busy?"

"Yes." Then she changed her mind. "Studying."

"How have you been?"

"All right." She said it in a way that meant something else. "Where are you?"

"In town. Uncle Eli needed to see me."

She knew him too well. "Everything okay?"

He fought to say it evenly. "No, he's dying."

"Oh, my God. You must feel awful."

"Anyway, he asked about you, and—"

"How nice of him. What did you say?"

"I told him we broke up."

She was quiet. When she spoke, her voice had changed again.

"So why are you calling?"

"I don't know."

"Are you at the Plaza? I could...be there in an hour."

His turn to be quiet; it had to come from her.

"No strings, Ricky, I swear. We never did say goodbye, you know. Not really, not that way."

There were strings, though—the layered pearls around her neck, the lines she'd murmur in a language all her own, the cries which lashed so tight they cut clean through, just missing his heart.

"You'll never find anyone as bad for you as me," she whispered after.

Then I won't bother looking, he thought.

She didn't stay the night. Rick watched her leave from his third-story window: the bellhop holding the door of the limo, bare legs scissoring from her skirt as she slid in, the black Cadillac motoring off.

He went back to bed, tossed for an hour between the damp sheets but it was no use, not with that thing burning in his jacket pocket on the chair a foot away.

And so, in a high-ceilinged room laden with Chanel and musk, the Zevi Coin had its way with him. He sat on the bed and caressed it, hefted it, marveling at its jewels and how they harvested the city light. He pictured the hands that must have held it as his did now, the men who must have hunted for it, lusted after it, the braided chains of circumstance that had linked its fate to Eli's and now to his.

He fetched his wallet from the night table and found the photo of Eli and him at the Sphinx, taken on that trip when he was twelve and which he'd carried ever since. He thought back to all that he'd learned from Eli a few hours before, the stories from his uncle's past and his family's, of Russia and strange encounters in the winter night, of mysteries Eli had solved and others he never could, and what his uncle had said to him at the end:

"Remember that crazy cabby who drove us to the pyramids, the guy who told you they used to shine like a mirror? When we got there you went running off and I paid the fare, and he must have liked the tip because it started him up again, on something he called the Fable of Zerzura. He probably didn't know it—at the time, I didn't either—but it's a rehash of a tale from the Talmud, one that's been passed on in countless versions over the ages.

"In any event, this Zerzura is supposedly an oasis of buried Egyptian gold, lost in the Sahara for thousands of years. Just another myth, though some still search for it to this day, but the story goes that once, long ago, a soldier of fortune actually found the place. He hurried back to Cairo to stake his claim, but as he was buying camels to carry away the treasure, he spotted Death standing in the marketplace. And Death saw him too and pointed at him with a look that froze the man's blood. He jumped on his horse and rode like the wind, all night and all the next day, until he reached Zerzura and safety.

"There he fell asleep, only to be awakened by the hand of Death. The soldier cried, 'You? But when you pointed at me in the marketplace, I was sure you'd come to Cairo for my soul.' To which Death replied, 'No, I was there for another's. I was merely startled to see you, for I knew we had an appointment tonight, here in Zerzura.'"

Eli had opened his arms then, and Rick felt again how they'd embraced for what they both knew was the last time.

"Well, it's only a story, son. And perhaps the Zevi Coin is only a piece of history. Or perhaps not. Just... watch carefully, now. Okay?"

Rick held the photo in his right hand, the coin in his left, and then, without willing them, both hands came together and he saw it. It was as if the coin and Eli and he were pieces of a puzzle, or words in some riddle that had been spoken long ago then forgotten, so the riddle had searched throughout eternity for someone to solve it, as if it couldn't rest until someone did.

He returned the photo to his wallet, secured the Zevi Coin in the lining of it. Yet the thing stayed with him as he fell asleep—rising in the sky of his dreams, above an oasis of gold in a sea of sand.

THREE

On a Slow Boat Made of China

Caroline Coast stole out of Duluth before Duluth could wake up and pity her. Bos'n Lou Sorine worked them hard, but it wasn't only the clean-up from loading grain and the squaring away for an Atlantic crossing. The haggard freighter was as caked with rust as a mime in makeup, and the bos'n had a mania about chipping and scraping it down then coating the steel with red lead. He liked to say that when they got through all the rust there wouldn't be any ship left, just a paint job.

On the second morning the sun blazed through a crosswind, nine knots from the north and gusting fifteen. Willis was at the wheel; the other two ordinary seamen, Freddy Sanders and Rolf Thurston, were pulling overtime for Ike Morris, the deck engineer, tearing down one of the winches. Nearby, Ike was commiserating with the bos'n and the new second mate, Abe Forbes, about the sorry state of the winches in general, and planning a renovation once they were at sea. Rick was bashing away at the rusted deck near the five-step ladder to the fo'c's'le—the raised portion of the foredeck where the anchor winches are, and where the lookout stands his watch in the "eyes."

"Hey, Wiseass! Come here!"

It was Whitehead, amidships between numbers one and two holds, repairing steel cable. Rick dropped his scraper and went over.

"What?"

Whitehead handed him an awl. "Stick this in there and lever it. No, not that way, shmuck!"

He grabbed it back and howled, clutching a punctured thumb; the awl dropped, banged to the deck. Everyone stared, but Whitehead only noticed Rolf.

"Whadda *you* lookin' at, faggot?"

Rolf ignored him; Rick returned to his work.

The three ordinaries were all young and new to *Caroline*—prime rib for Whitehead, who licked his chops whenever one of them was near enough to sniff. Rolf got it the worst, though. He had the cut physique of a decathlete and the temperament of a cloistered saint, so by some perverse logic all his own, Whitehead had pegged him as gay and taunted him incessantly. Whitehead was itching for a brawl, that much was plain, but it was also plain that Rolf's detachment was driving him around the bend. The more Rolf didn't rise to it, the more malicious the bait. Guys were placing bets.

Rick cocked an eye at Whitehead: Even the name suited—bush platinum hair, chewing-tobacco teeth, a solid lump of pink torso and pinkish eyes that were always watching, reckoning their prey for the high-speed hit-and-run or the cold-blooded carving up. He added his own judgment to Willis's: Whatever lurked inside Whitehead was ravenous, and to keep it from devouring himself he had to unchain it and let it feed.

Not that Rick couldn't handle a fight; Sid had taught him well and he'd held his own any number of times ashore and at sea. But JJ Whitehead? He was something Rick had never encountered, and when his time came, he wasn't at all sure he'd be able turn back the beast.

A bright blotch above: The Egyptian on the flying bridge in a billowing white tunic; he shaded his eyes, glanced at the sun and the horizon, on finding east sank behind the bulwark. Rick had seen him there yesterday doing the same—kneeling on a Persian rug, offering his prayers to Allah.

—⁓—

They were in Lake Erie, steaming through a muggy night. Rick was at the helm, and with him in the wheelhouse was Third Mate Bradford Tyler—six and a half feet of melancholy, as though the view from that height depressed him. He rarely spoke, chain-smoking instead and humming broadside ballads between drags, keeping the lyrics to himself. Tonight, it was "The Golden Vanity," slow and sad; when he finished each stanza, the ash would glow and fade, and the exhaled smoke would carry the start of the next.

Now the humming stopped as Captain Brace tripped in from the starboard wing and tottered towards the radar scope. He was a hulking type, handsome maybe when he was young, his brawn gone to fat. He leaned close to the glass and the reflection of the scope's red sweep crawled over his face, then he pushed off and wobbled to Rick's side.

"Pick them up on the next pass."

"Aye, captain."

He trained himself aft, swayed out to the chart house where he often spent the night, blind drunk on the watch bed until noon.

Saint Eves stepped onto the bridge, tailing Brace to make sure he didn't do damage. Though it was apparent now to Rick why the first mate presided over the captain's office—the bedroom was still used by Brace—he had to wonder what skeleton or rotten luck or worse was keeping Saint Eves from his own command and stuck on a decrepit tub like *Caroline Coast.*

He greeted Tyler, assessed the traffic on the lake, came to Rick's station and loitered by the binnacle where he could view the compass. Maybe the first mate was trying to rattle him—the scuttlebutt was that he considered any gyro variance in fair weather to be "steaming all over the ocean"—but Rick didn't mind. He knew his job.

"You getting on okay, Weisman?"

"Yes, sir."

"Glad to hear it."

During this the gyro compass had clicked off course a full degree. Rick responded with a touch of the wheel; the ship nudged a fraction; he held her steady and in a few seconds the needle clicked: dead on course. He touched the wheel the other direction to compensate.

Satisfied, Saint Eves shifted to face him.

"I believe the question was, why you chose the sea."

So much for his mind-your-own-business speech, Rick thought. And so much for my "usual reasons."

"One thing I could say, sir, is that I practically grew up on a sailboat."

"Really? What kind?"

"A cutter. Forty-foot double-ender, gaff rigged; built in Norway in 'thirty-eight, then fitted out at Camper-Nicholson's in England."

"Sounds like a Colin Archer."

"That's right. She'd already been around the world twice when my stepfather bought her."

"Was he in the Merchant Marine?" He was still angling for "why."

"Used to be a police detective. Retired now."

Saint Eves hadn't gotten what he wanted but it was all he was going to get, because Rick closed down in a way that let him know it. The first mate departed, following Captain Brace aft to the chart house.

—∞—

His trick at the wheel done, Rick was on lookout in the "eyes" atop the bow of the ship, the forward-most spot of the fo'c's'le. Nights like this, standing lookout is the best part of a watch—riding the easy swells, chasing down the moon and the Milky Way. He played his harmonica and surveyed the horizon for lights. Aboard a modern ship in good weather a lookout feels almost useless, knowing that vessels are marked on radar well before he can spot them. But not so on *Caroline*. The bos'n gave Rick, Rolf, and Freddy the heads-up the first day they sailed: *Caroline's* prehistoric equipment sometimes put a ship where it wasn't, like the night they'd almost rammed a swordfish boat that the radar showed as clear to port. He expected his lookouts to look *sharp*, and even here on the Great Lakes with orderly traffic lanes, Rick took him at his word and smacked the bell whenever a new light showed—one ring starboard, two rings port, three rings dead-ahead.

"Here's your java."

It was Whitehead, up from standby with coffee. He snubbed Rick's "thank you," retraced his steps down the ladder from the fo'c's'le deck. Rick warmed one hand around the mug, turned seaward and with the other held up his harmonica. The wind brushed through its reeds making arcane chords that it alone knew, wind music that needed no instrument yet played through his anyway.

—◊—

"Hi, Rick. Everything okay?"

"Yeah, Willis. Got six ships—one starboard, four ahead, one port."

"All right, then. You're relieved."

When you draw a JJ Whitehead on your watch, you'd better pray you draw a Willis Aloysius Fine too. Willis had a big rep as a classic boxer and a bigger one as a compulsive talker. Rick assumed the former was earned since the latter assuredly was. Willis Fine used to ship as bos'n until he got tired of the headaches and realized he didn't care about the money or the prestige; he missed the night watch and his daydreams, missed not having to worry so much. So he'd demoted himself to AB and said he was happy. He kept his life and the lore of the sea in a stack of journals, and he liked reading them to himself almost as much as he liked holding forth—smoking a Cuban cigar, squinting through granny magnifiers, lips mouthing words. A bit odd, like most seafarers, but he'd been straight and steady from the first and Rick was grateful for it.

He was on standby now, the last hour and twenty of the watch. There are three deck watches on a merchant ship: 8-12, 12-4, 4-8, each on duty day and night for its respective hours, plus whatever overtime the bos'n assigns, which is always welcome due to the good money. The 12-4 is called the dog watch—at night it's the blackest, the hours the most disorienting. The 4-8 is considered the plum because its night shift is just getting started when the sky begins lightening, and its day shift is just getting started when the crew breaks for dinner— work on a merchant ship ends at five, like an office. The 8-12 is in between: not too stressful on the inner clock, not too interesting either.

During the day it's all work—no standby or lookout needed, and each watch's two AB's take turns at the helm. The night watch is called the sea watch, and within it there's a rotation—tomorrow Rick would have first lookout, the next day first standby—which keeps men reasonably sane. But Rick dreaded this cycle of it, last standby.

You sit alone in the mess, bringing hot coffee up to the wheelhouse and forward to the lookout, and in theory staying alert for any emergency. In practice you do what you can to kill the eighty minutes before they kill you.

Tonight he'd been trying to read the guidebook Willis had lent him, about Tunisia, where they were headed, trying to ignore Eli's envelope, which he used as a bookmark, trying not to think about a world without Eli in it or the legend of the coin or what he'd learned from his mother about his father's death, trying and failing at everything because when you have last standby you keep drinking coffee as though someone's making you, cup after cup like a suspect under spotlights, hunched over a Formica table getting more tired with every sip and when it's like that you can't stop the thinking. So you try anything to get through it and tonight Rick was staring at the wall, counting the chip marks in the green paint that showed the grease gray beneath...sixty one, sixty-two...coffee narcosis thrumming with the pulse of the engines...one hundred six, one hundred seven...tapping a penny on the table rim, rocking against the ship's roll, muttering with each throb and pitch and counting, staring, tapping, sinking...

Finally, he opened Eli's letter, reading again of the man whose biography he found so troubling, though for what reason he couldn't say.

> ...which explains why the Tsar commissioned the coin. But the history really begins in 17th-century Poland, where there came among the Jews a

charismatic mystic named Sabbatai Zevi, who in 1648 proclaimed himself the Messiah. The Jews had been suffering merciless persecution and slaughter in central and eastern Europe, and over time Zevi attracted a multitude of followers. Among them was a humble and devout young man named Yaakov Ziskind. Like his father, he was a goldsmith by trade, and like Zevi he was from Smyrna. He became one of Sabbatai Zevi's first and most fervent disciples, spending more than seventeen years in the cause—until his so-called Messiah converted to Islam in 1666.

Oh, the depth of betrayal the poor man must have felt, Rick. On the brink of suicide, he experienced an overwhelming vision of the Christ and his mother Mary and converted to Catholicism. He became an ascetic after baptism, in self-imposed penance for believing in a false prophet, and journeyed on foot throughout Europe for decades. During his travels, the goldsmith would speak his witness to all who would listen, and when this wandering Hebrew Christian made his way to Russia, word of him attracted the notice of Peter the Great. The Tsar, then but twenty-five, had the man brought to court for what became the first of many private audiences, and eventually asked him to serve as Jeweler to the Imperial Crown. Yaakov accepted, yet he never stopped telling his story until the day he died, always praising the Lord for bringing forth Sabbatai Zevi—for it was Zevi's falseness that had opened Yaakov's eyes. Indeed, the Tsar, who was himself very religious, agreed to have Yaakov engrave on the coin's edge in Latin and

Cyrillic the phrase "Glory to God in the highest," and decreed that the object be known as the Zevi Coin, and from all this there arose the legend that he who bears it—

"Okay, Weisman." Joseph of the 12-4; the dog watch was taking over.

Down the passageway to 8-12; Whitehead and Willis arrived moments later. Rick opened his locker, undressed. Willis brushed his teeth and clamped open the port light; Whitehead was at the sink. When both were in their beds Rick washed, switched off the ceiling bulb, climbed into his bunk.

He closed his eyes and the lurid memory began its assault, yet this time he didn't punch it out as he usually did. Tonight, he needed to see it all, once more now that he knew the truth. Shifted onto his back and let it come:

Still life with blue sky and a streak of red, the Stearman biplane falling from it coughing and smoking, the sirens of fire truck and ambulance wailing across the runway after the plane drills itself in. And he saw himself below as his soul rose through the flames, the boy at the foot of the control tower, face screwed tight, not crying for trying so hard to understand:

Why didn't you take me with you, daddy? You always take me with you and give me flying lessons. Why not today? Why did you take your green leather binder instead, and hug me goodbye, and tell me you had to go alone? What did I do wrong?

And then it's Uncle Eli—emerging from the ruins, holding him by the hand, leading him through a blur of field trips and baseball games, opera and literature, art museums and magic shows and the sea and his ships, and always the simple talks about life and death and God until at last the screaming nightmares stopped.

FOUR

The Nature of the Beast

It was dawn, a Canadian chill in the August air. *Caroline Coast* glided out the steel doors of the final lock of the Saint Lawrence Seaway, the one called Saint Lambert, heading for open ocean. Rolf, Freddy, and Rick joined the line of men getting coffee.

The Seaway is a 2,300-mile chain of natural waterways, artificial canals, dredged channels, and the Thousand Islands of salad fame, all linked by sixteen locks that stair-step the 600-foot drop from Lake Superior to the Atlantic. Rick had been through it once before, which didn't make the forty-eight hours in traffic any easier, but at least he knew the drill: the ship enters a lock, men climb into bos'n's chairs fore and aft and get lowered to the wharf, catch the lead lines, haul down the mooring hawsers and secure them to the bollards, work the hawsers while the ship sinks to their level, scramble aboard as the lock doors open at the other end. The deck crew is on call for two days and nights, with only catnaps for rest.

The three ordinaries trudged up the foredeck to number one hold, sat warming hands around mugs. They barely knew each other, yet they were roughly the same age, had the same job and the same enemy...

"Anyone been to North Africa?" Freddy began.

"Saw Cairo once," Rick replied.

"No kidding? This is my first trip out of New York. How 'bout you, Rolf? Do any traveling?"

"Some. In the Marines. The Far East, mostly."

They drank their coffee. Mist floated on the Saint Lawrence River; fresh sunlight rayed through the trees on the near shore.

"Aw, ain't that cute. Little Lulu and her playmates."

They didn't have to look to know who it was but they did anyway, to make sure JJ was keeping his distance. He was—walking his coffee mug up the port side with one of his buddies, Forrest of the 4-8. The two ABs laughed, climbed the stairs to the fo'c's'le deck.

"You believe that muhtha?" Freddy's eyes bugged from a geekish face with red pimples and redder hair. He was five-nine and thin as pasta, but no wimp. "And you get to bunk with him," he finished, winking at Rick.

"True, but Rolf's his honey pie."

"Yeah, what about that?" Freddy pressed.

Rolf gauged him. "What about what?"

"I mean Whitehead—the way you keep shining him on. Like you don't know he's there. How long can you keep *that* going?"

"If you resist a force you tend to increase its strength; if you're indifferent, you tend to weaken it."

"Somehow," Rick put in, "that doesn't sound like it's from the Marine Corps training manual."

Rolf scratched a stubble of beard.

"Hardly. I got it from a wise man I once met, in Kashmir."

"That's where you were stationed?"

"No, but when I made corporal, I was tapped for embassy duty. Manila, Hong Kong, Singapore—from there I was sent on a mission to India. My last, actually." He nodded. "You can learn a lot in the Orient. Or nothing at all."

"Uh huh. Well, that aside," Freddy drew a money clip from his pocket, pulled a bill, "twenty bucks says you still end up fighting the putz."

"Sorry, I don't gamble."

"I'll take that action," Rick said, reaching for his—

"SANDERS YOU'RE ON WATCH! NOW GET BACK TO WORK!"

It was the bos'n, right behind them with the electric megaphone. They all flinched, and Rick lost hold of his wallet. It landed heavy, with a thump.

"I'm busted," Freddy hissed. "Later, gents."

"What do you have in there, brass knuckles?" Rolf asked, grinning.

Rick didn't blink; Sid always said people blink when they lie.

"Lucky charm," he answered, wagging the wallet.

They were steaming through the Cabot Strait, between Newfoundland and Cape Breton Island. Rick was at the wheel, Tyler was humming his tunes. A school of dolphins raced along with the ship, turquoise with bioluminescence beneath a sea of stardust, and every few seconds one would dive the keel then shoot out high above the waves on the other side.

"You really think you can pull it off?" The captain's voice, from the passageway aft; now he and Saint Eves entered the bridge with an eddy of cigar and pipe smoke.

"I hope so. Caroline deserves better."

"But what about my phosphate deal? There's more money in that for me," Brace said as they passed by.

Saint Eves sighed, as though tired of arguing. "Things should be clearer soon. We'll have dinner at Café Stella and talk it over, okay?"

They strolled out to the port wing. When they were beyond earshot, Tyler grumbled, "Deserves better? The Alang graveyard's too good."

Coming from the third mate, seven or eight words was a tirade, and Rick took the rare opportunity to speak.

"So what's the first mate doing, sir—looking to buy the ship or something?"

"Could be. Not the first comment I've heard that would make you think so, though for the life of me I don't see it. An old bag lady like Caroline Coast?"

"And the phosphates?"

Rick had pushed too far. Tyler swiveled the watch chair so his back was to the helm, then added, "That's why the Arab's on board." A snort. "Fertilizer. Would be the perfect cargo for Caroline."

Rick filled in from memory what he couldn't see in the gloom: the fogged windscreens, the flaking coats of paint and varnish, the obsolete instruments. She reminded him of the first freighter Eli and his brothers had bought in 1946—the *John L. Burns,* a Liberty Ship named for the septuagenarian civilian hero of the Battle of Gettysburg—and now he felt regret for the ungracious thoughts he'd had about *Caroline.* No matter what happened, no matter how tight things got for them, his uncles wouldn't scrap the *John L.,* wouldn't sell her. They kept her docked and turned her into a Merchant Marine museum for school kids. Maybe it was like that for Saint Eves. Maybe he'd known *Caroline* when she was young and strong, or more likely just her story—a tale of untold courage, perhaps, like many tales of war. Or maybe it was only that she'd been there, on the convoys, and made it through. Which for Rick's money was plenty.

Thousands of Liberty Ships and others like *Caroline Coast* had been built during World War II. Prefab sections railed from inland factories to the tireless yards, welded together on gargantuan assembly lines; some had been completed in as few as ten days, one had been launched in four. These were the ships that had held the Atlantic lifeline to Europe against impossible odds, and those who sleep in free beds now surely must owe them something.

So, the hell with Tyler, he fumed. This ship did deserve better—what forgotten hero doesn't? But who cares about one more hopeless bag lady on the skids? Who wants to know where she sleeps, where she came

from, or how she came to this? That's how it is with
these old ships, banished to some mothball fleet, or
hacked up for scrap at the Alang on the west coast of
India, or doddering like *Caroline* across the oceans of the
world—eyes glazed, awash in booze, steering their carts
full of cast-off junk into the bleakest back alleys of
commerce.

Yet still the dolphins danced with her, in the
kindness of the moonlight.

—〰—

A cloudless sky, the air so hot you could grill on it.
With no overtime after lunch, Rick was heading aft with
his rigger's knife and bag of wood. He passed by the lone
container cradled atop number four hold, came up
behind Rolf, who was on his knees by number five,
bashing rust with a scraper; grunted "Hey" and got the
same back.

Rick climbed the ladder to the poop deck; settled in
the shade of the paint locker, dug into his bag for a new
hunk of ebony, opened his rigging knife and started
whittling it. He'd learned the trick when he was a kid
and took it up again when he first shipped out. There
was no point to the work; a canoe was about the limit of
his talent. He just liked doing it, shaving the burrs,
smoothing the nicks, making it—

Like a grub from the mass of superstructure, a
shirtless Whitehead was spawned onto the after deck
and stood by the door, stretching. Now he spotted Rolf.
Even this far off, Rick could see his tongue snake out. He

hitched his jeans, cranked his strut, and when he got to Rolf he roughed up against him and waited for a reaction. As usual, nothing. Whitehead spat—a glob of chewing tobacco bubbled on the deck.

"Ain't you the lucky one, Wiseass," he drawled.

Rick kept whittling; the knife slipped and grazed a fingernail. Whitehead came up the ladder, bellied against the rail, opened a tin of Skol, stuck a plug into his cheek.

"Yeah, you do got yourself some view, here."

Another brown missile but this time at a target: it hit by Rolf's knee.

"She sure is a dish."

Rolf kept on as though he hadn't heard any of it, and that was pushing Whitehead right to the edge. Rick tried to rope him back.

"Give me a break, huh? I'm still digesting."

But nothing could stop him now, not till he got where he had to go.

"You know, Wiseass, all them muscle boys are faggots. That's why they's always in the gym, so's they can make it with their girlfriends. But muscle fags won't fight. It's all just for show."

Whitehead fired a third salvo and this one smacked Rolf's waist. He reached with a glove and wiped it, resumed scraping.

"See what I'm sayin'? All them muscles and she won't fight."

Enough with the Zen, already, Rolf! JJ's asking for it, why not let him have it?

He attacked the ebony as if it were Whitehead's throat.

"Hey, faggot. Get over here, I got a job for you." An ominous new tack—Whitehead was Rolf's senior.

Rolf kept working.

"Move it!"

Nothing.

"You hear me? I'm givin' you to three!" A pause. "One, two..."

He leaped down the ladder to the main deck, booted Rolf's butt and sent him sprawling. Now it was all half-speed and strobe-light fast, full throttle around the bend and crashing the guardrail, flying silently over the cliff.

"*Get up!*"

Rolf rose to his knees, spoke as to a wayward child. "If I get up, JJ, it's not going to be pretty. Better all-around if you just apologize and we both forget it."

Whitehead flushed, coiled to kick again but this time Rolf saw it with other eyes, whirled and caught the jeaned leg and jackknifed him *splat* to the deck—straddled his rump, locked up the left arm tight.

Whitehead seethed, brown saliva dripping out.

"I'd appreciate that apology, now."

"Up yours, faggot."

The arm splintered like a rotten branch and Whitehead blacked out.

Rolf looked up. "You're bleeding, Rick," he said.

—⁂—

Even for an ex-Navy pharmacist's mate like Bos'n Lou Sorine, it had been a taxing day of medicine—first

Whitehead's broken ulna and radius, now Rick's filleted index and the story that went with it—and he was fed up.

Stuck his coal-black face into Rick's: "All right, Weisman, you saw what you saw and that's that. I'm not saying you ought to lie the other way about it. I am saying you ought to shut the hell up. Rolf doesn't need anyone's help and that includes you." He wrapped the tape too tight. "Whitehead's on your watch and watchmates are supposed to stick together. Not to mention he's one vicious fiend, and if you throw in with Rolf whatever it is you think he'll do won't be half as bad as what he will do." Scooped up the first aids, dumped them in the kit. "So, if you can't shut up then you didn't see a thing, got it?" Stood and stowed the bag in the locker above his desk. "You were facing aft and whittling and daydreaming about some babe, and you didn't hear anything either till Rolf broke the arm."

Now he turned, jabbed a bony finger.

"Follow me? You get that story straight and don't change it no matter what. You've been at sea long enough to know the score. Blow this with JJ and you're dead meat."

—⁂—

Mess was tense, a work-shirted funk over steak and yams. Whitehead and Rolf sat as far apart as possible— one face gray, the other unreadable. No one knew for sure what had happened, but everyone was making his case anyway. The votes split along party lines: Whitehead was a dues-paying union man, Rolf just a two-bit ordinary; the majority of elders sided with JJ, though he was seen for what he was and they knew Rolf had put up with more from him than they ever would, if any of them had the nerve to take him on in the first place.

The buzzing died as King Tiny, the seven-foot, three-hundred-pound oiler, rumbled in late for dinner. By custom the Black Gang—oilers, firemen, water-tenders, wipers—should have its own area separate from the topsiders'. But here the adjacent engine-room mess lived up to its name, a shambles from a fire back in July, so both factions had to cram in and tolerate the other.

Caroline's Black Gang was ruled by the King, chief among the oilers, who are like bos'ns below decks. He sat at the head of the table where most of his sallow-skinned, oil-streaked roost crowded together. For all his phenomenal size, Tiny was a witty, literate man with a degree in mechanical engineering, and this evening it was obvious he was relishing more than just his food, particularly since he regarded topsiders as pansy prima donnas loath to get their hands dirty. The bos'n, the deck engineer, and the three deck watches less Forrest, who had the wheel for the 4-8, filled the remaining tables. The stewards, lowest of the low, served the food. Cautiously.

Freddy's Brooklyn accent thickened as he confided to Rick. "Our boy is toast. Whitehead will get him someway; sleeping, or ashore, or over the side even."

"My money's on Rolf."

"Yeah, maybe in broad daylight, but—"

"Care to make it interesting? I'd like to win back my twenty."

Freddy weighed the risk. "Nah, you saw 'em fight,

you should know."

"*What?* Who told you that?"

He glanced around. "JJ's spreading the word. Says you're backing his story that Rolf jumped him dirty."

Rick's mouth fell open.

Freddy nodded. "So it's *not* true. I guessed as much. What's the real dope?"

"Look, the bos'n told me to keep quiet, make like I didn't—"

He swallowed the rest as King Tiny stood up. The mess hushed; whatever he was about to say, no one was going to argue with it.

"Gentlemen, kindly join me in offering our gratitude to the, uh, 'Butcher' of Baton Rouge here," he began, raising his coffee mug.

The Black Gang smirked.

"He has generously provided us all with an expert tutorial on queer bashing."

The Black Gang chortled.

"Why, I'd lay odds poor old bloody, beaten Rolf here never even looks at a fella again."

The Black Gang cracked up; King Tiny sat amidst their applause; Whitehead huddled over his food. Gradually, conversations continued, and Freddy finished theirs.

"Going to be awkward, isn't it? To keep saying you saw nothing, with JJ saying you saw everything his way?"

Rick chewed his steak.

"And I kind of doubt friend Rolf's going to like it if you do." A shade lower. "You're in what they call a lose-lose situation, bub. You thought about that?"

— ᴍ —

Someone was hammering on deck, a slave gong. Above Rick's bunk the ceiling plates perspired in the heat, the welding seams streamed with rust that might be blood, the rivets dividing and multiplying like cells under a microscope. He wanted to sleep but couldn't. He wanted to believe that Freddy had it wrong—

"Nobody does me like that and gets away with it. *Nobody*. Break my arm? I'll break his stinking neck!"

—but the more Whitehead went on, his venom hissing on the air like a rattler's, the more Rick knew Freddy had it right.

"And I'll sneak on him like he done me, when he's sleepin' or ain't lookin', just like he done me. We'll see how he likes being a wheelchair faggot. Or a dead one."

"Well, you have been riding him mighty hard," Willis put in, with a judicial tone.

"Hey, whose watch you on? Sure, I was ridin' him, but only same as always! And later I was just snoozin' when he jumped me like *that*," he slapped the good hand on his thigh, "and broke my arm."

"Yeah, I got that part. What I can't reckon is...look, he's a nice enough guy, and no one else thinks—"

"You're not standin' with *him*, are you?"

Willis had almost had it. "I didn't say that."

"Dammit, I'm tellin' you how he took me out was he *sand*-bagged me, gave me no warnin'. I was only *ridin'* him, see, same as always, and then he's on me and..."

Now Rick saw them, there in the welding seams—

his demons clawing out from the rivers of rust.

"Come on, JJ," Willis interrupted, "we're talking this to death, don't you think? Let's get some sleep. Might make you feel better."

"You son of a—you ain't *with me,* are you?"

"You'd best mind your tongue, friend. No call to speak to me that way."

Soon, now. Very soon.

"You're right. I got no beef with you, Willis Fine. You're a fair man and we're watchmates, and watchmates got to hang together. If you don't believe me, ask Weisman. He was there. He saw the whole thing."

Whitehead punched his mattress.

"Hey, Weisman. Tell him." The fist punched again. "You hear me?"

"I'm trying to sleep."

Whitehead sprang from his bunk, his porcine face sweating, breath reeking. "Listen, *Jewboy*, I ain't takin' no lip from *you.* I'm sayin' Rolf did me dirty. You saw it, now tell *him!*" His thumb jabbed towards Willis.

The slave gong on deck stopped. The sea shone fire-crosses through the porthole. And though Rick tried to fight them with everything inside that sued for peace and sanity, finally nothing could stand to the devils in the rust.

He sat up, legs dangling off the side of the bed.

"All right, JJ, I'll tell him."

Rick looked at Willis; the AB shook his head, trying to stop him. But it was too late.

"He's lying, Willis. Every last lousy word of it." Now to Whitehead, "That about what you had in mind?"

Whitehead stared back, stunned. Willis sagged into the future, eyes rolling. Rick dropped from his bunk and headed for high ground.

FIVE

The Riddle

The bright afternoon turned to ragged dusk, and the occluded skies brought seas and a cold wind, and Rick had last lookout. There were no ship lights to mark, no company except stars that aren't there and a horizon he couldn't see and unfinished sentences that clash out of time and order, never resolving, never recanting, leaving him nothing to do but damn his demons and himself even more. You think you've got them licked, he said to no one, yet they're only dormant like locusts, biding their time, and when they come for you they come in force.

Now the sentences did resolve—into Eli's and his own from the night when the coin changed hands:

"A few years later you were born, and when your dad burned up in that crash I knew, just as Michael had predicted, that the Zevi Coin was to be yours. I meant to give it to you then, I was supposed to give it to you then, but I couldn't. I was too weak to let go of it. I'm mortified to have to say this, but I thought that if I did, my luck might run out."

Rick shivered, recalling how eerie it was, how much his uncle believed in it.

"I'm sorry, son. Sorry I'm so selfish and stupid. Maybe it would have changed things for you. Maybe you—"

"No, sir. It wouldn't have changed a thing. Not the Zevi Coin or a bucket of them. And no one's to blame but me."

Eli wasn't listening.

"After that I was too ashamed to give it to you, or so I told myself. But the sealed instructions have been attached to my will since the day you came home from the hospital. Thankfully it was God's will that I give it to you in person. I'm grateful for that. Spared me from a final act of cowardice."

"Uncle E, please—I can't stand you talking like this. Of all people, the way you've lived? We make our own destinies, you showed me that."

"And it's true. But it's not all that's true."

And then he told him about the soldier of fortune, and the lost oasis, and the appointment in Zerzura.

Rick shivered again.

After midnight he stayed up, figuring Whitehead would be snoring in an hour and it'd be safer. He went to the mess where Rolf was on standby and sat with a mug of coffee:

So now what? Tell the bos'n how you took his advice? Like maybe he'd let you switch watches with Freddy or swap jobs with a steward? No—you won't ask him, and he wouldn't let you anyway and it'd be no use even if he did. There's nowhere to hide on a ship; everyone hears everything and a move like that gets you branded gutless all around. In 8-12, at least you have Willis.

"Rick? You okay?" Rolf was peeking over his book, *The Interior Castle.*

No answer, just a fake grin.

"How 'bout some fresh joe?"

Rolf went to the pantry, expertly banged the top of the urn at the edge, which flipped off the lid. He caught it and set it on the counter, emptied the leftover brew and cleaned the grinds, began measuring in water and Yuban. Now Mr. Saint Eves entered and paused, spread-legged, just inside the door. Nodding at Rick, he flicked open his Zippo and lit his pipe. Rolf turned his head at the smell and the rest of him followed; he stood at ease, military-style, hands clasped behind his back. He knew what was coming.

"All right, Thurston, let's hear what you have to say for yourself."

"Yes, sir. It was like this: Whitehead kicked me when I was on my knees working. He tried to kick me again, so I took him down and locked his arm. I asked for an apology, he said, 'Up yours, faggot,' and—well, you know the rest."

Saint Eves slid onto a table edge, relit his pipe. "Not exactly how Whitehead tells it."

Rolf grimaced. "Which is to be expected, isn't it?"

"Possibly, but his allegations are serious, and so is his injury. I may have no choice but to take action if you can't substantiate your side."

"I've given you the facts, sir. That's as substantial as you can get."

The first mate weighed the case, but Rick didn't like Rolf's chances.

"Mind if I speak, sir?"

"Go ahead."

"I was there; I saw how it went."

"You're willing to make a statement? There could be repercussions."

"No, I'll make a statement. Rolf's telling it like it is except for what he left out. Ever since Duluth, Whitehead's been riding him with that faggot crap and worse. Anyone else would've blown his stack long ago."

"Okay. That part jibes with what Willis says." He appraised him through the smoke. "I appreciate getting the straight story, Weisman. Takes guts." He took an ashtray from the table, tapped the pipe bowl empty. "And, uh…if things get too rough on your watch, come see me."

The first mate left. The engines surged into the silence.

Rolf studied Rick for a second, turned and replaced the coffee urn lid, pushed the button, walked over and sat opposite—three-day beard, brownish eyes penetrating.

"Thanks."

Rick shrugged. "No big deal."

"It is to me. I hope you know how to defend yourself."

"I get by."

"Ever in the service?"

"My stepdad was a cop; he taught me some moves."

"Well, that's better than nothing. But from what I

hear, this guy's an expert with a knife and takes no prisoners. Think you can deal with that?"

Rick saw the white reptile below his bunk, staring up.

"Tell you what. Let me show you a couple of dirty tricks you can use in a pinch. Who knows what he might try tonight."

The moves were simple but deadly. He took Rick through them several times, then over coffee had him visualize everything again.

"Guess that's all we can do for now. It's not much."

"No, it's a lot. Consider us even."

"Whether or not *we're* even won't mean a thing when *JJ* decides to get even. Understand?" He checked the clock, scratched the bridge of his nose, decided. "Afternoons when our watch ends at four, Joseph and Driller go straight to King Tiny's for poker, then to dinner. Which leaves our cabin empty. You're free then too so it should work out."

"You're saying—?"

"Yeah. Fortunately, you learned some basics from your stepdad and you're in decent shape. We'll put mattresses on the floor, and I'll give you a crash course in martial arts. And bank on it, friend, you're going to need it."

—m—

First light. No sleep.

Rick slid down from his bunk, collected clothes and sneakers, dressed in the passageway. He headed for the mess and poured coffee into the biggest mug on the counter, added cold milk, gulped down half. And what about tonight, wise guy, he berated himself, and tomorrow? Even high-octane Colombian has its limits.

Out on deck the wind was freshening; he sucked in salt air, shook his head to broom the cobwebs. Leaden sky and swells, a fringe of red in the east: the Mistress of the Sea, up to no good. He knew her ways well enough—how fast she could jilt you or kick you out of bed. Her foul temper matched his own, and neither improved as the day wore on.

Right before four when he was heading for his first session with Rolf, the call for "All hands" crackled over the ship's loudspeakers. Rumor was they were in for a blow, a violent gale, the backing remnants of a Caribbean hurricane that had ravaged the eastern seaboard, caromed off a high-pressure system and shifted to the northeast. The deck engineer rounded up Rick, Joseph, and Driller, and took them to secure the lifeboats.

There was a bark from the after-end of the boat deck.

"Weisman!"

The bos'n had just climbed the ladder from below; Rick jogged over.

"We can't have no one-arm helmsman tonight; it's a sure thing Whitehead won't be able to hold onto Caroline in *that*," he thumbed at the Gothic front chasing them from the southwest. "So, I want you and Willis to divide your wheel—two hours each. He'll take it first 'cause she'll be all over us right about eight and who knows what'll happen. By the time you're at the helm we should be settled in, one way or the other."

"What do I do till then?"

"Stand by in the mess. Saint Eves has ordered lookouts on the wings so Whitehead will take one and Sanders the other after you relieve him. But mark my words, kid. You keep your slickers on and stay *ready*. Don't know what sort of ships you're used to, but things can get awful hairy awful quick on old Caroline."

Now he hailed the deck engineer. "Hey, Ike! When you're through here, have this bunch do the paint locker. After that you can knock off." He glanced at his watch, then the storm, then continued on his rounds.

—⁂—

The thundering came first.

Rick was resting before watch—in slickers, outside on an upper deck to avoid contact with Whitehead. He'd found a snug spot by a storage locker, facing the storm front so it wouldn't catch him napping, yet in spite of the rising gusts and heavy seas he'd dozed off when the sound shot his eyes wide:

A wall of water, where the horizon should have been.

He vaulted to the ladder, slid handrails down three decks to the main, yanked open the door to the passageway and slammed it closed. The ship pitched down and pitched him with it; he threw himself back at the door, caught the handle and sealed it shut just as the monster wave hit like a runaway freight, its engineer hanging from the steam whistle's rope. *Caroline* heeled hard over, lights browning out, bangs, bashings, and yells spilling everywhere from bunks and lockers—mere bird cries in the banshee wail. Rick was paralyzed against a bulkhead, goggling at King Tiny's cabin above him. The ship was paralyzed too, on the threshold of disaster in a forty-degree roll and for the first time in his life at sea Rick thought the Mistress might take him for her own. But then, clumsy like a drunk, *Caroline* righted herself and King Tiny burst out from his cabin, spewing obscenities as he dragged Rick to his feet and steamrolled through the engine-room door.

Rick groped towards the mess. Freddy was there, scared sweating witless; he met Rick's eyes then headlonged through the door, bound for a bridge wing and lookout. Rick wedged himself into a corner seat and dug in. After the first massive blow of the front there were mountainous following seas and he didn't like the way *Caroline* was riding them, didn't understand why she hadn't been heaved-to, didn't know how many cardiac wallows she could take before she foundered, and those worries plus the airless mess and the cannonades of rain and the surreal wind wound him white-knuckle tight—watching light bulbs fizzle and flare, stacks of dishes hurl from a latched pantry, a clock tick so slowly it seemed to run backwards and all the while he was watching he was waiting, for that one wave a ship can't shake off, that one last goodbye wave that would break her spine and stone her to the bottom.

Now *Caroline* came about, heeling over again as she exposed her beam, finally straining into the maw of the storm only to be flung into roller-coaster dives and teeth-chattering quakes and that's when he heard it, the most terrifying sound any seafarer can ever hear: the crying of his ship's mortal soul.

He staggered from the mess and out to the rain-blinding black, the seas walloping the deck and gushing through the freeing ports. His flashlight found it on the first pass—on the starboard side, six yards forward of the superstructure, the bulwark that extends up four feet from the hull to encircle the deck had torn open at a welding seam.

Ran back to the passageway:

"MAYDAY! MAYDAY!"

The bos'n flew out his door.

"She's splitting apart, Bos. Starboard rail by number three hold."

Rick lurched outside again as cabin doors opened and the bos'n rallied the troops. "Everyone forward! MOVE IT! Joseph, tell the bridge. Ike, we need the Lincoln."

Men tumbled from the passageway, each adding his flashlight's illumination to Rick's, each hooking onto something to keep his feet—a ventilator, a cable, anything—each trying to persuade himself that the ship disintegrating before his eyes was still alive, knowing if that tear reached the deck there would be no stopping it and *Caroline* would go down.

Now Ike and the bos'n lugged out the Lincoln arc-welder—tools, grinder, cables, flood lamp, and scrap iron heaped on its chassis, the live end of the power cord from the ship draped over Ike's arm. The spell snapped. There was just one chance to save their necks and everyone scrammed to grab it.

Rick fell in with Freddy and Rolf, wedging the

Lincoln against the bulwark; Ike, Jacky, and Driller lashed it and clamped the wheels. The bos'n tied its power cord in a knot with the ship's, rigged outlets for the light and the grinder, plugged everything in and wrapped the joints with electrical tape. Forrest and Joseph secured the flood lamp to a cargo boom and turned it on: as the ray riddled with bullets of rain drew every eye to the bulwark, *Caroline* plowed into a giant sea and the impact sawed seven more inches. Leaving two feet at most till the jig was up.

Second Mate Forbes stumbled from the passageway with arms full of welding gear, his uniform saturating in an instant. The bos'n helped him to the railing and Forbes dumped the load, hollering above the gale, "START GRINDING. NO TIME FOR PERFECT, OKAY?"

The bos'n plugged in the grinder and kneeled. Sparks fountained off like Roman candles as he cleaned to raw metal.

Forbes and Ike pulled helmets, rubber gloves, boots, and knee pads from the pile of gear and suited up. The second mate inspected the welding stick, Ike hefted the first patch plate; bos'n completed his prep and backed away. Joseph laid rubber mats on the deck and the team kneeled; Ike braced on a bollard, positioning the patch; the second mate supported by the Lincoln, his welding stick aimed at the plate's lower left quadrant. The moment was etched: fortress skies, harpoon rain, desperate men in a strobe of white.

The bos'n wound up the Lincoln's voltage and threw the switch: a bolt of 300-amp juice streaked out the electrode, sizzling like fried steak. Forbes shifted the stick, and the section of weld he'd finished cooled and hardened in a brume of steam. His back was arched, neck muscles taut below the helmet: electric-arc welding is tough enough, dangerous enough on its own, but having to fight force-11 winds and waves and the spastic fits of a ten-thousand-ton freighter—

"Go relieve Willis," the bos'n cupped his squawk into Rick's ear, "and tell him to hustle down here. Second mate's going to need a breather fast."

Rick let go the cable and catapulted at the superstructure, snagged the handrail as his feet ice-skated out. Climbed to the boat deck, clutched the lifeboat tackle going aft, upstairs again then aft again then up again to the starboard bridge wing, pointed for the wheelhouse doorknob but the ship took a colossal sea and knocked him flat. He rolled and skidded, finally struggling to his knees yet now the black night went maggot white, horrid white charging like a rhino. He launched himself at the legs of the beast and Whitehead sailed over him, thudding against the side of the wheelhouse. Rick scrambled to his feet, his flashlight for a club, hunkered at the ready but again *Caroline* pitched crazy and this time dangled him in mid-air. Bawling like bedlam, Whitehead lunged.

—⁓—

Am I dead? Dying?
He feels brisk, alert—gazing down at the self that he's vacated, strapped unconscious to the captain's watch

bed, six feet below him in the chart house.

The storm is muted to sighs; the bos'n is tying off stitches, swearing under his breath; Saint Eves sits beside him, assisting. Nearby, a jumble of slickers on a puddle of wet. A moan from Rick's body as they apply the bandages.

Sorine slumps in his chair. "That's it. Best I can do."

"First-rate job, Lou, as always."

"I hope so." He gets up, starts repacking his kit, "If it's all right, we ought to keep him here until the storm eases."

Saint Eves chews a lip. "What do you think? Do we need to radio the Coast Guard?"

"Difficult to tell. Along with the gash in his skull he probably has a concussion, and they can be tricky. But I'd say no."

"Okay. You'd better get back to work; I'll keep an eye on Weisman. And send someone up with the status of the repairs."

The repairs. Yes, I remem—

Just like that he's hovering by the welding crew. Willis is polishing off the final patch plate; the crisis has passed.

How long since Whitehead—?

Even as the question forms, he's back in the chart house, focused on the chronometer. He begins to get the idea: Saint Eves asks about the repairs, his curiosity is aroused, next moment he's viewing the men working on deck; he questions the time, in a heartbeat he's facing a clock. Whatever it is he's become, the slip of his mind seems to move him, instantaneously.

Lord, what a thought.

It hauls hard on his psyche, severing his human sense of *being here,* and he lifts to the ceiling and through it and out the top of the superstructure—soaring high above the ship, astonished to see everywhere at once: the raven ocean spanning to the horizons, the graybeards churning foam at their crests, the sky above teeming with miracles as in the dreams of mystics. Imagine, he wonders, to be higher, high enough to view the curvature of the earth, high enough to—

He's hurtling around the planet, seas and stratus and continents whip beneath, stupendous with color: day to night, night to day, faster till the blue-white nucleus blurs, faster till the colors blend to one, faster till the stars become strands of tinsel and the strands stretch into cracks and the universe drains out like bath water.

Now there is only emptiness, and a wind keening through it, and he fears for his soul for he knows that he's lost. Cast adrift on a primordial sea, surely here he is lost forever.

New sounds on the wind turn his sight: A black castle, black and red banners threshing at its turrets; in some vague other distance a sphere of luminous white and fabulous blue, like the earth from space yet not, familiar and welcoming and he wants to go towards it but cannot. He imagines being loosed from what holds him, yet it binds him still. He wrestles against the invisible, yet it flexes to the match.

"This black castle would have you for itself. Your desire for the light fuels its strength. Drop your struggle or it will devour you."

He does as he's told, and the contest stops.

Now he hears the voice again but calling from distant reaches, its repeats circling the space as if fueled by surrounding cliffs. "You listen well for one who has strayed so far. But you do not belong here, and I am charged by He who has no name to send you back."

The imagined cliffs materialize. He's in a desert canyon, the floor of it carpeted with sand, the peaks gorgeous with sunset, the sky cobalt. The author of the voice stands before him: gray and wine robes with gold thread interwoven, oxblood boots shined beneath the dust, ornate sword at his belt, white hair framing a gaunt face with hawk nose and hawk eyes lake powder blue, faceted dark as the ruthless sea.

"Nevertheless, one must play the hand one is dealt," he says, drawing the sword and, with it, a rectangle in the sand. "So, I shall leave you with this: There is only one thing I know, the only thing that needs to be known. If you can know this thing, then you need to know no other; if you cannot, then it matters not what else you know. Should it be given you to know this thing, you will believe it is because you have come to know all other things; yet until it is given, you are condemned to know nothing."

Within the rectangle drawn by the stranger Rick sees shadow pictures in the sand, swirling like trapped spirits in a genie's lamp: an alley with phantoms running, chasing; an old man's fists against a desert sky; a sea of huddled faces in streetlight red; a woman's tears, glistening on the coin in her palm.

"Watch carefully, now," the stranger says.

With a click the rectangle of sand coalesces and

clarifies and becomes as a pane of glass, and Rick looks through it to the sky and the sea and *Caroline Coast:*

In his cabin, at his desk, is Samir Abdessalam, writing in a notebook. To one side are a tin of cigarettes, an ashtray, a silver cigarette case and lighter. Before him is a map with red lines marked on it. The ship heaves and Abdessalam holds onto the desk, then closes the notebook and folds the map. He pushes back his chair and opens the center drawer: passport, wallet, pistol, box of ammunition. He deposits the map and notebook, shuts the drawer, exits the cabin. The watcher follows as Abdessalam wobbles along forward, holding the handrail until he's at the doorway to the chart house. Saint Eves is still seated by the body on the bed.

Abdessalam speaks, the first mate replies, the Egyptian departs. Saint Eves looks over his shoulder and scowls.

Tyler pokes in the doorway. "Bos'n says the welds are holding and they're stowing the gear. Willis Fine's back at the helm."

"Good. Tell Whitehead to get up here on the double."

"Aye, sir." He hesitates. "How's Rick doing?"

Saint Eves shakes his head. "Okay, I hope, and if so it's all thanks to you, Brad. You understand we may need you to testify."

"Don't know that it'll help much, sir. I heard a thump on the wheelhouse, came out and saw JJ by his side."

"And if you hadn't, no doubt he'd have chucked him over the side to finish the job."

Tyler leaves; soon Whitehead arrives, dripping. "Yeah?"

"What do you have to say about this?"

"About what?"

The first mate springs, mangling his collar.

"Listen, buster, I didn't see what you did to Weisman, but I've got a damn good idea and I'm warning you—you are *in my sights.* One more little thing, *anything,* and you have my personal guarantee that you'll never get a job at sea again. You read me?"

"You can't do that! I got seniority and you got no proof! I'll report your ass!"

"Be my guest. Nothing would suit me better than demolishing you in a hearing. I'm sure Rolf Thurston wouldn't mind helping out either, along with Weisman. And don't forget, your union rep on this ship is Willis Fine and watch mate or no, he's as pissed off as I am. Maybe more."

Whitehead starts to speak but doesn't.

Saint Eves lets go. "Got it?"

Whitehead melts away; shortly afterwards, Saint Eves does too.

Rick, still severed from himself, remains—transfixed on his body below. Now a single groan escapes; now a single limb moves; now the claim of bones and blood begins to reel him in and he begs the canyon for salvation yet finds only pinwheel galaxies shredding the rack of sky and stars showering napalm and trying to break free his chest seizes—lungs frozen, eyes peeling as the night rips open and through it there's an aqua sky with puffs of clouds. Suspended in mid-air is a crystal oval, smooth and level like a tabletop, its surface bare except for a crystal bowl filled with white-blue flame.

I've seen this before, it's called to me before—

He yearns to take the bowl and drink, and as the desire draws him closer a portal of sky swings out, a great door, and from beyond the door he hears the voices of many men, debating issues of grave importance. The voices grow louder and he realizes the men are about to come through and also that they mustn't find him there, and now there's a flux of noise and he panics—shouts and the voices from beyond and another that sounds like his own but from where he doesn't know, repeating the stranger's riddle until he looks back through the rectangle of glass to the ship: Abdessalam has returned, standing framed in the chart-house entrance, his face ashen as though witnessing the unthinkable. Now Saint Eves returns too, shoves the Egyptian aside and hurries to the bed. Rick watches as the first mate takes his wrist and counts the pulse, dabs sweat from his face with a towel, presses the bandage and pries open an eyelid and—

Oh, God, I can feel that.

Eons away, light years away, still the touch sends shock waves that shoot him out the canyon, slingshot like a stone from some impossible stretch fired down, down—shattering the glass, plummeting the stars, vanishing in one flash-funneled swoop through the night and the storm to the ship and the chart house except now it's different, the room beginning to spiral, the pain like a pile driver and he can't stop it, not this, never this—the falling like you fall in that dream, the long dream of falling that ends with the sledge strike to the floor and the stranger's sword held high by its blade and his voice orating the riddle again and again as though it's been searching eternity for someone to solve it, and won't ever rest until someone does.

SIX

News of the World

"Wake up, kid. There you go. Open those peepers."

Kelp stink and salt...rumbling engines...calm seas. The bos'n with a loaded tray; he set it at the foot of the bed, poured water from a pitcher, offered the mug.

Rick drank it all then croaked, "Gotta whiz."

"Left a soup pot for that. Here."

He took back the mug and Rick labored to his knees, positioned the pot, pulled aside his underwear, managed not to miss. The bos'n removed the pot and set it on the floor.

Rick crumpled down, groaning loud.

"Don't complain," the bos'n said, uncapping a bottle of Jack Daniels. "You have six stitches and a concussion, but it could have been worse. And on the bright side," he tipped a half shot into the mug, "seeing as how you survived and didn't tarnish my reputation, I'm not charging you for the surgery. Here, have a taste."

Rick's frayed nerves soaked up the splash of liquor

but he craved more. The bos'n saw that and smirked.

"Good stuff, huh?"

"Hard to say. Leave the bottle so I can make sure."

He chuckled, unscrewed a pill-bottle top, tapped two caps into Rick's hand.

"Pop these for a chaser and you're jake."

"I thought with a concussion you had to stay awake."

"Look, if you're not in a coma after all the sleep you been getting, no worries about that. The pain, now, that's going to hang in a while. But if you really don't want 'em—"

Rick took the pills and the bos'n gave him another swig of whiskey.

"Sweet dreams, kid. I'll drop in on you later."

He put the mug on the tray with the pitcher of water, jammed it against the bulkhead and rail by Rick's feet, stepped to the sink and rinsed out the soup pot, left it on the tray too. Took the pill bottle and Jack Daniels and was about to go.

"Hey, Bos—you think I'm okay? I mean, upstairs?"

"Given your screw-up with JJ, you were probably mental to begin with."

"Seriously."

He shrugged.

"You came out of it long enough for me to ask a couple questions and give you the once over. Reflexes were fine, you knew the year, where you were..." A slant to his expression. "You did spout some peculiar stuff, I will say that."

Rick's neck dry-iced.

"Peculiar how?"

"I don't know. Something about flying around space and falling through windows." He stepped, reached with his free hand, pressed the tape securing the bandage. "But like I said, not to worry. The brain can play tricks when it gets shook." He shrugged again, and as the door closed behind him a sluice fractured and the torrent of last night flooded in.

The bottom dwellers of the ocean have adapted to the pitch cold, the black, the crushing pressure. But what if you swept one to the surface? What if you showed him the sun and the world then sent him straight back? Suppose he lived and were able to tell the tale—what could he say? Who would believe? Maybe he'd be scarred by the vision, maybe he wouldn't believe it himself, maybe he'd have to try once more for the surface, even if it meant he'd never make it back.

Now Rick saw again what he'd seen through the napalm sky on the night of the storm, and remembered when he'd seen it before:

He was sixteen. He'd driven out to the beach on a friend's motorcycle, out from the city to the ocean with some wine and some codeine and a girl he'd just met. He'd come to the shore often that summer, for similar fleshy wallows, and sometimes the starlit sand would transform into allegories: time, because it can't remember your name; wisdom, because it falls through your fingers.

But tonight, it had all gone horribly wrong. Tonight, reclined against a log of driftwood with the laughter of the girl in the surf, he realized the naked truth:

There is nothing so trackless, nothing so helmeted as sand.

And with that, as though the road that led on from his father's crash had reached its dead end, he sat up, gulped a handful of pills and washed them down with wine. Soon he fell back flat and the star cloth above ripped apart: an aqua sky with puffs of clouds, and suspended within it a clear crystal oval, on its surface a bowl of white-blue flame. It called to him, and he yearned to drink from it, and he floated away from his life.

Is that what happened to my father? he thought now. Is it happening again to me? Is it all finally just scripted in blood and genes, and you can never escape? He tried to see his father's face but saw only his own, there in the red biplane and the terrible fire; felt the tide of fear yet the thrill of it too—lifting high above the storm, soaring across the universe, riding that rocket straight into...what? Insanity or infinity? Is there a difference?

At last, the bos'n's narcotic rippled up, soothing his skull the way honey cools the scald of curry. There was a voice from somewhere far off and words he couldn't understand, and the words were like wind chimes. He dreamed of a grove of palms, and a spring, and a face in the stars at the gates of Canaan.

—m—

He awoke to the snores of Willis and Whitehead. Switched on the reading lamp: his watch hands read 1:57, date window twenty-one.

Climbed down weak-kneed, wobbly. Three steps to the basin, the image in the moonlit mirror blurred. And now something else in the glass. Almost like...fog.

Splashed cold water on his face, looked again.

Still there, moving.

Leaned in closer—

Phantoms came streaming out, their looks of misery shoving him back to the lockers. He shut his eyes but the voice was repeating those words he couldn't understand so he opened them again, yet now the phantoms were coming with the voice, and the faces were of people he knew and others he didn't all entreating him the same, and certain he had to be going mad he grabbed for the only power he could, his link to Eli and the world before the storm.

He groped in the pillowcase—

Wait. It was with you last night, remember? In your jeans when you were on watch. Someone undressed you and put you to bed and put your clothes away.

To his locker. There they were, the Levi's on a hook, the bulge in the rear pocket. He exhaled, tuned in to Willis and Whitehead. Still snoring.

Reached for the wallet—

He knew it even as he tore at it, knew it from the weight as he pawed at the lining, knew it as he sank to his knees amidst paper bills and plastic cards and the wallet finally empty, fluttering from his hands.

The coin was gone.

—w—

He lost time after that. Now he found himself dressed and floundering up the foredeck in the dark.

Amidships he went dopey, sucking air, and held on to the starboard side railing. A beam of light shone from behind him—the dog watch standby coming to relieve the lookout.

Dog Days on the dog watch, Rick thought in a haze—drugged and trembling, a hollow corrosion in his throat and Eli in his mind, that summer they went to Egypt: "...comes from long ago, Ricky. The nomads of North Africa named this time for the rising of Sirius, the Dog Star. For them, the Dog Days meant terrible heat, disease, and suffering..."

Everything went gray and Rick went with it.

"Who's there?"

Flashlight white like a desert sun. Like Dog Days in the desert, a white dog hunting, hounding—

"Rick?" Rolf, on one knee. "You hurt?"

"I don't know. Don't think so."

"All right, stay put."

Rick watched Rolf's flashlight beam bobbing forward, up the four stairs to the fo'c's'le. A bubble of clarity through the gray goo: Can you trust him? Could even Rolf resist such temptation? Could anyone?

The flashlight was returning.

No. Trust nobody. Report nothing. Only you and the thief know about the coin. Keep it that way. Until we reach port it's not going anywhere, and neither is he. Enough time, maybe, to find out who it is and steal it back. Enough time to make him pay.

"Okay," Rolf said, bending over, lifting him up. "Joseph will clue in the bridge. Let's get you back; I have to stand lookout." Rick slung an arm around him, Rolf started in the direction of the main house.

"I'm not going to bed."

"Yeah, you are. You need rest."

"I've had rest; I need food. Come on, take me up to the eyes. I'll hold the fort, you raid the fridge."

Rolf weakened, sighed, walked Rick forward, helped him negotiate the steps to the fo'c's'le. Once at the eyes he propped the rubber body against the rail and Rick held on, panting and twitching.

"Jeez. You going to faint again?"

Rick breathed in and out, nodded.

"I'll be okay."

Rolf, skeptical, watched him for a few seconds then took off.

Rick scanned the sharp horizon, the ship cleaving towards it alone. But no, he thought, for there under sequined stars and a sly moon slept the Mistress—spent from her upheavals, a black-widow lover finally sated. *Quite a night you gave me,* he mused bitterly. *Quite a ride. And now look at you, lying there all purring and innocent across the sea's satin sheets.*

"Here, this should keep you till morning."

Rolf was back—a mug of coffee in one hand, in the other a platter of roast beef, Swiss, rye bread, grapes, and Cookie Fong's runaway rave, Chinese potato salad. Rick wolfed every crumb.

"Man, that was a lifesaver," he said finally, sipping hot coffee. "I owe you."

"Uh, quite the opposite."

"What? How do you mean?"

"Because if I'd just played it cool with JJ—"

"Come on, Rolf. Any cooler and you'd have frozen. And if I hadn't been so hot to get out of town, I wouldn't have ended up on Caroline in the first place. Ifs are worthless. Forget it."

"I wish it were that simple, but it's—" He mouthed a word, stopped.

Hold on a minute, Rick thought. That morning in the Seaway, when you dropped your wallet. Maybe last night he came to check how you were doing and then— no, not Rolf, not like that. Not Willis, either. Whitehead, Brace, even the bos'n and Saint Eves. And almost anyone else, since the whole crew had to know you were out cold. Good time for a little larceny, right? Didn't expect to hit the mother lode, though, did you? Still, Sid would mark Rolf on the list, for the wallet and the guilt. At the bottom, but there. At the top was the Egyptian. What was he into, anyhow? A pistol and red lines on a map? *Or did you really see that at all?*

"...begin your training, Rick."

"Huh?"

"I said I'd teach you, remember?"

"You're kidding."

"Don't worry, we'll take it easy till you're better. But if I have anything to say about it, next time Whitehead makes a move, you're going to be ready."

"I was hoping Saint Eves put the hex on him."

"Excuse me?"

"You know, when he let him have it for jumping me."

What's wrong? What am I saying?

"How did you know that? You were unconscious."

God, that's right—I was out.

"Oh, yeah…of course, but…Willis told me."

Rolf's antennae quivered. "Uh, huh. Well, if I were you, I wouldn't count on JJ backing off. He's not the sort who'd lose sleep over the threats of some officer, even one as formidable as Saint Eves. He'll wait his chance."

"What about the crew?"

"They've got him in deep freeze for now, though in the long run that could make matters worse."

"You're saying, he'd trash his career to finish me?"

"It's probably trashed anyway. You'd know better than I would, but who'd hire him after this?"

He has a point, Rick thought. Even in a code as raw as the Merchant Marine's there's a line, and Whitehead had crossed it. Harassing low-life ordinaries, beating a man silly over a card game, even knifing some poor local ashore—all that was one thing. But attacking a watch mate, at the height of a storm at sea?

"And if he's going down, he's definitely going to try to take you down too. So we've got to get rolling, today at four if you're game."

"Okay, I'll be there. And thanks, Rolf. If I can ever do anything for you—"

"Like, say, trusting me with the truth?"

Glints in his eyes, and Rick felt ashamed.

"Yeah, like that. As soon as I figure out what it is."

"Fair enough. I just hope you know it when you see it."

—⁀⁀—

A shaft of sun through the porthole, bright first then dulled by overcast.

9:14. Mid watch. Willis and Whitehead at work. Rick took stock: Better. Almost not bad.

He got down, stretched and stripped. It was warm in 8-12 but he shivered; thought about showering then remembered the bandage—which was moist and needed changing—used a wet towel instead. Dressed and finished washing up, shunned the mirror till he started shaving then hardly recognized the face in it. No phantoms were lurking there now, but his one-night stand with the Mistress had left its mark: dark bags, strands of gray hair, and her brand seared onto his mustache. He'd grown it when he shipped out three years ago—to hide something, though exactly what he couldn't remember anymore. Now, on the left side of it, there was a half-inch spike of silver.

Better go find the bos'n.

Still feeling chilly, he put on his leather jacket. At the end of the passageway, he saw Ike and Willis, and Rolf working overtime, rebuilding one of the cargo winches by number two hold.

The bos'n's cabin, the mess. No luck. Climbed the companionway to the boat deck. No bos'n, but he ran into Freddy lazing in the shade, reading a paperback thriller. Rick hadn't seen him since the night of the storm.

"Wow, I just love your new look. How're you feelin'?"

"Getting there. You see the bos'n around?"

"No way. Wherever he is, I'm not. I'm his pet project." He patted the deck. "Take a load off. Let's hear the happy tidings in eight-to-twelve."

"Later. I have to get this bandage changed."

Last flight to the bridge deck. Seamen aren't permitted in these hallowed halls unless they're on watch or ship's business, but Rick was betting his condition lent him a one-time pass.

The radio hut was at the top of the companionway. The operator, nicknamed Sparks like all radio men, was hunched at his workbench, tracing circuits on a sheet of schematic and muttering through his teeth, which had a pencil clamped between them like a racing bit. His hind drooped over the sides of his stool like a deflated inner tube; from there north he formed a triangle. He had the ship's transceiver in pieces and an array of test devices surrounding them, probes from which he inserted into the jumble of wires and tubes. A grunt of disgust, a pencil-aspirated "thiht," and back to the schematic with more mutterings. The radio was on the fritz from the drubbing it took during the storm. A critical state of affairs for any ship at sea.

"How's it going?" Rick ventured.

"Thihtty."

"You see the bos'n?"

No answer, and as Rick was about to press for one, Chief Engineer Briggs huffed his squat bulk up the companionway, blew past Rick to the Egyptian's quarters next to his own. Without knocking he barged in; Rick saw the captain there with Samir Abdessalam before the chief slammed the door.

A glance back at Sparks but he was still berating his electronics. The wind whistled, a little criminal pretending he's not. Rick sidled from the radio hut—

staying close to the bulkhead, eyeballing the Egyptian's door.

Sunlight rayed through the bridge windscreens and down the passageway. Rick was just outside the cabin now; the wind was white noise, the voices inside butting heads: Abdessalam's a drone, Brace's and Briggs' spiking and falling, only fragments audible.

"...where do you come off...that would be highly dange...only going to say this once, Brace..."

CRACK.

From the radio hut, the clipped, urgent words of a BBC reporter—so loud Rick couldn't hear the voices in Abdessalam's room. The stupefying news fought through atmospheres of static: "...early morning, Soviet troops in a violent confron...fired on civilian demonstra...reports confirm three dead...khail Gorbachev still held hostage in the military coup...ssian President Yeltsin at this hour...Red Square...rallying hundreds of thous..."

The radio voice died; ozone smell, a short circuit.

"Thiht, thiht, thiht," Sparks fumed. Now Rick could hear again the quarrel in Abdessalam's room: "... and without us...your big cheese Le Clerc...lousy shipmen...tlemen, do not forget I am here at the pleasure..."

CRACK. STATIC. CRAAACK. Electric smoke in the corridor; the stench of wood burning.

Rick took two fast paces and ducked into a storage closet, closed the door and peered through the slats. The smoke thickened and there was a shout; someone tripped the fire alarm and Sparks hollered over it, "IT'S OK! I'VE GOT IT!" The captain broke from Abdessalam's cabin with an extinguisher and the chief barreled out too. The Egyptian followed but chugged the other way past Rick's closet, bee-lining for the bridge; he'd closed the door to his cabin but hadn't locked it. Rick slipped out, screened by the smoke and clamor. Edged backwards into Abdessalam's quarters, left the door ajar, heeled around—

The knife slice of déjà vu split his head like a melon. Everything was as he'd seen it the night of the storm: the room, the desk, the tin of cigarettes, the ashtray.

So, it was real, it was all—

A whoosh of chemical foam.

"STOP IT!" Sparks yelled.

Rick went to the desk, opened the center drawer: the box of .45 caliber cartridges, the map and the pistol—a Colt automatic, chrome-plated, its ivory grips carved with arabesques. But the notebook wasn't there, and neither was the coin, and of interest only a worn, leather-bound book, volume one of *The Enigma of Faith* by Kenneth Carmody. He riffled backwards through the pages—numerous underlines and notes in the margins. Then on the title page, a jolt. It was a private edition, and there was a handwritten inscription: To my dear friend Samir, may this help you find your way. Kenneth.

Rick replaced the book, spread the map: a red line ran east from a town called Nefta to the port of Sfax; by the harbor was a red question mark. The line split in two over the water: one going north then west through the Strait of Gibraltar into the Atlantic, the line ending with an arrow tip pointing west; the other going east then north to Istanbul. Pointing at Nefta itself was a short red arrow with a question mark by it.

"DIDN'T YOU HEAR HIM SAY IT WAS OK?"

Strobes behind his eyes and stabs beneath his skull, he put the map back in the drawer and hefted the pistol, which felt like an old friend.

You're into something, Abdul—

"NO, I DIDN'T!"

—which means if you took my coin, I bet you won't raise the roof about your Colt being missing. Can't have people nosing around, can you—

"MAYBE IF YOU WEREN'T SO SOUSED YOU WOULD'VE!"

"DON'T YOU TALK TO ME LIKE THAT, BRIGGS!"

—and if not, thanks for the loan. Got a feeling I'm going to need it.

He tucked the pistol into the back of his jeans under his jacket. Dizzy with pain and adrenalin, he pocketed a handful of cartridges, closed the drawer, slid out into the smoke and away from the cabin as Sparks emerged from his shack, quilted with white muck.

"Thiht!" he sputtered.

Briggs and Brace gawked at the spectacle; the alarm silenced, and Saint Eves arrived, separating the two officers.

"You both promised you'd try make this run with a semblance of civility. And that goes double in front of the crew."

They all turned. Like a chump, Rick grinned.

"What's *he* doing up here?" the captain challenged Saint Eves.

"That's Weisman, the OS who was injured."

Brace glowered, and in his wrecked features Rick saw the relic of a commander.

"He shouldn't be here. Why's he *up* here?"

"I was just trying to find the bos'n, sir."

"Yeah? Well, you find something to *do,* mister, or I'll find it *for* you. And don't ever let me catch you loafing around on this deck again."

Saint Eves said "shove off" with a jerk of his thumb and Rick did, but at the top of the companionway there was Abdessalam with his Vaseline smirk. Hurried past him and down to the boat deck, head jackhammering, chest heaving; stopped at the rail to—

"Excusez moi, M'sieur Weisman."

Oozing from behind; now the Egyptian stood beside him.

"How gratifying to see you so improved so soon. Your distress was most lamentable the night of the storm. Yet here you are, appearing quite yourself."

Rick started to leave but Abdessalam blocked him.

"Step aside, Abdul."

"My given name is Samir."

"I'm not going to ask again."

"Nor is it necessary. But kindly permit me to ask you, if you might recall anything you said? At the time you regained consciousness?"

"What?"

"It was most unusual. If you please, m'sieur."

Rick pictured him that night at the chart house door, his look of—

Oh, no. Did I babble about what I'd seen in his room?

"It so happens I *don't* please, and what's more I don't know or care what the hell you're talking about."

Abdessalam glared. Rick held his ground and the Egyptian's high-calorie smile clicked on.

"My abject apologies, m'sieur. Truly, it is...nothing."

He bowed and waddled up the companionway yet Rick didn't notice, for at the instant the Egyptian had said it the word "nothing" had begun to echo, *if you can know this thing* except now Rick could hear the words *should it be given,* the riddle spoken that unharbored night and *it matters not what else* he held on to, the rail so he wouldn't faint and fall in because *you have come to know* the air's as white as clouds, as white above as the souls of saints, *yet condemned to know nothing* so blue below as the hawk eyes dark as the ruthless sea.

SEVEN

Flesh and Blood

Rick drifted down to the main deck. He didn't care about changing his bandage now, not after seeing again what he'd seen the night of the storm. Not with the .45 steel cold on his spine. Not with the news from the radio and Abdessalam's questions and Eli's words and those of the riddle, all looping together in his head.

Inside 8-12, he wrapped the Colt in a towel and hid it at the bottom of his laundry bag. Dumped the cartridges into the toe of a dirty sock, balled it and stuffed it in too, the detective in him mulling the squabble behind Abdesalam's door and "your big cheese Le Clerc" and the "shipment," then climbed up to his bunk and looked for signs in the rusting rivets as he had ages ago, before the storm and the riddle and the stranger in the desert.

It wasn't what the stranger's words meant or didn't, whether they meant something to the Egyptian or meant anything at all. No, it was the fact of them, or maybe the *sound* of them. Like an undertow, taking him out to deep water.

"Hey, there, lad."

Willis was at his bunk; Rick hadn't even heard the door open. Now Whitehead came in too. The 8-12 was off duty.

"How's the head?"

Rick talked with one but watched the other—JJ moving from sink to locker to bunk as though looking for what he'd lost. You haven't lost a thing, Rick thought. You've just arrived where you've always been headed.

"Well, fair to middling isn't bad, Rick."

Whitehead's game was an old, established one; most seafarers play it or sanction it to some degree or another. "Harass the Ordinary" is but a variation on an archaic dance as ritualistic as animal courtship: younger men, or less experienced men, enter circles of older, or more experienced men, and the ritual begins: find the newcomer's sore spot, rub it raw until there's a conflict, preferably a fight. Once he's trounced, the rookie is welcomed into the fraternal arms of the established crew; he can then take his revenge on the next sucker to come along. Simple.

"What you want now is some Cookie Fong chow."

And Whitehead had it all worked out. He'd skewed the rules to cover his butt, which was fine as long as he could kick everyone else's. He'd had quite a run at it too. Twelve years as able seaman, who knows how many before that; day by day, with his own hands, building the road that had brought him to Rolf, and Rick, and Saint Eves, and finally to exile in the outlands.

Rick climbed down and went to lunch with Willis. Footsteps behind them, like the tapping of a cane.

—m—

The bos'n didn't show for the meal but Rick located him after, in his quarters across the passageway from the mess. The door was open; he was standing over the desk in his combination office and dispensary.

"What," he barked to Rick's knock, not turning from his paperwork.

"Sorry, Bos, but my bandage needs changing."

"You need more than that changed, mister." Motioned him in, all eyeballs. "Why were you on the bridge deck this morning?"

"I was just trying to—"

"That deck's off limits and you know it. Thanks to you I got chewed by the captain." Squinting. "Abdessalam told Brace he thinks you were snooping around his cabin during the fire."

"That's a crock. And if he were sure of it, I wouldn't be standing here, would I?"

Sorine conceded the point before he said it. "Yeah, Saint Eves vouched for you and the Arab let it go. What with the smoke and all he couldn't swear to anything. But he's awful suspicious. Any idea why?"

Rick made it look like he was considering the question, while considering his own: *So Abdessalam didn't report his missing Colt. But with everything you saw in his quarters, can you be certain that means he has the coin? Maybe he just doesn't want Brace and Briggs to know he's armed, might upset them. And maybe the Colt's not his only weapon. Too much of a showpiece. So, if he bellyaches about it being stolen, maybe they'd poke through his stuff and find another...or what else?*

He gambled the race card. "Beats me. Maybe because I'm Jewish?"

It paid off; the bos'n frowned. "Let's have a gander."

Rick took the chair by the desk and bos'n started lifting the bandage; it stuck, and he had to tug and pry till it loosened.

"That Arab—he's quite the character, isn't he, Bos?"

Sorine snorted, dabbing with alcohol.

"Kind of cozy with Captain Brace and the chief, as well. For a passenger, I mean."

The bos'n bent over till they were face-to-face.

"And you seem nosy enough for me to believe him."

"He's making accusations about me; isn't it natural I'd be curious about him?"

"Natural or not, Weisman, when it comes to the Egyptian you can be curious or you can be healthy, not both." He straightened, opened a new bandage. "You didn't listen to me about JJ, though I can't say I blame you. But you'd better listen this time." He finished with the fresh dressing. "You heal fast. You're okay to stand watch. Don't get it wet, hear?"

He crouched, scissored the bandage off Rick's finger.

"By the way, Bos, did you notice anything fall out of my pants the night of the storm. You know, when I was brought to my bunk?"

"Why? Something missing?"

"Just a keepsake I had in my wallet."

Sorine's head snapped up and he didn't blink. "In your wallet? You saying you were robbed?"

"No, everything else is there."

"Well, try the lost-and-found. You might get lucky."

—⁓—

The floor of 12-4 was covered with mattresses. Rolf was sitting in the lotus position under the open porthole, barefoot and meditating. Rick closed the door and turned back to the room: A blur whizzed at him collarbone high; he chopped a forearm block, the thing banged against the wall, clattering down at his heels. A two-inch-wide, foot-long dowel.

"Good reflexes," Rolf explained, going to the sink.

"What about 'taking it easy'? You might have taken my eye out instead."

"If I'd wanted to do that, you'd be missing one," he said, washing his hands, assessing Rick in the mirror. "Besides, you're looking a lot better and there's too little time as is."

Rick emitted a whiff of vanity at passing the test; Rolf caught the odor, and his jaw tightened as he toweled dry. "Sit down."

Rick took a spot facing where Rolf had been; Rolf went to retrieve the dowel then positioned himself again under the porthole.

"Okay, listen up. As we move along with this it'll be easy to start feeling cocky. Don't. You have to keep your ego in check. Let Whitehead supply the energy to defeat himself...or he may do the same to you."

Offered the dowel.

"Here, this is for when you're sleeping. Keep it under your pillow."

"Not much of a stopper," Rick grumbled as he took it, thinking wistfully of the Colt, though he knew there was no way to keep it handy and still keep it safe.

"There are techniques that make it deadly. Volatile points—nose, ears, temples, neck—"

"But if he comes when I'm sleeping—"

"There's more than one way to sleep; I can teach you that too."

He toggled the toe of Rick's sneaker.

"Look, I understand you've had it rough lately, but if we're going to make this work you've got to open yourself to getting good at something very new, very fast. It can happen but you have to let it. I'll be showing you elements of Karate and Muay Thai and anything else I can come up with. Try to let it go past your mind and straight into your body. When we're not together, visualize. Every hour of every day you've got to see yourself defeating Whitehead." He leaned in. "And I mean *really* see it—see it until you can taste it. Visualize it any way you want, as long as you use the things we're doing, and you always win. All right, enough chit chat." They stood up. "We'll start with blocking and feinting. Think of yourself as a fighting rooster. Give ground using your wings but keep your talons ready for when your attacker makes a mistake. Watch carefully, now."

The phrase reverberated against the steel bulkheads, repeating in Rolf's voice and Eli's and the stranger's as Rolf curled to his stance and kept talking. Rick matched positions and tried to listen through the cascading echoes but couldn't so he stopped trying. Now his teacher moved and that made him move, as though their muscles and bones were bolted together, as though one set of hands set the other—like a clock spring, ticking.

—⁂—

It was after six; they'd missed dinner and Rick wanted to go scavenge for leftovers. Rolf wasn't interested in eating, only sleeping before his watch at midnight, so they remade the beds in 12-4 and Rick went to beg charity, stopping first in 8-12 for his windbreaker and harmonica. Cookie Fong swore at him in Chinese on general principal, in English for showing up in his galley all sweaty, then doled out a platter of Salisbury steak, spuds, and Caesar salad. Rick took it to the fo'c's'le, knowing it was too early and light for the 4-8 to post a lookout.

His head hurt but the training session had felt good. He ate his dinner beneath gathering overcast, watching the lights of ships converging toward the Strait of Gibraltar and the Mediterranean, yet all the while imagining himself fighting Whitehead as Rolf had told him to—outwitting the beast, pummeling him broken and bloody into oblivion. He didn't let him die, though; he needed the practice.

When the food was done Rick held up his harmonica and the wind played through it, long baleful notes that changed the scene: In place of him fighting JJ was a desert town with Bedouins on camels and

women of the night, and now whistling into the picture
from above came a silver biplane and Rick saw himself
in the pilot's seat, wild-eyed and fraught, wrestling
madly with the controls as the aircraft dove coughing
and smoking toward the dunes.

EIGHT

Into the Night

Rick had first standby; brewed a fresh vat of coffee, made himself a mug and chomped a brownie. The swells rolled easy; they were steaming through heavy fog. He found Nefta in Willis's guidebook.

A jewel in the barren *djerid*, Nefta is an ancient town, and as the center of Sufism in Tunisia, it is also a true religious capital with dozens of mosques and hundreds of shrines. Biblical legend tells us that when The Flood receded, it was in Nefta that water first boiled up from the earth...

A place like that, marked so prominently on the Egyptian's map? Didn't make sense.

...because of this it was inhabited by Kostel, the son of Shem, who was the son of Noah, and later became the site of Nepte, a Roman outpost. Its modern oasis of hundreds of thousands of palms was made viable by the boring of many deep wells...

Nor that a man like Sir Kenneth Carmody, a renowned historian whom Eli admired, would grant his friendship to a slug like Samir Abdessalam.

> ...In the Islamic religion, the Sufi is one who has attained direct, personal cognizance of God. For the citizens of Nefta, the way of the Sufi is the way of life...

He closed the book; Eli's envelope held the place. The coin was stolen, yes, but he wondered—was it still somehow his? Perhaps by its own rules until he gave it to the next? And if so, was it still leading him somewhere he couldn't imagine? Or was the legend just that and nothing more? He removed the envelope and unfolded Eli's notes, searching for clues.

> ...our family did very well in the lumber trade, as you know, yet we'd always lived more than modestly, paid our workers more than fairly, and when the Jewish pogroms began at the end of the 19th century, we were left alone. Then came the first World War, and with the country falling apart under Tsar Nicholas and the monster Rasputin, followed by the October revolution, your grandparents used up their wealth to help our neighbors in Babruisk. Those were desperate times, Rick, but we kept on as best we could. We brothers had our chores, our father ran the timber forests and lumber mill, and our mother held everything together.

Which brings us to the winter of 1926. I was eleven, the revolution was nine. The date was December 14th, the night before my father's birthday. My brothers and I were in the loft where we all slept, up late finishing the little gifts we'd made for him, when we heard horses and went to the window. A carriage had arrived in the snow; the driver held the door and out came two men who assisted a woman and a boy.

Next morning, there he was at breakfast—introduced as a poor cousin who was going to stay with us till spring. His first name was Michael, we weren't told his last, and though he'd come to us with little more than the clothes on his back they hardly looked poor. It was also evident that he wasn't Jewish and therefore couldn't be a cousin; the possibility of a mixed marriage was beyond our conception.

As far as we knew, then, this was the first time our mother and father had lied to us, yet that only made the intrigue more diverting. And Michael, though always deflecting our questions, proved an excellent companion. Whatever we did fascinated him, almost as if he'd never been with other boys. He was particularly taken with our fantasy world of the forest, which was ruled by awesome and dreadful spirits we believed in without question, and we were amazed by all of his stories—from Russian history, mostly, but the world's as well. He was a great raconteur, and though I was a few years his junior, we'd often talk for hours by candlelight after my brothers were asleep. But I could never get him to say who he was, where he'd come from, or why he was with us. 'It's for your own sake,' would be his final answer.

Rick rose from his seat and stretched, prepared two mugs of coffee and took them up to Whitehead on the bridge and Willis on lookout. Came back to the mess, refreshed his own mug and read on.

Early one morning in mid-April, Michael woke me and asked me to come to the kitchen pantry. I lit a candle and led the way downstairs. Hidden behind sacks of flour was a miniature chest of green amber; the lid of it was defaced in the center, as though something had been pried off it. We sat on the floor, the candle and box between us, and he took something from inside it. Then he told me I was the only real friend he'd ever had, and there was a gift he wanted to give me. I tried to refuse but he wouldn't hear of it. When I finally agreed he made me swear not to tell anyone. And then he opened his fist to my first sight of the Zevi Coin.

I can still recall the shadows on his face from the candlelight, the almost scary way he stared into my eyes. And after he told me the whole story, he finished with this: "My family has passed into history. If the Zevi Coin stays with me it may fall into the wrong hands, and who knows then how history itself might be wronged. Your life is just beginning, Eli; your heart is good. The coin will help you on your way. And when you are old and wise, you'll be shown who should have it next."

Can you even conceive the effect this had on me, son? A thousand thoughts came all at once: How could I hide the coin from my parents and brothers?

What disaster would befall our family if the communists found it? And then this—the realization that Michael must be a Romanov. Why else would such a treasure be in the possession of a mere boy? And that in turn led me to the deepest mysteries: Our parents had detested what the Tsar had become as intensely as they now did Stalin, so why would they help any relative of the Romanovs? How would the royal family even know us? And why would they hide Michael with, of all people, some country Jews in Babruisk?

I didn't ask Michael any of these things because I knew he didn't want me to, but what was in his face told me I'd guessed part of the truth and that he'd hoped I would.

Rick glanced at his watch then the wall clock: standby was almost over. Downed the last of his coffee.

That night, long after supper, the woman and the two men who'd brought Michael returned. We said our goodbyes to him, and as soon as he'd left the house our father declared the subject forbidden. So it remained until May of 1928, when we fled Russia aboard an ocean liner to America.

What a sad voyage for us all. The weather was miserable; not one decent day. Maybe that's why your grandmother's health failed, or maybe she'd been dying ever since Stalin took our land, I don't know. She was just painfully frail. One of us always with her, getting her things, trying to make her eat. What she wanted most was to spend time with her baby girl—your mother, Rick—and her sons. She knew she didn't have long. We all knew it too.

One night towards the end I was alone with her and feeling sorry for myself, so I mustered my courage and asked her if Michael was safe. She reminded me that I was never to mention that name, but now that I'd started, I couldn't stop. I blurted out that I loved him and missed him, that I knew he was a Romanov, that I worried about him so much. I cried and pleaded with her until she gave in. "I love him too, my darling," she said, "more than you can know. He has escaped from Russia, and though he may never be safe, God willing he'll be forgotten."

Father was with her when she died. We brothers stayed on deck, our baby sister in my arms as we sailed into New York harbor.

—◊—

Rick headed to lookout, a couple minutes early because of the fog. It was serious, swirling soup; the moonlight only let him see the fog itself, not into it, and even with a flashlight pointing down at the deck he went off track, knocking a knee against a bollard.

"Comin' up," he hailed at the top of the fo'c's'le stairs. Once he stood in the eyes he clicked off the flash: he could see Willis next to him, but there was no ship behind, no ocean surrounding.

"Don't like the feel of this," Willis warned, flicking on his own flashlight as he left to relieve Whitehead at the wheel. Rick zipped his windbreaker and turned seaward, seeking nowhere into nothing.

How often had Sid and he been through this, aboard *Moonraker* in those Long Island Sound fogs? Hugging the coast by dead reckoning, the confusion of buoy bells and boats' horns, the muffled chug of their own diesel, the sails draping slack; Rick would shimmy out to the tip of the bowsprit while Sid kept him talking to make sure he was okay, and more than once the extra margin had kept them from running aground. Radar is supposed to change things, but *Caroline's* left Rick with the same frightening lot that's been the lookout's for all the centuries men have gone to sea.

The hour crawled by like hard time in solitary.

—⚹—

"I'VE GOT A CONTACT. WATCH FOR LIGHTS STARBOARD."

It was Tyler over the electric megaphone; now came Caroline's steam whistle, deafening in the murk.

Five minutes. Six...

Four short blasts on the steam whistle. Danger. A motor at idle. Voices babbling. Bearing to port.

Rick went aft, past the anchor windlass to the bell, rang it twice; back to his post.

Dammit—bearing to starboard, now.

To the bell again; one ring this time.

"SEE ANYTHING?" Tyler called, edgy.

Rick swiveled, cupped hands and belted: "GOT SOUNDS, NO LIGHTS."

"I HAVE HIM STARBOARD."

The bridge searchlight switched on. *Caroline* steered to port; Rick could feel it in the airflow. And she was reducing speed; he felt that in his feet.

Four more blasts on the whistle.

They have to be hearing it. So why don't they signal?

Finally, a bell ting-tinged and the babblings clarified, into Italian, no French and...

The lunatics are drunk. Holy crap they're singing!

Rick reached back far into high school:

"ATTENTION! ATTENTION! VOUS ALLEZ MOURIR!"

The roar of a motor throttling up but getting nearer; they'd guessed it wrong.

"AUTRE DIRECTION! ALLEZ VITE!"

Now the ghost shape of a rogue trawler came through the fog—running lights dark, helmsman thrashing her wheel in the red glow of the bridge, his frenzied eyes and mouth beseeching heaven as hell itself loomed from the night of time.

And then time stopped.

Caroline quaked and shuddered and Rick stumbled aft to the bell, slammed the clapper bellowing "COLLISION! COLLISION!" as cries came from the water and the alarm rang the crew awake and the officers shouted from the bridge and Captain Brace called out on the ship's loudspeakers:

"MAN OVERBOARD!"

Everything hushed together—the bell, the alarm, the officers. The engines stopped too, but with people in the water they couldn't chance reversing the propellers which meant that *Caroline* was still moving. Rick went back to his post; the searchlight, arcing to starboard; life rings being dropped. Hopefully, whoever had fallen overboard from *Caroline* could see them blinking, could still swim for one and grab it. As for the louts they'd rammed, if any were alive, they were probably too drunk to—

Crying, from somewhere near.

Rick aimed his flashlight down the prow of the ship to the water thirty feet below, where *Caroline's* motion and bow wave scattered the fog: a heap of wooden hull was caught at the waterline. He shifted the beam and spotted words on a plank: *Cheval Marin*. Went further aft and...there. Small pale face, hair matted—a boy, clinging to the tangled frame and bedding of a wooden bunk. Any second now it would wash away and take him with it.

"GIMME SOME HELP! GOT A SURVIVOR!"

The only response was the rattle of the falls amidships, a lifeboat being launched. Rick snatched a rescue ring, hitched onto a cleat what he hoped was the right length of line, looped it around another cleat to prevent it from sliding aft. He lowered the ring one-handed, watching with the flashlight, and got it to stay where he wanted—grazing the water behind the boy.

He waved the flashlight at the bridge, shoved it in his jacket and grabbed hold of the rope. Yanked it taut and hopped up, astride the rail.

What in God's name am I doing?

Judging by the noises from below, he couldn't wait to find out.

He laid forward, groped for the line with his feet;

got one wrapped, rolled over the rail using the other as a brake, started his descent slowly but then it wasn't slow at all—he was slipping, the foot brake failing, his hands sliding on the rope slick from the damp and now he squeezed like crazy to stop. He swung through the air, strength dripping into the sea.

This answer came before the question. He relaxed and eased his grip enough to slide down the rope, ended with his feet planted on top of the life ring, his back to the boy. The rush of relief died fast. With the line stretched under his weight the ring rode deeper in the water and though she was losing speed, *Caroline's* bow wave still had enough power to push him aft. The ship jutted above, immense and malevolent in the fog.

Coiling the rope on a wrist, Rick pivoted around and shined the light: the remains of *Cheval Marin* were letting go and the boy knew it.

"Au secours," he begged.

Rick jammed the flash in his pocket again and slid down further, one foot through the ring and water to his neck and swells sloshing over his head when abruptly the pile of junk fractured and plowed right into him. Something sharp pierced his side as he clutched at the boy, first by his clothes then by an arm which made the boy shriek, the shrieking doused by the sea into retching and Rick yanked him onto the ring so his mouth cleared the water, fighting the boy's clothes caught somewhere in the planks, kicking with his free leg at the debris till it gave and he had him.

A cone of light from above.

"HANG ON, RICK!"

The bos'n; other voices too. And then they were rising, and Rick was hanging on—to the ring with every last ounce and to the boy like he was a sack of diamonds, and the boy was hanging onto Rick's neck with his good arm and weeping, "Merci, m'sieur, merci...merci mille fois."

Flashlights in the fog; the blanched faces of three men.

"He's hurt," Rick cautioned.

Freddy and the bos'n held them steady and Forrest tried to take the boy from Rick's arms.

"Non, non!" he protested, clamping tighter.

"Ça va, ça va bien," Rick reassured him.

At that he went limp; with great care they lifted him to safety. Rick, they hauled in and laid out like a dead fish. Sorine gave orders and the boy was carried to the chart house. Bos'n kneeled, examining where Rick's bandage had been.

"Weisman, you're a lot of trouble." He saw the rip in Rick's windbreaker, inspected the wound. "But luckier than a rabbit's foot. Wash it clean and with a little treatment this should heal up fine. And by the way, good job."

He gave Freddy instructions then left; Freddy helped Rick to his feet.

"What's got into you, bub? There are easier ways to kill yourself, you know."

They hobbled down the fo'c's'le.

"Who went overboard?"

"Chief Briggs."

—⁂—

Freddy went to get the first-aid kit from the bos'n while Rick took a hot shower—taking care not to drench his stitches again, washing his new wound with soap, trying to fathom what had happened to the chief given what he'd heard on the bridge this morning.

Freddy was waiting for him in 8-12; Rick dressed in jeans and two sweatshirts, sat on Willis's bunk.

"Anyone see the chief go over?" he asked, as Freddy painted the puncture with iodine.

"Word is, he came running out on deck when we rammed the trawler, and the captain saw him slip on a wet patch and fall. Freak accident."

Rolf stuck his head in from the passageway, thumped fist to chest.

"All hail the conquering hero. But you know what they say, my friend. When you save a life, you're responsible for it forever."

Freddy turned sideways. "Don't fall for that. The real dope is Weisman was so spooked by the crash he abandoned ship. The kid saved *him.*"

"Ah, that sounds more like it."

Rick crooked a finger. "Shut the door."

Rolf did, then leaned on the bunk bed. "What?"

"You know the rumor, that Abdessalam's on board for some deal involving a shipment of phosphates?" They nodded. "I don't think so. This morning, I overheard Chief Briggs and Captain Brace in the Arab's quarters. They were all at each other's throats, and they sure weren't talking about fertilizer."

"So, you're saying what?"

"That Brace knows exactly what happened to the chief, and it was no accident he was the one who called out 'man overboard.'"

They both stared; Rick pushed back.

"Think about it. Briggs was a lifelong seaman and sober as a judge. And he just slips and falls over the side? On a calm night? Sorry, no sale."

Freddy let him have it first. "You really are nuts, aren't you? I mean, that's one hell of a leap, isn't it? From a little argument to murder?"

Rolf came closer. "Listen, I realize your stepdad's a cop, so it's probably understandable you see things this way. But whatever's going on, if anything, frankly it's none of your business."

Freddy finished him off. "Not to mention, Sherlock, if Brace did do in the chief, he's the last guy on earth you should be messing with."

Rick looked them back and forth. "All right—fine."

"Sheesh," Freddy groused as he got up with the kit, leaving band-aids on the bed for Rick. "Oh, I almost forgot. Bos'n wants to give you a tetanus shot. Hopefully with a dull needle."

Rolf followed him out, made sure the passageway was empty, came back in.

"You know more than you're letting on, don't you?"

"Honestly? Since the storm, I don't know what I know."

"Good, I was hoping you'd say that. We can take it from there. I'll see you a little after four, my place."

He left and Rick went to find Sorine. It was going to be a long night.

—⋙—

Rick checked his watch: almost midnight, though that didn't mean a respite for 8-12; it was all-hands on duty until the search was over. He'd taken the helm so Willis could pitch in with the lifeboat crew. The bos'n was with the boy, who was bundled up and sleeping in the chart house, but aside from some lacerations and a partial dislocation the word was that the kid was okay.

Captain Brace slouched in the watch chair; Tyler stood by the radar. The first mate was out on the wing, and his voice crackled through the walkie-talkie after Forbes updated him from the lifeboat. Now Saint Eves entered the wheelhouse.

"They're bringing in two men, captain. Both dead. I'm heading below."

Tyler went to the steam-whistle lanyard and yanked it, held on for three seconds. "Steady as she goes, Weisman," he said, resuming his station at the radar screen. Even with the whistles and her searchlight, *Caroline* was lolling about in busy, fogged-in shipping routes, and as the ill-starred crew of *Cheval Marin* had found out, that could be lethal.

"Right in these waters," Brace slurred, his voice low. He wasn't speaking to Tyler or Rick; they just happened to be there. "Night like this one."

He sipped at rum-spiked coffee.

"Your whole life you love the sea, except now it's the enemy like the Krauts. You pray for bad weather but there's not a cloud in the sky. You can spot a rowboat at five miles and we're nineteen ships."

It was an old IOU stuck in some crypt of his soul, come due right when the fog and the night and the cross of x-latitude and y-longitude made a combination that tripped the lock, and the dead men in the sea made a lever that opened it.

"Prayers aren't answered much in a war. Everyone's praying to live, everyone dies anyway."

"A convoy, sir?" Tyler prompted, still concentrating on the radar screen.

"AG one nine one," Brace mumbled. "Liverpool to Gibraltar. August, nineteen forty-two."

He drank, seemed to have stopped, started again. "Your shaft bearings seize up. You have to make repairs. The convoy leaves you behind and you're drifting on that bathtub and the moon's like a blazing sun. Nine hours, all alone."

The captain paused as Saint Eves' voice sparked through the megaphone, wafting up while the lifeboat discharged its cargo, then continued.

"Yellow flashes on the horizon. U-boats attacking."

Forbes and Saint Eves spoke briefly, the exchange garbled; Brace went on when the boat cast off.

"You put on all the speed you can. You can do *that* much, right? And then you steam into fog, thick soot like this, and you can hide in it now so you want to feel good but you can't, because the fog is on fire and so is the water. You pick up men roasted like pigs but still alive. You pick up others barfing oil till they rip their lungs apart. And there's not a damn thing you can do for any of them except pray they all die fast. But prayers aren't answered much in a war."

—⁓—

"Here they come," Willis called out.

It was a steel-gray dawn with gilt edges, an odd slag smell in the air. The lifeboat pulled into view from the thinning fog; everyone craned for a glimpse, men so drugged with caffeine and fatigue that they stuttered when they talked. As the boat drew near, they could make out two bodies, though unlike the others these had been wrapped in the blankets intended for survivors. No one spoke, yet every man knew what every man wanted—that one of them would be Chief Briggs. If not, if both were from *Cheval Marin's* crew, two more to add to the three already laced in tarps and stored in the meat locker, then the search would go on. And they'd had their fill of it.

Forrest and Joseph manned the oars; Mr. Forbes guided them home at the tiller. He'd been on the job since the job began, though the crew with him had rotated twice during the night. The deck hands made ready to raise the launch.

"You find him, Forbes?" Saint Eves called down.

"Yes. I wish we hadn't."

The first mate didn't ask. "Okay, then. We're getting out of here." The winches wound the cables, the blocks groaned as the lifeboat rose. "Sanders, go tell Captain Brace we have the chief."

The lifeboat leveled at the top of the gunwales and the first body was passed over, the meaty corpse of Chief Briggs. Then the next, slight and lax. Another boy, Rick thought, not as fortunate as the one he'd saved. Now the crew came aboard, and with Joseph and Driller they secured the boat.

Forbes tried to caution Saint Eves, but the first mate insisted, "No, carry on," and his junior, after a scowl at the crowding men, stooped between the two bodies and uncovered the larger. Congealed by drying sea salt, the brains drooling from the chief's crushed skull caked his hair.

The crew murmured angrily. Forbes moved to the other body and laid aside the blanket. Now there were gasps, and someone gagged.

It was an Asian girl, in her mid-teens at most; wrists and ankles locked together in steel manacles, her gown and black hair caught in the chains. And she wore another chain—a gold mesh necklace with an opulent gold and jeweled pendant attached, a half-bird, half-human figure. She'd drowned with her sublime eyes open, and seemed almost to be smiling, as though at the end she'd beheld something angelic.

"You done there?" The captain, on the bridge wing.

"You—" Saint Eves hacked, looked up. "You'd better come down."

"Can we get going or what?"

"Yes, but you'd better come down."

Forbes covered her again and tucked the blanket, as if to comfort her without waking her. The bos'n told the crew to knock off; only he, Saint Eves, and Forbes stayed with the bodies, waiting for the captain. For the rest of them, the long night was over.

Rolf and Rick sleepwalked down the ladders.

Caroline was gaining speed. At the main deck they leaned out over the rail—the stiffening breeze eased the nausea though the odd smell was still in it, something charred and smoked leavening the sweet salt. The sun broke through and short minutes later the fog evaporated, and now atop a razor-cut horizon ballooned clouds of pristine white, like freshly washed sheets in the wind.

The ship dipped into a wave and spray splashed their faces.

"Look," Rolf said, pointing forward.

Rick wiped his eyes and shaded them: There in the near distance rose the first bluff of land, and he realized then that the burnt smell was Africa.

NINE

Lord Randall, My Son

Like the throne of the king of a race of giants, the Rock of Gibraltar ruled over the strait. A brisk wind white-capped the waves, the high sun beat down, and a three-masted tall ship, under full sail and flying the Swedish ensign, was heading west between *Caroline* and the Spanish coast. As word had spread, every hand who could break from work had come to see the sight—this rock, this storied channel, this splendid clipper—shining like a torch against the evils they'd witnessed.

Willis and Rick stood with a crowd at the port-side rail; Willis lit a half-smoked Cohiba. The tall ship was full abeam now, her crew waving from the deck and yardarms. *Caroline's* steam whistle blared in salute; *Caroline's* men waved back, watching as she passed astern. Willis and Rick turned away and strolled to the starboard side.

It was after lunch and there would be no overtime work today; Saint Eves knew that everyone needed a break. They leaned on the rail; Willis smoked his cigar and Rick chewed a toothpick. Facing them was the coast of Morocco, yet Rick could only see the face of that young girl. She was from an aristocratic family, he felt sure, maybe an important one. He guessed the slave-trawler's crew had left her necklace on her to prove who she was; the pervert who wanted her had to have paid a fortune, and likely knew everything about her. Another wave of nausea, imagining it all again: chained below decks, sleeping, perhaps with others they hadn't found because they were at the bottom with the wreckage, the dread and terror as *Caroline's* whistle and maybe his own yells woke her, the ripping crash and the ocean flooding in...

"At least we made some real money last night."

It wasn't strange that they were thinking about the same thing. No one was thinking about anything else.

"Too real for me, Willis."

"No, we did well, son. Those heinous slime deserved to die, and I'm sure the poor girl wanted to."

"And Chief Briggs?"

He nodded, smoked, tapped ashes. "All I'm saying is that men come up from the sea and men go back to the sea, and what occurs between is by the grace of God. Because the sea is God's hand, and I've never found rhyme nor reason to think of her any other way."

Rick didn't know then that Willis and the chief had been friends since the war.

"How can you talk like this? Like there's nothing we can do about anything? I don't believe that."

Willis chuckled. "The sea don't care. To her, what

men believe matters less than spit."

He rolled the cigar in his fingers and his Irish philosopher, always loitering backstage, mounted the podium.

"Listen, lad. When you been at sea as long as I, you'd have better learnt some things. Take you, for one. Shipping out only a few years and you still got the land in you, and troubles from the land, I could tell from the start. I don't need to know your troubles, but I do know this: Whatever it is you think you're about, whatever course you're on, the Almighty has your compass rigged for His purpose, not yours, and you're really on another course, for another shore, and you have no idea where. So, if the chief fell and cracked his skull on the way down, then there's naught to mourn. He was a man of the sea, and she took him when it was time. And if someone whacked him and tossed him over, then the sea will take care of that too, one way or another. Same way she took care of that little boy when she called you in to save him and brought that little girl home. I've seen it time and again, son. Because the sea is God's hand, and that's all there is to it."

Coming into view on the coast of Morocco, framed by the march of mountains behind, stood a city of white arches and domes.

"There's Ceuta, belongs to Spain. And Tetouan—south along the coast, see? The twin jewels of Morocco they're called."

A drag on the cigar; the smoke did a two-step in the breeze.

"Aah, don't mind me, son. I'm just a rootless,

shiftless rover. Love the life, wouldn't have no other. You
work hard, travel the globe, and share the fruits of your
labors with the good ladies waiting ashore. Meantime
the sea cleans your brass and sets you straight. All you
need to learn you can learn from the sea, and what can't
be learned from her you weren't..."

As Rick eyed the sun-stroked rim of North Africa
the droning of Willis's voice seemed to fade, and on the
wind came a sighing of wings that carried his vision far
into the past: a marble city on a vast continent...

"...I always try to get inland for a museum or a
palace or something. Even been to Paris once, when we
had engine trouble in Le Havre..."

...elaborate temples and courtyards, a bustling
harbor, a squadron of military galleys under full sail...

"...the old Galveston Star. Now *there* was a home
and a feeder. Don't know why I ever paid off that ship.
Dumbest thing I ever did. Ended up in the South Seas
for a year..."

The ancient day went dark, dead quiet yielding to
ear-splitting, earth-wracking convulsions and Rick felt
the horror as people fled in vain, volcanic ash and rock
flaming from a slate sky.

"...which goes without saying. Of course, your Latin
American countries are something else. If you can stand
the heat—and if you can stand it in Sfax you can stand it
anywhere; anyway, if you can—stand the heat, that is—
man alive but you can have a time. They got for instance
this bordello in Caracas..."

Now—sucking the sea dry, blotting out the sun, a
five-hundred-foot wave came crashing down on it all.

The temples and harbor, the galleys and city, the continent and its people—gone. Vanished forever, save for sagas in the scrolls.

"...but the one voyage I've never sailed is Romance Run. Hey, lend me a toothpick, will you?"

The vision flattened and blew away, a ribbon in the wind, and the coast of Morocco returned. Rick mopped his face with a shaking sleeve.

"How 'bout it?"

"Huh?"

"A toothpick, lad."

He fumbled for one; Willis dropped his cigar into the churning water.

"Thanks." He seesawed the pick into his molars. "Name has a ring, don't it? Like maybe you heard of it somewhere, except you didn't?"

"What?"

"Romance Run, lad. Aye, that's how it is. That's—"

"ATTENTION ALL HANDS. ATTENTION, PLEASE."

Saint Eves through the loudspeakers. Everyone on deck turned, craning up at the bridge.

"United States Coast Guard officials will board us in Sfax to conduct an inquiry into last night's collision. Moreover, due to the nature of the trawler's cargo, we've been directed to cooperate with Interpol. An inspector from their headquarters in Lyon is scheduled to arrive here by helicopter at eighteen hundred hours. He'll be lowered by harness and both off-duty watches will assist in bringing him aboard. Finally, on behalf of the captain, I'd like to commend you all for your steadiness and professionalism during our recent difficulties. Carry on."

Willis and Rick started towards the passageway; Willis continued where he'd left off.

"Aye, Romance Run. That's the Far East, lad. The Strait of Malacca, the Bay of Bengal, the Gulf of Siam. Islands like Java and Bali and Sumatra; harbors like Shanghai, Rangoon, and Khlong Toei. Places all smoky with opium and spice. And the women. Lord have mercy. Shaped and taught by Beelzebub himself."

"Thought you said you hadn't been there."

"No, but I gab with the men who have, and it's in them when they go on about it. The way they get superstitious at it. The way it hooks them and calls them back, looking for something they can never find. Makes them old, it does, even the young ones. They don't care, though. Once they got it in them, they want nothing else. Aye, I know Romance Run as well as any."

"But you won't ever go yourself?"

"Not by choice, but someday I wager the sea will bring me there all the same."

—⁂—

He's in a boat, floating down a river through a sapphire morning. There's the music of bells, and children playing in the shallows, and from both shores bend spires of gold.

A canoe comes alongside and bumps the boat. In the canoe is a toothless old man, a beggar in rags, his palm outstretched. "A blessing for today?"

"Will this be enough? It's all that I have."

He hands the beggar the Zevi Coin and the old man bows.

"For all that you have, I will tell you all that I know, which is the only thing that needs to be known. If you can know this thing, then you need to know no other; if you cannot, then it matters not—"

"Hey Jewboy."

Jarred from the dream, Rick shifted and gripped the dowel under his pillow.

"Got something to show you."

Willis was snoring; Whitehead rose from his bunk; Rick heard his breathing before he smelled it, the reek of rotten eggs.

"Don't be so nervous, kid. You're sweatin' BBs. I just want you to meet my best friend, that's all."

Rick saw the blade: This is it. Cry for help? No, he'll make his move before Willis reacts and you'll have lost your edge. Concentrate. Wait for it.

"What we got here is a Randall Model One, the best attack knife in the world, my daddy used to say. Lord Randall, he called it, had his name engraved on it: Sergeant Gary 'Scoot' Whitehead, United States Marine Corps, Semper Fi. Killed nine Japs on Guadalcanal with this knife. Got the Medal of Honor too. Gave me both on my thirteenth birthday. On my fourteenth I pawned the medal and scored some meth and that night when he was nappin' with the TV, I got even..."

Watch his eyes, wait for it.

"...snuck up with Randall here and tried to cut his throat. The old fart actually lived. Takes skill and muscle to kill someone and seein' as how I was new at it, I didn't wade into him like you got to. Plus, he was the toughest sucker I ever saw. My daddy. Squirtin' and blasphemin' and he nearly beat me to death anyhow, just like always. I got away, though, and I ain't been back."

The knife, vibrating. "Never made that mistake since. I won't start with you."

"Maybe not, but you kill me, and *you'll fry!*"

Rick had taken the opening and pumped up the last two words, hoping to wake Willis; Whitehead whipped his head towards the other bunk, saw nothing moving, snickered and faced Rick and—

Willis drove full force onto Whitehead's back, ramming him against the upper bunk. Rick kicked and the Randall flew into the sink; Willis turned Whitehead around and loosed an uppercut that dropped him cold. Rick climbed down and they both stood over the stiff.

"Fetch the bos'n, lad."

—⁓—

He was snoozing in his cabin, the door ajar. It creaked as Rick went in and one red eye opened.

"This had better be good."

Hearing the story he groaned, rubbed his cheeks.

"All right," he said through spread fingers. "Go up and tell Saint Eves. I'll get with Willis."

Rick climbed the companionways to the bridge deck, knocked at the captain's door. Voices inside. The anticipated "Come" didn't and Rick knocked again.

"Mister Saint Eves? I have a message, sir. From Bos'n

Sorine."

"Come."

On the couch, propped by a pillow and cocooned in adult-size sweats, sat the boy; his eyes opened wide at Rick's entrance. Saint Eves hunched at the desk with clasped hands and white fingers, flushed and choleric; Captain Brace slouched against the bookshelves, picking his nails with a pocket-knife. Dominating the tableau, close to the boy in a leather chair, was Samir Abdessalam. Red silk robe, red silk pajama legs crossed; his bald dome rotated, caterpillar mustache over moist lips.

"Ah, M'sieur Weisman. Your timing is perfect."

The Egyptian motioned for Rick to enter but he stayed put, holding onto the doorknob.

"What is it?" Saint Eves snapped.

"Excuse me, sir. Bos'n asked me to report that..."

While Rick recounted what had happened, his peripheral vision stayed with the boy, who also stayed fixated on him.

The first mate swore under his breath.

"Very well. Give the bos'n my compliments and tell him I want Whitehead locked up in the Black Gang mess. Find him a cot and a bucket."

"Aye, sir."

"S'il vous plaît, do not leave just yet," Abdessalam said, with authority.

Saint Eves' eye froze Rick where he stood.

"Mon capitaine," the Egyptian went on, speaking to Brace but looking at Rick, "perhaps if M'sieur Weisman could be spared from this urgent task, he might prove helpful with the child?"

The chronometer clicked loud seconds, each tick ratcheting Rick's tension—why the Arab was there, why he appeared to be in command, what he was after. To the first there was a surface answer—he spoke French as did the boy. As for the rest...

"Sit down next to the kid," Brace said. Incensed, Saint Eves stormed out. The captain, realizing too late he'd undercut his most senior officer, dumped on Rick. "Are you deaf? *Sit down!*"

As he did, the child leaned and took Rick's hand, covered it with his other, reprising his words from last night as though to give thanks again for his life.

"Merci, m'sieur. Merci mille fois," he whispered, though Rick heard a prayer underneath: that his savior had come to rescue him once more.

"Rien de tout," he replied, his heart going out to the boy. He looked to be ten or eleven, yet the smile that repaid Rick's words webbed lines in his weathered skin, too many to be from the sun alone, even North Africa's. He's been through far more than his share, and Rick didn't even want to guess what he'd seen aboard *Cheval Marin.*

"Je m'apelle Musa," the child said in a meek voice.

This galvanized the Egyptian; instantly rapt, he tried to cover it with a yawn, but Rick had noticed: *What does that mean? And how could it matter—the first name of a simple cabin boy?*

"Je m'apelle Rick. Comment ça va?"

Musa bit his lip and shrugged. Abdessalam observed, lids lowered.

"Get on with it, already!" Brace demanded, then

regretted it as the Egyptian's glance reminded him who
was boss. Point made, Abdessalam began gunning Musa
in rapid-fire Arabic mixed with French, from which the
most Rick could ascertain was that he wanted the boy to
reveal the identity of the owner of *Cheval Marin*. He
also seemed to be suggesting names. During the barrage,
Musa's grip on Rick's hand tightened but he said nothing.

Finally, Abdessalam broke off, turned to Rick.

"M'sieur," he implored, "you see why we require
your good offices? This unfortunate incident with what
was evidently a slave ship, it is a difficult knot to unravel.
And yet the boy will not speak."

"Why not leave it for Interpol? Isn't that why they're
coming here?"

"The issue is somewhat more complex. Captain
Brace has been directed by your Coast Guard to learn all
he can from the child before the inspector arrives." He
sniffed. "Puerile rivalries, but such are the ways of men.
Maintenant, kindly let Musa know how safe he is with us."

Another crossroads, as with Whitehead but worse.
Once again Rick wanted to turn aside, once again he
could not. The lie about the Coast Guard was so
transparent, the boy so clearly in harm's way, Rick's desire
to help him grown so strong though he couldn't have
said why—

He sat back and crossed his legs.

"Looks to me like he understands that just fine."

The Egyptian's mustache drooped.

"An intriguing word, 'understand.' Many degrees,
many shadings. But I believe you give this rodent more
credit than he deserves."

"I must defer to your knowledge of rats, of course."

"Watch it, mister," Brace snarled.

Rick ignored him, glued on Abdessalam, who was licking toxic waste from the corners of his mouth.

"It would be best if you left us, captain. I will deal with the redoubtable M'sieur Weisman in my own way."

Brace threw a parting jab as he walked out. "You're a goner, sailor."

Musa squeezed. Rick smiled at him with a confidence he didn't have.

"Now, isn't this more civilized?" Abdessalam fished into his robe, extracted the silver cigarette case and lighter.

"Balkan Sobranie?" he offered, case extended.

Before Rick could refuse, Musa let go his hand and held out one of his own.

"Oui, m'sieur. S'il vous plaît?"

The boy selected a stick and Abdessalam, sending Rick a triumphant sneer at the breakthrough, leaned over and lit it. Musa inhaled, his eyes rolling up.

"Our young friend disappoints you?" Abdessalam pontificated as he lit his own cigarette, reclining into the worn leather. "Americans, you're such a stupid cliché. What do you know of the world, much less North Africa?" One hand waved the cigarette, the other underscored. "We're just camels and sand dunes, nomads and pyramids, yes? But here is reality. There is the desert of the cinema, and there is the desert of the poet, and there is the desert that does not abide such pretensions. We Arabs say that Sahara is the Garden of Allah, from which the Lord of the Faithful cleansed all unnecessary life, that there might be one place where he could walk in peace. Believe me, my friend, in North Africa only Allah walks in peace."

During the infuriating sermon Rick had slid forward to the edge of his seat, wanting to strangle the Egyptian with his bare hands—everything he'd been through since his last night with Eli suddenly caving in, just as pieces of what he'd seen and heard aboard *Caroline* started falling into place.

"My, what a pretty speech, and from such a stinking bastard. May I translate? You're a two-bit crook. You work for a bigger one named Le Clerc, and both of you sucked Brace and Briggs and maybe others into some scheme involving this ship. Chief Briggs didn't like the way things were going so the captain got rid of him."

A blink at the mention of Le Clerc, but otherwise Rick's smoldering anger hadn't ruffled Abdessalam a bit.

"And my interest in Musa?"

"The owner of Cheval Marin must be your competition. Which means Le Clerc wants Caroline as transport for—"

He'd spoken the truth before he realized he knew it. Now Rick remembered the map, and the arrow that pointed west towards America.

The Egyptian applauded.

"Voila! At last, you think you see it all, though in fact you see very little. Nevertheless, it has been a most enjoyable analysis, m'sieur, absent but one crucial detail. That I have your coin."

"Actually, there's another—that I have your Colt."

"Hardly items of equivalent value."

"No, but the pistol carries the power of life and death, which in one respect puts it in the same league."

Abdessalam dropped the cigarette to the floor, squashed it with his slipper. His voice assumed another quality.

"Ah, M'sieur Weisman, here you are incorrect. I cannot conceive how you came into possession of such an extraordinary treasure, nor how you came to learn the hallowed and esoteric Riddle of Lazrag. Indeed, it was your repetition of the riddle while you were unconscious that provoked me to pry into your belongings. And since it is possible that you have not fully grasped the significance of the object you have been carrying, I must warn you—it is the long lost Zevi Coin, once part of the crown jewels of Russia, and worth more than any life. Even my own, and therefore most assuredly yours."

Nothing added up now, nothing at all. Rick looked at Musa, but the boy was engrossed in his smoke. Gravity failed as he stared at the Egyptian.

"Your face is pallid, m'sieur. You need to rest. You have rendered an invaluable service in uncovering the path to young Musa's affections, but please do not let me detain you any longer."

Rick stood. The cigarette dangled from Musa's bottom lip, any solace he'd gained from the nicotine forgotten. Rick squared off, weighing his options. Abdessalam shortened the list by reaching into his pocket and producing a miniature semi-automatic.

"As an old Tunisian proverb puts it, 'Better to see very little than be totally blind.' Good day, m'sieur."

Rick left but listened in the passageway. The

Egyptian's interrogation resumed, and soon Rick heard whimpering.

TEN

As Below, So Above

Whitehead was banging on the door of the Black Gang mess, loosing a fusillade of hair-raising howls, cursing the ship and his shipmates as he had since he'd been locked up. Rick was doing much the same to himself—livid at what had happened with Musa and Abdessalam, prowling the floor in 8-12 or glaring through the porthole at the coast of North Africa a few miles off:

Nice work, wise guy. You didn't help the boy at all, probably put him in more danger with that smug son of a bitch. See very little, he says? When he knows about the coin and the riddle? And one led him to the other? See almost nothing is more like it. Well, to hell with that and to hell with him. Almost nothing is still something, and for all his cool Abdessalam has to be in a panic with Interpol on the way. So, what's his scheme? How's he going to talk his way out of this, when Brace himself might throw him to the wolves to save his own skin? Thanks to me he's likely figured out who Musa is, and that he's not just some cabin boy. If that's true then the kid might well be his bargaining chip, and if that's true what use can I be? As for the coin, if Abdessalam's arrested by Interpol...

To these and a swarm of other questions he had just one answer: retrieved the Colt, filled the clip, rolled the pistol inside his windbreaker:

3:47. Two hours before the helicopter's due. Think, for God's sake. Think...

—∞—

"...his Randall's not only a weapon. He believes it has mojo, that it makes him invincible—which makes him weaker than he'd be without it."

Rick was in the 12-4 cabin for his training session, lunging at Rolf with the wooden dowel. Each lunge would bring a miss by him and a counter by Rolf that stopped short: foot to crotch, fist to nose, knee to solar plexus.

"Switch," Rolf said.

Rick gave him the dowel then set his stance. Rolf attacked in slow motion and Rick tried to match the moves Rolf had worked on him.

"Yes. That's it. No, more leverage. Nice. Take what I give you. Very nice. Relax and concentrate. Slow like the tide, swift like a flame thrower. No, I have you, see? Do it in one smooth motion. Each move of his is the start of yours; whatever he does you build on that. Okay, let's take a breather."

Rick went to the porthole, by the shelf where he'd

left his jacket, gulped fresh air and studied his watch:

Fifteen minutes since you got here. Give it ten more, allow thirty to tell Rolf, that'll push it to five—time enough before Interpol arrives at six. Time enough to snatch the boy at gunpoint and hand him over to the inspector. Time enough to get yourself good and killed, unless the Master Sensei here can come up with something better.

Because all his thinking had come down to just Rolf.

He served Rick a paper cup of rusty tap water. Rain began pouring on the flat sea like a jackpot of nickels and Rolf had to raise his voice.

"You're doing fine. You're visualizing, aren't you? Keep it up. Do it as often as you can. Do it—"

"Till I can taste it, right?" Rick crumpled the cup.

"Right. Now, here's another scenario. That cast on his arm could be useful to him. So what about this? Instead of face to face, he jumps you from behind. What's the force you have to work with? His thrust onto your back. Go with the momentum; his energy is your ally. Let it propel you forward and...here, I'll show you." He turned Rick around. "Like this, see? You grip here and...no, no, remember—first play the hand you're dealt."

This time Rick could hear the echo *before* Rolf spoke, and when the words did come, they sent him careening down a hall of mirrors—the numberless reflections not of him or Rolf but of the stranger. Rick pulled back, his mind in rags.

"Let's stop," he said. "It's time we had that little chat."

Rolf nodded, settled in cross-legged, spine like a rod. Rick brought over his windbreaker, sat down again and unwrapped it. The Colt gleamed on the field of blue nylon.

"Well, well. You've been busy. Whose is it?"

"The Arab's. But I'd better begin at the beginning."

The rain ended as abruptly as it had started. Cool air breezed through the porthole and Rick let it all out—his father's descent and death, his mother and Sid and his own overdose, finally Eli, Michael Romanov, and the Zevi Coin and at that point Rolf couldn't hold back.

"What a story. Your uncle ever hear from him again?"

"Once, almost thirty years ago."

Rick recounted the family fable in shorthand: 1962, the height of the Cold War. Seven months before the Cuban missile crisis, the Soviets had approached President Kennedy through back channels; for the first time, they were interested in purchasing grain from their enemy, and the president asked Eli to arrange the sale. He flew to Moscow alone and with no official brief, flew back one week later with a signed contract—a major achievement in itself. Even more significant, the size of the deal proved that the Soviet system was in trouble. Combined with Eli's war record and decorations, his leadership in the maritime industry, his distinguished philanthropy and critical, behind-the-scenes service to the government, it resulted in his being awarded the Medal of Freedom.

"The rest I learned from Eli when he gave me the coin. After the hoopla in D.C., he received a cable from the American Express office in Malta: 'Dearest Eli, My heartfelt congratulations, Michael.' Eli phoned the office and spoke to the clerk who'd taken the telegram, but he found out only that the person who'd sent the message was a fierce old crone with a Scottish accent, who paid in cash.

"Now he became obsessed with Michael. He was alive, but in Malta of all places? With some battle-axe to run his errands? Maybe he was in trouble or needed help. Fact is, Eli simply wanted to see him again on any terms, and enough years had passed, he rationalized, that he wouldn't be putting him in danger if he tried. Anastasia was in the news then—claiming to be the surviving daughter of the Romanovs—and that too would provide cover. He decided to ask an innocent question or two of his contacts in the State Department.

"As it turned out, a number of cousins were around, notably one Prince Rostislav 'Rusty' Romanov in Monaco, and a Duke or some such in Scandinavia—not to mention the presumptive head of the family who, go figure, lived in Miami. It didn't take many inquiries before Eli knew that none of them could be Michael."

Rick hadn't spent long on the episode and there was still plenty of time, yet he felt a new uneasiness. He went on with greater urgency: what had happened during the storm and since, what he knew about *Caroline* and the Egyptian and what he thought he knew, and throughout it all Rolf just listened. Until the end, when Rick told of his meeting with Abdessalam and Musa and laid out what he wanted to do. Then Rolf darkened.

"Damn. Wish you'd told me this part first. I hope

it's not too late."

Rick lost his wind, like he'd been gut punched:

What a fool you are. Abdessalam and Le Clerc are thugs. If the Arab's done questioning him then the boy's merely a liability to be disposed of. Unless—

"But what about Interpol, Rolf? They're expecting to talk to Musa, right?"

"Really? What makes you think the captain even mentioned a survivor in his report? With what they're up to? That's the last thing they'd want."

"And Saint Eves, or the other officers?"

"Get serious. With this bunch anyone who's trouble is history, Chief Briggs's murder proved that. And besides, we don't know who's in or out, do we? Including Saint Eves."

Rick stared at his watch: two minutes to five.

"My God. Musa's probably dead already."

Rolf brushed a hand over his forehead, closed his eyes. A moment later he opened them.

"I don't think so. But we've got to move it."

Rolf improvised a plan; Rick agreed as he hid the Colt in the back of his jeans, put on his jacket and zipped up. They stepped out from 12-4; the engine-room door roared open. It was Julio, one of the wipers, in a paisley bandanna. He closed the door and Whitehead bawled.

"That loco JJ still going?" he complained, then ambled forward towards the din of men at their food.

When he turned left into the mess, the two ordinaries split up: Rolf trotted into the companionway; Rick headed aft, outside and up the dripping ladders. He saw that the downpour hadn't ended, that *Caroline* had steamed out from below an expansive formation of stratus and was about to steam under another one. The rain still fell astern, gray curtains of it studded with—

A bug-like shape, a helicopter skimming over the weather: Interpol. A full hour early.

Rick ran up the last ladder and heard the thrum of rotors, crossed to the window of the starboard bridge-deck door: Rolf was at the top of the companionway, the corridor empty. Rick drew the Colt and went in, clued Rolf with hand signs that the helicopter was approaching. They bracketed the captain's door. From the port-side saloon came subdued table-talk: the officers at dinner. No one was about, which would change the instant there was word of the chopper. And if they got caught like this—

Rolf tested the knob, and it rotated. Nudged the door open and peeped in, shut it, shook his head.

Rick put away the Colt and they hustled out the door he'd come in. The sun broke through a chink: they had to squint to see except for the helicopter, which they couldn't help but see, and it figured that her pilot was already in contact with *Caroline's* bridge. They went to the ladder and down four stairs. Again, Rolf shook his head.

"Listen, our only chance was if the Arab and Musa were still in the captain's— Hold it, someone's coming."

They took another step down; Rolf inched up to see. A cheek muscle flexed, and he muttered, "It's the Arab; the kid's with him. He has a portable transceiver."

"What?"

"He's got to be talking to the chopper."

He ducked below the deck and Rick said, "Then it can't be Interpol, can it?" A moment later they heard the captain's voice: "What the *hell* is going on here?"

Rolf and Rick peeked together: Abdessalam, white-suited, a satchel strapped to his back; his pistol drawn, the dumped transceiver at his feet, the other hand controlling Musa. The helicopter maneuvered into position. Saint Eves and Tyler arrived from the saloon and stood behind Brace.

"DO NOT MOVE," a man with a megaphone ordered from the chopper door; another with a machine gun covered the men on deck as a harness and seat were lowered.

"Bon chance, mon capitaine!" Abdessalam shouted, barely audible in the racket.

Musa's eyes clamped shut, his lips and chin quavering. Abdessalam reached for the seat and caught it, spoke to Musa and the boy's eyes opened again, his face without hope and now Rick was lurching up the stairs with the Colt drawn, yelling at Abdessalam as bullets hurled from above and Rolf tripped his legs from behind and something frozen hot hit and he fell flat, the chromed pistol scuttering from his hand across the slick wet deck right at the captain, flecting sun like a signal mirror and Brace dove for it and sighted it at Abdessalam, who fired one shot that dropped the captain dead.

The Arab arced his pistol at Rolf and Rick, at Saint Eves and Tyler, at Second Mate Forbes who'd just exited the passageway with a carbine he wasn't rash enough to use—then buckled himself and the boy into the seat.

They rose aloft; the men brought them inside; the

Egyptian took up the megaphone: "Au revoir, M'sieur Weisman. You were amusing to the end!"

The helicopter banked and sped away.

Saint Eves went to Brace and knelt: a red pool was fanning out, like spilled paint in the bright sun. Rick's blood had spilled too, blackened by his shadow.

It's the poisons in my blood. None in the captain's blood, only mine.

Rolf rolled him over; his torso blocked the sun.

The halo is important. Why don't I know why?

Rolf stripped his tee shirt and pressured it on Rick's shoulder, called out, "Need some help here!"

Flares behind Rolf's halo, and clouds like cutouts on aqua paper, and Rick feels himself lifted not by Rolf and Forbes and Tyler but by the voices of many men. His Musa, his coin, his failures—these are the topics yet not the issue. Beyond the clouds a section of sky swings out: a great door, revealing a darkness from which one can't return, nor would he wish to. He slips free and goes towards it but now the stranger emerges, enraged at him, ordering him back, his sword slashing Rick's heart then lancing the tumor within, and Rick cries out as the poisons jet like squid ink. Below through the spreading bloom he sees a boy calling his name and a woman kneeling in grief and above them the stars—pacing the edge of heaven.

ELEVEN

Horse Latitudes

He was aware of his shoulder being worked on. The rotors of another helicopter. The bos'n's cabin. Yet he awoke somewhere else, on the watch bed in the chart house where they'd put him the night of the storm.

"What time is it?"

The bos'n was perched on the chart table—bandages, bottles, and his kit bag beside him.

"Six thirty. The man from Interpol just came aboard." He stood and clapped. "All right, let's get you out of here."

"What?"

"Look, the bullet only nicked you and I gave you a local anesthetic." His face was grim. "Saint Eves wants you ready to talk to the inspector. You've got a lot of explaining to do."

It didn't register. What explaining?

He helped Rick sit up, scrutinized his pupils with a flashlight.

"You're one of a kind, kid. First you cross JJ and get your brains bashed in…" Rick felt the spot—no dressing, just a large band-aid. "Yeah, your stitches dissolved; it looks okay." He took a wrist for a pulse. "…and then you play hero and catch a nail in the gut for your trouble. I can accept all that, but this last thing? That's a death wish." The bos'n motioned him to stand. "You keep working at it and it'll come true. Easy, now." Rick's knees went rickety and Sorine held him till they steadied. "You alright?"

Rick answered by leaving, went aft holding the rail that ran the length of the corridor. He'd almost reached the companionway when Saint Eves and Forbes came around from the port side, conferring with a man in a shabby tropical suit and Panama hat, carrying a dented aluminum briefcase.

Saint Eves called Rick over.

"Inspector, this is Rick Weisman, the seaman I referenced. Weisman, this is Inspector Jean Marc DuPonte of Interpol. He's going to question you."

The inspector didn't extend his hand.

"May I see some identification, sir?" Rick asked.

Saint Eves made to object; DuPonte waved him off. "Certainment, m'sieur."

He grubbed in his jacket, switched the briefcase to his other hand; reached into a pants pocket, found the billfold and flapped it open: the photo of the melancholy man in his late fifties looked even more hangdog and henpecked than the real one.

He shrugged at Rick's thank you, frowning with his eyes as much as his mouth; stuffed the wallet into a jacket pocket.

"How's the scratch?" Forbes asked Rick.

"Okay, I guess." To Saint Eves, "I'm sorry about the captain, sir."

The first mate took a step. "You're feeling good enough to speak with the inspector, right?"

Judging by Saint Eves' look, *however* Rick was feeling was good enough for him. And then, full force from the first mate's eyes, Rick understood everything he was facing: The pistol, and was it his—which if so would do him in. And if not his, whose, and how did he get it? And the big one—that if it hadn't been for him, Captain Brace would still be alive.

"You mean now? I don't know, sir. Maybe if I could have dinner first, I'd—"

"We can scare up a bite here."

He gripped Rick by his good arm, led him into the oblong saloon. Forbes and the inspector followed. A spruced-up steward Rick hadn't met before was on duty; Saint Eves greeted him as "Rawlings," spoke privately to him; he replied, "Right away, sir" and quick-stepped into the galley. Forbes called on the intercom phone to Tyler, who was covering the second mate's bridge watch, as the rest arranged themselves around one end of the lone table for eight—the inspector at the head, Saint Eves opposite Rick. Forbes hung up and sat next to Saint Eves; Rawlings reentered with a tray of bottled waters and sodas, tumblers, small plates, a can of cashews, a bowl of ice and a pitcher of iced coffee; placed the tray in the center of the table and returned to the galley.

"Inspector?" Saint Eves offered, tilting a bottle of

Evian water.

"Merci," he responded, and the first mate handed him the bottle. "Ice?" DuPonte refused; he emptied the Evian into a glass, drank most of it.

"Help yourself, Weisman," Saint Eves said. "Sandwiches are coming."

Rick filled a tumbler with ice, poured coffee, gulped it fast. He was in trouble, huge on the face of it, yet he sensed some wiggle room. Because Saint Eves also had a lot of explaining to do—to the Coast Guard and Interpol. It all depended on the game. And the rules.

DuPonte withdrew a zippered case from his jacket, selected a thick cigar with an elaborate ring. "Would it be offensive?" he inquired of the officers as he cut the tip. Saint Eves flicked his Zippo; DuPonte leaned over. "My wife hates cigars," he confided while getting it lit.

Saint Eves reached behind to the sideboard for two ashtrays, kept the inspector company by filling and lighting his pipe. The galley door swung in, the steward placed the platter of food, arranged the salt and pepper, mustard and relish, then said to Saint Eves, "Anything more, sir?"

"No, Rawlings. You're done here."

Rick put a roast beef on rye on his plate, didn't bother with the condiments, crammed in a mouthful.

"M'sieur Weisman," DuPonte led off as soon as the door to the galley stopped swinging, "I would like to hear first what you have learned of this Egyptian fellow, Samir Abdessalam. I admit he is a complete mystery to me, by which I deduce that, if he is associated with Emile Le Clerc, he must be exceptionally cunning, because I know a great deal about M'sieur Le Clerc."

Rick made a show of chewing and swallowing and drinking more coffee as his brain burned on overdrive: *Cheval Marin* and its cargo, ostensibly why DuPonte was here, were in the margins. Topic A was Emile Le Clerc and his cohort the Egyptian, which meant that Saint Eves must have known Le Clerc's name, reputation, and connection to Abdessalam and told DuPonte, and that meant Rick couldn't be sure of Saint Eves. The first mate's discussion with Brace about buying *Caroline Coast* and his outrage at Musa's interrogation by the Egyptian both implied he was clean. Rick's hunch had been that Saint Eves was ignorant of Le Clerc and of Abdessalam's real purpose on board. Now he saw that he'd blown it on that score, but on how many others? Which could mean he was in a different sort of trouble altogether. And piled on top, it looked like Saint Eves was betting that something had happened in Rick's meeting with Musa and Abdessalam after the first mate left, something that had driven Rick to take action. And he must have said as much to DuPonte.

So now he knew: the game was poker, bluff and feint. DuPonte had doubled the stakes by interrogating Rick with Saint Eves there. What was he holding? Doubts about the first mate, for which Rick was the foil?

Rick checked his cards: Some he needed to turn face up—what he knew about Musa, the Egyptian, Le Clerc. Some he needed to keep close—the coin and what he'd seen in Abdessalam's cabin the night of the storm, because they'd never buy anything else if he tried to sell a story that crazy, and because if DuPonte happened to believe there was such a coin it would become part of the official record, and then someone, he was certain, would see to it that he'd never get it back. And lastly there was one joker, the pistol.

He appraised the inspector. His opening move had been a classic, all traps and subtleties. He had no cause to suspect Rick had even heard the name Le Clerc; he was testing his mark before Rick could get his bearings. Sid would have loved him.

Another swallow, then, "I don't know much, and what I do know I found out today—except for the name Le Clerc, which I'd heard once before. In any event, what happened this afternoon convinced me that Musa was in danger, and I had to help him. Maybe it's that thing where you've saved someone's life and —"

DuPonte stopped him with a raised palm. He'd been blowing smoke rings and gauging Rick through them, but now he balanced his cigar on the ashtray, reached for his briefcase, put it on his lap, and unlatched it. He took out the Colt in a plastic evidence bag, laid it on the table.

"Is that yours?" he said, still fishing in the briefcase, not looking at Rick.

"No, it's Abdessalam's."

The inspector placed a ballpoint and steno pad by the gun, closed his briefcase and set it back on the floor.

"How it came into your possession will, no doubt, be a diverting narrative." He puffed the cigar, returned it to the ashtray. "But let us begin earlier," he said, flipping his pad open, writing "Weisman" at the top of the first page and underlining it twice. "Before the collision with

Cheval Marin. With emphasis on facts relating to our Egyptian friend."

Rick felt his way, using a second sandwich and more coffee for a crutch. He knew from the bos'n that Abdessalam had made noises about his snooping around during the radio fire. Saint Eves had to be reevaluating information like that regardless of where he stood, so Rick picked it up there: his search for the bos'n, talking to Sparks on the bridge deck, the events in Russia—

"Astounding, is it not?" DuPonte interjected, addressing Saint Eves and Forbes. "The Berlin Wall and now this. I did not dream that in my lifetime such things could be." His closing word on the subject was, inexplicably, directed at Rick. "The latest news from Moscow is encouraging, and we must all hope that freedom will prevail."

The inspector toasted the thought with his cigar. Rick assumed he was to go on and did—telling of Chief Briggs' entrance into Abdessalam's quarters, and his seeing the captain there. "I'm not a snoop, but they were arguing, and it was heated. That's when I caught the name Le Clerc."

"From the radio hut?" Forbes put in.

"Well, I...went closer after I heard what was going on." Saint Eves was turning purple. "I apologize, sir, but it stunk. The captain and the chief, in deep with this Arab, who was supposedly just a passenger?"

"How's that any of *your* affair?"

"Please," DuPonte umpired. "Maintenant, what more did you hear?"

"Only bits I couldn't decipher."

To Saint Eves again—Rick didn't want to lose him altogether; he might still be innocent. "Probably with the concussion I wasn't thinking clearly, sir. Or maybe it's because my stepfather was a detective."

That last was aimed at DuPonte, and it hit.

"C'est ça?" He looked up. "In the police?"

"Yes, but he's retired now." He wrote, Rick went on. "So, when Chief Briggs died in the collision, and the rumor was that the captain had been with him when he went over the side—" DuPonte stopped writing and sat erect, turning to Saint Eves. "—I thought back on the argument." Rick paused for effect. "I was there when they found his body. His skull was busted open."

A breather, at Saint Eves' expense; Rick had gambled that the first mate hadn't had the opportunity or the inclination to mention Briggs' death, knew that if he were right, it would be a bombshell.

DuPonte drew on the cigar.

"This has been a most interesting voyage, Captain Saint Eves."

It was uncomfortable for all of them, hearing DuPonte speak the first mate's new rank for the first time. Rick quizzed the inspector's profile: No, no accidents with this guy. The sonar was always on. He'd used the tension to send a ping; now he was reading the echo.

"I'd prefer you didn't call me that. Captain Brace was my friend, Chief Briggs as well."

"An old friendship?"

"Since the war." For men of his age, "the" war meant only one.

"Yes? How unusual. Kindly enlighten me."

It was evident that Saint Eves was not in the mood—not now, not with Rick there, not after everything.

"Shouldn't we get back to Weisman?"

DuPonte blew a smoke ring. "And we shall. But first I would be most gratified if you would humor me."

They locked eyes, struggled, then Saint Eves gave in. Maybe in spite of himself he wanted to talk—or needed to.

He told of a friendship and debt that spanned decades, to that convoy in 1942. Willis Fine, Walter Briggs, and he had all been teenagers new at sea, on different ships in the convoy when the wolf pack struck, all three saved by one young captain braving the danger to rescue scores of men dying in the water. Dakken Brace was that captain, a gifted third mate recently graduated from King's Point at the top of his class yet a veteran already of two convoys. The night before AG 191 was due to sail, his captain and senior officers, along with a dozen others from the convoy, had been killed in a dockside pub by a German bomb dropped during the blitz that exploded a year late. Brace was given temporary command of his ship, a new freighter named *Caroline Coast,* and in the desperate days of war if you could cut the job, you got the job. So, at the age of twenty-two, his pluck and cool duly commended, he became one of the youngest captains in the annals of the Merchant Marine. And, according to Saint Eves, in his prime one of the best.

"You are serious, m'sieur? He was master of this

same ship for so long?"

"He was offered others, but Caroline was his first love. She saw him through the war and never let him down, which is more than—" Saint Eves bit off the rest, a tremor in his cheek.

Forbes coughed. The inspector busied himself with a new page, cocked an eyebrow at Rick who plunged right in, not caring where he'd left off. During Saint Eves' account he'd taken another look at his cards and didn't like them, and with that poor a hand, he had to up the ante.

"I need to explain about Musa, because that's how I ended up with Abdessalam this afternoon. The bos'n had sent me to Mister Saint Eves' office on an errand. Abdessalam had been grilling the boy and didn't seem to be getting anywhere, so seeing me he improvised. Since I'd saved Musa's life the night before, he probably thought he would trust me and—"

"At the moment of the collision, you were where?"

They weren't going to be glossing over anything.

"The eyes—" DuPonte's pen paused, "—uh, that's up in front. I was standing lookout on the fo'c's'le."

"Merci. Please recount the incident."

Rick started to talk about rescuing the boy; the inspector had other ideas.

"From the beginning, s'il vous plaît."

Rick began again; twice he had to wait while DuPonte caught up.

"The name of the boat—how did you learn this?"

"It was on a piece of the wreckage."

"Um-hm. And the singing? This was en Français?"

"Yes. And they were definitely drunk, as—"

"You learned French when?"

"I had three years of it in high school."

"Yet you knew how to say—" he consulted his notes "—vous allez mourir, and allez vite, and also autre direction."

"So? I have an excellent memory." *What's your point?* read Rick's expression; the inspector trained a cold eye.

"To speak French well requires more than memory. You have also a tolerable accent. Forgive me, but Americans are not known for their, how shall I say, facility with languages. Even their own."

What a jerk, Rick thought. The inspector was needling him for a reaction, and he obliged.

"Au contraire, m'sieur. Why, a recent study of American seafarers revealed that, during a mid-ocean emergency, almost eighty percent will spontaneously—"

"That will *do,* Weisman!" Saint Eves snapped.

DuPonte smoked his cigar, sat back. "I have not heard of this study, but it sounds fascinating. You might find statistics on the Asian slave trade equally fascinating." He looked at the ceiling, continued as though discussing the weather. "Or perhaps I misjudge you. After all, numbers are so boring, are they not?" The weather turned, a squall brewing. "Numbers of teenagers bought or stolen, numbers of convicts and political prisoners disposed of for the benefit of particular governments, numbers of young girls and boys sold as sexual playthings to wealthy—"

"Now you hold it *right there,*" Forbes growled.

"What's this have to do with us? All we did was collide with a bunch of drunken louts. We had no idea what their cargo was."

DuPonte ruminated on his fingertips. The squall passed; the intercom buzzed. Saint Eves twisted, reached, lifted the phone from the wall; listened for a few seconds, gave an order and hung up.

"M'sieur Weisman," the inspector resumed, sipping Evian then crossing his legs, "you seem to have your wits about you, you have experience with such things from your stepfather—try to put yourself in my position. Knowing what we know of Cheval Marin, if you were to speculate as to why this type of boat would be idling in a foggy night with no lights on, and why her crew would be singing and drinking, what might you say?"

"I don't know. Could be they were drinking to forget what they were doing."

"Can you surmise another reason?"

"Hiding from a pursuer?"

"In which case I do not think they would be singing."

"Probably not."

"Or might they instead have been waiting for a vessel, so as to transfer their cargo? And might they not have become excited, contemplating treasure and the end of a dangerous enterprise, and started drinking? And in this hypothesis, would it not also be reasonable to suspect that the ship with which Cheval Marin had this collision might have been the very ship it was to meet?"

Now Rick understood the questions about his

French.

"No," Saint Eves said.

DuPonte, turning like a gun turret. "Pourquoi pas? You yourself stated earlier that the radar showed no other ships in the vicinity."

"What of it? Considering the fog and the crew's level of intoxication, it's a fair supposition that Cheval Marin was off course. Or maybe the other ship was. All I know is, the other ship was not *this* ship."

"Unfortunately, as to that I have only your assertion."

"No, inspector. Because to make such a hypothesis plausible the entire watch would have to be involved. The officer on duty, the helmsman, the lookout—"

"Plus the engine room," Forbes cut in, "because to execute the pickup the ship would have to stop."

"And when a ship stops in mid-ocean," Saint Eves added, "lots of people are likely to wake up, so in fact the *entire crew*—"

"It is conceivable."

Saint Eves slapped the table. "Then explain this. If it was our rendezvous, and everyone aboard was in on it, why did we stick around for hours recovering bodies, and why did we report the collision? All we had to do was sail on and no one would have known."

DuPonte laid his cigar in the ashtray. "You are quite correct," he conceded, completely unfazed, "yet such things have been known to transpire, and in my profession, one must pursue every...angle? Maintenant, M'sieur Weisman," he led in, apparently tickled with himself for the Americanism, referring to his notes, "after the collision, nothing was said between you and the boy Musa, or you and Samir Abdessalam, until this afternoon?"

"That's right."

"Were others present?"

"Captain Brace and Mister Saint Eves."

"Bon."

The bets were piling up, soon all bluffs would be called. Rick's shoulder was bothering him now and he realized he might easily miss a trick. Time to discard what he could and hope it was enough. He sketched the scene for DuPonte: the captain sending Saint Eves below, Abdessalam's verbal barrage at Musa, the lie about the Coast Guard ordering Brace to probe the boy—

"M'sieur Saint Eves, prior to your departure from the captain's quarters, the boy had been interrogated for how long?"

"Approximately fifteen minutes. Captain Brace had told me at the start about the directive from the Coast Guard. I didn't believe it any more than Weisman did, and when I left, I confirmed it was false. I, uh, have the record of that communication, by the way." Saint Eves knew now that he could be on the hot seat too.

Another complex Gallic frown—which in this case meant, "you wouldn't be reckless enough to make that up"—then DuPonte gave a nod to Rick.

"S'il vous plaît?"

Now came the tough part—how he got Abdessalam's pistol, how he'd learned what he'd learned from him, why the Egyptian would speak with a nonentity like Rick without the motivation of the coin and Rick's already *having* the pistol. Saint Eves hadn't been there so he couldn't challenge anything Rick said. He just had to persuade DuPonte, who could bloodhound bunko from a hundred yards.

"It was clear that Musa was petrified, and, as I mentioned earlier, as far as I could tell the boy hadn't said a thing before I got there. When I sat down, he took my hand, told me his name, and thanked me for saving his life. I told him mine, asked how he was feeling—"

"En Français? Bon. Tell me about the questioning."

"Abdessalam's French was mixed with Arabic, and coming faster than I could take in what little I could make out, but I did gather that he was pressing Musa hard for the owner of Cheval Marin. I also caught some names that he tossed out. One was Ahmed Hameed, which he repeated, I think, three times. Another was M'sieur Chabbi. Later—and I don't know if he was still on the same subject—I heard the words Ammi Zarga. I'm not sure that was a name," DuPonte's pen stopped, his face went alabaster; Rick sputtered to a halt, "although I think it was...because of the way he..."

The inspector laid down the pen and reached for his cigar; its ash was cold. Saint Eves lit his Zippo, but DuPonte was absorbed in the stub, held vertical in his quivering fingers. Finally, he began pulverizing it in the ashtray.

"How many times did he say Ammi Zarga?" He sounded metallic.

"Twice."

"His tone? Can you describe?"

"Same as usual, intimidating." Rick focused, added, "I believe he may have taken a deep breath before he said it the first time."

DuPonte finished the cigar's destruction. "Did it elicit a reply from the boy?" He took up the pen. "Did you notice if...his countenance registered...?"

The pen hovered; his hand steady. He hadn't completed the question, so Rick did.

"There was no reply, and as to the rest, I was concentrating on Abdessalam."

"I see. Continue, s'il vous plaît."

Rick needed to regroup, used the coffee. Whatever was signified by the wild card "Ammi Zarga," the stakes had been upped again, maybe the game itself changed. He'd proven useful to the inspector, that much he was sure of. Possibly enough to ease himself out of trouble provided he could deal with the pistol. He rechecked his cards: Did he still need to give DuPonte every item concerning the Egyptian—especially Nefta and the markings on the map? If he did, and they meant what he thought they did, all hell could break loose. And if that happened then what chance would he have of getting to the boy before he was dead or worse, or the coin before it was sold or bartered—which at best was a million-to-one chance anyway? On the other hand, it was a million-to-none if he couldn't get past this first, and a single bad bluff could sink him.

"By now Abdessalam was losing his patience. The boy was no closer to talking, so I presumed I was about to be dismissed. And what might the Egyptian do to him then?"

"One can imagine," DuPonte mused. Saint Eves and Forbes were buying it too. Now Rick had to *hold* them.

"I had nothing to lose so I decided to draw fire to myself. And the only thing that might do that was this name Le Clerc—who, based on what I'd heard, had to be Abdessalam's boss—and my theory that he and Abdessalam were conspiring with Captain Brace."

The heroics had been no-risk, and they clicked. They all stared at Rick like he was certifiable: Nothing to lose? Are you demented or dim-witted or both? Rick wanted to be seen that way, needed it for the bluff he'd been setting up and now laid his last bet: he told them of Musa and the cigarette and Abdessalam's sanctimonious soliloquy about Allah and the desert...

"That's when I said I knew the Coast Guard directive was a sham, that he really was raking the boy over because whoever owned Cheval Marin was competing with him and Le Clerc. His face told me I was on target, so I let him have it: he was on board Caroline to evaluate her as transport, for smuggling Asian slaves to America."

Rick had looked at each one in turn as he delivered the punch line, ending with DuPonte.

"How did you know this?" the inspector challenged.

"I didn't. I was gambling. But I'd pieced things together in a way that I hoped would press his buttons and give me an opening."

"Towards what end?" Forbes said.

"His, to put it bluntly. My plan was to kill him."

They all gaped. DuPonte sipped his Evian.

"And what was his reaction?" he asked.

Rick's shoulder throbbed and he fingered it. "More than I'd bargained for. He pulled a small-caliber pistol and sent me on my way. Maybe he would have pulled the trigger too, if he hadn't still needed the boy to talk."

"You are fortunate, m'sieur. He might well have decided that shooting you was the best way to accomplish that."

Rick sipped coffee, scanned them over the glass rim. The scenario had worked. Nearly home free...

"I was furious with myself. I hadn't made things better for Musa, and maybe I'd made them worse. That's when I went to case Abdessalam's quarters."

A sharp glare from Saint Eves.

What's he worried about? Something I saw in there, which might tie him to the plot?

"And you were hoping to find...what, m'sieur?"

"Exactly what I did find." Rick indicated the Colt. "He carried that little semi-auto the way most people carry keys." A warning bell in his mind but he was too close to cleaning-up to listen. "A made guy like him? He was bound to have a piece of serious artillery."

"And what else did you discover?"

"Nothing, but I wasn't looking. I needed a weapon to help me rescue the boy and that's all I could think of."

Rick was on a roll, DuPonte picking up every card he laid down. The gun story had gone perfectly, and now not only were his own secrets safe, but the map and Nefta too. He didn't get Saint Eves, though. Obviously, Rick had nothing on him, yet he was still in a state.

"I told everything to my buddy Rolf Thurston. He's a U.S. Marine and a martial arts expert, and I was hoping he'd throw in with me. But right away he saw what I hadn't—that they might get rid of Musa before Interpol arrived. I couldn't believe I'd been that blind. There was no time for planning. It was us against Abdessalam and maybe the captain—me with the Colt and Rolf with his black belt. If we were able to save Musa, we'd take our chances with the authorities..."

Rick sketched in the rest and DuPonte wrote.

"...then the helicopter came, the Arab showed up on deck with Musa—"

"That is sufficient." The inspector scrawled a line, reviewed backwards up the page and onto the prior two, jotting check marks.

"Tell me—why did you and Rolf Thurston think the conspirators could risk disposing of the boy? Would you not infer that they would be constrained by the coming of Interpol, who would be expecting to speak with him? Furthermore, why did you not trust one of the officers, or perhaps your friend the bos'n, rather than take matters into your own hands?"

Rick almost grinned. They were the same challenges he'd put to Rolf, and he answered them the same way.

"Bon. For the moment, that is all I have, M'sieur Weisman. I am grateful for your assistance. I do not know how the Coast Guard will judge your actions, but I shall recommend leniency." To the officers, "If there is nothing else?" To Rick with a perfunctory nod, "Then you may go, m'sieur."

Rick shoved back from the table, preparing to.

"I have a question," Saint Eves said, tapping spent tobacco from his pipe.

The floor fell away. He'd thoroughly misread the tells. Saint Eves hadn't been worried for himself; it was something about Rick's *story*. What had he missed?

"It's a minor point. I was just, uh..." he'd begun cleaning the pipe bowl with a gimlet on his pocket-knife, each grate shredding Ricks' nerves, "...confused as to how you got into Abdessalam's room. I tried the door myself after I went below to see the bos'n." Now he lifted his gaze to Rick's. "It was locked."

Forbes and the inspector completed the tribunal.

Rick railed at himself: *You moron. You've been too lucky, too damn lucky by half to mind that bell in your head when you said the word "keys," so smug with luck you forgot how lucky it was that the Egyptian's door was open when you did take the Colt, left that way because of the alarm and the radio fire but anyone with half a brain and knowing what he had in there of course he'd—*

Bluff called, no cards, only one play.

"I picked the lock."

The game was over. Everything would be good if he could jimmy the door, nothing would if he couldn't.

DuPonte jumped in, sniffing what might be blood in the water. "And you learned this skill from your stepfather, the police detective?"

"No, from my friend Max, the juvenile delinquent."

"Ah," Saint Eves said, suspending disbelief as long as possible.

"Perhaps you would be good enough to demonstrate, m'sieur?"

"Thought you'd never ask."

Rick still couldn't feel the floor as they marched him from the saloon, down the passageway to execution. Saint Eves led like the priest, DuPonte and Forbes the warden and guard bringing up the rear. The cabin doors passed like death-row cells, the engines droning his last rites because there was no Max and no one had ever taught him but there had to be something somewhere he could use, from a movie or an encyclopedia or a magazine or Sid but there wasn't. Instead, he came to Abdessalam's door in his mind's eye: smoke from the radio fire. He zoomed in closer: no dead bolt, simple keyhole. His hand on the knob, the slack in it: fifty-year-old ship, cheaply made. *Focus.* Inside the Egyptian's room now, the key chain on his desk: *there*, the large brass one—that must be it, a notch on either side. So, one lever or two? If one you might catch it, if two you probably won't, and the thing is if you knew how to do this you could do it blindfolded but you don't and you can't, so you've got to see into the keyhole and how are you going to do *that?*

7:46. Less than an hour to sunset. The Egyptian's stateroom faced aft, his door opposite two port lights. A single hope. If the sun had sunk below the overcast, if the curtains weren't closed, if the light came in just the right way at just the right moment—

They'd arrived at the door. DuPonte peeled away his police tape.

—but that was one towering spire of ifs, and it made a house of cards look like a cathedral.

"Would you like to borrow this?" Saint Eves asked, offering his pocket-knife.

"Always carry my own, thanks."

Rick kneeled. He had to go slow; every second could be precious. Slipped the rigger's knife from his jeans, peered into the keyhole—the mechanism black as pitch, not a hint showing. He shifted his gaze to the room: a curve of porthole, the hem of curtains split and yes! a glorious shaft of celestial sunlight moving nearer. He snapped open the sailmaker's awl and, turning towards the inspector, exhibited it, then did the same to Saint Eves, all the while praying for one tiny glimpse, for one breath of grace to one so undeserving.

He turned back to the door and set the awl at the keyhole, prepared to ram it in and flail away when he saw it—a glint of edges.

With one hand on the doorknob, he inserted the awl, navigating by the snapshot in his mind and the clicks of metal on metal. He encountered the lever and pushed up—no go; reset and pushed down, skidded off and caught it again, joggling the knob till with a clunk the awl point bit; the knob rotated, and the door opened.

Though he hadn't been to a synagogue since he was a child, didn't keep the Sabbath or the Holy Days, didn't know the Torah and wouldn't have obeyed its laws if he did, even a wayward soul like his had to acknowledge when a prayer had been heard and answered.

"Okay, son," Saint Eves said as Rick got to his feet. "It's almost time for your watch. Thanks for putting up with us."

"Not at all, sir. And I'm truly sorry about the captain." Saint Eves acknowledged. "Inspector DuPonte, Mister Forbes..."

Rick walked on air to the aft port-side door, stepped outside.

Hovering above the smooth, drowsy sea was the gray mass of stratus, but the sun was still hidden by it. It *hadn't* sunk below the cover, Rick realized. There must have been a break—at the exact second, at the precise angle...

Trembling now, he thanked God, and in return received the palpable sense that someone was listening.

"Yo, lad!"

Willis was with Rolf on the main deck, at the starboard rail. Rick climbed down the ladders; they'd come over and were waiting for him at the bottom. Willis held a coffee cup.

"Reprieved?" Rolf asked.

Rick could only shrug; Willis and Rolf exchanged a glance; Willis put a hand on his shoulder.

"For a man who's cheated the gallows, son, you look more like you just met your maker."

"Could be," Rick managed to say.

They each hooked one of his arms and guided him to the rail. Willis slid a Cohiba from behind his ear and lit it, passed it to Rick.

"Go on, it'll do you good. First time for everything."

The smoke tasted silky. Another drag. A third and fourth.

"That's enough. You might get queasy, even on a shy sea like this."

They switched coffee and cigar. Rick didn't drink, though; he was savoring the nicotine, which seemed to loosen the unendurable presence.

"Time for me to get some sleep," Rolf said, patting Rick's back. "We'll talk later, okay? I'd like to hear the gory details."

Willis smoked, Rick eyed the coast of Algeria and the Atlas Mountains beyond; the pastel haze of day's end seemed to atomize the view, like a painting by Seurat.

"Mighty calm, eh? Smooth as glass."

Rick read the signs—a story was brewing, though he hoped Willis would spare him.

"I was just thinking I never seen the like. Not this kind of dead calm, not here in the Mediterranean."

Rick sipped coffee.

"Reminds me of the Horse Latitudes. You've heard tell, lad?"

He gave up. "Yeah."

"And how do you reckon it came by such a name?"

"I don't know. Sea horses?"

"Aye, sea horses. But not like you're thinking."

A deep drag on his cigar.

"It was back in the fifteen hundreds, when the Spanish sent their galleons to the Americas in search of gold and plunder—the greatest ships carrying the greatest conquistadors of the greatest empire in the world. But a strange thing would occur on their passage. As the ships sailed below twenty-five degrees north, plenty times the wind would die, and they'd be stranded. Sometimes after a day or so a breeze would stir, and they'd be on their way west. Other times the Almighty let 'em stew, even for weeks. Do you have any idea how brutal the sun is there? The water supplies would get so low there'd be none to spare for the war horses. The animals went berserk, and the caballeros had no choice but to herd them overboard. What a wrenching thing it must have been, watching those pitiful creatures drown, hearing them..."

He trailed off, seeing.

"The soldiers loved their war horses something fierce, so it's no wonder they were deviled with nightmares, the spirits of the horses galloping over the waves. And the seafarers in turn were so dismayed learning of the soldiers' dreams that they swore they could see the angry beasts bearing down on them. They began to call the region the Horse Latitudes, and it's stuck for all these centuries."

He smoked his cigar.

"What was the name of that trawler we sank?"

"Cheval Marin."

"Aye. Frenchy for 'sea horse.' Makes you think, eh?"

It fit together for Willis in some way only he could understand. He left and ascended the same ladders Rick had descended minutes before, going to the bridge deck for his trick at the wheel.

Rick went forward to relieve the lookout, holding the coffee cup before him—a castaway with his tin can of rain.

TWELVE

Of Captains and Kings

Caroline steamed east. Rick's two hours on lookout had been quiet and easy and here at the helm it was too—the ship steering herself, Tyler humming, the moonlight on the foredeck. Now Rick saw a flame in the eyes: Willis had his back to the breeze, lighting a cigar.

Saint Eves entered from the port wing, carrying two mugs of coffee. With Whitehead in the brig the 8-12 had no standby, but still it was a gesture, a senior officer taking up the slack.

"Evening, captain," Tyler said. The title was in general use, whether Saint Eves liked it or not.

"Why don't you knock off early, Brad? I'll take the rest of your watch; we can get together in the morning with Abe to plan the service."

"All right, sir. Good night, Weisman."

"G'night, Mister Tyler."

Saint Eves brought Rick one of the mugs then slid onto the watch chair, prepared his pipe and lit it. Waft of cherry smoke.

"I thought you'd like to know, as it stands now the Coast Guard's not electing to press charges in your case."

"That's good news, sir. Thank you. I was afraid I might lose my papers."

"At the minimum, Rick. At the very minimum. But there's a catch. They want you to cooperate with DuPonte when we get to Sfax."

"Excuse me?"

"It has to do with the boy. Musa trusts you, and the inspector thinks Abdessalam wouldn't have bothered to take him along unless he was important. DuPonte has an operative who's in with Le Clerc, and he wants to start by arranging a meeting. After that, he says he may need you for a couple of days. Since we're scheduled to be in port for three, at most four, there's an end to it."

Rick didn't respond; Saint Eves read into the silence.

"Look, I don't like this any more than you do. But the fact is we've run smack into one devil of a mess. According to DuPonte, the high end of the Asian slave traffic is booming, so much so that the big guns have moved in—organized crime families, terrorist fronts, some transport groups that also run heroin and weapons and Lord knows what else. Turf wars are flaring up everywhere. In North Africa, it's about to blow sky high."

Pipe smoke eddied inside a tube of moonlight.

"I understand, sir."

"No gripes?"

"None worth mentioning. I wanted to help the kid before and didn't do very well. I've been trying to think of how I might help him once we get to Tunisia, but I'm not doing very well with that, either. Maybe now I can."

"Maybe so. Any questions?"

"Not really." Rick sipped his coffee, saw an opening to work on the jigsaw puzzle, the entwined unknowns of *Caroline Coast*. "But I have been concerned...since you were so close, about how you're doing—regarding the captain and the chief."

Saint Eves exhaled, combed fingers through thinning hair, silvery in the moonlight. "Well, I thought we were."

"How did you all get together on Caroline? If you don't mind my asking."

"No, you've earned yourself a few answers."

He smoked and the pipe bowl glowed.

"After the war, Briggs, Willis and I stayed in touch as best we could. We had a reunion with the captain in 'forty-seven, on the fifth anniversary of the convoy, but after that it was cards and letters and not many of those. Six years ago, I got a message from Willis. He'd heard Brace was in bad shape. His missus had walked out; the kids wouldn't answer his calls. Plus, he was stuck in the Gulf, unable get senior officers to sail with him, and pretty soon Caroline's owner would pull the trigger and he'd be finished. We couldn't allow him to be disgraced along with everything else, so we sent Briggs a telegram and it was like it was meant to be. I was between commands and the chief was in the market for something coastwise, which is where Caroline was contracted, and Willis was in Miami. We dropped what we were doing and signed on, and our reputations lent the ship just enough credibility to shore up hers."

He paused but didn't smoke.

"Six years. It must have gone well. Till now, I mean."

"Reasonably well, and in spite of the worst owner in the world we've kept Caroline afloat. Unfortunately, after three years the company lost half the coastwise contract, and we found ourselves trucking grain to North Africa. Merchant ships go wherever the money is. Doubly true for this ship."

Rick thought he might shut down, with a slew of puzzle pieces still missing, so he mentioned something he never did.

"I know the industry, sir. My uncles are in it."

For seafarers, a familial connection to ownership was akin to leprosy; Rick was trusting Saint Eves not to make things even worse for him.

"Yes? Then you do know. Willis and Briggs have a lot of seniority, obviously I hold a master's ticket, and our families expect us to use what we've earned over so long to stay as close to them as we can. That's made the last few years very rough. My wife and sons support me, though. If they didn't..."

He relit his pipe; Rick prompted again, "So how did all this happen, sir?"

A sigh. "What I do know is that it started ten months ago. We were having dinner at Café Stella, our hangout in Sfax, and Willis and I left early. Brace and Briggs wanted one more for the road." A snort. "Some road. They didn't come back for thirty-six hours. I actually phoned the police."

He shook his head.

"Ever since that night something's been eating them. They'd go off together when we were in Sfax, be at each other's throats when we weren't. Yet as much bad blood as there was between them, they'd still keep to themselves and exclude me and Willis. In retrospect it adds up, though. The grain contract is done. This is the tail leg of a pair of runs to complete it, which means Caroline's future is more dicey than ever..."

The day before *Caroline Coast* sailed to the States to pick up the last load of grain, Brace brought Abdessalam aboard. He told Saint Eves that he and the chief had a hot deal percolating with the Egyptian and his partner Emile Le Clerc, who were looking for a ship to carry phosphates from Tunisia. Saint Eves tried to give them the benefit of the doubt, of which he had plenty, which is where things stood until *Cheval Marin*. Then came Brace's story about how the chief went overboard, and the lie about the Coast Guard directing the captain to interrogate the boy.

Saint Eves pushed off the watch chair, went to the windscreens. "By that time, it was too late. All I'd wanted for Captain Brace was to give him back a little self-esteem when he retired. Evidently it wasn't enough."

"So that's why you've been trying to buy the ship?"

He swiveled. "How did you know about that?"

"Scuttlebutt, sir. And things I overheard."

"I see. More eavesdropping." He faced forward again. "You're partly right. It's the main reason but not the only one. Early last year I was retained as a consultant for an import-export group looking to get their feet wet on the shipping side. One thing led to another, and they asked me to join them; put a nice equity position on the table as well. I saw an opportunity to help Brace, save a good ship, and build a bit of capital myself, which I could use after all these years as first mate. I convinced them that Caroline could be a low-cost, low-risk initial investment, and we went from there."

"So that deal's off now?"

"Not sure my heart's in it anymore, not sure theirs is either, but theoretically it's still on—that is, if I have any reputation left. Naturally, there's no guarantee the current owner will sell. Our offer's thin or it wouldn't pencil out, not with the work she needs. So far he hasn't been biting because a ship like Caroline can be a real cash cow. No debt, no maintenance, just drive her till she dies. But he's been under a lot of heat from the Coast Guard, and now with everything on this passage he may decide to get out while he can."

"What then?"

"First, back home for a refit. Then my group has the inside track on a regular coastwise run—not exceptionally profitable, but Caroline wouldn't get torn apart and I'd be near my family. That's something."

He sat, went through his pipe rituals; Rick lapsed into his own thoughts.

One quadrant of Rick's jigsaw puzzle was complete: Brace and Briggs, angling for a fast, easy score; *Caroline Coast,* a haven for bad actors yet with her standing as an honest wreck propped up by Saint Eves. All of which made her ideal for Le Clerc's purposes. Rick took some comfort there; at least he'd helped to save the ship from such a despicable fate. He moved around the rest of the pieces—map, coin, Musa, the inspector and his operative—but couldn't fit them together. Too many others were missing.

"Do you think you could play 'Holy, Holy, Holy' on that harmonica of yours?"

"I don't know it, sir. Never heard of it."

"No? Oh, that's right, I forgot you're— I just thought it might be good to have music at the service tomorrow."

"How about 'Amazing Grace'? I wouldn't embarrass you on that one."

"'Amazing Grace' would be fine. Thanks."

He smoked his pipe and Rick surveyed the sea. Nothing more was said until Rolf relieved him at twelve.

That night he dreamed he was flying, in a silver biplane over a moonlit desert. A white stallion raced the plane's shadow across the dunes.

—◆—

The next day dawned savagely hot and humid. *Caroline* had no air conditioning, and what little breeze there was followed from the southwest, which seemed to counter any airflow through the portholes and also rolled the ship in long, quartering swells.

Unsurprisingly, the barometer at breakfast was low and falling. Everyone had heard about the crimes and conspiracy involving Brace, Briggs, and the Egyptian, but topping that and even the heat was Whitehead. Though his vocal cords had finally blown out he could still pound on the door during meals; he was doing it now and it was getting through, and Rick was getting the blame. Sitting with Willis, Rolf, and the bos'n, he caught stony stares thrown his direction—from the deck engineer, from a Filipino oiler named Diego, and conspicuously from Forrest and Jacky. Even a steward hazarded a leer when he dolloped Rick's eggs.

King Tiny had set up his shortwave radio and tuned in the BBC's dry recitation of the latest news from Russia. The leaders of the coup had been arrested, Gorbachev released from custody; troops and tanks were withdrawing from Moscow; Estonia, Lithuania, and Latvia had declared their independence. Yet the two pundits introduced after the summary were by no means sanguine as they speculated about the future: the dangers posed by a demoralized Soviet military; the high stakes of the inevitable Kremlin purge; the lightning rumors, among which were a new coup and the resurgence of the communists, the rise of a dictator, or even the return of the monarchy.

The bos'n got to his feet at the adjacent table.

"Turn that off, will you, Tiny? Listen up, gents. The captain sends his compliments. He's canceled work today; we'll only be standing sea watches."

Scattered applause, one ballpark whistle.

"I also have two announcements. First, our ETA in port is oh-one-hundred—"

General groans though it was no surprise; the collision and search had delayed them more than seven hours.

"—and we're not sure yet what the tug situation is so we may have to anchor in the harbor. Second, at four this afternoon there's going to be a service on the fo'c's'le for Captain Brace and Chief Briggs. Tiny, please assign a skeleton crew below. And let me see, someone's got to be on the bridge with Mister Forbes..." He glanced around. "Looks like Sanders has the wheel now and since it'll be his watch, he's elected. The rest of you, you're expected to be there."

More grumbling.

"Okay, enough. Doesn't matter what you think of them. This is important to the captain, and you'd better show up, or you'll regret it."

"Same goes for my crew," King Tiny chimed in.

Not a sound from the Black Gang.

"All right then, that's all."

The bos'n sat and was forking sausage when Jacky sang out, "What about JJ? Don't he get to go to the service?"

Eye contact between Willis and the bos'n; they'd been expecting something like this. Willis took the ball because it was union rep territory.

"You have a grievance?" he said through a yawn, letting everyone know where he stood. "The floor is yours."

Jacky got up holding his mug and took a swig, his eyes darting side to side. Now he banged it down and the coffee spilled out. He put one boot on his chair, leaned a forearm on his knee.

"Okay, I'll speak my piece. I say JJ's gettin' the *shaft!*" Approval from Forrest and Ike but no one else. Jacky punched a finger from table to table, a claw of greased hair scything across his forehead. "Started when Weisman there took Rolf Thurston's part against his own watch mate, sayin' JJ came at Rolf when JJ says the other way. You see how thick them two are—who's to say JJ didn't have it right?" More ayes choruses with Forrest, the tide turning. "So, you can't fault JJ for comin' at Weisman, can ya? After what he done to him?" Forgotten was the storm, the ship about to founder. "And now *this.*" His fingers spread wide, and his arm swept aft, at the Black Gang mess. "You know why he's locked up? Because Willis overheard him tellin' Weisman here how he came by his knife. That's right! How many here heard that story?" Jacky waved his hand and several more affirmed. "And for that they keel haul a twelve-year AB, lock him in that hot box, and let him yowl his guts out? And now they're going to give him to the Coast Guard?" To Willis, jabbing his index, "It's wrong, I'm sayin'— dead wrong. He ain't had a fair hearing and I'm puttin' it on you to make my complaint up top. You tell Saint Eves we want justice for JJ, our union brother."

Jacky had them. He'd tapped a keg of TNT and lit the fuse. Then he snuffed it out.

"Or I swear I'll file a complaint on *you!*"

A fork scraped a plate. Someone sneezed.

Willis yawned again.

"Why Jacky, if I didn't know better, I'd think you were sassing me."

Jacky shrunk into his chair. Willis could have left it there and everyone would have shuffled off, but though Jacky had lost his case at the close, things had been said that couldn't be unsaid, and if not dealt with might spell trouble later.

Willis, still seated, canvassed the crowd.

"Anyone else?"

King Tiny rose from his throne, sweaty black tee shirt plastered like hot asphalt.

"Go to it," Willis said.

Tiny mopped his face with a napkin, skirted out from the Black Gang table until he was standing behind Jacky's chair. He put his hands on the back of it.

"I just want to acknowledge friend Jacky here for that moving soliloquy. You missed your calling, pal; you should have been a D.C. spin doctor. Fortunately, I'm proud to say, your shipmates are men of true grit and character." He grabbed a fistful of Jacky's shirt, lifted him right out of his seat and held him up like a buckshot rabbit. "Men who can't be swayed by *bilge scum* such as this!"

In one oiled motion, Jacky drew a stiletto, slicked out the blade, and flung his arm at the King, who dodged by a millimeter then slammed Jacky into the bulkhead and clamped his neck with gigantic hams. Everyone was hollering and jumping from their seats, four men grappling with the King and three more joining in until he had to let go.

Jacky rag-dolled to the deck.

"UNHAND ME, KNAVES!" King Tiny commanded as he shook off the Lilliputians.

"Let's go," Rolf said to Rick.

They trotted down the passageway aft; outside, the sun was a hammer, the deck an anvil. Rolf led them up the ladder to the poop deck and behind the paint locker.

"All right, listen good. Last night Driller and Joseph were talking about what they were going to do in port when Driller turns to me and says, 'Tough town, Sfax, awful tough town. Sailor goes ashore, gets drunk, gets rolled, disappears. It's laid on the local A-rabs and no one's the wiser. You tell your friend to watch his back.' After that scene in the mess, Rick, I'd take it as gospel. So, when we make port, you'd better stay with me and Freddy, or just stay on board."

Rick started to laugh, and then, thinking he might not be able to stop, instead told him what he'd agreed to do in Sfax with DuPonte.

Rolf's expression was answer enough.

—∿—

"'No man is an Island, entire of itself; every man is a piece of the continent, a part of the maine...'"

Beneath a mercury sun in a stainless sky, the air steamy with brine and seaweed, the men of *Caroline Coast* had assembled on the fo'c's'le—officers and crew, deck and engineering, stewards and cooks alike. The guests of honor, though, were absent. There would be no solemn rites, no caskets draped in flags. The dead would have one more journey, home to America for burial.

They'd arranged themselves in the shape of an arch in ruins, at the base of which—forward of the anchor windlass, flanked by its chains—Saint Eves held forth, his worn, dog-eared Bible in hand, opened to a page of notes. Willis was beside him, at parade rest. Rick clutched his harmonica, waiting for the sign from Saint Eves; he stood with Freddy at the apex of the arch, their backs to the ship's eyes. The stack and superstructure and cargo masts towered beyond, as though *Caroline* were there too, saying farewell.

"'If a clod be washed away by the sea, Europe is the less, as well as if a promontory were, as well as if a manor of thy friends or of thine own were. Any man's death diminishes me, because I am involved in Mankind. And therefore, never send to know for whom the bell tolls; it tolls for thee.'"

Saint Eves closed the Bible. "John Donne wrote those lines four hundred years ago, and they are no less true today. We stand here in respect for the memory of Captain Dakken Brace and Chief Engineer Walter Briggs, yet who among us is not also standing in judgment?"

As Saint Eves gazed severely about the circle, Rick looked off to sea. They'd rounded Cap Bon and were heading south. Astern, to port, the hazy outlines of an aircraft carrier and three escorts patrolled past the distant coast of Sicily; to starboard sloped the lowland shores of Tunisia.

"These men were my friends. I knew them. Their lives were long and their burdens heavy, and finally they succumbed to the weight. For this are they to be summarily condemned? Every courageous act and selfless deed expunged? Every sacrifice, goodness, and charity dismissed? Would we want God to judge us in this way when we face Him? No—and yet mankind's is a more intolerant court than Heaven's, for our vision is short, our perception weak, our love conditional. We rejoice in our conceit at the descent of others. We reject the gifts of men such as these when they fall from grace, though among their gifts to us is their fall from grace itself. For the descent of any man is a reminder from God: that evil whispers in every ear, patient and eternal. Let He who made them judge the souls of Dakken Brace and Walter Briggs. Let us judge our own. I invite you to join me in the Lord's Prayer."

He bowed his head.

"Please!" Inspector DuPonte stepped forward from the rear of the port-side crowd, in the same rumpled tropical suit he'd worn yesterday, Panama hat in hand.

"I know it is not my place, mon capitaine, and I intend no disrespect, but I beg leave to speak. The testament you have given for your friends, it impels me to bear witness on behalf of the young girl who died in Cheval Marin."

Saint Eves assented; DuPonte hunched his body and planted his feet. Now with one hand in a fist and the other crushing the brim of his hat he branched his arms—like some prophet who'd wandered the world finding all ears deaf to his message, yet pressing on reduced to audiences of bums and beggars and men such as these, common men plying a common trade, as if they might see what others refused to, might awaken others and make them see too.

"And I beg to speak also for uncounted multitudes, whose lives are a dying that does not end, a living death whose every sunrise is shame and every sunset despair." Sweat fell like tears down his cheeks. "No—I cannot feel charity, even towards once-good men such as your captain and chief. If it were within my power, I would enslave those who enslave others, make them suffer every agony, every degradation—"

His body swayed, his shaking hands opened, and the hat fell to the deck.

"Whatever punishment may await me for my un-Christian malice, I will never have to stand before God accused of compassion for those who became Satan's creatures, *while the Lord's children cried out for deliverance from them!*"

The prophet's knees buckled; Ike caught him under the arms. The bos'n shoved through the crowd to his side and the arch of men parted. Ike and the bos'n helped DuPonte down to the main deck and aft to shelter.

The service was over; there would be no prayer or hymn; the crew began filing from the fo'c's'le. Saint Eves stayed behind, and as the men passed amidships, he tolled the bell—once, then twice, then once again.

THIRTEEN

Mission to Kashmir

Caroline steamed into the channel offshore from Sfax. Rising from the flat Tunisian coast, the lights of the city and its harbor fused through stifling vapors of chemical dust, the phosphate depot and oil refinery and the ancient medina at the heart of town resembling clusters of bonfires in the smog.

When the order came to drop anchor, the windlass dug in like a bad mule. It was half past midnight—earlier than projected because of a strong southerly current—and Willis and Rick were tapped for overtime to help the 12-4. Finally, with much cursing, banging of wrenches, sloshing of lube oil, and gnashing of gears, the anchor went down. Once it grabbed and the engines were cut to idle, *Caroline* began swinging around the chain until her bow pointed north, as though she'd realized where she was and was ready to leave.

It was past 1:30 before the 8-12 knocked off. Rick climbed up to his bunk and found a note from DuPonte:

the inspector wanted to see him in the morning. He sank into the pillow, wretched from exhaustion, but the lone fan by the open porthole was worthless against the corrosive stench and humidity, and what with Willis's snores and *Caroline's* slosh, his own ravaged nerves and the riddle repeating over and over, once more he lay there thinking   about Musa and the coin, Abdessalam and Le Clerc, that young girl's face...

After an hour of it he was wide awake, got dressed and went to the mess for coffee. Joseph and Driller were on standby playing cards; Rolf had to be on lookout. Rick poured two mugs halfway, added milk, chocolate, and sugar, filled ice cubes to the rims and went forward to find him.

Outside, the pancake archipelago of the Kerkennah Islands, nine miles to starboard, was marked by pinhole lights like fallen stars. Rolf was at the port-side rail, silhouetted by the glow of the city—no point standing watch in the eyes, he was surveying the shore. He turned as he heard footsteps.

"Sheesh, Weisman, don't you ever sleep?"

Rick handed him a mug. "Any word on the tugboats?"

"Not yet, but the Coast Guard's due soon."

They drank, leaning on the rail; Rolf had things on his mind.

"I've been mulling over everything you told me this afternoon. Even tried to handicap the odds."

"What's the line?"

"I don't know, Rick. I couldn't count that high."

No rejoinder and he went on.

"Look at this dump. You're so far out of your league it's ludicrous. If DuPonte hadn't asked for your help you wouldn't have a clue where to start, and when he's done with you, what do you do next?"

"The point is, Rolf, he did ask, and that puts me in the game. It's not much but I'll take it." Rick spat over the side. "I don't care how it looks to you or anyone else. I'm going for the kid."

Rolf gave him a second to cool down. "We never did finish our talk, about the night of the storm. You've changed since. Maybe with some help?"

Rick looked over. "Not sure I'd call it that."

"And now you know what you're supposed to do, right? And you can't turn loose of it. You can't even figure out why you can't."

Rick shrugged.

"In the east they'd say that's your dharma, your duty in the cosmic order. Christians would say you're following the call of the Holy Spirit."

"Well, I'm Jewish, so I guess I'm just meshuga."

Rolf chuckled. "Maybe so. In any case, I feel sorry for you, pilgrim."

They sipped at their mugs. A bell buoy clanged.

"Hell, who am I to talk?" Rolf started in again. "I'm always kicking myself about Josie, and here I am trying to give *you* advice."

"Who's Josie?"

"You mean I've never mentioned her?"

"No, but then we only talk about me."

"Good point."

"So?"

"Told her I'd make a lousy husband, that I was breaking it off for her own good. She said if I really loved her I wouldn't be so worried about her future."

"Smart lady."

"Too smart for me. Too good for me too. But she gets what I'm after. In fact, she's after the same things herself." He crunched an ice cube. "Truth is, I fell for her the first time I saw her."

"Which was?"

"Last December. I'd been through a lot recently—badly wounded in action, missing for a couple of months, and I also had to decide whether to re-up. I took a bunch of leave time and went home to Monterey to be with the family. They'd been worried sick about me, of course, and anyway my folks are devout Catholics, and it means a lot to them to have all their children and grandchildren home for Christmas. Particularly the black sheep."

He glanced at Rick, explained.

"I'm the only one who's lapsed from the faith, but they have so much of it they're not concerned. They know I'm searching and trying to find my way, and that's good enough for them. It's weird, though—lately I've had this feeling that I'm circling right back to where I started."

He drank his coffee, seemed lost in his thoughts. The moment stretched and Rick nudged him with an elbow.

"Josie?"

"Oh, yeah, sorry. I met her at a friend's New Year's Eve party. Five minutes later I'd given up on the Marines. Five minutes after that I was thinking job, house, kids, and Josie forever. Talking with her, being with her...it was like...I don't know."

"Zerzura," Rick said under his breath.

"What?"

"Nothing, it's just an old fable my uncle told me about—a lost oasis of gold in the Sahara. Everyone knows it's a myth, yet some still search for it."

"Zerzura," Rolf repeated, raising his eyes as though hoping to see its mirage. He drank and went on. "Yeah, that sounds about right, except it was no myth. When midnight came and the gang started singing 'Auld Lang Syne,' I took her into the kitchen and kissed her as sweetly as I knew how. Then I told her everything I was feeling. I was smashed enough to make it okay if it wasn't with her, but sober enough to know what I was saying. When I was done, she put her arms around me, and this time we really kissed."

He wavered before the memory. After a moment Rick asked, "If it was all that, why did you let go?"

"Because you can't run if you're holding on. And I had to keep running."

"From what?"

He answered as though someone might hear who shouldn't.

"The hound of heaven."

His story tumbled out. It was July 1990, and Rolf was stationed in Singapore. As part of the American embassy's military contingent, he'd been assigned to accompany the ambassador to a strategic conference in New Delhi, but during the week of meetings the troubles in Kashmir boiled over again: eighty-two people killed in a clash between Indian military and secessionists; Srinigar shut down by a protest strike; Pakistani and Indian troops exchanging fire across the border. Sliding towards their third war over the province, both sides through back channels petitioned Washington to intercede. The President dispatched his envoy to the New Delhi conference, Deputy National Security Adviser Brooks Sauter, a Green Beret Brigadier General, to Srinigar, and Rolf was assigned to the elite joint-service escort.

"So ironic. For years I'd wanted to visit the Vale of Kashmir, one of the most beautiful and spiritual places on earth, and now I was going in the middle of a fight. We took off in the early morning, planning to arrive at dawn. I was in the rear chopper, General Sauter in the lead; two others spread right and left. The moon was bright, and they were laying for us with heavy machine guns and a Stinger missile. I don't know much more—whether they were Indian or Pakistani military out to sabotage the mission, or Kashmiri separatists, or rogue agents; whether they had the wrong information or simply gambled wrong about where General Sauter would be. What I do know is that they fired the fifty-calibers on the lead ship and used the Stinger on ours."

A launch was departing the harbor, headed for *Caroline*.

"When I woke up, I knew I was finished. I had a rack of broken ribs, both legs were useless, and one was ripped from the knee up. My left hand was waggling in the breeze. I dragged my carcass around by my right to see if anyone else had made it. They hadn't, so I wedged myself against some wreckage with an M-16 and two grenades. That's the last thing I remember until I woke up the second time, and then I was sure I was dead."

He was feeling no pain—lying on a cot, covered by a quilt that was covered with aromatic herbs. The cot was on the porch of a cabin in the foothills, surrounded by stands of fir trees and fields of flowers and snow-capped mountains. In the valley below were two rivers with gondolas on them, and a village, and a white temple in the distance.

Rolf crunched another ice cube.

"And then he came out. His name was Preeta Das. He spoke in that singsong English you get from educated Indians, and though he sort-of looked like he was in his late thirties, he just as easily could have been in his sixties. An average, clean-shaven guy with glasses, wearing slacks and a shirt. Like an accountant, or maybe a dentist. He told me the valley was known as Pahalgam, about ninety-five klicks east of Srinigar, and that I'd been brought to him by the men who'd shot me down. When I asked why they would do that he said, 'They saw that God had chosen to spare you, and in their faith he who saves another for the sake of God makes for himself a sanctuary in Paradise.'"

Rolf stayed in the valley for what turned out to be nine weeks—cared for by his host who also became his mentor, unaware of what had happened to General Sauter's mission, cut off from the world that reported him missing but presumed him dead.

"So, this Preeta Das. He was like...what? A yogi or something?"

"He didn't volunteer, and I didn't ask. Seemed irrelevant, you know? Before I left he helped me to see my dharma, my path. It frightened me like nothing else ever has, and when I asked him what would happen if I wasn't equal to it, if I gave up along the way, he told me this: 'Give up every fear but one, and you need not fear anything else.' At the time, I thought I knew what he meant. After a while, I wasn't so sure."

Rolf emptied his mug into the sea.

"He had a driver take me to New Delhi. Four hundred miles in a junk Jeep with a guy who couldn't speak English, through territory on red alert—man, I came back to reality in a hurry. He dropped me at the U.S. Embassy, and you cannot believe the uproar when I walked in."

"Wait a minute. I think I read about this somewhere."

"You probably did. A hero back from the dead? The press ate it up."

The launch neared; two Coast Guard officers were with the helmsman.

"A few months later I was waiting for a ship, all torn to pieces about Josie, and I tried to find him. Really wanted to talk. The phone company was no help, but eventually I reached some bureaucrat in Pahalgam. According to him there was no Preeta Das. I said he was a healer and a teacher and that he'd saved my life, and that I needed to find him—had he ever heard of such a man, anywhere? The guy hung up. I tried a bunch more times and packed it in. I went to the library and found some photos of the place. There was a valley with two rivers, but aside from that it didn't look at all the way I remembered it."

Saint Eves megaphoned from the bridge, "Lend a hand at the gangway, Thurston; I'm coming down." Rolf hailed back and he and Rick strolled aft to the portal in the midships rail; they watched the launch as it putt-putted alongside.

"That's some yarn, Rolf."

"Ain't it, though?"

"Too bad things didn't work out with you and Josie. You sure this dharma of yours doesn't include her?"

"No, I'm not." Rolf grinned. "Just like I don't know whether hers includes me. Maybe someday I'll stop running long enough to find out."

FOURTEEN

The Wheel of God

At dawn, Arab voices began warbling over loud-speakers—the Muslim call to prayer, from minarets within the walled medina.

Rick stood at the forward rail of *Caroline's* flying bridge. He'd had just one miserable hour of sleep, ended by the noise of the tugboats; showered and changed his bandages, got coffee and the morning gossip, then climbed up here, trying to take it all in as the sky lightened and the ship moved closer to the wharves: the fleet of local fishing boats—lateen-rigged, engines chugging and smoking—passing on their way out to sea; the bickering of the longshoremen docking *Caroline;* and the medina, the Old City of Sfax, unmasked from its nocturnal aspect by the first rays of North African sun—white and ochre domes and arches, blue doors like chips of broken tile, mosques and their minarets aspiring in the midst.

Now *Caroline* was secured, and Rick studied the

port: Fronting the quay were donkeys attached to milk wagons, dock alleys filled with skids of sponges, rows of ramshackle warehouses and machinery, and stacks of cargo containers, including a powder-blue forty footer bearing the white-laurelled logo of UNICEF. But unlike Duluth, there was no phalanx of silos and vacuum chutes—they had their own quaint technique for off-loading grain in the Bay of Gabes. Beyond the waterfront spread the French-grid modern city and the medina; straight ahead were storage tanks, the oil refinery inshore, and two ships at the phosphate depot. In the harbor, a tug pushed a Russian freighter, half again *Caroline's* size but in not much better shape, towards the quay. The longshoremen, disregarding the call to prayer, lined up to secure the new arrival at the slip forward of *Caroline*.

A clanking on the gangway: the harbormaster was coming aboard, his uniform bone dry in the ninety percent humidity; starched creases and a grandiose hat with a patent-leather brim. Mr. Tyler came to greet him and only then did Rick realize how small he was; he could have been Tyler's monkey. They clasped hands and the harbormaster bent his neck to view the tall American, baring bad teeth. His arrival meant the ship would soon be cleared; Rick trotted down to the bridge deck to see Inspector DuPonte.

Mr. Forbes passed him on his way outside and to the rail; Rick heard *Caroline's* new first mate greet the harbormaster by name as the official came up. Sparks was in his hut, working on the ship-to-shore hookup. Seeping through the saloon door slats were muddled voices and a funk of coffee, tobacco, and body odor: the

Coast Guard inquiry. Saint Eves was still in there, Rick was sure, and he heard someone say the name Newton, the First Assistant Engineer who'd taken over from Chief Briggs. Scuttlebutt was that the officials had set straight to work last night, hearing DuPonte's report and taking statements from Saint Eves and Tyler, and now were looking further into the deaths of the two officers.

DuPonte's cabin was open; his bag was packed, and he was knotting his tie. Rick knocked at the doorway.

"Ah, bonjour, M'sieur Weisman. You received my note. And you are willing to assist?"

"Anything that might help the boy."

Pinched his tie, centered it. "A worthy ambition, though I fear it is unwise to expect much advancement towards it. Yet you may indeed help many others. Maintenant, tonight at Café Stella—"

The name threw Rick, and the inspector noticed. "What is it?"

"That's the restaurant Saint Eves told me about, where the captain and the chief got mixed up with Le Clerc."

DuPonte squinted at him, began combing his hair. "It is that sort of place, m'sieur; perhaps you will understand after this evening. Our meeting is at ten o'clock—I regret that it must be so late, but my operative has been away in the north." Admonished Rick with the comb. "I will be at the gangway at quarter to ten, with a car."

"Should I bring a change of clothes? I was told—"

"That is not necessary for now. Later we shall see."

With that he closed the door and Rick headed below for chow.

Men were still wandering into the mess and taking their seats, in good humor. The horrendous passage was over, Whitehead remained quiet and had given up his door banging, and once the stevedores started unloading the ship's cargo, the crew would be free to unload theirs on the town. Rick ate with Willis and Freddy; Rolf was sacked out.

"What's the story in this burg, Willis?" Freddy asked, mouth full.

"Things are a tad dicier for Americans than they used to be, since the Gulf War." He crooked his brow. "But you should feel right at home, Rick—the people of Sfax are known as the Jews of Tunisia."

"Really? What could they have done to rate such a compliment?"

"Well, say for instance a merchant from another town tries to open a shop. Two locals will set up on both sides and squeeze him right out. The rest of the country calls them ruthless, but they don't care; they're better at business and richer and always have been. So, listen up, lads, and tell Rolf too—watch your step, mind your manners, and keep hold of your wallets. These folks can carve you up so neat, you'll think you like it."

The bos'n came in carrying a leather-wrapped Billy club; he approached their table and banged it down in front of Rick.

"Weisman, you've got first gangway watch, eight to four. Somewhere down the road, maybe this afternoon, the Coast Guard may want to speak with you, but I hear most likely not. Either way," hands on the table, he lowered his voice, "after that you'll have all the time you need."

He was in on the deal with DuPonte, didn't want to say more than necessary in front of the others while still letting Rick know he'd be off duty until *Caroline* left Sfax.

"And take care with this thing, it's deadly. Sprung steel with a lead-filled tip."

He stood erect with a groan, palm to lumbar, looked around for a seat and found one.

"He'd better not give me the four to midnight," Freddy grumbled to Rick. "I'm up for some serious partying. How 'bout you?"

"I don't know. Think I'd better pass."

Freddy punched him in the arm. "That's your problem, bub—you think too much. What you need is a major splurge, and me and Rolf are going to make sure you get it. Trust me, tonight's the night."

—⁓—

At eight, armed with towel, hat, sunglasses, a thermos of ice water, and the Billy club, Rick headed out to the foredeck. It was a Bessemer oven—one hundred twelve in the shade, the humidity like invisible rain.

The watch station was a wooden stool under a jerry-rigged awning not far from the gangway, where Tyler was still stationed. Before Rick could get settled, Forbes and the harbormaster arrived from the bridge deck, the first mate with a wrapped gift of liquor—taboo for Muslims—tucked under his arm.

"When the stevedores come, Rick, stay on your toes."

"They are thieves and scoundrels," the Tunisian elaborated, giggling.

"Any of them so much as looks at you queer, let him have it."

"What is written," the Tunisian agreed, "is written."

They continued to the top of the gangway, where Tyler was watching the proceedings on the wharf; Forbes gave the harbormaster the liquor and he marched down with his treasure; moments later an air horn blasted and both officers motioned Rick over to see:

From across the quay, streaming by the hundreds out of the warehouses and alleys, the native stevedores came—begging for a ticket to work, crowding the boss man who stood at the foot of the gangway, flanked by two henchmen and a cart full of wooden scoops. The boss extracted friends and family and ushered them aside, then divided the remainder of the tickets between his henchmen. They waded into the mob, callously shoving against it, handing tickets to their cronies and those who'd agreed to a kickback.

When it was all over the boss man led one crew up the gangway, leaving another below with his boys to handle the dockside chores. He stepped on deck then stood so every man would have to pass by him, intimidating both his top workers who'd operate the machinery but mostly the throngs—each man with a scoop—who'd work the cargo. They milled about the three forward holds, smoking cigarettes and arguing as some of them peeled away the canvas tarps that seal out water from the holds. The winches were then fired up, the cargo boom cables hooked to the hatch covers, and the mammoth iron slabs were raised then deposited on the deck.

Finally, they lowered down pallets of burlap sacks and the men jumped into the holds, sinking to their knees in the hills of grain, chattering nonstop. As sacks were filled, they tied their strings and piled them on a pallet; when the pallets filled, they were winched aloft by the cargo booms, swung over the side to the wharf; the sacks unloaded there from the pallets and stacked up by the shore-side crew.

Caroline would be cleaned out in just a few days of this lunacy, though Rick had heard that on her past calls in Sfax it had sometimes taken ten days or more, depending on what else was happening in the harbor. He did the math: seven thousand tons of grain unloaded by, roughly, two hundred fifty men; twenty-eight tons each or about nine tons a day for three days; maybe one hundred pounds per sack, so that was one hundred eighty sacks per day per man, or fourteen for every hour of their thirteen-hour shift. Which equaled one sack every five minutes, every man, and he didn't bother to calculate lunch.

It had to be one hundred thirty degrees in the holds, and each worker was making a thousand milliemes a day. A little more than a dinar. About a buck.

Welfare program, Sfax style.

—⁂—

The day crept by, and when the grain dust wasn't making him chain sneeze, when he wasn't mopping sweat with a towel that was saturated with it or splashing water on his itching eyes, Rick observed the comings and goings. There was a lot of them.

Inspector DuPonte left soon after the harbormaster. He was met on the wharf by a tan Rover with a European driver, who got out and held open the passenger door. Later, a parade of crewmen that included Rolf and Freddy traipsed ashore, wallets fat with draws from their pay. Around noon a police van arrived, and two uniformed men came aboard with body bags. The Coast Guard officers took off next, scheduled to return tomorrow to deal with Whitehead and the transport of Brace and Briggs to the States. They were followed by Ike, the bos'n, the police, and several stewards, lugging down to the van three of the six body bags, now with bodies inside. On the second trip, the stewards were replaced by Mr. Forbes, who carried the bag with the young girl, cradled in his arms.

Other than that, Rick watched the workers from his post in the relative luxury of shade, marveling at their morale. He couldn't reconcile it with what Tyler and the harbormaster had told him, until the afternoon call to prayer crackled through the loudspeakers. He was half dozing behind his sunglasses; as the chant began, he pictured muezzin leaning from their towers all over North Africa, exhorting with the same phrases, when abruptly there was a disturbance on deck and he jumped off the stool, Billy club ready.

Someone had collapsed in number two hold; Rick watched as they hauled him up on a pallet: a white-haired geezer, skin and bones. They laid him on deck and the boss dumped a bucket of water on his head. The man didn't come to, and before Rick could grasp what was happening two winch operators carried him to the starboard side and heaved him over. Rick ran to the railing: the smack of the sea hadn't roused the old man and one of the winch operators turned and made a slit-throat sign to the boss, who then went to the port side and hollered orders down to the quay. A trio of longshoremen rowed around in a skiff and fished out the body.

CPR, Sfax style.

—⁓—

At 3:10, Mr. Forbes showed up at Rick's post.

"Captain wants to see you." He held out his hand for the Billy club but avoided Rick's eyes. "His office in five minutes. I'll take the rest of your watch."

The edginess from the usually up-front Forbes was odd. Rick didn't know why Saint Eves had sent for him but assumed it was for an update on his status with the Merchant Marine; he told himself that the report had to be okay, or he'd have been called on the carpet with the Coast Guard. So, what was wrong with Forbes? He went to 8-12 to wash and put on a clean tee, then realized he'd be free to leave the ship after he spoke to the captain—a chance to get oriented in Sfax before meeting with DuPonte. He showered fast, did his bandage routine, dressed in his shore clothes: khaki slacks, loafers, gray silk shirt. He took the wallet from his jeans and the passport from his duffel, buttoned them into his pants pockets, hurried up the companionways to the bridge deck and the captain's office.

"Come," was the reply to his rap.

Saint Eves was sitting on the edge of his desk, holding a piece of paper. The curtains were drawn, the desk lamp lit, three fans whirring.

"Sorry I took so long, sir. Had to clean up."

The captain offered the paper—a telex.

"From KBS, son. It's...bad news."

TO OS RICK WEISMAN, SS CAROLINE COAST. ELI DIED THIS MORNING. PLEASE CALL. WE'RE ALL AT RHODA'S. UNCLE MILTON.

Saint Eves led him to the couch. "You'd better sit down. Was this unexpected?"

Rick was reading it again, word by word—

"I didn't realize...didn't know that when you said you had uncles in the industry, you were talking about the Kagan brothers."

—but nothing changed. Everything already had.

"I once got to shake Eli Kagan's hand, after a speech he gave at Seatrade twelve years ago. He was a giant. Were you close to him?"

Matching the edges evenly, Rick folded the paper.

"Yes."

"Then you've been fortunate to know such a great man so well. And from what I've seen of how you conduct yourself, I'm sure he was proud of you."

Rick tucked the telex into his shirt pocket.

"I've taken the liberty of arranging the call. You can use this office; Sparks has an operator standing by. Just give me the phone number."

Saint Eves provided him pen and paper, got what he needed and left.

Alone now in the quiet, Rick felt the borders of his skin lifting, as if by treaty with the air. The telephone rang and he went to the desk, took the call standing. It was his mother, sniffling but composed. She talked about Eli's dying hours, his refusal to go to the hospital so he could remain with the family, the kind words he'd spoken to each.

"When his time was near, Ricky, he asked for you. Milton told him you were at sea, and Eli demanded to know why you were away from the office. He said you needed to be here to run KBS. I don't mean to make you feel bad, darling. He wasn't himself and—"

"It's okay, Mom."

"Milton told him he'd bring you home. It made Eli so happy. He said—" She stifled a sob. "He said, 'Rick will know what to do. He'll take care of everything.'"

She broke down; he heard the phone pass to another.

"Ricky? It's Uncle Milton. If you want to come to the funeral, I've got your emergency release approved; the telex to your captain is on its way—give him the word and you can pay off immediately. There's a commuter flight from Sfax to Tunis this evening, a red eye for London tonight; you could be home on the Concorde tomorrow. I'm holding the reservations. It's up to you."

Rick thought about what he'd miss if he stayed. He

wondered if somehow Eli was trying in his death to save him from his own, as if maybe Eli knew that Musa and the coin were beyond reach and beyond hope, that Rick should turn aside now to be with the family who needed him and take the seat his uncle had prepared for him, at the table he and his brothers had built with their own hands from nothing.

He thanked Milton and told him he'd phone again if he decided to come, but that if he didn't call within the hour he should cancel the flights. Rick sent his love to Sid and everyone and said goodbye.

He stood still in the captain's office, imagining how it would be: the scores of mourners and dignitaries at the memorial service, the cables from friends and well-wishers, the President's call to Rhoda, the politicians, statesmen, and business leaders who would make their tributes to an incandescent life.

Descending from the bridge to 8-12, Rick made his own: Remembering how, the day after Pearl Harbor, the brothers had enlisted in the Navy, all serving the duration with distinction. How Milton was in submarines, rose to lieutenant commander and earned the Navy Cross; how Ernie and Alf, both gunnery officers on the *Missouri,* had been present at the signing of the Japanese surrender; how Eli had finished the war a decorated full commander in the Office of Naval Intelligence. He remembered then how the brothers had finagled a $10,000 loan to buy the *John L. Burns,* and from such beginnings had built the second-largest American merchant fleet, blazed the trail into the age of container ships, become compulsive philanthropists, and earned the veneration of their employees, their competitors, and their country.

What would men such as these do in my place?

Now as never before, Rick Weisman felt his obligation and accepted it:

Yes Eli, I will take that seat, just as you've always wanted. But when?

He toppled onto Willis's bunk and closed his eyes:

Into the dark he swims, seeking shelter and answers but also the place where tears begin, which he'd never found for his father and wants to so much for Eli, far into the dark until there's an aqua sky with puffs of clouds, and suspended within it a clear crystal oval, its surface bare save for a crystal bowl filled with white-blue flame. Now a section of sky swings out and coming from beyond it are the voices of many men. He senses their voices growing louder, as if the men are about to walk through the door but instead it's Eli who does. He moves towards Rick, young and smiling.

"Don't be sad, son."

"But I love you, Eli. And I don't know what to do."

"Well, dear boy, there's only one thing I can tell you, because it's the only thing I know." As though to explain he spreads his arms wide, dissolves into Rick's heart and brings him sleep.

—m—

"Snap out of it, bub."

Freddy close. Rolf behind, watching.

"Hey, there you are. You okay? You had us worried for a minute."

"We came home to take you out," Rolf said, "and heard the news from Mister Forbes." He sat on the bed, patted Rick's knee. "Maybe you need to be alone."

"No way," Freddy insisted. "Dude needs his crew."

Rick stared off, blank. *Eli, Eli—*

Suddenly, electrifying 3D images pulsed against the ceiling: an army of terrified children in chains, whipped by men on horseback into a river of red, with only their heads, as though severed, bobbing above the flood.

Rick launched off the bunk and bolted out the door. He knew exactly what he needed, and he needed it now.

FIFTEEN

Smoke and Mirrors

The Café de Paris was the harbor joint, marooned on a cobblestone island ringed by warehouses and potholed streets. Under a tin roof and signs for Chartreuse and Cinzano—captions for the comic strip below—a mob of seamen at the outdoor bar shouted for drinks; others sat at surrounding tables where red-vested waiters jockeyed in French and pidgin English.

Freddy and Rolf had come running after Rick, catching up when he'd hesitated at the foot of the gangway. He told them what he wanted, and since it meshed with their plans, they'd brought him straight here, to a table on the outskirts. Rolf snagged a passing waiter carrying a tray of drinks from the well and each took a fizzed gin; Rick gulped his as Rolf ordered the second and third rounds. When Rick's double scotch arrived, he drank that too and started on the next, and only then did the horrifying images begin to fade.

"By your leave, gents. Apologies for being so late."

The Tunisian stranger, his American English startling, turned the empty chair and mounted it saddle style—eyes bemused, hair pomaded, narrow frame slung inside a white polo shirt and madras shorts.

"How can you be late?" Freddy ventured. "We weren't told when you'd show, just to wait for you here."

The man put his fingertips together.

"But consider. If a train is behind schedule, is it any less so just because we don't know when it's due? Ah, Moncef!" he cried to the waiter, who hurried over. "Cointreau!" They shared a jest in that medley of Tunisia's two languages Rick had first heard from Abdessalam. The name of it was as smashed together as the sound: Frarabic.

"All that aside, I am delighted," the Tunisian's hands encompassed the world, "to be your chaperone to the manifold pleasures of Sfax." He looked from Freddy, to Rick, then settled on Rolf. "The arrangement that Iftikhar offered was satisfactory?"

"Assuming the quality is top drawer."

"Only the very best for my customers."

The waiter returned with a glass of the liqueur and a chit; the Tunisian signed, joked again with Moncef, sipped.

"Mmm, nectar of the gods."

"I thought Muslims weren't supposed to drink," Freddy put in.

The Tunisian's mouth fell open. "No—is that true?"

Rolf took over. "Where did you learn your English?"

Another sip.

"Facts of life cost extra. One dinar, please."

Rolf held up the bill. "Let's start with a name."

"Ah. The truth costs two dinar."

Flexing a bicep that did not go unnoticed, Rolf extracted another. "No more bull, okay?"

"Yet that is my forte. Shall we finish here and proceed? The famed medina of Sfax awaits."

The three of them polished off their drinks and stood; Rick didn't do either and Rolf leaned over. "You coming? It's all right if you'd rather not."

Rick processed this then concentrated on his watch, working to make the dial focus: Two hours till DuPonte—what the hell. He downed the whiskey, pushed to his feet, and the Tunisian set a quick pace from the bar, zigzagging side streets to a main drag called Avenue Habib Bourgiba. He paused outside a busy brasserie.

"Excuse me, but I have a phone call to make. Details, you know."

He stepped through the doorway; the maître d' met him, attentive.

"Our fates are sealed," Freddy said.

"Think we're being hustled?"

"May wee, Rolf. But as Willis said, maybe we'll like it."

They made room for a Bedouin walking his camel along the street. The Tunisian exited the café and took leave of the maître d', who ceded the three Americans a curt nod.

"Ready?" their chaperone asked, leading them before anyone could respond across the wide, palm-tree lined avenue, darting between cars and bicycles and mostly prosperous-looking, Western-attired citizens.

Rolf took a fresh stab at the name issue. "I believe I

paid for something you haven't delivered. Not the best way to begin a relationship, is it?"

"Ah yes, my name. A thousand pardons." The Tunisian locked his fingers and cracked the joints. "Typically, I prefer anonymity all-around, a prudent policy in my line of work, yes? Nonetheless, I will keep our bargain, but fair is fair—afterwards you must also introduce yourselves. Agreed? Very well, then. In Arabic my name is Bir E'Ness. You may call me that if you wish, though you'd probably sound exceedingly droll. Or, if you choose, my dear tutor had a transliteration of it I've always been fond of: 'Manwell.' That's M-a-n-w-e-l-l. 'Because you, dear boy,' she would say, 'shall serve mankind.' As you can see, I have fulfilled her prophecy."

—m—

"...a city is like a girl, young friends. She doesn't become a woman until she has been conquered. Preferably often. Which is why you Americans are so drawn to the world's hoary metropolises. It's the attraction of an adolescent to a painted lady with tired eyes. He may adore his high-school sweetheart, but, after all, an expert is an expert, yes? Such a city is Sfax..."

They hadn't heard it in the modern section, but inside the medina there was Arabic music everywhere. Strange quarter-tone scales. A recorder or woodwind. A lute. A drum, perhaps clay.

"...violated many times, by many invaders over the ages. She has watched her suitors come and go, their great civilizations wax and wane, yet she remains behind these walls much as she always has. What you see is a painted lady with tired eyes, but within her heart is a virgin waiting without hope for a love that will never come. Perhaps I gush, but this city has a soul. So, when you tread here, tread with care..."

Manwell was guiding them along winding, cobblestone streets — each with a medieval gutter in its center, like indigo veins in the medina's flesh. Sailors from the ships in harbor strutted for action; an occasional tourist couple took photos or haggled for bargains. The craftsmen and merchants seemed to know their guide well—most would greet him, cordially or enthusiastically, and then either disdain the three Americans or glance at a spot above their heads and return to their work, all questions answered.

"...exceptional artisans here, and they make good use of the cooler evenings. To your left—that's esparto grass being fashioned into mats. To your right—silk weavers and embroiderers. And here's one of our best saddle makers. Salaam, Yousef! Sfax also has renowned metalworkers—engraved brass vases and trays, jewelry in copper, silver, and gold. See the iron grilles about the windows?"

They entered a red-light district: disconsolate young harlots posed on the front stoops of stucco houses, limp flowers pinned to oily hair, their fathers, brothers, and sisters scouting for johns. As their group passed, each girl tried to work up a semblance of seduction—a gartered thigh, a heartless pout, a curved tongue.

"If you think we're stopping here," Rolf growled, clutching Manwell's arm. The Tunisian removed Rolf's hand and steered them through the venereal streets.

They came to a square. A Bedouin in robes gave way before their entourage, face caved inside his kufiya. Manwell led across the square into a long alley; out the other end of it the houses were stately, the streets wider yet almost empty of traffic, the pavement clean. And still there was that music—malouf, Manwell had called it.

"You see?" he said with a flourish. "As promised, only the very best."

"Tell me, Manwell," Rolf asked. "What's a smart guy like you—?"

"—doing in a job like this?" he finished for him. "Too personal?"

"A trifle, but you have paid for the concession. In Tunisia we say that all is mektub; one cannot escape one's fate. 'Elli mektub fejbin lazem tsufu elayn,' sayeth the proverb: 'What is written on the forehead must be seen by the eye.' I come from a wealthy family, yet wealth does not necessarily imply, how shall I say...adherence to the strict letter of the law, if you catch my meaning.

"My dear papa, however, had higher aspirations for me. I was given the finest education at American schools and colleges, chose government and made good, was the pride of my clan. Then disaster. Three years ago, I fell in love with a incomparable beauty, proposed marriage but was spurned, a calamity which commenced my decline. I accepted bribes though I did not need the money, drank to excess, sought comfort in the arms of professionals. Ultimately, I lost my sinecure and took up with the dubious crowd that introduced me to my current métier. Yet still I am the pride of my family and still I do not need the money."

"So why—?"

"One cannot dither away the days, can one? In Sfax, everyone must be busy, everyone must work. This too is tradition. Furthermore, my occupation allows me to assay human nature in all its intricacies, human weakness in all its caprice. The clash of cultures, the desires of men, the mysteries of women—an epic saga, which someday I will set down in the pages of a book. Ah, here we are."

A Moorish villa. The arched door, framed by spiral-fluted marble columns, was the same blue as most doors in Sfax except here ornamented with arabesque carvings. The walls were stucco; the marble motif was fulfilled in cornerstones.

Manwell unlocked the door and ushered them in.

A courtyard, open air. Dwarf cypress trees grew from white marble planters on a black marble floor. Framed by marble columns matching those outside, were more arched, arabesque-carved doors. Moonlight and malouf flowed in from above, draping the Andalusian frescoes adorning the walls.

In the center of the court was a cylindrical brass table and four gold-tasseled pillows. On the tabletop burned three candles in brass goblets, and there was a brass and glass hookah with four pipe hoses. At the foot of the water pipe were two tiny brownish cubes, set like cupcakes on lace doilies.

Freddy whistled low. "When you make a phone call you don't mess around."

"Thank you," Manwell replied, bowing. "If you are pleased, I am pleased. Come in, come in."

He closed the door and latched it. Imitating him, they removed their shoes before walking across the glossy tiles.

"Where are we?" Rick asked as they sat.

"Ah, the silent one speaks at last."

"He's just had a death in the family," Freddy explained.

"Oh, I see. My condolences."

Manwell picked up one of the cubes, displayed it to Rick in his palm.

"Have you ever tried kef?"

"No, I— Never. What is it?"

"The golden pollen of the hemp plant, for which our state of kayf, or dreamlike tranquility, is named. It is the finest smoke of the cannabis family, and this is the finest kef in the world. You are in for a treat, my friend. And more."

Rick glowered at Rolf—disillusioned with him and distraught at himself, though not sure why on either count.

Manwell split the cube and crumbled it into the bowl of the water pipe; Rolf and Freddy took up their hoses; Rick raised his then froze: On the screen of his mind the stranger had come again: standing at attention, holding his sword before him by the blade, its grip pointing up crossed by its guard, fixing him with a gaze at once fiery and forgiving. Rick recoiled before the vision, biting down hard on the mouthpiece.

The Tunisian applied a match.

"A word of advice. Do not hold the smoke in your lungs. Breathe with it normally. In this way the kef will detect your own rhythms and merely enhance them. If you try to trap her, she may become surly."

The kef bubbled in the water pipe.

Somewhere a clock struck the hour, the sequence of bells dissonant, as if they should mean something to Rick though he couldn't remember what. He continued to smoke, hoping he wouldn't.

Rolf fumbled for his wallet and handed sixty dollars to Manwell, who argued, "But you owe me only fifty. And you have not yet seen—"

"The women who keep a house like this are bound to be okay for pugs like us. And regardless, the kef is more than worth it."

"You are a connoisseur, Rolf. Salaam."

They breathed the smoke—entranced by the lyric of architecture, the mystique of their pilot, the canvas of sky, the sensate music. No one spoke; Manwell reclined on his cushion; the clock chimed the half hour.

"And so, it is time for tales. The women I have chosen for you tonight are truly artists of the first rank. Thus, you must hear and appreciate their stories before you presume to partake of their talent.

"Freddy, yours shall be Sophia. She was born twenty-two years ago on the island of Sicily yet is strikingly fair. At seventeen she was deflowered by her second cousin, who then proposed marriage. The young man to whom she was betrothed by arrangement called vendetta on the cousin and the two families obliterated each other. Sophia was given into the care of nuns, but she escaped across the Malta channel and thence to Sfax. Her skills are folklore. She will cost you eighty American dollars."

Freddy blinked at the sum. Manwell clapped once. A door opened and she stepped out—holding a candle that illuminated her features, her blonde hair straight, her figure explicit by lamp light through a transparent gown. She turned and retired to the room. Freddy gave Manwell the bills and followed her in, the door closing as if by sorcery.

The clop of a horse's hooves on cobblestones; Manwell resumed the introductions. "Now to yours, Rolf. Her name is Fan. Born in Dakar, Senegal, of Wolof nobility, she disgraced her family by having an affair with the hated Moroccan envoy. Disowned by her father they eloped to Rabat, but the Moroccan was abusive and publicly unfaithful. After a year of humiliation, Fan murdered him during sexual congress. Something about a well-placed digitalis capsule? I'm fuzzy on the details. In any event, with a price on her head, she eluded capture by throwing in with a caravan of Rif Berber, eventually settling in Gafsa where she learned to ply her craft. Two years ago, she heard of this house and came to Sfax. She, as well, costs eighty dollars."

Rolf laid the bills on the table as Manwell clapped three times. The light cast from a door behind drew them like moths. She was bald, red-lipped, clad above the waist in the skin and fur of a panther, tribal symbols painted in gold on her thighs and hips. Rolf started towards her, stopped.

"You okay, Rick? Not too stoned, are you?"

Too stoned for what? Compared to what? In the nine years since his overdose, he hadn't touched anything but alcohol—and now something was rushing the ends of every nerve, and something was dancing a belly dance on hot coals, and something was telling him to run for his—

"Rick?"

"Huh? Yeah, I'm fine. Just great. See you later."

Rolf went to Fan, encased her head with his fingers. She rolled it beneath them then led him into her room.

"Finally, we come to you, my friend. I have saved the best for last because you are in pain, and I would like to ease this pain. It has often been said that the most ardent women of the world are those of the Sahara, and the one who shall be yours is its blossom. Her father deserted before she was born, and for spite her mother sold the babe to..."

Manwell's speech drowned in the roar of jets. His mouth continued moving and Rick tried to lip-read what he could no longer hear as three fighters in formation sliced the moon-bright sky. The stars dripped.

"...she booked passage home to Tunisia to search for her father—not for revenge, as with her mother, but to thank him for giving her the lusty nature that had enabled her to prosper and buy her freedom. She didn't find him, however, and as her quest ended in Sfax she remained here. Her name is Magdalena, after the consort of the Nazarene. She will cost you one hundred dollars."

Rick sat up. "I...I've never paid for a woman before."

"Are you certain? A woman who costs you nothing may in fact cost you everything."

The jets rumbled into the distance and a white dove glided through the open roof; it landed and waddled to a cypress tree, fluttered up to the planter rim and began preening its feathers.

"Listen, before you clap or anything, is there a bathroom I can use?"

Manwell ducked his head, his hand arching toward a door off the courtyard.

The burnished black floor squished like mud; Rick opened the door, found the light switch: white tile and porcelain, strong bite of disinfectant. Rick closed the door, leaned over the claw-foot tub, raised the window—putrid air whiffed in from the alley. He urinated, gargled water, washed his face, stared in the mirror:

The shroud of a hollow man.

In the cabinet were toiletries and a box of disposable razors. He dabbed cream on his mustache and with a few fast strokes and a scatter of cuts it was gone. Stared in the mirror again and got punched hard.

Nowhere to hide now, Weis guy. What did Saint Eves say? About Eli being proud of you? Some joke. Some—

Bells, chiming from outside.

Oh, no. How many the last time? Eight, right? Couldn't be nine, could it? Not nine... Because that would mean—

Rick had to hold the sink to keep from falling, each of the clock's ten bells like heavyweight blows hammering the liquor and kef to the mat.

He flung open the bathroom door.

Manwell was waiting, holding Rick's loafers.

"Don't forget these."

"Look, I'm sorry—can I pay for your trouble?"

"No regrets," he said, amiable as ever, escorting Rick to the entrance. "In Tunisia we say, 'Each bird sings according to the shape of its beak.' If this is not for you, I'm gratified that you realize it."

They were at the door; Rick wriggled into his shoes.

"Can you find the way to your ship?"

"I guess, but do you know of a place called Café Stella?"

"Café *Stella?*" Manwell grabbed Rick's arm, roughed him out into the street. "Why do you want to go *there?*"

Rick wrestled loose; his lie was lame but sufficient.

"Because I'm hungry, dammit, and a shipmate said they had good food. What's your problem?"

"Ah." Manwell mulled that, nodded, shook his head. "Your friend is quite correct. You will find their menu decidedly to your liking."

He gave directions; Rick tried to follow the jumble of nonsense but drifted to another thought.

"Can I get a taxi?"

"Difficult at this hour—try the Hotel Triki, one block from the medina gate."

He extended his hand and Rick took it.

"Tell Rolf and Freddy I had to go, okay?"

"Of course. And now I bid you farewell, Mister Rick of America. I ask but one favor in exchange for the inconvenience occasioned by your departure. Should anyone at Café Stella happen to inquire after me, please say only that—"

A wry grin.

"But I'm being foolish. Why should anyone think to ask you about me?"

With that he bowed and backed into the villa, closing its door through ripples of moonlight.

SIXTEEN

Year of the Rat, Year of the Goat

Rick was lost, stranded at the shore by a pier just south of the harbor. One boat was tied up there, a white sloop with *Lorraine* scripted on her transom, rocking in the light chop. The boat reminded him of *Moonraker* and Sid and Eli, and that led for the hundredth time to all he'd promised to do then forsaken for nothing: DuPonte and Musa, the herd of children, the coin.

He shuffled onto the pier, sat on a piling and hung his head...

He'd located the Hotel Triki outside the medina but found no taxis, not at the hotel nor anywhere else. With that frustration the kef had come scuffling back after its knockdown in the mirror, and what he could remember of Manwell's rights and lefts and French and Arabic street-names tumbled together like Bingo balls. He wound up at the train station on the wrong side of town, flogging himself all over again. Reversed course, kept the harbor to his left, followed Avenue Habib Bourgiba to the modern section. Everyone spoke in Frarabic, and their answers to the manic American's "Où est la Café Stella?" brought only frustration for him and confusion for them. Finally, he snared a shrewd-looking street scamp and waved a five-dollar bill in his face, which purchased just enough English to get him here—within view of *Caroline* and the harbor, in the general area where, according to the kid, Café Stella was supposed to be.

He might as well have been in Tangiers. He jogged around searching the deserted residential streets, which were lined with parked cars, periodic palms, and the rare landscaping of a wealthier home. He circled each lap towards the sea to keep his bearings, sweating himself sober—the acrid, sodden air, the guilt and hunger and lack of sleep finally wearing him down until he was undone, wasted and washed up...

11:25. Got to go again. Maybe DuPonte is still at—
A flashlight, approaching from the road.
"Hey, you!" Rick called out, too beat to try French.
The light zeroed in.
"What are you doing here? That is our pier; you cannot stay here."
English had never sounded so good to him.
"I'm looking for a place called Café Stella, but I'm lost. Can you help me?"
The flashlight switched off. Rick stood and as his vision adjusted again to the moonlight a young man strode up: late teens, Rick's size, black shirt and slacks, keeping his distance.

"Café Stella? What is your business there?"

Again, with this?

"No business—my friends tell me the food is good."

"And who are your friends?"

"Who's asking?"

He took a step, bristling. "I am Christian Bouché, son of Antoine Bouché, the owner of Café Stella. Now, I ask again, who are your friends?"

"Richard Saint Eves and Willis Fine of the SS Caroline Coast, which is right there." Twisting, he pointed to the harbor; twisted back and Christian had transfigured.

"Pardon, m'sieur!" Rick noticed now the intelligent eyes, tinged Asian. "We must be very cautious of strangers these days; that is why each evening I come outside to inspect our property and our sailboat. But a friend of Messieurs Saint Eves and Fine is always welcome. Maintenant," he swept an arm, "shall we go? The café is near, though I am not surprised you could not find it."

The land end of the pier led onto a grass sward with a brick path; Christian followed it to the boulevard that ran adjacent to the shore, curving away by a rocky breakwater. There were no streetlights, but the houses were whitewashed with moon glow.

"I have neglected to ask your name."

"Rick Weisman."

Christian whirled. "You have been *false* with me, sir! Because of you, there has been much anger and trouble tonight."

"Look, I realize I'm late, but—"

"Do not insult me further! You accused Ammi

Zarga of collaboration with Emile Le Clerc!"

"*What?* That's garbage! I don't even know who Ammi Zarga is."

"Then explain why my sister has cursed your name and vowed revenge."

"I can't. I have no idea. I'd swear it on a stack of Bibles."

"Very well, m'sieur. But now I swear to you: if you are again being false, you will pay dearly."

He was already, reeling: Why would DuPonte lie about him, and how does this kid know about it, and even if it were true, why would his sister want to demolish him for it?

Christian continued across the boulevard. A man on a bicycle spoke a genial word but got no reply. A block further and they went left into an alley Rick had dismissed as impossible for a restaurant—too narrow, no sign, more like a driveway.

Four houses down they turned right and there it was: at the end of a short street, with a cul-de-sac that served for parking, currently crammed, a stone building with a wooden sign by the door that read in painted script, "Café Stella." The sign was lit by a spotlight dug into a patch of lawn; below it was an illuminated glass box. Nearing, Rick could see that mounted inside the box were painted depictions of the house specialties; the names written below each were in the same feminine script as the sign. They arrived at the door and Christian held it open, yet despite the intensity of the moment the artistry of the illustrations drew Rick closer.

"You stop for *pictures?*"

"Why, is that a capital offense around here?" Rick shot back, realizing he must have looked ridiculous.

Christian probed his features.

"What is the date of your birth?"

Rick couldn't have been more fogged if he'd been asked for his shoe size, but Christian wasn't joking, and Rick didn't need any more problems. He answered and then was ushered through the café door—out of the North African tropics and into the brio of France:

Every table was taken and nearly every chair, the patrons pegged as much by their hands in conversation as the hands on the clock: these were night people— musicians, writers, artists, glitterati, and their hangers- on. The cult was the west, the language French not Frarabic, the smoke thick, the arguments impassioned, the laughter triumphant. Gounod's *Faust* trio sung over unseen speakers.

Christian acknowledged the maître d'—a swarthy, toothy ferret—at the entry podium, and guided Rick through the crowd: plank flooring, padded wrought- iron chairs, oak-topped tables with iron legs, white stoneware on black placemats emblazoned with gold fleur-de-lis, short cloisonné candelabra with a lit candle in each. An archway in the wall to the right opened to a bar and lounge. Four expert waiters worked the room. A glamorous woman turned to her date to greet Christian, flirting with him as did two others, but he was oblivious. Snubbed, the women assessed Rick, though their expressions were unreadable to him.

They came to the only empty table—adjacent to the kitchen, in an alcove by an exit door with a sign above it that read "Sortie"; another sign, above the table yet below a lit miniature painting on the alcove wall, read, "Réservé à la Gestion." Four chairs, small cloisonné table lamp, ashtray with a graveyard of butts, empty coffee cup on a saucer, half-empty glass of water on a linen napkin, notepad and pen; the door was jammed open a foot, allowing a draft of cooler air.

"Sit, m'sieur. I will tell my father you are here."

Faust gave way to Lauretta's "O mio babino caro" from Puccini's *Gianni Schicchi*. Rick sat so his back was to the wall, thankful for the chair and the music and the current of sea air. He gulped water from the unused side of the glass, poured the rest into a cupped hand and rinsed his face, dried off with the napkin. Christian pushed through the swinging doors from the kitchen, held one of them for a waiter, then approached.

"M'sieur, my father and sister are on the telephone with Ammi Zarga," he said as he bussed the table. "They ask for you to wait. And might I offer refreshment? A Perrier?"

Ask? Offer? Inexplicably, an inch had been given and Rick was far too gone to question why, or care how it would seem if he took a mile.

"Yes, thank you, but actually I'm very hungry."

Christian was embarrassed. "Excusez-moi. I will bring you some supper."

"Merci beaucoup. Et, uh—faire vous avez... espresso?"

Amusement at Rick's French, but his status definitely clicked up.

"Mais, oui."

"Un grande tasse, s'il vous plaît," Rick specified, fingers horizontal.

Christian went back to the kitchen and Rick surveyed the scene. Several customers stood out: a bearded grizzly bear; an inebriated artist with paint in her perm and on her jump suit; a denim-and-diamonds couple who now rose from their table and prepared to leave, clucked over by a waiter who'd doubtless been big-tipped; four rock-star wannabees in leather. But what he spent the most time looking at were six large oils on the papered walls, especially one of Berber children playing in an olive grove, and another of a desert sky with an old man shaking his fists at it. The bold signatures read, simply, "Lorraine," as on the Bouchés' sloop. By style, she was the same artist who'd drawn the illustrations outside, and it was a fair bet the artist was either Christian's sister or mother.

The well-to-do couple reached the foyer, waved to the maître d' but he was intent on the phone and didn't respond. Rick turned in his chair, appraised the miniature hanging at his table: a sunset with fishing boats, heavy canvas sails dusted bronze in the rays, striped hulls mirrored in the refracted darkener of the sea. A lone form in the foreground boat was gathering his nets off the stern, leering like a half-wit.

Rick tried to gather what was left of his:

Okay, you can still get on track. Explain things here, find out what you can, maybe meet with DuPonte and his operative tomorrow—

"Weisman!"

The shout came from the front door, hushing the

crowd; it was Mr. Forbes and Willis, sidearms strapped to their hips, walkie-talkies clipped to their belts. They were coming full tilt past the maître d's podium, which now was unattended, and their guns and grim jaws spelled trouble. Mr. Forbes let Rick have both barrels of it from six feet away.

"Good grief, man, we've been all over this whole town looking for you!"

Willis pitched in, venting steam. "And if we hadn't run into your friends on their way home to Caroline, we'd *still* be lookin'!"

"I messed up, I know. We got loaded and I— What did DuPonte say?"

"What *didn't* he say," Forbes fumed. "The man was fit to be tied. Saint Eves tried to cover your rear by telling him about your uncle."

Willis plopped a foot on the chair opposite. "Which didn't help much, lad. 'Cause yours is hanging in the breeze with a bull's-eye on it."

"Look, I left the old city a little after ten, couldn't find a cab, got completely lost..." Rick tapered off as they stared at each other. "What?"

"So, you've been wandering around Sfax for the last hour and a half?"

"Yeah, until a few minutes ago. Why?"

Willis sighed. "Rick, on the day your luck runs out..."

Forbes sat down and said, "Whitehead escaped."

"You're not serious."

"Was sprung is more like it," Willis corrected.

The first mate went on. "Forrest had gangway tonight and Jacky was hanging out with him. They deny it, of course, but the captain has evidence and he's turning them over to the Coast Guard. He wants them off the ship."

"Here's the thing, lad. Whitehead's through and he knows it. But I don't think he's through with you."

"How 'bout the police?"

Forbes wiped sweat from his forehead. "They've had us up to here, what with Interpol and the body count from the collision and that whole mess. The Coast Guard's leaving JJ to them and they're fatalistic about it, figure he'll run into the local bad element, and it'll be curtains. Maybe they're right, but Saint Eves is taking no chances."

A hand on his pistol to make the point.

"So, let's get going, sailor. You're coming with us."

"Excusez-moi, M'sieur Fine."

The voice came from behind Willis, and he moved sideways, his foot coming off the chair. It was a young woman with a tray of food, in an emerald jebba shift. She tossed the sheen of black hair obscuring her face. The food steamed but Rick couldn't smell it.

"Lorraine! What a sight you are for sore, old eyes."

Flattered, she rolled hers and addressed the table, placing silver and napkin, a plate of sliced grilled beef and roast baby potatoes, bread and salad, Perrier and espresso. Whatever happiness Willis had given her drained as she looked at Rick.

Forbes had risen to his feet at Lorraine's arrival—unlike Rick, who'd lost his manners along with his senses.

Lorraine beamed dazzlingly at him.

"Bon soir, m'sieur. I have not had the privilege of

meeting you."

"Oh, perdition," Willis said, chagrined. "Lorraine, may I present First Mate Abraham Forbes. Mister Forbes, this is Mad'moiselle Lorraine Bouché."

Forbes doffed his officer's cap.

"A pleasure, miss. I begin to see why so many speak so well of your café."

She dipped her brow. "I thank you for your kindness, but I must also ask your indulgence. It is very important," a flip of her wrist, as though shooing away a fly, "that I speak with this man."

Forbes almost said no then reconsidered, conferred with Willis; Lorraine put the tray on the table, glaring icily at Rick for an instant, as if that was all she could stomach. Christian hurried from the kitchen then spied the maître d's absence. Looking puzzled and irritated, he went to man the podium himself and got on the phone. Rick seized the opportunity to gulp coffee. He was going to have to think and dodge and hold his own before a blazing sun—debatable whether even espresso could get him through that, but it was all he had.

Forbes gave in.

"All right, Miss Bouché, but not too long; we need to get back. Weisman, we'll be in the bar."

They weaved between the tables, Forbes updating the ship with his walkie-talkie. Lorraine sat in the chair across, buttressed elbows and clasped hands as Rick finished the mug of espresso in two more gulps.

"First, I must know, m'sieur: Why did you fail DuPonte? He directed me to return from Tunis specifically to meet with you."

The obvious dawned. *"You're* his operative?"

"Not anymore, not after tonight. Anyone who doubts Ammi Zarga is not welcome here. And you have not answered me."

"My apologies, mad'moiselle. It's no excuse, but this afternoon I received bad news from home. I had too much to drink and forgot the hour. I'm sorry."

She pursed her lips. "Your eyes are red, m'sieur, but not, I believe, from an excess of tears. Perhaps wine was not the only drug to ease your distress?"

"Listen, missy. I'm doing my best to be polite, I said I'm sorry—if you want more than that, you're going to be disappointed. If you want to talk, let's talk."

A curl toyed at the corner of her mouth. She shifted her position: hands into lap, legs crossing under the ankle-length jebba. The motion released her scent, and he felt dizzy. His sense of smell was still alive, he realized, but only to—

"Your dinner is getting cold."

Those eyes softened slightly, and Rick let his do the same. He laid the napkin on his lap, cut a piece of steak, forked a potato with it, put it in his mouth and went haywire. If he'd been alone or in the company of anyone else, he would have devoured the exquisite cuisine like a piranha, but given Lorraine, he forced himself to sip Perrier after each swallow. She sat back, judging his every move, and soon it became intolerable. He needed to change the game.

"May I compliment you on your pictures?"

She'd heard this line too often.

"You are a...lover of art, m'sieur?"

Rick expected the sarcasm, was ready for it. "I have no talent myself, so I try to appreciate the talent of others."

His frankness disarmed her a bit; she decided to test him. "Can you say why you appreciate mine?"

Holding a hunk of baguette, he pondered the miniature again; chewed and swallowed, let himself slide into it as Eli had taught him. Even with her charged presence across the table, the brilliance of the painting made it easy.

"First of all, the light is just wonderful. It reminds me of Georges de la Tour, one of my favorites, and the emotion it brings out keeps pulling me further in."

"Yet the feeling is too somber, non?"

Her head cocked, critical as she looked at her work, and a fall of hair caught in a gold mesh chain that was her sole ornament; it glittered about her neck, vanishing into the jebba.

"In Tunisia don't you say, 'Each bird sings according to the shape of its beak'? Your tune is a sad one, yes, but there's humor too, I think, and even the bitterness has a sweetness all its own."

Now on the heartbeat she smiled, holding his eyes as he smiled back, then got down to business.

"DuPonte claims that you made accusations against Ammi Zarga, linking him to Emile Le Clerc."

Her smile remained, frozen.

"Not true. Like I told Christian—"

"I am not as trusting as my baby brother."

"I'll keep that in mind. I assume you're aware of the circumstances?"

She didn't answer but Rick guessed that DuPonte

hadn't gotten that far before she threw him out. Letting Rick know as much would have weakened her position; her face said she wanted Rick to proceed as though DuPonte had told her, and he did, which strengthened his.

"Ammi Zarga was one of a handfull of names I heard from Samir Abdessalam during his interrogation of the boy. It was in French, of which I understand little, combined with Arabic, of which I understand none, so I can't be positive about the context. But as best I could tell, he wanted to learn what the boy knew of the ownership of Cheval Marin and was suggesting possibilities."

He cut a piece of steak. "Just the mention of Ammi Zarga by a henchman of Le Clerc's was enough, evidently, to arouse DuPonte's suspicions." Forked the meat, pointed with it. "You seem to be sure he's wrong and maybe you're right. But for my money, the inspector is a dedicated pro who knows his stuff."

She flushed yet stayed focused. "Since you are such a great admirer of his, then explain why he would lie about you, if lying it was."

"I can't. He was angry that I missed our appointment, but I doubt that's it. Frankly, based on my own dealings with him I'd say he was..." Rick's attention was drawn to the kitchen, "trying to get a reaction..."

Lorraine swiveled. "These are my parents, m'sieur."

An older man was heading towards them, wiping his hands on a towel; a petite Asian woman in shiny black pants and smock followed two steps behind. Belying the medicine-ball gut bulging behind his apron, Antoine Bouché had an athletic gait and was handsome in a haggard way. Rick saw his children in him—their composure and bearing—but their looks had come from the matriarch. He stood and prepared to offer a hand, but Antoine continued to wipe his, making sure Rick didn't, looking the American head to toe and back. Madame Bouché scooted the chair on Rick's right until it was next to his and sat. Antoine took the seat to his left.

"Madame Bouché, M'sieur Bouché," Rick began, sitting as he did, nodding from one to the other. "Je suis désolé. I deeply regret the trouble I've caused here tonight."

"You speak as a gentleman," Antoine snapped, "but that does not make you one. So, we will speak as one bastard to another. In English—the *language* of bastards."

He pulled a pack of Gauloises from his shirt, shook out a cigarette, slapped his apron pockets for matches, found them and lit up. Meanwhile, with Lorraine surveilling from under lowered lids, Madame Bouché occupied herself with a fingertip evaluation of Rick's face and ear. He flinched at her touch but tried to stay calm throughout the bizarre exam—sensing the ageless machinery of her belief system, his grades marked against factors of which he had no conception and over which he had no control, as though generations of her line's past were guiding the marks, working the abacus, calling the tally, their readings noted in her throaty noises impervious to translation.

Antoine scowled. "Do you have any *idea* of the danger my daughter lives with every day? How much she has sacrificed for her family?"

"Papa, non," Lorraine protested.

"It is on *your* head what has happened with her and

DuPonte, no matter what Zarga says!"

Lorraine patted his hand.

"It could be that Ammi Zarga is right, that M'sieur Weisman is blameless. Inspector DuPonte may have altered the facts to fit his own agenda."

The love between them was stronger than his rage.

"Peut-être, cheri, yet he could not have done so, had this man been here to dispute him."

She was about to argue but Rick inserted, "Your father's right," before she could.

Her reaction to that was interrupted by Madame Bouché, who'd paused to bend towards her daughter. "L'anée du rat, l'anée de la chèvre," she muttered. Lorraine, after a sharp glance Rick's way that he pretended to miss, chinned and bug-eyed "shut up" to her mother, which made her look like a schoolgirl. Madame Bouché shrugged then upturned Rick's palms. Neither husband nor daughter seemed to care what she did with him.

"How did you leave it with Zarga, papa?"

Antoine inhaled, held it; his reply rode the smoke.

"You must go to him tonight and take the American."

Lorraine lapsed into staccato French.

"Papa, ça ne peut pas être! Tu a mal comprise."

"Non, ma fille. C'est le plus urgent."

They went back and forth, and Rick got the gist.

"With all due respect, people, I'm not about to—"

Antoine riveted on the front door.

Lorraine and Rick looked too, and saw an Arab dandy enter, smoking a thin cheroot. Christian stepped from the podium; he wasn't going to let the newcomer into the café and the man didn't force the issue, though he had the air and build of someone who could and usually did. Retreating, he waved to Antoine with his cigar hand and bowed. Christian closed the door, resumed his post, sought his father but the sight line was blocked by his mother—she'd risen from her seat, finished with her examination. Rick stood, pulled back her chair; Madame Bouché moved to her daughter's side and whispered in her ear; now she retired to the kitchen, a sorceress in satin.

Rick sat down; Lorraine stared at him and shook her head, dumbfounded, then leaned towards Antoine: "What was Hameed's top man doing here?"

Her father took her chin, rotating it so her eyes were on his; she blanched at what she saw in them.

"The roads are not safe. Take the boat to Jerba, go to Mustafa's. Zarga will have a plane waiting for you."

Antoine had said more with his tone than his words, yet Lorraine understood.

"So I was right. Cheval Marin was Hameed's." Her eyebrows furrowed. "But the sinking—it was an accident, non? We had nothing to do with it, Papa." Then a new idea struck, launching her into another flurry of French. Rick was forgotten.

Just as well. The more you talk the stupider you look. You guessed wrong about how much Lorraine had learned from DuPonte because she played you to guess wrong. When they told Zarga of DuPonte's accusations he took your part, but why? Like Rolf said, you're so far out of your league it's ludicrous.

While the other two consulted, Rick finished his meal, resolving not to be played anymore. True, Lorraine had been working for the inspector, undercover in Le Clerc's operation, and if she were going to remain in Sfax maybe in time Rick could enlist her help. But he didn't have time, and anyway she'd stated that, as of tonight, she was no longer DuPonte's operative, which likely meant she was done with her undercover work too. Rick now knew that she'd been with Le Clerc in Tunis, so if Musa were alive, it was possible, though by no means certain, that Abdessalam would have taken him there, whereas Lorraine was now bound for Ammi Zarga's. And even if they told him who Zarga was and where he was and why he wanted Lorraine to bring him there, and even if it all seemed to fit Rick's purpose, the fact was he couldn't be sure about *anything* they chose to tell him.

Forbes signaled from the archway to the bar, tapped his watch. Rick held one finger aloft; Forbes twirled his in reply as Willis joined him. They were going to stand there and wait, but not for long.

Lorraine and Antoine were still at it, heads together.

"Excuse me?" Rick interjected. They turned in unison. "I'm being told that I must leave now, but I just wanted to say...merci—for the dinner, the hospitality, and the, uh, fascinating chat. Again, my apologies for the trouble I've caused, but you seem more than capable of handling it without me."

He scraped back his chair until it hit the wall; what Antoine said next nailed him to it.

"You refuse to go to Nefta, m'sieur?"

Antoine hunted with his cigarette, sparks and embers in the ashtray.

"Then perhaps this might change your mind. Ammi

Zarga says that you and he must meet," his eyes slanted up, "regarding the coin."

Now this opera unto itself like every family's— comic and tragic, banal and profound—went terribly *unlike*. In one fringe of Rick's vision: Forbes and Willis, drawing their pistols. In the other, through the exit door: a black silencer trained on Lorraine.

Rick flung the table over, toppling father and daughter as Willis and Forbes fired and the assassin's shot ricocheted and struck Antoine in the forehead; Rick lunged sideways at the gun re-targeting Lorraine and slammed his fist on the barrel. The semi-automatic clattered down; the crowd screaming and rioting; Rick got to his knees, aimed through the doorway and squeezed the trigger: the running assassin clutched at his leg but stumbled out of sight before Rick could fire again. Wheeled with the pistol to the café: Lorraine on the floor holding her dead father, more gunshots now from somewhere near and—

The clap of explosion, a cannonball of scourging fire from the kitchen.

Dogs barking...little dogs behind thick doors.

A siren in the distance, another and a third.

Gravel...gasoline... He was on his back, outside where he'd been blown through the exit, the pistol still in his hand. The door was broken, hanging off its top hinge, cast in shadow crosses by the hooded lamp above.

Funny how it moves, splintered and holy like that.

His hearing popped—the sirens got louder and the dogs bigger; cries from the smoking restaurant. Forbes and Willis staggered out, each crutching another person, all coughing. Forbes was bleeding from the hand holding his sidearm; Willis had no weapon—holster empty, forearm charred. The two patrons they'd helped went their separate ways into the night.

Willis reached Rick's side first, hauled him to his feet. Rick tried to head back to Café Stella but Forbes barred the way.

"No, son, the cops and medics will—"

Rick made to push past; Forbes grabbed his sleeve.

"Are you nuts?"

"Yes, sir."

Forbes yanked him nose-to-nose.

"Surrender that weapon."

Rick propellered his arm, put the pistol to the first mate's temple.

"Surrender yours."

Willis made a move; Rick shifted so he was behind Forbes.

"Don't, Willis. This has nothing to do with either of you. Tell Saint Eves I'm keeping my promise. He'll understand."

Forbes shook his head, gave up the 9mm and Rick tucked it in his belt.

"Your extra clips."

They handed them over as Willis pleaded, "Rick, you've got to *listen* to me."

"Can't, my ears are still ringing. Now your money. If I don't show up before we sail, you can dun my pay."

Rick pocketed the bills. The sirens were close; lights going on in the surrounding houses, windows opening.

He stepped back. "Better shove off." Forbes wheeled; Rick saluted with the gun barrel. "I wouldn't have pulled the trigger, sir. I just didn't want you to get in trouble for letting me go."

"Yeah, I know. Otherwise, I'd have decked you."

"Even your luck can't save you now, son," Willis finished. "Only the good Lord can."

They trotted down the alley and out of sight. Rick went to the exit door, peered into the smoke: flames licked from the kitchen and climbed the archway to the bar; he made out Antoine's body but not Lorraine's. Ventured inside and, with an arm shielding his face, checked the kitchen inferno: no chance Lorraine's mother had survived that. To the café proper: some people were still struggling to their feet, others dragging or being dragged towards—

There, limping along the wall...

He didn't want to call her name, afraid of who might hear, so he followed her, passing over the pleas of the wounded, telling himself they'd be cared for soon, knowing he had to get her out of this place because the assassins might well come back to make sure they'd finished the job.

Lorraine found Christian in the foyer and collapsed to her knees, cradling her massacred brother, her jebba blotted with blood.

The sirens, very close. Rick squatted beside her.

"Lorraine. We have to go."

Skin sooted, hair singed, face blank, comprehending neither Rick nor her own name, everything that gave substance to life, everything that sustained it, gone. Now her eyelids closed, her head rolled back, and she was gone too.

Through the window, he saw two police cruisers escorting an ambulance. The Arab dandy waved his arms in the headlights; the lead cruiser and the ambulance went on until barricaded by the parked vehicles in the cul-de-sac; the rear cruiser stopped, and the dandy leaned on its driver-side door, talking through the window.

Rick extracted Christian, hefted Lorraine over his good shoulder and stood; she was weightless, like dry leaves. He gripped her with one arm, kept the pistol ready with the other, picked his way over bodies to the exit and looked out, checking both ways. He went right, paused at the back of the building and peeked around: smoke belched from the kitchen, the service doors flat on the ground. Slunk across a strip of lawn and down the driveway of an adjacent house, crouched by a row of garbage cans; he recognized the facing street from his search for the café.

Should be a beeline to the dock.

Cats and dogs yowling; more lights going on all the time. Twenty yards away, six neighbors were prattling in the street. He had to risk it; adjusted Lorraine, skulked by some bushes then angled to a tree. The group of neighbors was heading to the café. New sirens sounded. Rick speed-walked the rest of the block to the boulevard fronting the water, spotted the sloop. No options, though the sirens might come wailing down this very road—and how would *that* look in their headlights, with him fleeing the scene carrying a body? But he couldn't wait. He didn't know how badly Lorraine had been hurt and had to find out fast. He belted the assassin's pistol with Forbes', hugged her legs, and sprinted to the other side, taking cover at the foot of the piling where Christian had discovered him.

All still clear.

He carried her the length of the pier to the sailboat; the tide was high, and the boat's scuppers were flush with the dock. Over the cable railing to the deck then into the cockpit; Lorraine groaned as he laid her down. He slid aside the gold chain and peeked under the top of the shift: her chest was all right, the stains there must have been from Antoine and Christian. An ear to her heart: regular but slow. He pulled up the jebba. In the moonlight he could see that she'd been cut at the hip; a shard of glass glinted, and he pinched it out: she gasped, and her eyes opened; looked around, determined where she was, fixed on Rick as he pressed the dress against her wound to coagulate the blood while watching her. She put a hand in place of his and nodded; gently he sat her up, leaning her against the port-side cockpit seat. Her eyelids closed again.

Rick toed off his shoes, went on hands and knees to the helmsman's well and dropped onto the starboard seat, set the pistols and clips in a corner of the well, checked towards the land: The café was obstructed by houses, but he could see its smoke and flame curling skyward; a fire truck sped along the boulevard from the north. No one nearby.

Back to work. The instruments and ignition keyhole were clustered to one side of the wheel; the maker's nameplate read "Nautor's Swan." He stooped forward to the deck house—as expected, the hatch and door were locked.

Rested on his heels, considering.

There was a breeze from the northeast; no jib forward but the mainsail was furled on the boom, except hoisting it might easily attract notice. The alternative was to kick in the door and grub about for a spare engine key inside, though the racket could be more dangerous than the sail, with no guarantee he'd find what he needed. Sailing was it, then, but it was going to be tricky, even trickier just to get away from the dock with no engine if the current that had turned *Caroline* when they arrived here was running. Plus, he was unfamiliar with the waters and the channel, which meant that, even with high tide and a bright moon, he could stray into shoals or reefs. And though he knew Swans were bred for performance, this refined thirty-five-footer was way outside his experience in *Moonraker*, and he couldn't be sure how she'd perform without a jib in light winds.

Scanned the sea: a lit buoy, maybe a hundred yards out. He'd bear for that—

"There are keys. Here."

Lorraine's hoarse voice was accompanied by her hand on Rick's ankle. He looked and she indicated the cushion behind her. He lifted it, no keys.

"In the locker...the medical kit."

He raised the lid: life vests, foul-weather gear, emergency flares, empty canvas duffel, white metal box with red cross. One fire truck siren whined to a wheeze; others still blared. He removed the kit, closed the lid, set the box on the cushion, located the ring—only two on it. Unlocked the door and hatch first, returned to the helm, keyed the ignition to on: the instrument dials lit up, fuel gauge at three-quarters.

Lorraine exerted herself to get the kit off the cushion, breathing hard after.

"Do you...see the buoy?"

"Yes."

"Keep it...close to starboard and...you will stay in the channel...then come around to...course two-one-seven."

Staying low, Rick padded forward and untied the bow line from the dock cleat, carefully pulled the rope in; came back amidships and did the same with the spring line; he noticed that the boat wasn't drifting from the dock: the southerly current was running. Finally, he released the stern line, coiled it quickly so it wouldn't get in his way, stepped into the helmsman's well and made one more sweep of the boulevard. Still nothing near; they'd attracted no attention. Nudged the Swan's throttle and buttoned the starter: her engine coughed, caught, rumbled; he helmed to port and powered to half. The boat forged ahead but the current was strong; he steered into it, the buoy light steady on the starboard quarter.

With the first-aid kit under one arm, Lorraine crawled the few feet to the main house; she set down the box, opened the door, backed onto the stairs then stopped—staring long at the receding shore, the fire-flashed smoke twining crimson wraiths in her eyes, her lips quivering and expression twisting, and now in this maiden farewell to all she held dear her tears began, raining down as though to fill the sea.

SEVENTEEN

The Prisoner of Phuping

The Swan glided south, her mast rising to an opaline moon on a plate of astral gems. Rick wished he could rise there too, above everything as in the night of the storm, because maybe then he would see and understand and be able to comfort her. But it was no use. When so much has been lost it's like counting stars, and you can never rise high enough or see far enough for that.

Almost three a.m. Lorraine remained below. For a long time after they'd left the harbor her wracking sobs had pierced his soul; since then, the softer sounds of her weeping still reached him, though for the last half hour he'd only heard her moving about. He couldn't deal with the idea of disturbing her, yet he didn't know how much longer he should chance it—cruising in strange waters at night without reference to a chart. To starboard, several pairs of headlights snailed along a coast road; earlier the shoreline had curved away then straightened yet her course kept them roughly parallel. His seafarer's sense told him they were all right for the present, so he let her be.

Yet Rick needed help too. The survival adrenalin had long since subsided and a raw craving for sleep had taken its place—he was fighting to keep his eyes open. Now for something to hold onto he reached for his wallet and the photo of Eli and him by the Sphinx. He angled it into the light from the binnacle, but it was their last night together he thought of, and that there would never again be another.

The hatch opened; Lorraine was carrying two mugs, her hair combed wet after a shower, dressed in jeans and a sweatshirt. She'd darkened the cabin first, saving Rick's night vision—a small point, more about seamanship than courtesy, but he noted it, just as she noted the photo he tucked into his shirt pocket.

"It is my—" She cleared her throat. "It is my turn at the helm."

He accepted a mug and Lorraine sat—gingerly, because of her hip—on the port-side cushion. She put her hand on the wheel and Rick let go. He sipped the coffee: she'd taken the time and trouble to make espresso, and though it had been served black at the café this was topped with frothed milk and chocolate. As if she knew that's how he liked it, which he did.

He studied her sideways, her swollen eyes and cheeks: *What in the world can I say?* Whatever makeshift shelter she'd fashioned before she came up on deck had to be rickety; best not to weigh it down with lame sympathies and clichés, he decided, when there were issues they had to deal with that might support it.

"Who is Mustafa?" he began.

"An old family friend, Mustafa Murad."

"And when will we make Jerba?"

"We are headed for Gabes."

He didn't know what that meant, let it slide.

"You think the assassins have figured it out? That your boat is gone?"

Her voice strengthened. "If not yet they will soon, and in either case they will search by aircraft at first light. Savages like Ahmed Hameed do not accept failure. I am sure his men are already in pursuit in town and on the roads—even if they know of the boat, in case it was set adrift as a ruse."

The espresso ice-picked Rick's intestines; he held his breath until it eased.

"Shouldn't we call anyone? Someone you trust?"

"I trust only Mustafa and Ammi Zarga. Yet I cannot risk using the ship-to-shore and the marine operator. Hameed's tentacles spread everywhere, within the police, the military—far more than Le Clerc's." Her mouth was grim. "Yet we Bouchés as well are not without influence in Tunis. For Hameed to assault us this way, he must not rest until I am dead, because only I can connect him to Café Stella. And if you are with me..."

Their eyes met.

"I'm trying not to think about that."

"But you must! I made our course for Gabes *because* of it. There you may take the morning train to Sfax and rejoin your ship. This is not your war, M'sieur Weisman, it is mine."

She turned away and he stared at her profile. After such a catastrophe, the unspeakable slaughter of her family, wounded and just emerged from unconsciousness, she'd had the self-control to plan with clarity for the sake of a stranger. The pause went on too long and she glanced over.

"What?"

"Nothing. Aren't you forgetting about Zarga?"

"Non, m'sieur, but everything is different now."

"Not for me. I have my own reasons for going."

"This *coin* my father spoke of?" she asked, tainting it.

It would have to be handled delicately, and in stages, yet even so he knew it might destroy her: Zarga's mention to Antoine about the coin, the knowledge of which could have come only from Abdessalam, meaning DuPonte had to be right about Zarga's connection to Abdessalam and Le Clerc. After all she'd lost, to have to lose her faith in Zarga too...

"It's not what you think it is, but anyway I wouldn't risk my life just for that. There's the boy, Musa, who means a great deal to me. And then there's— Well, like I said, I have my reasons."

He'd stopped himself from saying "you," yet she'd heard it. She blinked a few times, appeared to study the compass. Though the course was rock steady she steered to port, as though she'd read it wrong, then to starboard, as though noticing the error and correcting.

"What is it, then?"

"Something precious my Uncle Eli gave me. It was stolen at sea."

"But then—how would Ammi Zarga...? Why did he...?" Her mouth kept working; nothing came out.

"Yes, it's odd, isn't it? That a Tunisian I've never

met, a man of some importance, apparently, would want to talk with me, a nobody, just an American merchant seaman, about an article that was taken from me on my ship? Can you explain this, Lorraine?"

The awful truth tried to break and enter, and she shot it on sight. "I cannot. We were asked by Ammi Zarga to accept it without question. C'est tout."

But that was not all, not for Rick, because once his questions started, they had to run their course, as they had again and again since they'd sailed from Sfax:

If Zarga had the Zevi Coin, or even knew of it, then he must also have Abdessalam's loyalty, likely more than Le Clerc did—and likely had Musa too. So, of what possible use could Rick be? Why would Zarga tell Antoine that Lorraine had to bring him to Nefta?

Who am I?

"Then can you explain what happened tonight?"

"I can only speculate, m'sieur. This man no one knows, this Samir Abdessalam—he was aboard your ship, and you learned that he is loyal to Le Clerc, so though it is without logic, Hameed must blame him and therefore Le Clerc for the sinking of his Cheval Marin."

"But why target you and your family? You were working with DuPonte *against* Le Clerc."

"I do not think that Hameed, though he seems to know all, could have known of my work with Interpol. My..." she sifted for the word, "...liaison with Emile Le Clerc has been established only recently, and granting that Hameed learned of it, there would be no reason for him to suspect my motives. But here is what I cannot grasp: Even if Hameed believed Emile in some way responsible for sinking Cheval Marin, given both my family's station in Tunisia and my involvement with Emile, why risk war with both Le Clerc *and* the government to avenge one insignificant vessel and a handful of slaves," her features contorted, "when there are so many more?"

The mild breeze freshened; she shivered, gulped hot coffee, set the mug aside, shifted her weight to take a bearing on a blinking light broad to starboard. Shifted back and the pain got her; a quick sharp inhale, a hand to her hip, then she forced it down.

"If we are not going to Gabes, m'sieur, I must now alter course for Jerba to arrive there by dawn."

"Then you'd better do it."

She hesitated, almost started to speak again, gave up, turned the wheel. The Swan answered smartly; Lorraine finessed the heading to one-six-two.

"Have you—" her voice broke, "—nothing to live for?" She looked at him and her eyes were glittering. "Not your parents? Or your best girl in the photograph?"

She wiped her cheeks with a sleeve. Rick fingered into his shirt pocket, felt the telex but retrieved the photo of the Sphinx, handed it to her. In spite of herself, a brief smile.

"You were a boy when this was taken."

"Twelve going on fifty."

"And this is your father?"

"My Uncle Eli."

"He must be very dear to you."

"Yes. That was the bad news I mentioned to you at the café. I had just heard that he'd died."

"Oh, non!" Rick showed her the telex. She turned it so it caught the light, read the few words then put it and the photo on the center cushion between them, holding them down with her fingers until he slipped them into his pocket.

Now she leaned across, laid a hand on his arm and squeezed.

"And I was so cruel to you. Please forgive me, Rick."

As she touched him and spoke his name for the first time, he almost found it, the place where tears begin.

"Nothing to forgive, Lorraine."

She heard it in his voice, patted with her hand.

"What an adventure for a young American, to see the pyramids."

A swallow of espresso rescued him. "And more so with Uncle Eli. Ever since my father's death he'd taught me to appreciate so much—history and architecture, great music and great art. Eli brought everything to life."

One more wisp of a smile; she removed her hand, but he still felt it.

"I have lived in Tunisia since my childhood yet still I have not been to Egypt. Would you tell me about your visit, or is it too long ago?"

Just for an interlude, she wanted to be swept away from unbearable grief and whatever fate awaited them both. Rick wanted the same and dove into it, grateful for the chance to talk about Eli. A eulogy of sorts.

"No, I remember it like it was yesterday. My uncle had meetings in Cairo and, unbeknownst to me, had arranged everything with my mother weeks in advance. Next thing I knew, a typical New York City summer day had turned into magic. That was so Eli."

Rick filled in some background: who his uncle was, what he'd achieved and what he meant to him. Then the layover in London and the three days they spent there, the West End production of *Pirates of Penzance,* the historic places, the excursion to Stonehenge.

At last, they flew to Cairo; Eli had vetted and hired a guide so his nephew could see the sights while he was working—anything Rick was interested in except the pyramids and the Sphinx. Those he wanted to see with him, and on their last day they took a taxi there.

How disappointed he felt at first, he told Lorraine, to see their specters brooding over the main street of Giza; he'd fantasized that they'd have to ride camels miles into the desert to find them. That feeling went away, though, as their cab honked along the congested boulevard—the cars, dust, noise, and throngs of people; the camel dung, exhaust fumes, and caustic cigarettes by the truckload; the scrawl of modern times signed everywhere—and was replaced by an unearthly sense of the pyramids' presence, as though they were judging it all from beyond the city skyline.

The traffic jammed to a halt. The driver turned to Eli and said, "In ancient Egypt they shine like mirror. Yes?" He showed gold teeth, fetched a rag from the glove box, buffed his chrome bracelet till it sparkled. "Yes?" the man asked Rick. "Yes. Thank you," Rick replied, nodding. Satisfied, the driver turned back to the wheel, honking the horn like crazy. Rick asked Eli if what the driver had said was correct and it was.

He knew from his history books that, until later

pharaohs had cannibalized it, and centuries of invaders and thieves had demolished it, a smooth limestone facade had covered the pyramids' enormous stone blocks, which now lie exposed. Today, one can still see a corroded remnant of it. But never before had he heard of this, this fact so extraordinary it had the quality of myth. It stayed with him as they hunched down a narrow tunnel to the entombment chambers. It stayed with him as they fought off the trinket dealers and camel-ride sellers. It stayed with him as they took their photos by the Sphinx and Eli stumped Rick with its famous riddle. When they drove back to Giza, he asked his uncle to tell him more.

"'I don't know much more, Ricky. But try to see them as they were: on fire in the sunlight or shimmering under the stars—so fearsome in their perfection. Small wonder the hordes tried to tear them down. But the pyramids could not be torn down—not by one invader, not by thousands of years of them. They could only hack away that facing of mirror, to salve the vanity of their own malefic gods.'"

Hearing his uncle's words, freeze-dried in memory until stirred to life for her, it was as though Eli himself were speaking, in Rick's voice as Rolf had in the stranger's.

"I wish I could have met your uncle, Rick. I am sure Ammi Zarga would feel the same. They have so much in common."

She trusted him enough now to open a window to her heart. How would she feel, he thought, when he drove a stake through it?

"They do? In what way?"

"Oh, many ways, even from the little you have said. Your uncle was honored by President Kennedy; Ammi Zarga has been honored by Habib Bourguiba and Zine al-Abidine ben Ali, and he is revered by the Sufis and treated as one of their elders, though he himself is not Sufi, nor does he follow their faith. Your uncle was a humanitarian and philanthropist, had a love of culture and attained a doctorate in history and accomplished so much in his life. It is the same with Ammi Zarga. He is the master of nine languages—I strive to improve with only five—and he is an eminent historian and author. My favorite book is his one novel, The King and the Cross, about the Knights of Saint John, but he has also written about the mystic poet Rumi, and the Sufi Berber, and of course there's his great masterpiece—"

Another corner of Rick's jigsaw puzzle locked together, her astounding pieces fitting into others on the board as he completed her sentence.

"The Enigma of Faith?"

Their eyes met again and something new passed between them. He still had to say it. "Ammi Zarga is...Sir Kenneth Carmody?"

"You are familiar with his work?"

"Just by reputation. Why did he change his name?"

"Oh, no, Rick, you misunderstand. He is truly humble and never would have bestowed upon himself a term of high respect such as Ammi, much less Zarga, which in the Tunisian dialect means Blue One, as in the white-blue flame of the Holy Spirit. Though Muslims do not recognize the ministry of the Spirit, the Sufis know that Zarga does, and they honor that as they honor him.

They gave him this name long ago, though I'm not sure when or how it began, and some prefer to call him Lazrag instead of Zarga, because while Lazrag means Blue One as does Zarga, Lazrag evokes as well the blue of the mightiest sea, and the white foam of its power."

The pulse of the engine and the rhythm of the waves became a pounding heart and sighing wings, the fabric of sound shaped by luminous threads of white and blue, a murmur of *nothing* on the wind.

"I'm sorry, Lorraine. I need to go below."

"Are you ill? Have I offended you?"

"No, it's... I have to wash up. Please excuse me."

"The light switch is to your right. In the forward cabin you will find a shower and the clothes of my—" She'd almost said father or brother but couldn't. "Some clothes that may fit you, if you wish."

She'd left the hatch open when she'd come on deck; he closed it and the door behind him before groping for the switch and flicking it on—teak, stainless, brass, a chart and plotting devices, three votive candles no longer lit but with not a moment to spare to take it all in he scuttled forward to the loo and sat, had to clutch at his flesh to keep from crying out loud. Finally uncramping, he stripped and cranked the shower valve all the way hot, stood comatose under the stream.

Carmody is Zarga, Zarga is Lazrag, Lazrag is the Blue One. The Riddle of Lazrag and the eyes of the stranger, the flame of the Holy Spirit and the bowl of flame on the night of the storm...

He dried off with a towel still moist from Lorraine and still fragrant with her.

...the white-blue light at my father's funeral and the flame when I almost died and the Blue One is Lazrag and Lazrag is Zarga and Zarga is...

He rummaged through the closet and drawers, found Lorraine's clothes before he found Christian's. Took out sneakers, jockeys, jeans, and a safari shirt. The jeans looked to be the right size and were, as were the rest. He noted Lorraine's bloodied jebba in the trash can, the first-aid kit on the vanity top, with antiseptic and gauze packages, scissors and tape, lotions and toiletries. And kinked black hairs—she'd trimmed what had been singed. He re-bandaged his side and shoulder, put fresh band-aids on his finger and head, ignored the spectacle of himself in the mirror; closed the kit and a glint of gold mesh under her hairbrush caught his eye. He lifted it up: It was the chain that had been about Lorraine's neck, and from it hung a jeweled pendant carved in gold—a half-bird, half-human figure.

It seemed to recede as it gyrated. For long seconds he couldn't move, couldn't breathe, couldn't shake the dread that was buckling his knees and threatened to drive him to them.

Somehow, he finished dressing and made his way back to the deck, took his seat on the starboard side.

"Do you feel better, Rick?"

He didn't answer, instead offered her the necklace, dangling it by its chain.

"You left this."

Disbelieving, she clapped a hand to her breast and scrunched her sweatshirt.

"Mon Dieu!"

Rick held the wheel as she fastened it about her neck and kissed it.

"The, uh, winged figure—is that from mythology?"

She took back the wheel.

"It is Garuda, the steed of Vishnu."

A ray of hope. "So, it's...part of your religion?"

"My religion. Such simple words, yet for me they are as split as my blood, my heritage. I pray to Christ Jesus, my Lord and Savior, as my father taught me; yet I cannot fully forsake the beliefs of Thailand because of the love in my heart for my dear mother. I am torn in two, Rick, stitched together only by the grace of the Holy Spirit. And lately by this as well."

"Why do you say that?"

"Because this Garuda is a cherished treasure, an heirloom handed down from ancestral aunts who were beloved twins. There is but one other like it, and it is worn by my younger sister Nanteya."

The ray of hope snuffed out, as her family had been, and the votive candles she'd lit for them.

She faced him, anxious to justify herself.

"That is why I approached Interpol. Nanteya lives in Thailand; she was kidnapped in Chiang Mai after a visit to the Phuping Palace. Police informants pointed to Le Clerc's organization. I had to *do* something." Chest heaving, she clasped the amulet once more. "Le Clerc has pursued me for five years, since I was sixteen, the same age as my sister is now." She hung her head. "It was a simple thing...God forgive me...to let him have what he desired."

Rick understood now what Antoine had meant,

how much she had sacrificed. He reached across and gentled her back; she glanced over, thankful, and he spoke kindly.

"But if he wanted you, why would you believe he'd harm Nanteya?"

"He does not know of her relation to me, Rick. So many Thai children have been bought or stolen and sold into slavery by monsters like Hameed and Le Clerc. I am sure that, to Emile, Nanteya was just one more," her mouth distorted with contempt, "though a *princely* prize indeed—a lovely, innocent aristocrat who would command a fortune."

She needed a moment; Rick waited for several then prompted, "An aristocrat?"

"My mother's family is Thai nobility. Because of Nanteya's birth animals, mother said she must bear her family's hereditary name. And though it was so painful for us all, when we moved to Tunisia to help my father's brother, she insisted that Nanteya stay in Thailand. My mother is...was...very definite about such things."

She wiped her eyes.

"My sister has lived in Bangkok with my uncle and aunt since we left. They have no children of their own and have been very good to her. We see her but twice each year. Yet even after Nanteya was kidnapped, my mother remained serene, confident that all would be for the best."

More questions would have to wait; the truth could no longer. "You didn't learn a thing from Le Clerc, did you. I mean, about Nanteya."

"No, but I will not stop. I will find her and save her

and—" She finally heard what he'd said. "How did you know this?"

Rick memorized those eyes, and the lantern in them she carried for her sister, about to flicker out.

"Because it was not Le Clerc who took her. It was Hameed."

Her lips parted. "What are you saying?"

"I've seen this Garuda before, on a young girl who looked a lot like you. She was a prisoner aboard Cheval Marin. We...we found her body after the collision."

Lorraine began to quake, and Rick took her hand.

"I swear to you she seemed at peace. As though she knew she was free."

But he was holding only a black abyss, and like a feather into it, Lorraine Bouché fell.

EIGHTEEN

Land of the Lotus Eaters

The liqueur was called laghmi, the hotel called Le Paradis, and the day in Jerba was called by the prayers that rose from the mosque of Sidi Sa'id.

Rick sat at the open window and wondered: a room by the sea, a whitewashed village, a woman from heaven—this morning was his. He'd seen it somewhere, sometime long ago, and it had come true; and before it was gone, he had to find out what truly was his and what was not.

He sipped liqueur from a paper cup, watched the waves and remembered...

Her head in his lap, the surge of energy through his fingertips as he soothed her shoulders, how that calmed her and let her sleep while the Swan sailed on, and he was left alone with his thoughts: How many choices by how many people had to be made just right to bring them to this? Or perhaps they were all irrelevant, everything leading to the same end regardless. Ile de Jerba rimmed the horizon. The sky was lightening to a new dawn, colored like every dawn with hope and peril. But driven by what? Destiny? Free will? Pure chance? Now Lorraine's hand in sleep found his and held it to her lips, and suddenly the answer didn't matter at all.

He throttled down the engine, slid aside and laid her head onto the cushion, went below and got the chart; returned to the helmsman's well and read it by flashlight. She'd drawn their course to bear for a spit on the northern coast above the airport, some miles west of the island's main town of Houmt Souk. And there it was—the lighthouse of Borj Djellidj, off the starboard bow where it should be.

With the engine again at full revs he followed the coast, picking through shallows until the chart showed a breech. Steered the boat around twin tongs of land into a sheltered cove with a mass of overhanging palms; slowed and inched as close to shore as he dared, roughly thirty yards given that the tide had ebbed, reversed the engine then idled it; headed forward and dropped the hook—it dug into the sandy bottom and the chain tightened. He guessed enough length for high tide, paid it out, went aft to the cockpit.

Lorraine was awake, inflating the dinghy. Rick retrieved the canvas duffel from the deck box and went below: put his loafers, the first-aid kit, toiletries from the bathroom on the bottom. Took the wallet from his khakis and stuffed in his shipmates' cash, pocketed it and his passport, packed the pants in with his silk shirt and added water bottles from the galley, leaving room for Lorraine's clothes and the pistols.

He came on deck with the duffel and went to the helmsman's well; Lorraine went below. The guns and spare clips were where he'd left them; he brought everything up to the cushion: the assassin's was a subcompact, 9mm Glock; the first mate's a fifteen-shot Beretta, also 9mm. He discarded the silencer from the Glock, filled its ten-shot clip with shells from one of Willis's clips, did the same with the Beretta's. Shoved both weapons and the clips into the duffel.

Lorraine returned with a pile of clothes and a zippered purse jingling with coins, gave them to Rick and he finished packing the duffel. She locked the hatch and shoved the key ring into her jeans; they launched the dinghy and paddled ashore, pulled the air plug, turned the boat over and covered it with palm brush and driftwood. Now they started on the mile hike east, to the place she called Sidi Sa'id, visible in the brightening distance. Lorraine was limping yet insisted they keep a fast pace—they were in view from the coast road.

They came to the outskirts of the village and then to Le Paradis, its white-domed cottages strung along a crescent beach.

No one was at the desk; Rick banged the bell on the counter and after a minute the proprietor arrived, annoyed at the hour and suspicious—they had no car, Lorraine had no ID—but though Rick also had no idea what she said to the man in Frarabic, the dollars she told Rick to dole out cinched the deal and elevated his frame of mind. With the room key he gave Rick a souvenir bottle of laghmi—the date liqueur of Jerba, the "lotus" that, according to folklore, had inspired Homer. Then

came a handshake, a wink, and a roll of eyes at the
ceiling, all in admiration of Lorraine and envy of Rick's
spectacular status with Allah.

The suite was Berber-style and the best they had.
Rick flopped into an armchair in the sitting area by the
windows; Lorraine tried to call Mustafa Murad. Nobody
home and she slammed down the phone; picked it up
again, rang the desk, asked for a wake-up call in one
hour. She got the kit from the duffel and, standing with
her back to Rick, stripped off her sweatshirt revealing a
short tee underneath, then stepped from her jeans. A
flood of white-water lust swamped his chest, and he was
disgusted with himself for it. She attended to her hip;
Rick kicked off his sneakers, stretched...drifted...

The creak of springs.

"There is room for us both," said a small voice.

He was too fatigued to even consider refusing, laid
down on the other side. She rolled and snuggled against
him, wanting to be held, and with his arm around her
she fell asleep. He tried to close his eyes but couldn't
resist drinking her in, her face and hair and hand on his
chest, the tee shirt above her waist, one bare leg crooked
over his jeans. After a while she shifted, and he was able
to extract his arm. He found paper cups in the bathroom,
went to the window and sipped laghmi for solace...

A private plane, droning; two early tourists, strolling
at the water's edge; a flock of white pelicans. The sun
rose higher in the sky, but he felt instead the earth
rotating in space, saw his life and Lorraine's rotating with
it a half world away from the other. And the world goes

round, and they are drawn ever closer, never guessing, never imagining until the moment they meet, and the heavens pause.

Is it for us to ever know the how or why? He turned away from the sea to gaze at Lorraine sleeping curled on the bedspread. *Perhaps that's all there is to anything. If so, it really is quite simple. Not much of a riddle at all.*

The phone was on Lorraine's side of the bed; it rang three times before Rick could get there. "Yes?"

"Bonjour, m'sieur," said a brisk female voice. Then she hung up.

Lorraine had slept through the noise; Rick sat on the mattress and touched her neck. She moaned and shook and woke, staring at the bedspread. When she looked up, there were tears from a source that might never run dry, yet even so she thought of him.

"Did you sleep?"

"No, I couldn't. Glad you did, though."

With a corner of sheet, he dabbed her cheek; she sat up and kissed his then hurried to the bathroom, grabbing her clothes and the duffel on the way.

Rick went to the chair and tied on Christian's sneakers, heard the water running, the toilet flushing. Presently Lorraine came out—a white blouse loose over her jeans, hair in a ponytail, a hint of makeup, eyes red. She got on the phone and Rick went to the bathroom. When he was done, she was sitting on one side of the windowsill, sipping laghmi from his cup, her sandals on the floor. He sat on the other side, and she crumpled the cup, put a foot onto his lap, wiggled it with a plaintive look through her sadness.

A minute of massage seemed to make her stronger. She replaced the first foot with the other. "This one feels lonely." Another minute and she took it away.

"Thank you, Rick. You have healing hands." Her face changed. "There is a restaurant named De Caravans. I have been there." She reached down for her sandals, putting them on and sliding closer to him as she did. "We can have breakfast and Mustafa will join us. Poor Mustafa. He and his wife and children—they are so upset. They were at his mother's when I called earlier; the radio and television are full of what happened at Café Stella, and they have been up all night. They were convinced I was dead too." Her voice lowered. "But because of you, my life has been spared. I will not be so kind with M'sieurs Le Clerc and Hameed."

"So, it's revenge, then."

No answer.

"And if you still have a life afterwards?"

He thought she might cry, again, but she had no tears for herself.

"I do not know. It is not important."

"It's important to me, Lorraine."

She swallowed. "My aunt and uncle have lost Nanteya, whom they raised as a daughter. It is right that I should try to bring them comfort." She turned to him, finding her way, "And is it not right as well that I should work against the evils that have destroyed my family? What I have learned of Le Clerc, his associates throughout Asia, his ties to the al Qaeda in Khartoum, his alliance with Qadaffi, his leverage with key Thai officials—this would be most useful to the authorities." She sighed as it sank in. "I suppose, then, that I do know. I shall go to Bangkok. It is where I belong."

It was starting to evaporate, everything he'd come to believe about the two of them, and he wanted to rail against it like the old man in her painting at the café.

"But what about you?" he said instead. "And your art? Don't you have your own dreams?"

She looked out to sea.

"Since we left Thailand, I often dream of the wats, the golden temples, and the monks in their saffron robes. I dream of the klongs, the canals of Bangkok in the morning, and of jasmine blooms in the night. My Lord Jesus is always with me, guiding me through the veils, yet still I dream of it, almost as if I am there. Often, I am painting, pictures I could never paint now, and as I work there is the music of bells." Another sigh. "My aunt and uncle have a cottage on Doi Suthep, high above Chiang Mai where many Thai artists live. My sister went to this place often; she was an artist too. She liked to paint nearby at the monastery of Wat Phrathat, and the Palace at Phuping. It is very serene there." She shook her head. "Perhaps someday I will go to Chiang Mai and paint, as Nanteya did. If it is meant to be. But you are most kind to think of it."

She reached for his hand.

"And you? After Musa…if you are still alive?"

Now through the window the answer he thought he'd found had dissolved. All that was left was the sky, as opaque as the riddle itself.

"I'm needed at home, in New York—at my uncle's company. I owe that to him. I owe it to everyone."

Her thumb caressed his.

"We are both still young, yet we are young no more."

"You're right, Lorraine. And I wouldn't mind so much except—except this morning I saw things I've never seen, wanted things I've never wanted."

She searched inside him. "What things?"

"A house on Long Island Sound, a boat we could sail together; you'd have a studio overlooking the water, I'd work hard at my job. Maybe we'd have children." The dark of her eyes, glistening. "I know, Lorraine. We've just met and it's...only an American dream, not grand like yours and I—"

"No, Rick, it is beautiful. As beautiful as a dream can be."

"But it won't come true, will it?"

She heard the thickening in his voice, put fingers to his lips.

"Did you understand what my mother said to me at the table in Café Stella?"

"Something about rats and goats?"

"Yes. You were born the year of the goat, I the year of the rat. In Thailand the issue of birth animals is very solemn, very complex. According to my mother, if we were to marry you would become a deva, which is like an angel, and our children would be thrice blessed. That is why she pored over the signs of your karma, read your palm and your aura. I am sure it was most strange to you, but in her beliefs, there is a great deal to learn about someone beyond their birth animals. She could always see so far, my mother. And what she said...her last words to me...that we would..."

Tears came and doused her voice, and she lifted her face to his and they kissed—sweet with laghmi and lipstick, salted with longing and loss, deepening and hungering till their souls melted and flowed and merged into a river, and when at last the kiss was done, they hugged each other tight, floating on its waters.

"Are there angels in New York City?" she whispered.

He could not say, or even speak.

She took both his hands and kissed the palms, then stood with one in hers and pulled him up.

It was time to go.

NINETEEN

A Psalm for Someone

Sidi Sa'id straddled the two-lane coast road that ringed Ile de Jerba, a frayed old village with its pride intact. The street was clean except for sand blown by the hot breeze. Lorraine and Rick crossed past a clothing shop, over the front of which were strung embroidered tunics, to the elaborate arched entrance of De Caravans. Inside it was all stucco, slow fans, and more arches, the breakfast clientele a mix of locals and visitors. Lorraine spoke to the maître d' and tipped him; he led them to a private table secluded by potted palms. She then mentioned Mustafa Murad and tipped him again. A teenage waiter—genial, olive-skinned, in traditional garb like his boss—stationed himself at the chair between them, placed two menus.

Lorraine browsed hers then shut it.

"Would you mind if I order for us?" she asked Rick, taking his. She handed the waiter the menus, favored him with her eyes and gave instructions in Frarabic. To each of his replies she'd add a note about preparation, and he'd jot it on his pad. Discharged, he bustled off but returned with bottled water and steaming hot Turkish-style coffee.

"They do not have espresso, Rick, but I hope this will please you."

Which it did, as anything would have in her presence. They watched each other over their coffee cups, saying little, what they'd felt and shared in Le Paradis saying it for them until a shadow passed over her face and she looked away.

The food arrived on two platters and Lorraine, visibly shucking her mood, pointed out the specialties as the waiter arranged plates and silver: "These triangle pastries are spinach and egg brik; this is makhroud, a honey cake with dates; and ojja is like scrambled eggs with peppers and onions, but seasoned with—"

The odor of sandalwood...

"Et voila! The irrepressible M'sieur Weisman!"

...and the mordant tongue of Samir Abdessalam.

His teal-suited bulk had sidled from the palms; he removed the red tarboosh from his head, spoke to the waiter in Frarabic as Rick rasped "the Egyptian" to an unsettled Lorraine, using his motion towards her to cover a reach into the duffel at his feet—located the Beretta, set it upside down in his crotch, concealed by the tablecloth.

The waiter left. Abdessalam, with ill-disguised delight, ensconced himself in the empty chair; perched his hat on the table, undressed Lorraine with his eyes, dabbed sweat from his forehead and cheeks with a monogrammed handkerchief.

"And this, if I am not mistaken, is the celebrated Mad'moiselle Bouché." He stuffed the handkerchief back into his breast pocket, arranged the points. "One hears such lavish reports of your beauty, yet perhaps they have become, how shall I say, a touch exaggerated in the telling? But I forget myself. Please allow a stranger to offer condolences for the demise of your family." He sat back, smug, lacing his fingers over straining vest buttons.

Lorraine was cold steel. "What have you done to Mustafa?"

"Done? You wound me, mad'moiselle. He awaits us at the airport, seeing to the plane."

Rick was colder still. "And why should we believe you?"

"Why, indeed. Our last farewell was, I admit, not of a variety that would encourage such trust." He pinched into a vest pocket. "Therefore, Ammi Zarga asked me to reunite you with this, by way of alleviating your concerns."

He produced the Zevi Coin, turned it side to side. Lorraine registered the knockout combo: the hook of Abdessalam's cozy familiarity with Ammi Zarga, followed by the uppercut of her first glimpse of the fabulous object.

"And the boy?"

"Musa's fate, I fear, is in your hands, m'sieur. And just as this coin will soon pass from mine, too soon shall his life pass from yours."

"Meaning exactly...what?"

Abdessalam palmed the coin as the waiter came back, placing a glass of mint tea and a third setting.

When he departed, the Egyptian opened his hand, laid the coin on the table and, with a wink at Rick, slid it to Lorraine.

"Would mad'moiselle be good enough to keep this? Your seafaring friend seems reluctant to take possession of it again, and the priceless bauble is a dire temptation. My failings, which are legion, have on occasion subjugated even my loftiest virtues."

Lorraine glanced; Rick nodded. She tucked it into a front pocket of her jeans.

"How romantic. Now he will always keep you near."

The Egyptian sipped his tea.

"I asked you a question," Rick pressed.

"Ah. And the answer is that Musa Hameed is in the dubious care of Emile Le Clerc, on the verge of a most untimely end. May I?"

Not waiting for the invitation, knowing he had stunned them both, he helped himself to a piece of brik.

Lorraine found her voice first. "Musa *Hameed?*"

"Oui, Ahmed Hameed's only child. It would seem," he remarked to Rick with pleasure, "that Emile did not divulge *everything* to mad'moiselle." His eyelids closed after a swallow. "Mmm...exceptional."

Rick still couldn't grasp it. "Hameed's *son,* aboard Cheval Marin? But why?"

"Adopted son, to be accurate. Ahmed long ago lost the ability to extend his line—an accident during a youthful prank. Turned him quite bitter." The Egyptian selected another morsel.

"You were about to say—"

"Patience, m'sieur. The advent of baby Musa in

Hameed's life was occasion for great joy, but his doting father has grown most vexed with the child. Though Musa tries his best, and so wishes to gain the approval of dear papa, he has no feel for the business." Bit into the food, spoke with his mouth full. "His loves are poetry, music, art—revolting." Shook his jelly jowls, continued as he assayed the platters. "It was his hapless mother who named the child after Moses, perhaps in the hope that he would be her deliverer, for her first marriage was not a felicitous one either. Soon after Musa was born, her husband, himself engaged in an affair, denounced her falsely for adultery, leaving her destitute and disgraced among her own. Fortunately, or perhaps not, she was a beauty like mad'moiselle, which at least gave her something to bargain with. Still, a Jewess marrying the likes of Ahmed Hameed?" He shuddered. "Scandalous. The poor creature made the best of her lot and cultivated the boy's tender proclivities, yet since her death last year—of a broken heart and soul, it was said—Ahmed has spared no effort to toughen his son and teach him the trade. Such paternal love and devotion, it is poignant, yes?"

Rick tried to recover.

"If you knew who Musa was, why did you have to grill him?"

"I did not know who he was, m'sieur—until, with your obliging assistance, he let slip his first name. Whereupon I posited that he *might* be the son of Hameed and acted accordingly."

"But why bring up Ammi Zarga when you spoke to the boy?" Lorraine put in. "Zarga had nothing to do with Cheval Marin."

"No, but making Musa believe that one of Tunisia's most revered elders had, shall we say, his eye on him, was bound to inspire a useful level of respect."

"You mean fear," she corrected.

"If you prefer. In any case—"

Abruptly it clicked and Rick cut in: "Wait a second. Are you saying Hameed hasn't been told? That his son is alive?"

"An astute deduction. Le Clerc has not yet determined how best to profit from the boy; moreover, he enjoys making the father suffer. Judging by Ahmed's rash behavior at Café Stella last night, the wretched man believes that his son died in the wreck of Cheval Marin and is indeed suffering frightfully."

Lorraine's face was chalk, Abdessalam went on.

"Nor at this time has Emile Le Clerc learned that mad'moiselle eluded the assault on the café. This I know personally. It must be inferred, however, that Hameed does know, from his informants in the police, and is very angry at the delay in his revenge—just as Emile is very angry over mad'moiselle's death, by what certainly must be the hand of his rival in crime." He chuckled. "Everyone is very angry about everything this morning."

"You sick son of a—"

"Come, come, m'sieur. Give credit where it is due. The collision was not my handiwork, it was the hand of Allah—or perhaps," a smirk, "the Zevi Coin? Guiding you to mad'moiselle? If one believes in such things." A shrug. "And who could have known that Hameed was aware both of my voyage on your ship and that I work for Le Clerc, and that subsequently he would link the ship to Emile and blame him for the crash and the death of his only son? No, m'sieur. Not even Ammi Zarga can divine everything, but one must adjust to circumstances. Adaptability—that is the key. Once the boy fell into my lap I had to make a decision, fit him into the scheme of things. Sadly, there were repercussions."

Lorraine spit it out. "You gave him to Le Clerc? His father's worst enemy? What sort of devil are you?"

He finished chewing and wiped his plump fingertips, all the while matching her intensity with his own.

"Merely the poor working sort, mad'moiselle."

He sipped tea, consulted his Rolex; the hand continued on into his suit jacket pocket for his cigarette case and lighter. He lit up.

"Do not be duped, young friends, by my girth," he said on the exhale, which he pointed at the dome. "That is testament to my wife's beguiling culinary arts, but my stock in trade is threading needles. So, though I am Le Clerc's agent, Emile does not know that I also work for Ammi Zarga. Ammi Zarga, however, endorses my office and is secure that I am his man and only maintain the demeanor of loyalty to Emile. Both are pleased with Samir and Samir gets paid twice, which pleases his wife and sons."

"Who do you really work for?" Lorraine challenged.

He took a drag of the cigarette, exhaled through his nose. "Myself, naturelment, as does every man. But my allegiance to Ammi Zarga derives from a higher plane."

"Yet he has never mentioned you to me."

"Again, mad'moiselle, of what use is a confidence if it is not kept? Ammi Zarga knows that the eye of my needle is dismayingly narrow. Though I count on my service to him to commend me in the afterlife, this life must not be neglected in pursuit of the next, and Le Clerc pays me far more than Zarga. If Emile should someday realize that my loyalty is not fully his—or worse, that my master is Ammi Zarga when their stratagems conflict—then swiftly would come the doom of Samir. Yet that is why I enjoy my work."

"So you're saying you gave Musa to Le Clerc because you had to give him *something?*"

"Excellent, M'sieur Weisman! Yes, Emile had high hopes for Caroline Coast. Imagine his irritation when events dashed them. To be sure, this was not entirely by chance; my mandate from Ammi Zarga was to do all I could to sabotage Emile's designs on your ship. Which is why I escalated the tensions between Captain Brace and Chief Briggs, bringing about their fatal rift. Had the collision not intervened, I would have ensured that whichever one killed the other was implicated in the murder, and in this way achieve Zarga's aim."

"You're quite clever, aren't you?"

"I try, m'sieur, though I am but a lowly Arab and cannot compare to a scion of the great United States. Nevertheless, despite the unforeseeable loss of the Bouchés—" briefly to Lorraine, with a bow, "again, my condolences, mad'moiselle—and the unfortunate disposition of Master Musa, Ammi Zarga is satisfied with Samir's performance. Moreover, Emile's frustration over your ship has been mollified by acquiring the boy, knowing he can use him to advantage against Hameed. Regrettably, after the tragedy at the cafe, his ideas in this regard have taken a turn for the worse. Yet even this fits Ammi Zarga's purpose."

He drank his tea and puffed his Sobranie. Lorraine seemed numb, staring vacantly at her coffee. Rick looked up at the dome, where the Egyptian's smoke rose to pear-shaped skylights of blue.

"Garçon!" Abdessalam snapped for the waiter, directed the kid to wrap the food. Then to Rick and Lorraine, "We must leave for the airport. My apologies for interrupting your breakfast but it may be for the best. The flight from Nefta was somewhat turbulent."

Lorraine excused herself, asking Rick for the duffel. He squeezed her hand as he gave it to her, but she didn't respond. The Egyptian stubbed his cigarette, lit another, pocketed the lighter and case.

"Speaking of trust, m'sieur, I perceive that you draw from a reservoir of it."

"Only when it's deserved."

"Ah. And perhaps in mad'moiselle's mind she also deserves...compensation? For her loss? Do not forget, she now has the coin."

"I don't forget much. I forgive even less."

The Egyptian curtsied his forehead.

"The desert becomes you."

Lorraine returned, passed Rick the bag under the table. The waiter brought the foil-wrapped leftovers and the tab; Rick made for his wallet, but Abdessalam pooh-poohed him and counted cash onto the tray. Rick foraged in the duffel. As he'd assumed, the subcompact Glock was missing, undoubtedly residing in the rear waistband of her jeans, hidden by her blouse. She drank coffee but locked onto Rick, her eyes flicking at Abdessalam: notwithstanding all his mentions of Zarga, or because of them, she was afraid. Or was there something more?

Rick lifted the bag onto his lap, letting the Beretta show as he zipped it in; if the Egyptian knew he was packing one pistol, he'd be less likely to suspect another.

"Quel dommage," Abdessalam commented, unruffled, as they stood to leave. "I was hoping you might still have my Colt. Sentimental value, you know."

"Inspector DuPonte insisted on keeping it."

"Yes? Then I shall press my case when, finally, we meet. Which, if events transpire as planned, will be soon enough."

He fitted the tarboosh on his head and led them out. At the curb was a beat-up Peugeot with windows open; Abdessalam held the rear door for Lorraine, shut it and went around the trunk. Rick sat in the front, the duffel at his feet; he watched as the Egyptian sucked in his gut to squeeze behind the wheel, started the engine.

Now he swung a U-turn and motored west on the coast road. Rick shifted sideways with his arm on the seat back, allowing Lorraine and him to stay in contact. But she was in her own world.

Abdessalam was whistling to himself.

"Aren't you forgetting something?" Rick said. "What happens next?"

"Oh, how thoughtless of me. We shall proceed to the house of Ammi Zarga, where Musa and mad'moiselle will form the springs, and Inspector DuPonte the jaws, of our hunter's trap."

Rick was as baffled as Abdessalam wanted him to be, though it didn't touch his poker face.

"So, what's the bait?"

"You are greedy. And after I have been so generous."

"Generous? Now you listen to me, you—"

Sharp pinch of female nails, stopping him cold. Lorraine had scooted forward; Rick turned to catch a head shake and another flick of her eyes, some of which the Egyptian must have seen in the rearview mirror.

"Mad'moiselle is wise beyond her years," he observed. Lorraine pushed back, irate with herself. "You would do well to emulate her forbearance."

"Sorry, but I like to know the game before I make my play."

Abdessalam's face darkened. "You are a gambling man, m'sieur? Then remember that you are also a stranger at our table, an uninvited and most troublesome guest. And know this: The rules change as circumstances change, which they do by the hour; and as you yourself have seen, the stakes are extremely high. Therefore, should you choose to remain, you must accept the cards you are given when they are given. Otherwise, your property has been restored and you are free to rejoin your ship."

Rick looked at Lorraine, replied as much to her as to him. "Am I?"

She didn't seem to hear, gazing out the window.

"Precisely," Abdessalam answered. "Each of us is compelled by his own motives to enter the valley of the shadow of death. What can we do except walk in faith? With that and the beneficence of Allah, the journey's end may yet prove a joyous one."

Rick leaned over. "By whose definition?"

The Egyptian giggled, considered, then threw back his head and laughed.

TWENTY

The Stalking Horse

The runway of Jerba Aerodrome aligned east-west, seeming to end in the sea. The Peugeot followed a taxi through the gate. A Tunis Air turboprop was on its glide path out of the sun, and as they passed the parking lot it landed behind the white domes that comprised the main terminal.

The taxi stopped at the entrance; Abdessalam drove by to a service road, turned and parked at the hangars of the general aviation area. Standing in the shade of the third of three buildings, a man waved: threadbare suit jacket and pants that didn't match, battered checheya nesting on a wick of wiry hair. Lorraine vaulted from the car with a cry of "Mustafa!" and ran to his arms, crying for her family all over again, though perhaps, Rick imagined, also for Mustafa himself, that he'd come to no harm from the Egyptian.

"How touching," Abdessalam drawled, handing Rick the keys. "Kindly return these to M'sieur Murad. I will find our pilot."

He exited with the food and minced his way toward the side of the building; Rick got out with the duffel. Lorraine spoke of him to Mustafa in Frarabic, and after a few words the old man squeezed his hand hard and shook it harder, repeating "Sank yuh, sank yuh." Rick said, "De rien" and gave him the keys. Lorraine said, "I will be only a moment," and she and Murad huddled together again.

Rick drifted off, following Abdessalam's path to the tarmac. A propeller and cowling came into view; ringing the massive radial engine were unmistakable teardrop bulges, and Rick knew right away what he was looking at: a classic tail dragger, a Cessna 195. Except for the graphics—the registration number, the logo of "Sahara Safaris" on the fuselage, with Arabic lettering below it— she was all buffed aluminum, not a speck of paint on her. As if she'd been born yesterday.

The pilot was as neat as his aircraft, a compact man with a buzz cut, in overalls with the company logo across the back. He and Abdessalam were talking by the tail, then the Egyptian walked behind it. Rick stepped over the wheel skirt into the shade of the wing, looked in through the pilot's window: seats of saddle leather with cream trim, cream-colored panel highlighting the instrument dials and rack of radios; everything—the twin control yoke, the chrome, the rudder pedals— immaculate.

"She's a beauty, isn't she? You like airplanes?"

The accent was Midwest U.S., but with a cluck of German that hadn't been flattened by the Great Plains.

"Even if I didn't, I'd like this one," Rick replied.

"Horst Langer."

His handshake was precise; no doubt his flying was too, Rick thought. Crow's-feet, ruddy complexion, late forties and street-fight slim.

"Rick Weisman." The sound of Abdessalam opening the luggage compartment. "What's her vintage?"

"Nineteen fifty-two."

"With a two-seventy-five Jacobs, as I recall."

"Actually, a custom three-thirty. You a pilot?"

"No, but my dad taught me when I was a kid. He had a Stearman we flew on weekends."

"Now there's a great airplane. Hard to believe you didn't keep after it, with that kind of background."

His head turned, taking Rick's with it: Lorraine was approaching.

Rick made the introductions—the pilot's stiff "Ammi Zarga speaks highly of you, miss," her polite "Merci, m'sieur"—and then Langer led them to the right side of the aircraft. Abdessalam was jamming himself into the copilot's seat. The pilot made to take Rick's duffel.

"I'll hang onto it, Mister Langer, if that's okay."

"Not a problem. And call me Horst."

Langer locked the luggage compartment then helped Lorraine; she set a foot onto the step-up and slid in, buckled her belt. The pilot was next and Rick last; he secured the cockpit door and his seat belt. The pilot put on his headset, strapped a clipboard with flight plans and chart to his thigh, began his preflight check and tower dialogue.

Lorraine, close across the duffel. "I am so relieved,

Rick. Mustafa is taking care of the funeral arrangements for my family."

He laced his fingers with hers; she welcomed it yet at the same time clouded over—for Nanteya, he felt sure, whose body would be out of Mustafa's reach, still in the custody of Interpol.

She turned aside so Rick couldn't see another of her falls, but he was already well into his own: *When was the last time you slept—yesterday? The day before? The few winks on the morning we arrived in Sfax? When was that?* He forced himself to think about the Cessna: Cruising speed had to be one seventy, with the extra horses maybe one eighty. He pictured the map of Tunisia from Willis's book—Jerba to Nefta, a hundred fifty or two hundred miles. Something like an hour until they—

"CLEAR!" called Langer through his window.

Rick's eyelids dropped like barbells.

The machine whine of the starter, the backfire and roar and oil-smoking stench of brute radial horsepower, the gnarl, surge, and jolts as the Cessna taxied over cracked cement, and now pivoting to the runway and howling down it the plane took off and took Rick into the heart of it all:

His father—the flying getting sloppy, the near air-show debacle because he couldn't sleep, the pills supposed to keep him awake except sometimes they didn't; the chewing out in that trailer when he was fired, never to work in the sky again; the decorated Korean War ace and test pilot and would-be inventor; the spendthrift dreamer whose every idea was worth sinking every dime into. His mother—hating the shows he flew to make a living when test pilot days were done; the travel, the uncertainty, the fear; seeing him lose and lose until she lost respect. And Rick—idolizing him and loving the carnival atmosphere, the World War I leathers and goggles and white scarf; his stunts and aerobatics in the Stearman, the flying they'd do together after the shows while she— *But no, that isn't her. It's Lorraine weeping with Mustafa* at Rick's father's funeral, after the long steep dive had ended because the dreaming had changed from money and inventions to something else, the dreams too real taking him too far away. Yet he refuses help from Eli and the Kagan brothers and has to sell the plane, but it's to a friend and war buddy who lets him keep flying it, so Rick never knows. But now the dreams begin to haunt him when he's wide awake, the spirits hovering about, the blood seeping from ordinary things like fever sweat, like the blood on Antoine and Christian and— *Yes, like that,* running from Mustafa's nose and bruises though he keeps babbling and *you're scared and I can't help you, Lorraine. Nor Mustafa nor anyone because I'm too small and can't even help my daddy* as he fades away, knowing that though he's holding on tight it won't be enough, holding on as his father dies slowly at the desk in the office where he has to work. And then comes the green leather binder where he writes down the dreams, each morning on the kitchen table before dawn can break the spell, and he keeps the writing from Rick and his mother yet she wants to believe it's all right because he's quit the pills and he's steady at the job and there's a promotion and a new refrigerator *and please don't cry, Lorraine. This is all gone ages ago and you've lost so much more than I've ever had, and Mustafa needs you now* though he still takes Rick flying and still to his son he walks on water until that day when the water can hold him up no more, that blue-sky Saturday at the airfield when he climbs into the red Stearman with his green-leather dreams and the salute of the hero who once—

Oh, dear God. No.

Lorraine, still dozing. Checked his watch: *Almost forty-five minutes since we left Jerba?* Altimeter at 2500 feet. *Think.* Lorraine, sensing him, was waking up now but he made sure she couldn't see his face. The desert—shimmering below. The chotts, the salt lakes that in summer bake to white mica— *Think, think.* A line of one-hump camels led by a Bedouin, three trucks and workers raking salt, a rusty car along the charcoal road and finally the thinking was done, and Rick knew.

Unlatched his seat belt, pushed himself forward, knocked aside the pilot's headset. "We've got to get off this course! Fly anywhere but west!"

Langer spun around. *"What?"*

"And take us down—the shine from the salt might give us cover."

Abdessalam had half-turned, weary and aggravated, and to convince them all Rick confronted Lorraine. She recoiled at what she saw in him, but this was no time for niceties. He bored in, shouting, "You said Mustafa was making the funeral arrangements, right? So, he'd have to deal with the police, wouldn't he? To claim the bodies?"

The Egyptian got it before Rick could finish.

"Do as he says, M'sieur Langer!"

The pilot snap-rolled into a thirty-degree dive,

banking south. The engine wailed and Lorraine, horrified at her wing pointing down and the ground hurtling up, rammed both feet onto an imaginary brake.

Rick turned her chin, so she faced him. "Don't worry, the airplane's fine. When did Mustafa phone Sfax?"

"This morning, after I called him from Le Paradis. I do not understand, Rick. What is wrong?"

"You said he was astonished that you were alive, didn't you?"

"Mais oui. The television was reporting that all my family—"

Now it shattered her, the conclusion Abdessalam had jumped to: the police in Hameed's pocket rigging the news of Café Stella's end; Mustafa Murad's knowledge that only three Bouchés were dead, which he must have let on when he spoke to the police and which would disclose in turn that he must have heard from Lorraine; the tip from the cops to Hameed and the black chopper that would be dispatched, the men at his door, the beating until he talked.

"But Mustafa is loyal, to us *and* Ammi Zarga. He would never—"

Again, she saw it. He might be prepared to sacrifice himself, but his wife and family? Desperately, to anyone, "Can we not try to call him? On the radio?"

Abdessalam, scouring the skies.

"I am sorry, mad'moiselle, but it is almost indisputably too late."

She looked to Rick, but found no refuge there, either.

"We'd have to radio Jerba airport, Lorraine, and ask the tower to make the connection. We can't take that chance, just like we couldn't on the boat. As you said, Hameed's tentacles are everywhere."

"Then there is *nothing* we can do?"

The drop in engine noise answered her as Langer pulled out of the dive. Now they were skimming at a mere hundred-fifty feet above the white glass; thermals mushroomed off it like speed bumps. The pilot riched the fuel mixture and adjusted trim, extracted a chart from the board on his leg, flipped it over and clipped it—peeking ahead and at his instruments, yet so attuned to his plane and its stability that even at this altitude he could pencil in a crude, horseshoe-shaped flight plan: south deep into the Grand Erg Oriental, west to the Algerian border, north to Nefta.

Rick realized he was still half off his seat, leaning forward. He fell back and buckled himself in, exhaustion swelling like the dunes of the desert in far-off waves to the south, the swells of the seas that once rolled over it. His eyes closed yet the chott stayed with him, conjuring mirages of water and palm trees. Why those? he wondered. Shouldn't you see an oasis only if you're crawling on your belly from thirst? Unless mirages aren't tricks of the mind at all. Maybe they're phantoms of things that were and are no more, ghost writers of Sahara's long-forgotten tales.

Parched throat. Gnawing gut. Lorraine sleeping. His watch said 10:51—he'd been unconscious for more than an hour. He sat straight. They were heading north-northwest, still skimming the dunes but not as low as before; altimeter at two hundred, attitude indicator rock steady. He opened a water bottle, drank all of it. Now he noticed they seemed to be following the tracks of a large vehicle, which was either somewhere ahead or behind.

He tapped Langer's right-side headphone; the pilot held it off his ear.

"What is it, Horst?" Rick said.

"Don't know. We picked it up at the hind end of the westerly leg."

"How far to Nefta?"

"ETA is fifteen to twenty minutes."

Rick asked for the foil package from Abdessalam, ate the leftover brik and honey cake. The aromas roused Lorraine, and she scrutinized the food, as though she had no idea what it was for. He offered her the ojja but it repulsed her. The apocalypse of the past twelve hours and the specter of what was happening now to Mustafa—she was on the brink. Would revenge alone be enough to hold her up? For how long? At what cost? As if to answer his questions though in a way that didn't, Rick glimpsed another mirage: a white stallion racing the plane, matching its shadow stride for stride.

Now the Cessna hurtled over a giant dune and Langer said, "There it is."

It was the vehicle making the tracks, a white splotch on the chopped-off rear of a blue box. White and blue again, he thought, blue and white but flat and familiar like something he'd seen somewhere else— *On the wharf, in Sfax.* And with that the puzzle pieces started falling, closer like the sand thrown from the vehicle's rear, closer with the splotch on the blue more defined now, a logo of white laurels and though the plane's cowling blocked it as they scorched past, still he saw it all:

The trap. The bait.

Rick ripped off his seat belt, got next to the Egyptian.

"UNICEF," he yelled in his ear.

Abdessalam jumped. *"Merde!"*

"The truck, the white logo."

"Go away, M'sieur Weisman. Your charms are wearing quite thin."

Rick unzipped the duffel, got the Beretta, pushed the muzzle into Abdessalam's neck. Langer saw it and began fulminating in German; Abdessalam cautioned him with a finger, then unbuckled his belt and rotated towards Rick.

"On further consideration, I am at your service."

"Make another pass," Rick ordered. "Broadside, to get a good look at it."

Wordless, the pilot and Abdessalam traded options, and the Egyptian nodded. Lorraine was frantic but Rick couldn't be bothered with her. Langer gained altitude for the maneuver, banked left.

"Will you now explain yourself, m'sieur, or shall we simply presume you've taken leave of your senses?"

Squatting, Rick watched through Lorraine's window for the first sight of it. "When you were on Caroline, you weren't just rating her, were you, Abdul? Le Clerc was planning an actual shipment for our passage home."

The Egyptian gaped.

"But you didn't have a clue where it was coming from, or how it would come aboard, did you?"

"How do you know all this?"

"I saw the map when I took your Colt. The question marks. And you sure made it plain when we left the café that something's up right now."

Base leg of the turn. The vehicle hauling the UNICEF container looked like some type of military transport, with tank tracks for the desert.

"You are quite correct. Emile has been more than unusually guarded in this affair. Each of his lieutenants has been told only the—"

His computer started whirring.

Rick confirmed with Lorraine. "You said Le Clerc had made an alliance with Qadaffi?" Then to Langer, "Those tracks—if you trace them back, where would they lead?"

He glanced at his chart. "Daraj. In Libya."

"But this means nothing, Rick," Lorraine objected, unlocking her seat belt and squatting next to him. "UNICEF would never engage with a fiend like Le Clerc."

"Maybe so, maybe not, but it would be a perfect front. Just like Nefta is the perfect front for his operation."

Abdcssalam was almost there. "Because as with UNICEF, Nefta is beyond suspicion. Who would dare defile a Sufi holy city? Your reasoning is cogent, m'sieur, yet I fear it may have taken one leap too many."

Langer completed the circuit, leveled again at two-hundred feet then glided down towards the vehicle. It stopped now and the driver pointed up, bearded mouth moving. Another bearded face, above the roof on the other side.

"And what would you say if I told you I saw an identical UNICEF container, dockside by Caroline Coast?"

"Yes? Well, that is interesting, but—"

He halted as the man who was not the driver hefted out something black and set it on the roof and beamed a red dot of laser—

"Jesus!" Langer hollered, yanking on his wheel.

Machine gun fire whacking the Cessna, her hard climb hurling Rick and Lorraine back and the Beretta to the floor; oil splattering, Langer soaked in blood still clamping the wheel to his chest and the stall warning blaring and Rick clawing himself to the front. Wedged between Langer's spilling innards and the gurgling Abdessalam, he wrestled the wheel and pushed it, drew the throttle to full and the Cessna came over the top but the reversal in force threw the unbelted Abdessalam forward—pinning the wheel yoke against the control panel, sending the plane into a full power dive, seconds from the sand when the gored engine seized and now there was only the wheeze thrash of scalding wind, Rick battling Langer's wheel with all he had though not enough and at the end of everything came Lorraine—on her knees up Rick's back, locking hands around Abdessalam's neck, screaming until the wheel was freed and the Cessna swooped skyward for the last time, wings stalling and tail catching a dune and in the final split instant Rick switched off the fuel as the plane dropped dead, burrowing into its grave.

Sand poured through the remains of the windshield. Rick spit and coughed and pushed up; Lorraine clutched his shirt and pulled as she fell off his back; both of them tumbling into the rear of the Cessna.

Oil...blood...broken glass and ripped leather...tubes of sun through half-dollar holes in the fuselage. They eyed the holes then each other, then checked on Langer and Abdessalam, knowing it was hopeless. Now Rick heaved his weight at the door, leveraging against the sand as he went. Lorraine shoved out the duffel and he helped her through.

They were surrounded by dunes like the one that had caught the Cessna's tail, and on the hot Sahara wind came shouting in Arabic—from two apparitions above, with weapons.

Lorraine translated: "They want you to drop the bag." She called something in reply, then muttered to Rick as they scrambled up, "You are my cousin from America, we were on a tour of the sights."

At the crest. The vehicle was fifty yards off, engine idling; one of the men was easily six-two, with a pistol; the other much shorter, pointing an assault rifle—Rick recognized the Kalashnikov, an AK-47; both men had cropped beards and mustaches, kufiyas wrapped on their heads, long knives in scabbards on their belts.

Lorraine started right in, imploring, gesticulating from Rick to the Cessna. The shorter man spotted her gold chain; he snarled at her and she shut up. He shouldered the AK, stepped forward a pace, snarled again. She slipped the Garuda from inside her blouse and let it hang outside. He grabbed the chain and broke the clasp with one pull, swung the amulet before her face as his free hand snaked between her legs and rubbed. He chortled once, then louder at his partner's wisecrack, then backed away.

Now he brandished the AK at Rick and spoke fast to Lorraine; she kept her translation calm though Rick could feel her fury: "Give him your wallet."

Both men were excited by the cash, but Rick gathered what was next—they were deciding what to do with the infidels, and he had to turn the tide.

He lunged for Lorraine, shook her so violently she fell down.

"You filthy whore! This is going to get us killed! We've got to give it up!"

She spewed a Frarabic cesspool as Rick wrenched her to her knees. The one with the pistol fired two rounds in the air. The other waved Rick off with the AK and started ranting at Lorraine. The act was working. They seemed confused, probably didn't speak much if any English, demanded to know from Lorraine what was wrong.

She answered through tortured lips and Rick growled across at her, menacing.

"I hope you know how to use that thing. Give him the coin!"

She spat at him and fished it from her jeans. The taller one squealed "Aieee," snatched the treasure and the two of them gloated stone blind, and with Rick spying sideways while he and Lorraine still swore at each other he cried, "Now!"

She drew the Glock and fired fast, nailing the taller with a shot to the spine, the shorter with one to the gut. Sprang to her feet and killed the tall one with a bullet between the eyes. Rick kicked the AK from the other; she stepped forward and, standing above him as he writhed in agony, finished him too.

Her blouse, rippling.

The engine of the vehicle, clanking.

She was fixated on her pistol, and Rick thought she might drop it in horror. Instead, as though it were a stone of runes, she spidered fingertips along its barrel, extended it arm's length with a squint, then tucked it back in her jeans. Rick retrieved the coin, wallet, necklace; confiscated the AK-47 and two clips, the knives, and the pistol—an older but well-kept Luger. It would replace his Beretta, which was buried in the Cessna. He piled the ordnance between the two dead men and gave Lorraine the Garuda.

"Sorry about my language."

She took it, inspected the broken clasp. "Would you tie it on?" As he did, "You have saved my life again, Rick. How many times is that?"

"I'm not sure who's saving who. We'll add it up later."

He went down to the plane for the duffel, scrambled up, found her by the bigger corpse—struggling with his left boot, the right already off.

"On the journey, I will try to mend his uniform with material from the other's. Possibly there is tape or a sewing kit in the truck. Then you will wear his clothes."

"Okay," Rick said, crouching to help. He'd gotten

that far himself but no further. "And, uh, what happened to his sidekick?"

Chewing her lip, she moved over to the tunic.

"Perhaps he was killed by the pilot of the crashed plane?"

"Works for me," he replied, pulling off the pants.

A grimace as she undid the buttons.

"That is not a good sign."

Lorraine used one of the knives to cut patches of unstained cloth from the shorter man's pants and shirt. Then they heaped sand on both men. Lorraine kneeled and, surprising Rick again, said a prayer for them—her hands in a steeple, her soft invocation taken by the wind.

When she'd finished, Rick slung the assault rifle, put the clips and knives in the boots, took them and the duffel, let her carry the clothes. They started for the vehicle. Rick knew her feet had to be broiling in those sandals, and she was still limping from her hip, and she had to be as banged up as he was from the crash. No complaints, though.

"Where did you learn to handle a gun?"

"Inspector DuPonte taught me, before I...before I went undercover."

"Remind me to thank him someday. Sure glad you decided to take the Glock."

"I was fearful, Rick. Abdessalam possessed so many intimate details of Hameed and Musa. How could he have obtained such information?"

"Any number of ways. That's what he does."

"Yes, though if the account of his commission from Ammi Zarga is true, its success would result in the death or imprisonment of Le Clerc. A man such as Abdessalam might do anything to offset the loss of so much income, even ally himself with Hameed."

"Still, he obeyed Zarga and returned the coin, which is priceless. He could have just run off with it. Doesn't that prove anything?"

"He had *us,* Rick, and thereby the coin as well. What might he have done next? And now he is gone, yes, but we have seen that we are mere pawns in a much larger game. Even with Ammi Zarga as a player, how many moves remain before someone sweeps us from the board?"

The UNICEF logo was only yards off; over a rise and they were in the shadow of the blue box. They set the gear on the sand, spoke under the noise of the idling engine.

"There may be another man inside."

"Or several."

Ears to the container: not a sound except whirring that wasn't the engine. An air conditioner? Though the exhaust pipe vented vertically, the diesel fumes were dense, swirled down by the breeze. They moved to the rear; Rick tripped the latch and backed away, ready to fire; Lorraine started the door clattering up and ducked.

A wall of cardboard boxes, each stamped with "UNICEF" in white.

They unhitched the straps holding them and two plopped onto the sand; there was another stack behind. Lorraine tore open one box: sponges. Rick kept his AK-47 ready while Lorraine hoisted herself to the truck bed, threw the boxes off to get at the next tier then dumped those as well, which exposed an inner door.

Rick gave her the nod, trained the assault rifle; she muscled the bolt and pulled back the door, using it for a shield. From behind it, on a wave of cool air—a single female cry.

Rick lowered the firearm, for he and Lorraine were standing at the maw of a netherworld: Arrayed on two tiers of padded platforms, which ran the length of the container on both sides, were perhaps a hundred Asian children—gagged, their hands tied, sitting upright and strapped in. Their ages appeared to be in the range of eight to eleven; mostly girls, a third boys. Those whose eyes weren't frozen wide looked glazed, like snared animals.

At the other end: refrigerator, pantry, a toilet visible behind a half-open curtain, and the source of the cry— an oriental nurse at a built-in desk and stool. She rose and came towards them, shaky and mumbling, hands in supplication, and when Lorraine laid into her in what Rick conjectured was Thai, the woman broke down in tears.

He walked the length of the container; the children's eyes followed. Three things were apparent: the rig was new, its owners had spent for durability, and it wasn't the only one of its kind—there was a large Roman numeral "IV" painted in white, neatly above the nurse's station.

He came back to Lorraine; she was on one knee grilling the nurse, who'd collapsed onto the deck of the container.

"Shouldn't we untie the kids?"

Lorraine pushed a hand at him, continuing to

interrogate the nurse though she didn't seem to be getting much back.

"Okay, then. I'm going up front."

Out and down into the mess of boxes. Around the side, he collected the duffel, boots, and clothing, went to the cab, and set them on the running board. A high-riding metal door, military cockpit, bench seat, truck-like controls, manual stick; the only distinguishing items were a window-mounted compass, an amber light fastened to the dash—likely so the nurse could signal the driver, Rick thought—and a civilian-style transceiver with microphone. It was on, crackling static. The fuel gauge read one-half. On the seat and floor were a map, three pairs of sunglasses, a jug of water, toolbox, large binoculars, carton of cigarettes, and garbage: cigarette butts, half-eaten candy bars, bread crusts, stomped lettuce leaves, and two empty liters of beer.

Rick tidied the cab, chucking junk and litter onto the sand, and worked the problem: *Langer had said ETA fifteen minutes or so; airspeed was about one-sixty per hour, so maybe forty miles. To where, though?*

He spread the map: no markings. Noted an airport, yet it was fifteen miles east of Nefta, in Tozeur. *Was Langer headed there, or to some private strip near Nefta from which he operated Sahara Safaris?* He had to discuss that with Lorraine, but the forty miles was in the ballpark, so reckoning the speed of this crate at twenty-five on the dunes, he estimated ninety minutes or two hours to Zarga's.

Loaded in their stuff, rummaged behind the bench. Along with the big-bore rifle that had demolished the

Cessna were knapsacks with extra clothes, though from the smell they were laundry. *Good. Lorraine won't have to bother with—*

The radio sparked in Arabic.

The tone of someone used to absolute obedience.

Idiot! Why didn't you think of that when you saw the transceiver?—he leaped down—*of course with this cargo they'd have to stay in close touch with Le Clerc's people, and of course they must have reported seeing the Cessna—*running for the rear—*and this guy on the radio probably told them to shoot it down and dispose of survivors and—hell, it could be Le Clerc himself!—knowing someone had to reply quick or they'd send helicopters and God knows what else and—Lorraine should say she was on that plane, tell him she was safe but in danger, tell him that Hameed... or maybe Abdessalam or...what, for pity's sake? What?*

He hit ground zero. Lorraine would have to find the answers—all by herself, up on that tightrope.

She was holding the nurse, calming her. Rick jerked his thumb to get her going: "Someone's on the radio. Might be Le Clerc."

Lorraine stared at him, instructed the nurse then jumped to the sand; they ran together to the cockpit. The radio voice was vehement. Rick boosted her up and she listened, not breathing.

"It is him."

"What are you going to say?"

She glanced skyward, lips moving in prayer, grabbed the microphone and pressed the talk button—began in Frarabic, repeating "Emile" helplessly, then stopped with a gasp as though someone were threatening her, went on in French. She morphed into another person, what she'd pretended to be when she was with him, riffing her improvised scenarios of which Rick caught mentions of Hameed and Café Stella and Abdessalam, cascading her words like someone in fear for her life. She released the talk button so Le Clerc could respond, heard him escalate from amazement to puzzlement to anger, becoming more upset as he went on. She waded in again, invoking Zarga's name and Musa's—then another gasp and her voice peaked; she let Le Clerc react, interrupted him, finally cut herself off as though the mike had been ripped away. Le Clerc, trying to restore contact...

Rick clicked the button and the radio went silent. She was trembling, hyperventilating. How much more could she take before she cracked?

He took her hand with both of his.

"We'd better get moving, Lorraine."

He helped her down and, with arms around each other, they walked back.

The nurse, per Lorraine's instructions, had freed all but a few of the children, most of whom were jabbering as Lorraine and Rick clambered up to the container bed; they assisted the nurse with the rest. When all the children were untied and un-gagged, Lorraine made a sign to the nurse, who clapped twice. Disciplined by parents and culture, every child hushed as though a fuse had blown, braking their banter and visits wherever they were sitting or standing—a flock of utter innocence, posed in sable hair and perfect features.

The nurse made a brief speech, introducing the newcomers with marked deference. Now Lorraine, composed once more through sheer force of will, circulated among them and began her own address. Rick knew that the armed strangers gooped with blood and oil must have composed a grisly picture, yet with her lilting voice and mothering warmth, Lorraine had them in her palm.

Done, she spoke with the nurse; the woman went to the refrigerator, bagged some food and gave it to her; by now she was surrounded by a gaggle of the less-shy girls. A group of the more daring boys likewise approached Rick, intrigued by the machine-gun toting American.

Lorraine said her goodbyes, she and Rick waved, and the children waved back, and they left, closing the inner door. Rick hopped down, tossed up the bogus boxes, and together they stacked them as they'd found them; he shut the outer door, they jogged forward and climbed into the cockpit.

Nerves vibrating with the engine, they sat there stock still for a moment; through the windshield, the desert undulated to three dervish twisters and a hazy horizon. Abruptly Lorraine dove into her bag of food, devoured rice and chicken with grimy fingers, oil and peanut sauce smearing her cheeks. Rick wiped the lenses of one pair of sunglasses, put them on, and the white-gold glare was crisped by the polarizer.

He clutched and located the gears, eased into first but nearly stalled, revved and pumped and as they lurched forward, Lorraine between chews and swallows told him what she'd told Le Clerc. Rick doubled back to the tracks they'd seen from the plane, in awe once more of her wit and poise under unthinkable stress, yet as he steered north for Nefta he knew that their lives and Musa's, the children's and even Zarga's were now in free fall—like bird's eggs from a tall pine, with only one small patch of needles below to save the shells.

TWENTY-ONE

The Garden of Allah

In the desert of the cinema, it's the sun and the sand, but in the real Sahara it's always the wind, a headless Hydra of many guises—scirocco, simoon, harmattan, and more, each the seed of legends best taken with liquor.

If they'd had any Rick would have guzzled it. Because while the wind was quiet here, an ominous brown band was belting the horizon to the north; in the few seconds he'd watched, it had moved closer.

"What is that, Lorraine?"

She slid near with the binoculars.

They'd stopped on the crest of a high dune, three-quarters of a mile west of Nefta, its white minarets and domes rising among thousands of palm trees. Below them was Zarga's house—a nondescript block structure with a dome and a porch, set within the frontier of the palms, at the threshold of the desert. A black helicopter was parked to the left of the house, in a clearing some distance away from it, guarded by four men.

An hour before, and in sight of a four-camel caravan, Rick had pulled into one of a string of oases they'd come across on the trip, the engine left running for the sake of the air-conditioning. When the caravan passed behind the dunes, he and Lorraine had gone back to the container so she could explain to the nurse and the children what was going to happen and what she and the children were to do. Then, with the sponge boxes strewn on the sand—the outer door raised, the inner door left unlatched—Lorraine and Rick had worked in the shade of two bedraggled palms, making their preparations.

Now as Lorraine examined the horizon through his window, Rick was stinking of another man's body odor and maybe his own fear, sweating in dirty fatigues and kufiya and the cramp of boots a half size small. The microphone he'd cut from the transceiver was fixed to his chest with duct tape from the toolbox, its talk button in the role of trigger, its wire taped around to his back as though attached to a wireless detonator. A pack of cigarettes supplied the shape for that, a section of the transceiver's antenna playing the part of the detonator. Lorraine hadn't changed clothes or washed her face; her look was just right. Rick fiddled with the Luger bulging in the back of his pants, under an untucked shirttail.

"I believe it may be a sand wind," she decided.

"Dangerous?"

"Not unless you are an animal, or a young child and cannot find shelter." She resumed her side of the seat, surveying Zarga's house through the binoculars. "But it is very strange, and I do not like it—it moves over the ground like a serpent..." She trailed off, scanning the grove of palms, the helicopter and the guards.

"They must all be indoors," she commented.

'Must' is a bit of a stretch, Rick thought.

The brazen fantasy she'd told Le Clerc keyed on Samir Abdessalam. His mercenaries, she'd said, had kidnapped her as protection from Emile just prior to Hameed's attack on the Café Stella. From that, she hoped, Le Clerc would deduce that Abdessalam could only have known about the attack if he were in with Hameed, and since Lorraine saw Abdessalam as capable of double-crossing everyone, she was counting on Le Clerc to, as well.

There was a pistol at her head, she'd told Emile, held by the last of Abdessalam's men. The pilot, Abdessalam, and his other mercenary had been killed in the crash, after the Egyptian's plane had circled the truck and Le Clerc's men had shot it down. When they came to investigate, her captor had ambushed them; now he'd wired the container with C4 plastique and had promised to destroy everyone at the first hint of trouble. He was demanding, she'd said, a helicopter and pilot at Ammi Zarga's house, and safe passage for him with Zarga as hostage. Plus, a briefcase—delivered in person by Ahmed Hameed, to rule out a trap—filled with the half-million American dollars that, her captor said, Hameed had agreed to pay Abdessalam for intercepting Le Clerc's shipment and transferring it to Hameed. For this the mercenary would swap the children and Lorraine, unharmed.

Hearing all this, Le Clerc almost came unglued. Lorraine closed in: She was sure Zarga would agree to be the hostage because of his relationship to her family—and most assuredly now, with her being the only Bouché left. And Abdessalam had told her that Hameed's son Musa was being held by Le Clerc. Wouldn't that be enough to entice Hameed to Zarga's with the money? Even though Hameed would deny being party to some alleged plot to hijack Le Clerc's shipment? If all went well, she urged, Emile and she would be reunited, Hameed would get his son, and Le Clerc and Hameed could then decide how to minimize everyone's losses with the profits from the shipment. At the end, Lorraine had begged him to do exactly as instructed, coating her goodbye with enough loathing to make it sound like love.

"If only we knew who was here," she said, lowering the binoculars.

"We'll know more than that, soon enough."

Because of course, Rick realized, her whole brilliant structure was a castle made of sand, built too near the sea: Was Musa still alive, or had Le Clerc already taken his revenge for Lorraine's death? And if Musa were alive, why would Le Clerc bother to deal with Hameed? Why not have a sniper take Rick out? One bullet so he couldn't even twitch his thumb, giving Le Clerc both the shipment and Lorraine, and retaining Musa for the further torment of Hameed. And if not that, what else might he try? What had he told Zarga? Even if Le Clerc had played it straight, was Ammi Zarga as wise as Lorraine believed? Did Zarga trust Abdessalam enough to see through Lorraine's fiction? And would he bring together all the forces she was praying he would? And what about DuPonte? Hameed had the police in his pocket; did he also know what the inspector was up to? Such as the original trap, of which Abdessalam said Lorraine and Rick were such a critical part? And if *that* were true, how many other ways could everything blow up?

So many it didn't matter.

Lorraine's eyes, bending the world, as though she'd been listening to his thoughts.

"I am so sorry, Rick."

"Why?"

"If anything should go wrong, I— I wish that..."

She faltered and he pulled her to him.

"Tell me tonight, over a glass of wine."

A kiss, brushed on his cheek.

"I would prefer a bottle of champagne."

"Mad'moiselle, you have yourself a date."

Another kiss and she turned away, put her wrists behind her back. He tied them with a length of shirt he'd ripped for the purpose; the Glock in her jeans was hidden by her blouse and her hands. They tested the knot. She could free herself with just a tug and Rick retied it the same way.

He opened the door, stood on the running board with the AK-47, fired off a burst, got in again and picked up the binoculars: nothing at the house yet, the roofed porch empty, except for a table and four chairs. He panned left to watch the helicopter—

"The guards have their guns drawn, Lorraine."

Magnified, the aircraft was recognizable as the one that had taken the Egyptian and Musa from *Caroline*.

"Two men, Rick! From the house!"

"Got 'em."

"*Describe* them," she pressed.

He did and she made the identification: "Ammi Zarga and Emile Le Clerc. No Musa or Hameed?"

"I wouldn't expect the kid, not till—wait. In the palms, with the four men..."

"What?"

"A huge guy just joined, their leader by how they're protecting him, though he looks like a peasant."

"That is him, Ahmed Hameed. He favors the humble dress of his tribe, nomad Berber. According to Le Clerc this swells his rapture when he takes his revenge."

"For what?"

"For everything. For nothing. And he never carries a gun; he murders with his bare hands. Is he holding a briefcase?"

"No, but we shouldn't necessarily expect that either."

He studied the group in the binoculars as they walked from the grove. Hameed's top lieutenant, the dandy from the café, was among them; Ahmed himself was a imposing figure with the head and mane of a lion, and Rick's take was that he was in a decent state...for a criminal psychotic. And why not? he thought. He wouldn't have shown up unless he was sure his son was alive. Plus, with his share of the shipment he stood to recoup his losses on *Cheval Marin* and make a profit, and Rick was positive that the man had no intention of letting anyone get away with a dime of his half-million, least of all some bottom-feeding mercenary. As to being accused of conspiring with Abdessalam against Le Clerc, what of it? Probably added to his prestige.

Rick finally dumped the binoculars.

"Kudos, Lorraine. All your guests have arrived."

She didn't reply and he looked over: her inhales were short and sharp, her color pale, the enormity of what might happen now overwhelming her. She was close to the end.

Rick glanced left. The sand wind was nearer, darker. He gunned the engine, and they tracked down the slope of the high dune, surfing the lesser waves to the plateau fronting Zarga's place. Two of the helicopter guards took stations on either side of the house steps. The Hameed group staked their territory to the right. Zarga and Le Clerc remained on the porch—unnaturally close to each other, framed by the front door. Rick assumed Le Clerc had a pistol on Zarga and said so to Lorraine. She stayed riveted on the scene, her face already in character, getting ready for her entrance.

They reached the plateau; Rick U-turned and reversed the truck, braked when the back end faced the house, some fifty feet away. He killed the engine, immediately leaned across her and opened the passenger door—his left hand in position on the microphone button. With his right he took up the AK and forced her out with its muzzle. For effect she tripped on the running board and sprawled onto the sand, got to her feet as Rick jumped to the ground. He shoved her towards the rear of the vehicle with the machine gun stuck in her kidney. Rick was exposed to the two helicopter thugs; if they'd had the command, he'd be dead, he knew, so her story was holding their fire. But for how long? How long before someone saw through it—the taped microphone and cigarette pack?

He stopped Lorraine at the corner of the container. Like Le Clerc's men by the porch and the chopper, Hameed's men had their weapons drawn, dwarfed by their boss who stood before them with his legs spread, fists on hips.

Rick turned his focus to Le Clerc: Italian suit, alligator shoes, slicked hair and slicker mustache, kinks and fetishes grooved deep into a bronzed face. With Zarga under his control, he was descending the stairs from the porch; now as they walked towards Rick and Lorraine the sand wind hit, whooshing like a freshly opened coffee can across the plateau and into the grove. Torsos and guns rode above the eerie tingling, ships of war on an inland tide.

"That's far enough!" Rick ordered; they were fifteen feet off.

"You're an American," Zarga said, with an upper crust English accent. The information was for Le Clerc's sake, Rick guessed; he sensed Zarga knew exactly who the "mercenary" was.

But Rick couldn't say the same. In the second he'd had to take in Sir Kenneth Carmody—linen slacks and shirt; slender and quite ordinary, like Rolf's Preeta Das—he didn't see at all what he imagined he might: his voice was not like the stranger's, his face more otter than hawk, his eyes in the sunlight not blue but hazel like Eli's.

"You have a problem with that?"

"Not at all. As for the matter at hand, to facilitate the transaction, both these men will want to see the children."

"Fine, but the money first. And let's have everyone lower their guns, shall we? I'm sure no one wants to see the children in...bits and pieces."

Le Clerc ordered his soldiers then translated for Hameed, who in turn spoke to his men and nodded to the dandy. Rick played their last bluff—cursing viciously at Lorraine, pretending to be incensed because Le Clerc spoke English, which implied she'd lied to Rick, which pleased the gangster. Lorraine shuddered in response, though Rick wasn't sure that was an act. Hameed's lieutenant trotted through the sand wind to the grove of palms, came back with a briefcase that he gave to his boss. Hameed stepped forward and stood by Zarga, towering over him and Le Clerc.

"Open it," Rick said.

Hameed didn't need an interpreter for that; cradled the case and popped the latches: banded stacks of U.S. bills. Shut the lid, lowered it to his side, only his hand still visible above the moving sand.

Le Clerc's cheek muscle, flexing.

"Maintenant, you must show yours, m'sieur."

Rick looked from him to Hameed and back again. Whatever gifts they'd brought were about to be unwrapped. He raised the barrel of the AK, placed it against the metal siding of the UNICEF container.

Two fast bangs, a pause, then two more.

The door flung open and a mob of skinny bodies raced out at full speed, screaming as they'd been told to as though terrified, which they were anyway and now more so by the sand wind, some tumbling into it when they landed, leaping up spitting but still fleeing with the others for the palms, the rack of little heads like billiard balls blasted in every direction. Hameed and Le Clerc started yelling orders, their men scattering while more children poured from the vehicle and now it was Le Clerc—raising the pistol from behind Zarga yet keeping him as a shield; Lorraine—whirling and crying out in Thai, which stopped the last few kids yet Le Clerc fired regardless; the nurse—struck in the heart pitching to her knees in the sand wind and Lorraine—forgetting she was supposed to be tied up diving to help and Rick flinching as if to stop her.

His thumb slipped from the microphone button.

"Drop your weapon, hands on your neck!" Le Clerc barked.

Lorraine surfaced, dragging the nurse up with her. The children, screeching. Rick heaved the assault rifle.

"You are a poor maker of knots, m'sieur," Le Clerc sneered; he turned on Lorraine: "Lâche la femme, et viens ici!"

She stared at Rick then assessed the nurse, laid her down dead into the sand wind. She walked towards Le Clerc, deliberately in his line of vision.

The chop of helicopters.

Hameed's eyes went wide and he let go the briefcase, and with one stride and swipe of his arm corralled Lorraine in a hammer lock. He felt her pistol against his belly and snatched it out, aiming around her at Le Clerc, who forgot Rick and Zarga both as he backed away, weapon trained on his enemy.

From the palm grove—the mouse squeaks of children; gunfire and angry shouts. Hameed said something that included Musa's name; Le Clerc spoke to Zarga who hurried off behind the house.

The choppers, louder.

Now the sand wind slithered away, and Ammi Zarga returned—with an ashen Musa and an armed Inspector DuPonte and Lorraine gasping at the sight, which made Le Clerc wheel about and Hameed realize he'd been tricked just as Rick realized that Musa's father would never be taken alive. Rick whipped out the Luger, fired two shots over Lorraine: Hameed's head exploded. DuPonte fired too, pulverizing the gun hand of Emile Le Clerc.

Two military helicopters, arriving.

Zarga fell to his knees, wrapped Musa in a hug.

DuPonte went and stood over Le Clerc as Rick ran to Lorraine. She was pinned under Hameed; Rick shoved him off her and she sat up, throwing her arms around him. The choppers hovered fifty yards off and descended, settling into cyclones of sand. A stout old woman slammed open the screen door and waddled down the stairs to Zarga and Musa, lifted the boy and carried him indoors. Rick helped Lorraine to her feet.

Scores of DuPonte's commandos began emerging from the trees—some with men in custody, some with groups of dazed children in tow, in shock or weeping, others converging on the truck to help those still inside, two relieving DuPonte of Le Clerc. One sobbing girl who'd been wounded was on a stretcher, being taken to the helicopters. Plainclothes Interpol men, uniformed Tunisian soldiers and a medical team with doctors and nurses deployed from the aircraft.

The inspector retrieved Hameed's briefcase; Zarga joined him as he came to Rick and Lorraine. But it was Le Clerc, in his wrath, who sought Rick's attention and got it.

"I was her *first,* you American swine! And I will always be her best!"

DuPonte pivoted, slicing a sharp command to a subaltern, and the man's rifle stock whacked the bloody pulp of Le Clerc's hand. The guards hauled him wailing towards the helicopters.

"Êtes-vous indemne, mad'moiselle?" the inspector inquired.

She didn't respond, pushed herself away from Rick, wiping entrails from her face with a sleeve. DuPonte went on, addressing them both.

"I am mortified that you had to hear such vile things at such a moment. Your courage has yielded a great victory. Not only for these children, but for many others we can now rescue with what we have learned. Perhaps even the sister of mad'moiselle', if we have good fortune and the grace of—"

"Inspector," Rick interrupted. "The girl who died in the collision...was Lorraine's sister."

DuPonte gawked, stupefied.

Zarga stepped in. "Leave everything to me," he said, placing an arm about Lorraine's waist and a hand on Rick's, guiding them away from DuPonte and the noise of the helicopter engines idling, and the police and soldiers, doctors and nurses doing their work with the prisoners and children. They rounded the porch of the house into the shade of the palms. A pond, fed by a bubbling stream. A path. Wind chimes moved in a breeze left by the sand wind. They shuffled along, slowed by Lorraine.

"Mustafa Murad...I am so worried," she whimpered, staring at the ground.

"We are trying to locate him, and I promise that we will. But for the present you must both rest. I should hear something by dinner."

Rick slowed, on the brink now himself.

"I need to go back...to get our—"

"No, I'll have your things brought to you shortly, and some clean clothes too."

Zarga turned his charges onto a side trail, at the end of which stood a small house of similar design to his.

"In the cottage are toiletries, mineral water, fresh fruit." His hand to Lorraine's cheek. "When you sleep, dearest child, you will see your family. They wish to say their farewells." Fighting tears, she looked down; he raised her face again. "As you wish to say yours." She broke away and ran; Rick started to follow but Zarga held him up.

"Please, Mister Weisman. There are two loving wives and six darling children anxious for their husbands and fathers. I fear the worst, but can you tell me—what has become of Horst Langer and Samir Abdessalam?"

"I'm sorry," Rick said, and Zarga sagged.

"So much death and sacrifice. And yet it is always thus when good men and women stand firm against the forces of Satan. Which is why so many choose not to, and then are vanquished by him."

He extended his hand and Rick took it; the wind

chimes tinkled.

"I should like to add my gratitude and admiration to Inspector DuPonte's, yet I cannot find the words. You have come all this way to rescue these poor children, and save Musa's life, and you have saved as well, someone most dear to me, whom I sense has become dear to you." A tonic, channeling from his hand. "Quite a journey indeed. Had you any idea when you departed what awaited you?"

"No, sir. Not at all. But I believe my Uncle Eli did."

Zarga's eyes twinkled.

"That doesn't surprise me. I remember how, in his youth, Eli seemed to have access to understanding that far surpassed his own."

He smiled at Rick's expression, his grip tightening.

"Didn't you guess, dear boy?"

Rick Weisman shook his head, and Michael Romanov folded him into his arms.

TWENTY-TWO

A Drummer in the Dunes

Rocks form a crude arch, and carved into the keystone at the apex is a chiseled vee, and kneeling before it and looking along it, his vision cuts to the horizon. Spread below is a valley of sand, and on a raised oasis are countless eagles. The stranger stands behind him, one hand on his shoulder.

"Watch carefully, now."

The first crescent appears. No illusion that the sun is rising, it is they who are turning majestically in space.

"Yes, I—"

The stranger grips him tight yet there is nothing more, nothing the dreamer can see or understand. The birds riot into flight and the horizon slides beneath the sun, and now as the stranger's hand lifts, the wings of the flock beat like drums across the sky...

The sound in his dream awakened Rick, yet perhaps only from one dream to another. For here lit with fire pastels through the cottage window there was also a drumming: zoom-thoom...zoom-thoom it sounded on the sands of Sahara—as though the drummer marked the parade of ages or the passage of souls.

Now it woke Lorraine, and they listened together.

They were lying close on the quilt covering the four-post bed. Rick was on his side wrapped in a towel, facing the window; Lorraine was on her back in the lemon silk kimono Zarga's woman had brought.

After a time the drumming stopped, leaving only the wind and the sunset.

Her face turned towards him, her voice husky from sleep.

"You are blessed. Many who live here in Nefta have never heard the beating of Sahara's heart. But though you are new to her, she offers it willingly."

"The sound woke me up. It was like the sound in my dream."

"As it was in mine. I was with my family. We were hugging and laughing. They told me they were happy and wanted me to be happy. The last words my mother spoke to me were of you, just as she did before she died. When we embraced, the beating of her heart became Sahara's heart."

She turned onto her side, replied to his question without being asked.

"No one knows why it happens, Rick. No scientist has ever explained it. It simply is."

A breeze; her damp hair and the scent of jasmine; the aurora of light behind; her finger, tracing his upper lip.

"What are you thinking, Lorraine?"

"I was remembering the cuts that were here when

we first met."

"I had just shaved off my mustache."

"So I thought. And because I do not like mustaches, I felt that you did it for me, as though you knew we would meet."

"I was using it to hide. I didn't want to, anymore."

Brows knitted, she weighed this.

"That is even better," she decided. Her gaze wandered over his dressings. "So many wounds."

He laid his fingers on her hip, softly on the ridge of bandage under the hem of the kimono.

"Is yours still hurting?"

Her eyelids dipped and fluttered.

"Not when you touch me."

His hand stroked her lambent skin; she moved, and the silk slid up.

"Will you make believe?" she whispered. "That… you are my first?"

He crawled from the desert to the oasis—praying she wasn't a mirage, taking his cure from her waters, falling to unfathomed depths and a secret place she needed him to reach, so she could surrender at last what she'd kept there safe. Yet something more was surrendered too, though neither could have said what or by whom. Not even after, when they'd died apart and been reborn together, when they'd given all they had and more than either thought anyone ever could. They fell asleep again and dreamed—perhaps the same dream, fused to each other as they still were, the oneness that they'd become:

Lying with her on a bed of feathers, and the bed is in a canoe, and spires of gold curve above the sounds of bells and children yet now this dream he'd dreamt before meant something new and it woke him, and he pulled away.

How can you even think that? Walk away from Eli's legacy, all that he's built, abandon your mother and Sid and everyone else? And for what? Some two-bit life in some disease-ridden, crime-infested backwater of the world? Just because...you're in love?

Yes, there was that, and there had never been that before. But was it enough? He tried to see it—actually being there, living an alien life in an alien land, cut off from everything that told him who he was, how to judge and categorize, how to know what he'd do and what he wouldn't, what was good and what was not.

It's not fair, Lorraine. Because America's a lot more like France and Tunisia than Thailand is like America, and if you came to New York, you could learn the ropes fast, but if I go to Bangkok—

He listened to her sleeping, breathed her scent. As in Sidi Sa'id, he didn't want to look but couldn't stop himself, felt weak and shut his eyes.

Get serious. When it comes to countries, America's in a class by itself. You can move on, but you can't move up. We're the center of the action, where the rest of the world wants to be, no matter how they gripe. Let 'em gripe. They're just spectators at the panoply of great powers and I'm an American, by God, and I want to be on that field, not stuck in the cheap seats where you can barely see the show. Who cares about Thailand, anyhow? Has a Thai movie ever come to the U.S.? Has a Thai artist ever been dissed in the Times? I mean, you've got Anna and the King of Siam and then what?

Wearied by his crazed rant, he dozed off into a limo heading to the Met:

A clear night after a snowfall, and outside were ladies minked and jeweled on the arms of escorts in tuxedos. Even these New Yorkers would stare at her, he knew. They who had seen everything—the wealth, the fame, the power, who pretended they didn't notice any of it yet worshiped it all—even they would stare at Lorraine, and they'd feel it, something in her they couldn't buy or take.

The driver pulled up, they stepped out and the crowd surrounded her, oohing and pawing. Across the street Rick spied a snickering Bronx Le Clerc, cigar in his teeth, slouching against a lamp post, wearing tropic Armani and twirling a chain.

"Hey, you've had swell time, kid. But don't go *overboard.*"

Now, wide awake, he faced facts: Lorraine Bouché would never live in America, and Rick Weisman would never live in Thailand. But the real reason why? He didn't have the guts to face that.

He got out of bed and went to the window, pulled back the curtain yet instead of Sahara saw himself in Eli's office: the Brooklyn Bridge and East River and a bottle of Chivas late at night, and in the city sky are memories of Café Stella and the Swan and Sidi Sa'id like knife wounds in his chest, and he can't go home for comfort because he doesn't have the guts to face that either—the house by the sea with the unused rooms and the unsailed boat, nor even to turn and look at Eli's Mary Cassatt, the painting at the beach of a mother and child.

—⚮—

They left the cottage and walked to Zarga's house, the way lit by lanterns in the sand. It was getting chilly in the palm grove and halfway down the path Lorraine took Rick's arm. She was wearing a broad-sleeved, embroidered jebba; Rick was in his own khakis and musty gray shirt. He'd covered the odor with a linen jacket of Zarga's, but the rest of the clothes their host had sent for him hadn't felt right.

"How did he find this place?"

"He did not, really. Several years ago, he became weary of his teaching at the University in Tunis. He was restless. He spoke to Habib Bourguiba and told him he was thinking he might retire to England. It was Bourguiba's idea to make for him a home where he could be among his Sufi friends and write and live out his days. He has stayed here since."

They were past the pond and the spring and stood by the roofed porch. It was a starry night, and there were stars in the sand too.

"I can see why."

"At the blessing ceremony, the marabout, the holy man of Nefta, said the Sufis wished the house to stand for what Ammi Zarga meant to them, a bridge between their faiths. So they had built it at the place where the oasis meets the desert, and the desert meets the sky."

Zarga came out to the porch. He closed the wood door, let the screen door whack shut.

"Ah, there you are, child."

Lorraine flew up the steps and threw herself into his arms, her heart tearing open once more, finally releasing the deepest pain that only his love could begin to heal, this surrogate father she adored who was her only father now.

Rick stayed at the foot of the stairs while Sir Kenneth held her. After a time, her sobs eased; Rick heard him speak and her mumbled reply; he gave her a handkerchief. She blew her nose then said, "Please join us, Rick."

On the table was a candle; light came through the curtained windows and the holes carved in the door, the star and quarter-moon of Tunisia. Lorraine introduced the two men—as though they hadn't met before, or that she wanted to forget the way they had and start afresh, and both understood and went along.

"Uncle Zarga, this is Mister Rick Weisman of New York City. Rick, my beloved friend and revered teacher, Sir Kenneth Carmody." She hadn't referred to him that way before, as her uncle.

Sir Kenneth extended his hand. "I'm honored to make your acquaintance," he said as they shook.

"The honor is all mine, sir."

"Come, let us enjoy the evening."

He held the chair facing west for Lorraine, wiping her cheeks with his handkerchief; he and Rick arranged themselves north and south. Sir Kenneth lit the candle and at that moment Rick realized how comfortable he felt, as if he'd been to this house a hundred times and this man was his oldest, closest friend.

Shaking the match, their host turned to Lorraine. "Do you need a shawl, dear?"

She smiled at Rick and his pulse jumped.

"No, Uncle Zarga, I am quite warm."

"May I get you both a glass—wine or champagne?"

"Champagne, please," she said.

He rose and entered the house; Rick caught a glimpse of the décor—a hodgepodge of casbah and crown colony.

"He likes you," Lorraine said, her voice breaking.

"I like him."

He came back with a tray, three flutes and a bottle.

"This was a gift from the president of my publishing house on my eightieth birthday. Very expensive, he made a point of telling me, so I've been saving it for a special occasion. Can't envision one more special than this. Rick, would you uncork it for us?"

He set the tray on the table and stood behind Lorraine, hands on her shoulders. She reached up with one of hers and held one of his. Rick cradled the frigid bottle—Veuve Cliquot, vintage 1947—peeled the foil, unclamped the wire, held down the cork, and twisted the bottle until the first air hissed and the gas was spent. He let the wine settle, extracted the cork, and poured.

"Lorraine, we are in the presence of a master."

Their host resumed his chair; they all raised glasses and clinked. "To courage," toasted Sir Kenneth, "the quarry of faith."

Chimes from the palm grove. What wind was moving them? Rick thought. There was none here.

"I should help Molly in the kitchen," Lorraine said

after drinking a quarter of her glass.

"How thoughtful of you, dear. But unnecessary."

"I want to."

The men stood as she left. Seated again, Rick finished his champagne, poured another, noted that Sir Kenneth's first glass remained full.

"How is Musa, sir?"

"Given what he's endured, rather well I'd say."

"He must hate me now."

"No, I don't think so. There's no hate in him, and though he had affection for his adoptive father, he knew what he was. Besides, I'm the one to blame for what happened, if anyone is." He shrugged. "Truth is, after your ship's collision with Cheval Marin, our plans went spinning out of control. As such plans usually do."

The chink of dishes and silver.

"I'd like to say a word to him, if I could, sir."

"He's sleeping. Perhaps in the morning."

With the reminder of tomorrow, Rick drank the rest of his second glass and poured a third. Sir Kenneth lifted his flute, seemed to take a sip.

"What will become of him?"

"I've been considering that very issue, Rick. I've never married, though I was engaged once during the war. She was an ambulance driver and got caught in a bombing raid. I still miss her." He sighed. "I've been close to some of my students and Lorraine is like a daughter to me, but I've always wished I could have had a son of my own. I thought perhaps Musa and I might make a go of it together. If the lad is agreeable, that is, and you're willing to entrust him to me."

"Me?"

"You saved his life. It's a solemn bond."

Rick contemplated the night, sipped champagne.

"Things work out in strange ways, don't they, sir?"

"Yet just as they should, despite how it may seem."

Rick fished in his pocket, put the coin on the table.

"If Eli were here, I think he'd want you to have this."

"After so long, the Zevi Coin itself." Sir Kenneth picked it up, appraised it in the candlelight. "I must say, for even the few days it was in my possession, it proved extremely useful." He glanced at Rick. "You're aware of the situation in Moscow? Much has been stirring under the headlines, including a movement to reestablish the monarchy. My producing the coin at the critical juncture confirmed my standing within the family, whereupon I asserted to those behind the movement that I would actively and publicly denounce any such effort. It's challenging enough for people accustomed to tyranny to strive for freedom. Many hard days lie in the future, but the day of the tsars is long past."

He squinted one eye at the coin as if it were a target.

"I've always kept close tabs on Eli's family, so once Samir gave me the coin and described how he'd come by it, I recognized your last name and realized you must be Eli's nephew and heir. It distressed me that it had been taken from you, though I sympathized with Samir's motives. Then came the crushing phone call about Eli's death from my friends in New York, and I was seized with the desire to speak with you and return it in person. That desire changed to alarm when, through Antoine, I realized you'd become involved."

He turned it, evaluating both sides.

"And it served a further purpose as well, that of inspiring Samir to new heights of deceit..."

Rick had been wrong about the bait—it wasn't the children. It was the Zevi Coin, Zarga said, that Abdessalam had been dangling to catch both Le Clerc and Hameed. And while the Egyptian finessed his plan, Zarga's job was to get Lorraine to Nefta and get DuPonte to leave Sfax, in order to throw off Hameed.

"The inspector was quite stubborn. Fortuitously, I still have arrows in my quiver from the old days..."

Orders came for DuPonte from Interpol HQ in Lyon. He left after his meeting with Lorraine at Café Stella—officially for France, but in reality to rendezvous with military assets in the north of Tunisia.

"Then my dear friends were murdered at the café and the world fell off its axis. I had discerned danger afoot, but nothing of this magnitude..."

Zarga's associates in the police called him at one a.m.—Lorraine's body wasn't among the dead and her sailboat was missing; Zarga presumed she was following his instructions. He sent Abdessalam with Horst Langer to retrieve her and, hopefully, Rick, and told DuPonte to marshal his forces in Nefta before dawn. The inspector stationed his men in the grove, choppers camouflaged on the outskirts of town.

"Then we waited. When we heard from Le Clerc, the inspector and I knew that, once again, something had gone horribly awry. Yet it was possible that you were still alive, and Lorraine might still survive, and that our endeavoring to accomplish the mission might help you both. The rest you know."

"But I don't get it—how did the coin figure in?"

"Oh, I thought I'd told you. The coin was the key. With it, Samir could persuade Hameed and Le Clerc that he could manipulate me by threatening to betray my identity. A prospect which would be vastly appealing to them."

"Why, are you rich?"

"Not that way. But ever since the Bolshevik revolution there have been persistent rumors of Romanov treasure—the famed Amber Chamber, lost crown jewels like the Zevi Coin, a cache of thirty thousand gold ingots. I have no idea if the rumors are based in fact, yet one fact is incontrovertible: the Soviets have never stopped searching, most recently earlier this year in Kaliningrad, the former Prussian city of Königsberg, where the Amber Chamber was last seen. Samir planned to use the coin to validate both the treasure's existence and my knowledge of its whereabouts. It would be self-evident to Hameed and Le Clerc that every scrap of their combined resources would be required to get it out of Russia. With literally billions on the table Samir would propose an alliance of their operations, including the slave trade, with himself as a full partner. Unquestonably, such a union would have had fatal consequences for all concerned, but that was beside the point. We just needed to get them and the children here, and today, if we were to intercept the shipment. Samir was betting that with the lure of Musa, Lorraine, and more riches than even Le Clerc and Hameed could conceive—"

"Dinner is served," Molly called from the house.

"—we'd bag the lot."

He flipped the coin in the air, set it back on the table.

"Did Eli tell you about its legend, Rick?"

"Yes, sir."

"And what do you make of it now?"

"I really don't know. But looking back...well, you have to wonder."

"Yes, I suspect you would. We mustn't be disparaging about such matters, yet what the legend predicts is really not so remarkable. Each of us is led to whatever his soul is seeking, yet by our own choices, for good or evil; one doesn't need a mystical talisman for that. And in some way, by the ineffable gift of grace, most roads lead to God's love anyway."

"Even if you've seen things, and want to believe, but still find that you can't?"

"Especially then." A grin. "It doesn't hurt, you know."

"What?"

"Having faith."

He slid the coin across the table; Rick protested but Sir Kenneth wouldn't hear of it.

"No, it's yours. I gave it to Eli out of fear. He gave it to you because you were worthy of it. I hereby relinquish it with my undying thanks, though it's nothing to the gifts you've endowed on me."

"I don't understand."

"My pardon if this is too personal, but Lorraine's life is very important to me, more so now than ever, and you in your short time together have touched her heart and rescued her from bitterness and despair. Such a debt I can never discharge. Now please, take it." Rick did, from beneath his fingers. "Do with it as you see fit—I know that you'll be guided, as I was, and Eli was." A sly air. "Our bloodline has always been a tad fey."

The chimes and the spring, and Rick heard his own words from afar.

"*Our* bloodline?"

"Yes, dear boy. You see, Eli's mother was not only a distant Romanov cousin, but also my own birth mother. Which I believe makes me something of an uncle to you, and you a fitting bearer of our legacy." He sat back, raised his glass and tipped it, took his first sip of champagne. "But that's a tale for another time."

Enthralled by the cipher of his grandmother's past, Rick pocketed the coin. The door opened; the housekeeper's stout form silhouetted behind the screen, fists on hips.

"Have you lost your hearing altogether?"

"Only when you call me, Molly."

"If you hadn't said it, I would have. Now, are you going to properly introduce Miss Lorraine's young man, or must I bear another of your shameful lapses in manners?"

She came out, the screen door banged behind her, and Sir Kenneth ushered Rick over. Earlier, when Lorraine was showering and Molly had brought the clean clothes and their duffel, Rick was sitting on the cottage porch, trying with useless fingers to peel an orange. She'd brought the clothes inside, returned with a plate, taken the fruit, skinned it and split it and handed him the dish, then sauntered off without a word.

"Rick, allow me to introduce Miss Molly Macquarie, the Queen of Scots, my cook, confessor, typist, and loyal opposition. We've been together more years than either of us cares to recall."

She couldn't have been more than five feet, yet her grip was iron.

"Good to know you, laddy. Come in and let me give you a taste of honest food. None of this local rubbish they feed you."

Rick held the screen door for her and Sir Kenneth, who carried the tray. Inside, the house was even more of a potpourri than Rick had glimpsed from the porch, and if he'd been comfortable there, here he felt completely at home.

There was a spacious hall under the dome that served as dining room, living room, and office; as best he could tell without being shown around, there were three additional rooms aside from the kitchen, two of which had to be Sir Kenneth's and Molly's bedrooms. Perhaps the other, Rick thought, was where Musa was sleeping. The main hall was cluttered with memorabilia—honors, awards, and photos from Sir Kenneth's career as soldier and historian, his service to Tunisia and his life among the Berber—and shelf upon shelf of books. The office ware was modern and the office area, though stacked with manuscripts and legal pads, reference books and international newspapers, was well organized. The rest of the furniture was of superb quality, apparently handmade in North Africa. An ornate sword was mounted above the fireplace, and centered on the mantelpiece in a silver frame was a photo of Habib Bourguiba presenting the sword to Sir Kenneth. He didn't seem inclined to give the grand tour of his life, however, so Rick took the lead.

"I'm curious, sir," he said, helping Molly into her chair; Sir Kenneth held Lorraine's. "Almost every door I saw in Sfax and Jerba was blue. Yours is half white, half blue."

Rick sat opposite Lorraine; Sir Kenneth settled into the armchair at the head.

"The aesthetic of Tunisian architecture is based on practicality. White to ward off the heat, domes to circulate the cool air, 'lucky blue' doors to repel the insects. When my Sufi friends gave me this house I fretted because of the door. But they insisted on the two colors and promised we'd have no trouble with the insects, and we haven't. Of course," he added with a wink, "the screen door I installed did help. Now, let us open the doors of our hearts to God. Lorraine, will you lead us in prayer?"

She bowed her head, clasped hands at her chest; Sir Kenneth and Molly did the same after crossing themselves. Rick closed his eyes.

"Dear Lord, I love my family so much. Bless them and forgive them and take care of them always. Thank you, Lord, for saving our lives. Thank you for these dear friends and...thank you for Rick. And *please* help all the children, Lord...help them to...help them—"

She couldn't continue. Sir Kenneth said the amen for her and Rick opened his eyes, but the three remained in prayer. At last Lorraine looked up—her eyes brimming with tears yet with a light on her face, and he wondered what it was. The others lifted their heads, Molly began passing the food, and after the dishes and wine had made their rounds Sir Kenneth started the conversation again—cautiously at first, attentive to Lorraine.

"Tell me, Rick, how are you enjoying your visit to the Land of the Lotus Eaters? I'm curious if you know how Tunisia came by that name."

"Homer's Odyssey, wasn't it?"

Lorraine was pleased and even Sir Kenneth seemed impressed. Rick didn't bother to mention the guidebook he'd read aboard ship, content to seem more lettered in history than he was.

"Quite so, quite so. Yet a number of locales claim identity with Homer's mythos, testament to man's abiding preoccupation with the concept: life freed of cares through the ingestion of a magical substance. It is Herodotus, the godfather of historians, whose description of the Land of the Lotus Eaters gives Tunisia, indeed the specific area of Jerba, its right to the title. Compare if you will..."

He was off and running and, just as Eli had described him as a child, he was a captivating storyteller. By contrast, dinner was almost inedible. Molly might have been an atrocious cook, but in between Sir Kenneth's ramblings Rick found her a charming dinner partner.

"...can't get used to this confounded heat. Do you think his lordship here cares a whit? I had to tell him I'd resign before he'd buy me my air-cooling machine."

"Such a ghastly thing. There ought to be a law," Sir Kenneth put in.

"It's for my room only!" she declared, continuing a standing argument. "And frankly, it's no affair of his."

So it went. Lorraine had regained her composure once more, contributing enough to keep things easy and familiar, yet it was obvious to Rick how important it was to her that these two people approve of him. For his part he told Molly what she wanted to know about his life at sea and chuckled at her chronicles of school days in Edinburgh. Then, with the women chatting at one end of the table, Rick and Sir Kenneth filled in more details of the day.

Rick told him of their flight from Nefta, and why they'd taken the route that had crossed them with Le Clerc's truck and the UNICEF container. Sir Kenneth dealt with Lorraine's question—how Abdessalam had gleaned the inside information on Hameed and Musa: it was from Le Clerc himself, who'd once seduced Musa's tutor for that very reason. Hameed had made the young woman pay for her indiscretion with her life.

The two men cut short their conversation when Lorraine caught on, frowning. Rick then tried to nudge the topic to the years after Michael Romanov came to England as a boy and his name was changed to protect him. Sir Kenneth wouldn't bite but Molly took over, and though the master of the house looked bored and embarrassed, he still corrected her if she veered off course.

Eton, Cambridge, military intelligence in World War II—like Eli, Rick noted. In 1946, he joined a climbing expedition to the Himalayas, fell ill and had to stay behind in a Tibetan Buddhist monastery. The recuperation in rarefied air did him good. He found his calling, began to write, and went to Tunisia. He'd been stationed there for a time during the war and had grown fascinated with the Sufi Berber; now he wanted to chronicle their heritage and history.

In the mid- to late-fifties, as Tunisia battled for independence from France, he became an important ally of Habib Bourguiba's and a national hero. In the early sixties he lived for three years in Malta—where Eli had last heard from him—and while researching the Knights of Saint John he'd embraced anew, and with the passion for a lost love found, the Russian Orthodoxy of his youth. That took him to Jerusalem where he began to explore the mysteries at the heart of all religions. He then accepted a seat at the University of Tunis and dug in to write his six-volume masterwork, *The Enigma of Faith,* for which, as the crowning achievement of an illustrious life, he was knighted.

Molly served coffee with a passable rice pudding. The phone rang and Sir Kenneth took it in the office. Returning to the table, he stood at his chair.

"Thanks be to God, Mustafa Murad has regained consciousness. The doctors predict a full recovery."

It was too much too fast for Lorraine. Sir Kenneth hurried to her side, stooped by it and spoke privately to her, which seemed to help.

"I'm sorry, dear," he said now, so the others could hear. "I shouldn't have startled you that way,"

Molly offered champagne. "Here, lass."

"Yes," Sir Kenneth agreed, standing straight, "and in fact, let's all drink a toast. For now that Mustafa is safe, I can tell you another piece of news." He went to his chair again and sat, hands clasped on the table. "President Zine al-Abidine ben Ali has spoken to His Royal Highness, King Adulyadej of Thailand. The children will be flying home soon, with the body of Lorraine's sister. The King has invited you both to accompany them and to be his guests for the state funeral, and then to remain with him and the royal family for a festival of gratitude in your honor. I'm told it will surpass any celebration in recent memory."

Molly clapped and Sir Kenneth joined in; Lorraine looked bewildered; Rick acted his role but it didn't fool his host. When dessert was finished, Molly shooed the men to the porch and the women cleared the table.

The candle flame had snuffed out in the breeze. They stood next to each other at the porch railing, watched by the stars.

"Has Lorraine told you how we met?"

Rick didn't reply.

"Her father, Antoine, had an older brother—Marcel, a reputable businessman in Tunis. During the troubles, informal congeries of community leaders were held; we both attended and, despite our differences, struck up a friendship. Though he was loyal to France, and his business was anchored there, eventually I helped him to see the justice of Tunisian independence and he became a covert supporter of the cause.

"Unfortunately, two decades later a rival in business learned of this and betrayed him. Marcel was ruined. His health began to fail, and as he was a bachelor I cared for him. The doctors did their best, but his spirit was broken. Finally, after years of his hiding his predicament from his family, and against Marcel's wishes, I contacted Antoine. He moved his family from Thailand to be with his brother, and I can console myself a little because, even though he was dying, Marcel's last years were relatively peaceful ones. Yet I've always done what I could to help the Bouchés, such is my guilt over Marcel and the uprooting of Antoine's family. And now they are dead, everyone save for Lorraine, and once again it is my actions that are largely the cause."

He looked over.

"We can never know the effects even our best intentions will have. All we can do is to try to keep a humble heart, trust in God's forgiveness, and pray."

What he was trying to say was wasted on Rick, and he knew it.

"You're not going to Thailand, are you?"

"No, sir. I have to get home."

"I see. What a pity. And when does your ship sail?"

"First light, day after tomorrow, I believe. But Eli's company has arranged for my release; I just have to see the captain before the ship sails. I'll fly to London the following morning and catch the Concorde from there." He tried to make it sound better than it was. "Time for me to grow up, I guess."

A finger of Sir Kenneth's, tapping.

"The entire trip wouldn't be more than a few weeks. Couldn't you perhaps grow up afterwards?"

Rick didn't react and Sir Kenneth regretted the jibe immediately.

"Please pardon me. That was entirely uncalled for,

to say the least. It's only that this is such a singular honor, the kind rarely afforded even once in a lifetime, yet one to which you are so eminently entitled. And think of Lorraine, Rick, and all she has lost, all at once. Can either of us begin to comprehend it? Yet by the grace of God you were brought to her side, to save her life and transform her heartbreak into hope. You're everything to her now."

Again Rick said nothing. The wind awoke.

"It's not really about having to get home, is it, son? I understand. It's difficult, sometimes, to feel we deserve the cards we've been dealt—particularly when they are so good. But then, every man has to play them as he sees them."

A gust of wind gyred sand into a cone, and with this last echo of the stranger's words, they faced each other and shook hands. Lorraine came out to the porch, meeting Sir Kenneth as he retired to his house; she kissed him on both cheeks, went to Rick and hugged him close.

"Thank you, mon cher."

"For what, Lorraine?"

"For giving me your strength, when I had none left."

—⁂—

It was the wind that roused him from a dreamless sleep. He dressed and went barefoot out to the porch, the morning cold before sunrise. He stood and listened to the wind—so much it lamented, so much it had lost. It called him away, to the grove and past Zarga's house, across the plateau and into the desert.

He climbed the dune they'd descended in the truck. At its crest he slumped to his knees, the wind carrying the words Lorraine had spoken last night, after they'd said everything there was to say then made love as though they never would again:

"The people of Chiang Mai have a proverb. 'He who has heard, must listen. He who seeks, must look with his heart.' What are you seeking, Rick?"

And after all this, he had no more of an answer for her than he'd had for Eli. She rolled away then, and the darkness rolled in.

Hands under his arms, lifting him to his feet.

"Are you alright?"

It was Sir Kenneth, wearing the blue robes of a desert chieftain, and a white kufiya with a blue band; the sword from his mantel was in its scabbard on his belt.

"I saw you from the house and—"

"Is this why they call you that?"

"What?"

"Zarga. The Blue One."

"You mean the robes? No, they're just another of my many eccentricities. I like to wear them when I write. You see, I'm working on a book about—"

"Then why?" His voice was hoarse and intense; Sir Kenneth backed off a step, turned and started down the far side of the dune. Rick went with him.

"I've heard there are those who, in their spiritual exercises, believe they have seen me, along with a white-blue light. I don't know much more about it."

"Your face, is it the same?"

"I don't know that either. I haven't seen myself."

"And why the other name—Lazrag?"

"Who can say? Some call me one, some the other."

They climbed another dune; a rim of sun shone above the palms.

"One night aboard ship, during a storm, I was knocked unconscious. I came to a desert canyon. I mean, I was *there*—it wasn't a dream. I met a stranger with blue eyes and a sword. He told me this riddle, which Samir said is called the Riddle of Lazrag. Was he you?"

"I have no idea, dear boy, nor is it important. Why not tell me what's really bothering you and let's see if we can sort it out together."

He steered them through the desert, and as Rick lost sense of where they were or where they were going, he told everything that wanted to be told. He didn't know how long he spoke but finally he stopped.

"Are you certain the plane crash wasn't an accident?"

"Everyone accepted that it was, sir. Just another airplane accident, like so many others. Yet I always supposed it wasn't, because I saw my father take his green binder with him, his dream journal, and he hadn't ever done that before. But I only found out the rest of the story recently, from my mother.

"One of the local detectives—this great guy named Sid Stein, who ended up marrying her—found the journal not far from the wreck and delivered it to our home. It must have been blown out of the cockpit when the plane crashed because it was mostly intact. My mother hid it from me all these years; I didn't even know it had survived. Thank God Sid got his hands on it before anyone else and took it upon himself to spare us any more anguish. To an insurance investigator, what was in that book would have spelled suicide. Maybe not explicitly, but—"

"So, there was insurance?"

"Yes, and they paid up. Thank God for that too."

"And the official cause of the crash?"

"A fuel leak, then one of the control wires snapped and the spark ignited it."

"Well, there you are."

"No, sir. My father restored that plane and maintained it himself, and he was a great mechanic. Never put so much as a scratch on an aircraft, not once—not even as a test pilot, even when he was hooked on pills—and a Stearman is nearly unbreakable. There's just no way around it. He rigged the whole thing."

They walked in silence.

"It could be taken as an act of love, Rick."

"I've tried to see it that way, like he did it for the life insurance, so that we'd be okay. That's what my mom and Sid think but it doesn't hold up. Why not sneak off with his stupid book of dreams and do what he had to? Why bring me along—just to screw me up *good?*"

Sir Kenneth gave him time to calm down, himself time to collect his thoughts.

"No man wants to face death alone. I'm sure he was scared, maybe he was wavering, or perhaps he surmised that it would be more credible to the insurance company if you were there. Many explanations are possible, and possibly more than one was in your father's mind, including the most likely: that he wished you, his son, whom he loved more than any person on earth, to be witness to his sacrifice, so that someday you'd understand."

"Gee, what a guy."

"But there's another aspect as well. Could it be that your father's soul was trying to tell you something, even as his mind and persona failed? And that this urgency made him bring you along, and his book of dreams too—in order to leave you his legacy, as Eli and I have left you ours?"

"What, that you can get rid of your problems by killing yourself? Thanks, I've been there."

"No, Rick. I think perhaps he was saying that sometimes our dreams are worth dying for."

It stopped him cold. He'd never looked at it that way, would never have accepted it if he had. And, after a moment or two, he didn't now.

"You make it sound almost noble. But what if the dreams are due to mental illness? It's one thing if you're a pioneer or an inventor or you want to save the world, and nobody cares. It's another if you're crazy. I'm sorry. I just can't see the beauty in suicide."

"Oh, please don't mistake me, Rick, neither can I. It's a dreadful sin, a dreadful transgression. God intends us to grow closer to Him through our sufferings, not to give up. Yet even from the ashes of suicide, the phoenix of wisdom may rise. For the dying of which I speak is not of the body at all, and I think therein may lie the gift your father left for you. Yet such is its value that a bill must be settled before you can claim it, and this bill must be paid in the coin of the realm."

They'd returned to the porch of his house. Sir Kenneth unhitched his sword and stood it against the rail. They sat on the first step with their feet in the sand.

"The coin of the realm? Which is...what?"

"I'm afraid I can't answer that for you, Rick. Each man has to make his own way to it. But as the riddle says, should you come to know this one thing, then you'll need to know no other."

From the grove, the crunch of a door shutting; Lorraine had left the cottage.

"That lousy riddle. I thought I'd solved it back in Sidi Sa'id. My big, cosmic revelation. And now I've lost her."

Sir Kenneth patted his back, and Rick saw in his mind the land where men such as this walked, where men such as he never would.

"I'm sure you'll find the answer someday, or perhaps it will find you—though in either case I imagine it won't be...what you might expect. Are there words to explain the fragrance of a rose? Would you pluck the petals to learn why it's so sweet? That's the way it'll be, Rick. Somehow, you'll just know, and it will be enough."

Lorraine arrived at the porch; she kissed her uncle's head, ducked her brow at Rick, turned and kneeled on the sand; Sir Kenneth began to massage her neck and shoulders. The screen door banged. Molly came out with a broom and swept, grumbling about the beastly desert. She banged in again without a word to anyone.

Sir Kenneth sighed. "She's always grouchy in the morning. On the other hand, her breakfasts are better than her dinners."

"Ammi Zarga! Ammi Zarga!"

A boy's shout came from behind the house, and then the child himself ran full speed into view, sandals flapping and shirt flying. It was Musa, a lizard he'd caught squirming in his hand. He pulled up short at the sight of Rick, and their eyes held each other's while their hearts stopped, and Rick found the place where tears begin. The boy freed the lizard and climbed into his lap, smiling up at him.

"Merci, Musa," Rick said. "Merci mille fois."

TWENTY-THREE

Zerzura

Inside a car in the rain, in the night with no stars, the lights from the waterfront and the swish-thunk of the wipers—this is how you say goodbye.

Lorraine guided Sir Kenneth's Citroen through the untended gate to *Caroline's* gangway, switched off the engine. Now there was only the patter on windshield and roof, and she and Rick sat in silence as they had for most of the drive from the desert. He remembered another rainy night, and a taxi in another harbor, and Willie Nelson on the radio. But there was no music here. He stared at the gangway and the rusted hulk of the ship, knowing what he would do when he got out of the car. He would stand there and watch her drive away. He would tramp up and ask Saint Eves for his release. He would pack his things and board an airplane and go to sleep for the rest of his life.

"Well," he said.

He glanced over but she'd turned aside.

"Will you write to me?" she asked, muffled.

"Sure."

She opened the glove compartment for a tissue and a pen and pad. Blew her nose, clicked on the map light, wrote five lines and tore off the page, then gave Rick the pen and pad and he wrote his, care of Kagan Brothers Shipping. They traded; she looked at Rick's address until a tear fell on the paper, then creased it in half. He didn't look at hers but did the same, put it in his shirt pocket.

She took another tissue, dabbed her eyes.

"I am sorry. I do not mean to act this way."

"I know. I'm sorry too. Listen, Lorraine, maybe I'll take a trip, come visit you in Bangkok, see what it's—"

"Would you? Would you truly?"

He wanted to hate himself, but he'd fallen too low for that. He couldn't reach for her, had nothing left to give except all that he had. He leaned for his wallet.

"Tell you what—you keep this until I do."

Slipped out the coin; it gleamed in the map light.

"Oh, no. I could not."

He took her hand, laid the coin on top of the paper with his address.

"Uncle Eli and Ammi Zarga both said I'd know what was to happen with it, and they were right. I want you to have it; you're *meant* to have it," he wrapped his hands around hers, "for the work that calls you." Now he let go. "And at least it'll remind you of me—at least for a while."

"I will never forget, Rick."

"Never is a long time."

"Yes, and Thailand is a very old place," she replied,

as though she'd just realized it, her features traced with rain shadows. She opened her hand and looked at the coin. "I will do as you wish, if you promise what you said. That we will see each other again."

She turned and gazed not at him but into him, just as Eli had so long ago, and the words burned on his tongue. Saying them to her eyes was like hurling acid.

"I promise."

She took his hand, bent to it and kissed the palm— as she had once before, by the sea in Sidi Sa'id.

"Then I shall wait for you."

He imitated what he thought a last kiss should be like, and a tender caress as in the movies.

"Goodbye, Lorraine."

She was so serene now, returning his kiss with one of her own.

"Au revoir, mon cher."

Rick stepped into the rain and shut the door.

The ignition strained and caught, the car reversed then accelerated forward—bumped potholes, crossed rails, and disappeared through the gate.

A bell buoy sounded from the harbor. The rain eased to a drizzle. He turned and started up the gangway then stopped. Plenty of time to talk to Saint Eves. Nothing but time.

He walked the wharf alongside the Russian ship, went left into an alley where three of her sailors were wobbling back to it, singing. Past warehouse blocks to the streets and cobblestones that led to Café de Paris, wanting to drown more than thirst until the morning found him passed out in the airport and *Caroline* went sliding into the mist. How many mornings like that does it take before a seafarer is through with the land? Maybe just one, he thought, if it's the right one. One morning with the harbor fading in the wake of his ship, fading away until there's just the ocean and the dawn and the gulls tagging along like beggars, which at last must give him up for good.

—⁓—

Even if he hadn't known where it was, he could have found the café that night. Even if he'd been blind. It was some party.

As he reached the far side of the street that skirted the court, Rick spotted Rolf and Freddy with a group of Russians—one tall blond muscleman and his three shipmates, guzzling their drinks. Their clothes were wet like everyone's; crossing the street, Rick saw Rolf take off his tee and tuck it in his jeans. One of the Russians pointed at Rolf's muscles, then their comrade's, and all of them roared at the joke. Rick waded into the crowd; what with the fog of alcohol nobody recognized him until he shoved in next to his friends.

"It's the wise man!" Rolf slurred.

"YO, BUB!" Freddy cried.

The Russians were sniggering like loons at the Americans.

"Give me the news," Rolf said, so close that Rick could smell the fumes.

"Later, I'm thirsty."

"Here." Rolf gave him his whiskey and Rick drained

the dregs. Freddy raised his glass: "To the end of Communism!" Everyone toasted including Rolf, who was without a drink but didn't notice.

"Tovarich! Friend!" bellowed the big blond, putting out his paw to Rick. As they shook the Russian said his name, Yevgeny, and Rick reciprocated.

"Tell me now, Rick," Rolf commanded.

"No dice—have to get drunk first."

"And it's about damn time," Freddy said grinning as he offered his drink. Rick set down Rolf's glass, took the gin and tonic, drank it in gulps and finished it. He tried to hand the empty to a waiter but just then the man took a fall, his tray flying and crashing. General cheers and applause.

Willis was with a group that included King Tiny; the commotion made him look their way and he saw Rick, began to weave over through the tables. Two men in Bedouin garb slowed as they walked the street, probably cursing the foreigners and their blasphemy. A quartet of local stevedore types hung at the edge of the revelry, stewing.

"Let's go," Rolf insisted, towing him to the street. Willis hailed again from the flank; Rick waved. Another robed Bedouin, hunkered under a bale of straw, tottered from the direction of the wharfs. Rolf stumbled but Rick caught him, propped him up against a warehouse wall.

"Tell me the whole 'n nothing but."

"Not much to tell, Rolf."

"What about the boy, and that coin?"

"Both safe."

"Then you've done well, pilgrim. Better than I

thought you could."

"How goes it with you?"

Rolf reached in a pants pocket, pulled out a wrinkled envelope.

"Wrote to Josie. Asked her to marry me."

"That's great! Why haven't you sent it?"

He was stumped, then solved it.

"*You* mail it for me. I got real Tunisian stamps on it." Rolf clamped Rick's skull in his hands. "You can run, but you can't...ever...hide." He stepped back, nodding, and slapped the envelope onto Rick's shirt.

Rick took it, looked at the address.

"Rolf, you're going to be home before this even—"

"No, you have to *mail* it for me!"

Rick pocketed the letter. "It's as good as there."

"Thanks, buddy. Thanks for everything."

Willis and Yevgeny, each with an arm around the other, barged from the crowd and swayed over with drinks in their free hands. Willis let go the Russian and hugged his watch mate.

"Great to see you, lad!" he boomed.

Yevgeny yanked Rolf by the wrist. "Come, tovarich. We drink."

Rolf was drunker than the Russian and losing the tug of war, and Rick turned from Willis because the Bedouin who'd been approaching with the bale of hay had dumped it behind him and suddenly was right behind Rolf, and something began to scream in Rick's mind as the Bedouin reached into his robes—something about the hidden face and shape Rick had seen before, known before in every nightmare of terror he'd ever dreamed and now he screamed out loud and lunged as the blade flashed and ripped Rolf's throat to the bone.

The Russian let go. Rolf collapsed into Rick's arms through a gusher of blood, his last gaze witness to some immutable truth. The Bedouin jerked backwards and the kufiya fell off: horrid white skin under brown dye, pink eyes insane as he whirled and ran.

Rick lowered Rolf to the pavement and raced after him, through the bleak streets to the warehouses and dock alleys—thirty feet and gaining, fifteen feet and Rolf raging inside him, five as Whitehead veered through an archway and Rick followed. A deserted warehouse, reeking of rot.

Whitehead wheeled, knife ready, and in the stodge of street light Rick saw it was the Randall and knew that whoever had set the beast loose had gotten it to him. Now Rick coiled up as Rolf had taught him, and Rick Weisman the soul dead and Rolf Thurston the body dead became one, unstoppable—because the dead can't be killed and the dead fear nothing and the dead love to teach.

They circled.

Shouts and orders coming closer, then waning.

Whitehead charged.

Rick juked and faked and punched his temple; the beast staggered, circled again and parried but this time the knife was a decoy and on the lunge his plaster cast struck hard, hammering his prey to the ground but with Rolf warning *Watch out!* Rick rolled and walloped Whitehead's knife arm then kicked a foot at his crotch. The beast keeled to his knees and Rick got to his,

pounding his fists like jackhammers and though the
Randall twice slashed his flesh he kept on pummeling—
nose and ears and temples to pulp till Whitehead
dropped flat and the knife did too. Now Rick straddled
his back and reamed it in—through the ribs to the heart
if there was one, digging deep then raising it high and
with Rolf's hand on his he plunged it into the neck of
the beast, buried to the hilt then out again and in again
until the beast was no more.

Whitehead was still. Rolf gone.
Rick struggled up and limped outside, crumpled to
the street. A lake of wine oozed from his wounds onto
the cobblestones, and reflected in its surface were clouds
on the moon as the lake flooded over him.

Inside is nothing, no sound or light.
He swims through until he breaks out, soaring
above the streets of Sfax. There below are men carrying
Rolf, others running the maze of the wharfs and
warehouses. There is the ship and Café Stella and above
it all is—
A black castle, banners threshing in the wind,
turrets rising aloft to the floors of Eden; its drawbridge
lowers, the portcullis rises to reveal an aqua sky with
fleeting clouds. He enters across the bridge above a gorge
of ink with demons louring up at him: suspended in
mid-air is a clear crystal oval, on its surface a crystal bowl
filled with white-blue flame. A section of sky swings out,
a great door, and coming from the infinite beyond are
the voices of many men. He prepares to meet them, to

join them. He has a lot to add to their discussion; he would need eternity to say it all.

But now his father emerges, alone with his leather binder. He sees Rick and comes towards him—young, as he was before he went mad, and Rick is as he was before his father died. At the crystal oval his father sets down the book of dreams and takes up the bowl of flame, and Rick extends his child's hand, feeling the misery his father feels at his son's being there. They both grow older through that misery until Rick ages into himself, and his father into the stranger, and with that it all vanishes— the castle and the clouds, the voices and the sky, the stranger and the darkness. Where the wind had been is a symphony of wings, and where the bowl of flame had been is a cup of glistering gold, held aloft in the coruscating firmament by hands that bleed from ancient wounds. A face and a form and a halo of thorns issue from the feast of heavens, and his voice is the cleansing water, and his eyes are the lamp of the world.

"Drink now, or thirst forever."

Rick takes the cup and drinks, and then there is only light.

—*m*—

"There he is!"
"Man, look at that blood."
"But he's alive, right?"
"Well, he's breathin."
"Hey, here's Whitehead."
"Dead?"

"Yeah, with a knife in the neck like he did Rolf."

"And good riddance too. Leave him for the cops."

"Let's get Rick on his feet." The bos'n, blurred.

"Anybody home, bub?" Freddy.

"Don't bother about him, son," said Willis. "Try to walk."

His legs were rubber-bands and he couldn't.

"We've got you, buddy."

Six arms carried him to the waterfront and *Caroline*, up the gangway and down to 8-12. They laid him on Willis's bunk; the bos'n ripped away his shirt, cut open his pants, checked his hand.

"Someone go get my kit. Saints, what a mess." He cleaned the wounds with water and a towel. "But I swear you have more lives than a cat, Weisman. Looks worse than it is."

Willis returned with the kit; the bos'n began his work and Willis took the towel, finished washing off the bad blood and the good.

—⚬⚬⚬—

He awoke to the hues of early morning. Someone had dressed him in sweats and cotton socks. He was alone in 8-12—the sky through the open porthole, the pitch and thrum of a ship under way.

Saint Eves peeked in and saw he wasn't sleeping, came and sat on the bed.

"How are you doing?"

His knuckles were bruised and swollen, his bandaged hand and ribs throbbing, his face raw where he'd been hit.

"Better than JJ. Not as good as Rolf."

Saint Eves shrugged. "Makes no sense. A fine fellow like him, going like that? Makes no sense at all."

"It does to me, sir. If I'd only—"

"Don't do that, son. Don't. There's nothing down that road, take it from someone who knows. It was Whitehead who caused this, no one else, and now the world's better off without him. That's some consolation, isn't it?"

What world? Rick thought.

The silence stretched; Saint Eves coughed.

"Look, I'm...going to be writing to Rolf's parents— by telegram first, to get there before he does, and a long letter after. You knew him best, so maybe you can help me fill in some details."

Rick nodded.

"Also, Sanders says Rolf mentioned last night that he had a fiancé or a girlfriend. He thought you might know something about it."

"Josie Winokur. He gave me his last letter to her, to mail for him. I'd like to handle that myself, sir, if it's okay with you."

Saint Eves smiled kindly.

"Let me know if you need any pointers on what to write."

"Actually, I thought I'd fly out to Monterey and tell her in person." Saint Eves' smile wilted. "That would be better, wouldn't it?"

"Yes, it would. In fact, it would be right decent of you. Unfortunately, I don't think it can wait that long."

"I could be there in a week or so."

"No, more like a month, given the monsoons." The

captain rolled his eyes. "Look, Rick, I figured if you made it back to the ship you'd be wanting to fly home. But I couldn't be sure, could I? Next thing I know, you're injured but not bad enough to leave you behind, and you've already missed your uncle's funeral, plus we're very shorthanded, so..."

He rubbed his forehead.

"What I'm trying to say is—you remember that deal we talked about? After my partners got news of the collision, turns out they'd put it on ice, not that anyone bothered to tell me. Of course, they also had to let go of our hold on that nice coastal run. It's funny, though—" his jaw flexed, "—when they heard that Captain Brace had been killed, things started cooking again, and fast. I suppose we have you to thank—"

Their eyes locked.

"Sorry. That didn't come out right. Anyway, the good news is, Caroline is under new ownership, which includes me. The bad news for both of us is that my partners have landed a much more lucrative contract, short hauling freight around the South China Sea. Which means we're not going back to the States. We're headed to K.T. for repairs and upgrades, our new officers and crew will—"

Rick gripped Saint Eves' arm hard, hard enough to hurt it.

"What's the matter, Rick?"

He could barely find his voice. "What did you say?"

"What?"

A heartbeat.

"K.T.—that's...Khlong Toei, isn't it?"

"Yes, the port of Bangkok. Why?"

Rick stared.

"What's wrong, son?"

He let go of Saint Eves and shook his head. The captain shook his too.

"So, there it is. If you want to contact your people, I'll arrange it. If you want your release when we dock in K.T., you've got it. But that's the best I can do. Sorry things worked out like this."

"It's alright, sir."

"You're a good man," Saint Eves said, standing to leave. "We'll hold a service this afternoon. If you're up to it, I'd like you to play 'Amazing Grace.'"

After a while Rick got to his feet, found his loafers in the locker, hobbled into the passageway and out to the foredeck.

The air was cool after the night's rain, the sea rolling easy. It was dawn, and clear, and the lookout had already quit his post. Rick climbed the ladder to the fo'c's'le; a gull swooped overhead, hovered and cawed then winged for home. And now as he reached the eyes of the ship the sun rose higher and lifted into the blue, and in his own filled eyes its light appeared as crossing beams that spread wide above the world: north to Russia and south to Arabia, west to America and east to Romance Run— where the children of the klong play by its waters, and the artists paint to the music of bells, and jasmine blooms in the night.

He knew one thing, and it was enough.

ACKNOWLEDGEMENTS

First, my profound thanks go to authors Anthony Eglin and Roy Schoeman, for agreeing to read the manuscript and write advance reviews. Thanks also to Moncef Belgacen, who jogged my dimming memories of Tunisia; and Rolly Flaviano, who shared his expertise in the martial arts.

Further acknowledgments and apologies: to the crew of the tramp freighter *SS John C.,* with whom I sailed so long ago; to my late uncles Joe Kahn and Sam Kahn, the joint inspiration for the character Eli Kagan; to my mother, sisters, and late father and stepfather—Tanya, Ellen, Barbara, Sy, and Lou—for their love and support; and to my old buddies Wil Baril, Fred Foos, Marty Kenney, and Hugh O'Reilly, for more than I can say.

Finally I come to my wife Barbara—a wonderful artist and storyteller, who worked tirelessly on the last and most critical read-through, and to whom this book is dedicated— and our children, daughter Erin and son Jaid. Thank you with all my heart for always believing in me, and thanks be to God for letting me be in your lives.

—*Roger Dubin*

After a stint in the Merchant Marine at age sixteen, and several forays into college, New York City-born Roger Dubin worked on and off for a decade as a guitarist and songwriter. Between gigs he wrote news copy and ad copy, which led to an award-winning career as a marketing executive and consultant in the cruise and travel industries, principally in San Francisco, Hawaii, and New York. He now lives in northern Arizona; *The Coin of the Realm* is his first novel.

www.ingramcontent.com/pod-product-compliance
Lightning Source LLC
Chambersburg PA
CBHW051228260626
47162CB00002B/322